Torn

Torn

Eleanor Green

Contact information: contact@authoreleanorgreen.com

Cover Art by: Kiley Murphy

Cover Photo: Rachael Jane

Published in the United States of America

Torn by Eleanor Green

www.authoreleanorgreen.com

For my husband, Kiley—the best of both worlds.

Acknowledgements:

I owe a debt of gratitude to those who were so generous with their time and expertise:

My beta readers, critique partners, bloggers, and book reviewers—thank you for your honesty and support.

Liz Aguilar with Book Peddler's Editing for the countless hours spent tweaking this book.

For my author friends who took time away from telling their own stories to promote, email, participate in giveaways, join my pity parties, and throw confetti across the states when it was time to celebrate. Your friendship is invaluable.

To the readers, friends, and family that have shared their excitement in this journey.

I would especially like to thank my family for allowing me to disappear into my fictional world, fending for themselves until I came back to reality again. The stories in this book wouldn't have been told if it weren't for the virtually infinite cups of Earl Grey, brewed and brought to me by my wonderful assistants/children, Jordan Olivia and Hunter.

You call me still your life—oh! Change the word—
Life is as transient as the inconstant sigh:
Say rather I'm your soul; more just that name,
For like the soul, my love can never die.
~Byron

One

Apprehension overpowered Katie. Her heart beat rapidly in her chest, encouraging her notion to run. Before she could flee the lobby and seek refuge in the stairwell, the office door swung open.

"Please, come in," Dr. Laura Burkhart said, her mauve painted lips curled up in an inviting smile. She was a petite woman with a heart shaped face and flaxen hair.

Katie stepped into the psychologist's office and glanced around the room. The office was simply decorated in creams and light blues. A side table adorned with a lamp, box of tissues, and a burning candle, hugged each chair. The aroma of pumpkin spice wafted through the room, struggling to mask the smell of fresh paint. Katie took the offered seat across from Dr. Burkhart and accepted a glass of water.

Katie nervously picked at a hangnail as she watched the condensation drip down the glass of water sitting on the table next to her. Her muscles tensed, finding it difficult to relax in the overstuffed cream chair. Taking refuge behind the curtain of her long, dark hair, she resisted the urge to tuck it behind her ear.

Dr. Burkhart sat down. She tucked her right foot behind her left heel, causing her knees to fall slightly to the right. Aware of her own legs, Katie drew her knees together. It was an effort to keep them together, her muscles fought against the unnatural position.

The session began slowly at first, a getting-to-know-you period, and then the hard questions came.

"What can you tell me about your past, Katie?"

"I'm not sure I'm ready to talk about it," she answered, concentrating on the dead skin surrounding her over-picked thumb.

"I understand you're having nightmares—how often, and are they different or recurring?"

"It's usually one of two nightmares. I'm either a little girl being pulled out of the arms of my mother and taken away, or someone's hurting me—that's the one that wakes my grandmother."

"Everything you tell me is kept in confidence," Dr. Burkhart affirmed. "I will not, and cannot legally, repeat anything you say to me." She waited for her response, but Katie remained stoic. When she saw the vacancy in the girl's eyes, she knew Katie wasn't going to open up, but it wasn't necessary to get the job done. "Would you like to heal, and stop the horrors of your past from ever haunting your mind again?"

Katie nodded. "How can you do that?"

"Through hypnosis."

"I thought shrinks liked to rehash past memories," Katie began as she looked quizzically at Dr. Burkhart. "Make you talk about them forever, and finally teach you how to deal with it." She slumped back in the chair and folded her arms.

"In most cases, yes. Yours is different. You've experienced too much pain and horror. I think it would be in your best interest if we calmed the storm in your mind—give you a fighting chance at a normal life."

"Are you telling me you can just make it all go away . . . what's the catch?" Katie narrowed her eyes. Nothing in life was easy or free. There was always a cost or a tradeoff.

"No catch, Katie. I only need your verbal consent. I know you've not had any reason to trust, but I give you my word . . . I *can* help you."

Katie shrugged. *I guess I don't have anything to lose.* "Okay."

"Come and lie down," she said, directing Katie to the sofa against the wall. Careful not to rush her, she waited for Katie's slow gait to cross the room and descent onto the couch. She could see the lack of trust and insecurity in Katie's muscles and her clenched jaw. If she pushed too fast, too far, she was sure her client would bolt.

Dr. Burkhart spoke in a soft, calming tone, "Just relax and listen to the sound of my voice. Starting with your legs, feel your muscles relax. Moving upward, let your abdomen calm. Now your shoulders are completely relaxed, feel the tension in your neck loosen, your arms feel weightless. You feel so light you could float through the air. That's it, relax, and feel your eyes getting heavy. You've been through a lot and your body is tired, so very tired. All you want to do is relax and sleep. You're so sleepy . . . very sleepy . . ."

It took nearly ten minutes to put Katie under. Dr. Burkhart kept her voice soft and calm when she spoke, "Katie, I want you to go back to when you were seven years old. Envision your parents' faces. Do you see them?"

"Yes." Her voice sounded distant and monotone.

"I want you to make them disappear." She watched Katie's body tense. "It's okay, they're not real. They're only images, like drawings. You can take your hand and erase them."

Dr. Burkhart spent two hours erasing each bad memory. "Now we're going to fill in the blanks, Katie. Your parents, Daniel and Celia Harrington were in a car accident when you were two years old."

Katie's body tensed and tears pooled in the corner of her closed lids. "It's all right, you've had a wonderful life with your grandmother . . . you and Gram have a special bond. Let's talk about your childhood growing up with Gram. Every Christmas you see the *Nutcracker* ballet and come home to Wassail. You love the smell of hot cider and cloves wafting through the house. Your favorite game is Scrabble and your favorite movie is *Pride and Prejudice.*"

Dr. Burkhart went over the list of memories that were typed out for her, carefully installing them in Katie's mind. She had to cover the recent move from Raleigh, North Carolina to York, Maine, so Katie could have a fresh start in a new town. "You're excited about the new move, an opportunity to meet new people and make new friends. You weren't happy in Raleigh, it was hard for you to make friends when you didn't make the cheer squad. But you'll miss your friend, Abigail, and will continue to keep in touch with her through email for a short time." Dr. Burkhart smirked at the genius behind the detailed plan. She wondered how long, if at all, her boss's friend, Elizabeth would be able to keep up the farce of emailing her own granddaughter under the alias of Abigail.

"Abigail," Katie repeated, each syllable rolling off her thick-with-sleep tongue.

Four hours was the longest Dr. Burkhart had ever kept anyone under hypnosis. There were so many details to cover, and she hoped Katie's mind could handle all of the new information.

"Katie, you're going to wake up soon. We've had a nice meeting about college choices. You'll apply to Princeton, Yale, Harvard, and Cornell. I'm going to count backwards from five. When I say one, you will wake up feeling refreshed and happy. Five . . . four . . . three . . . two . . . one."

Katie opened her eyes and yawned. She covered her mouth and apologized, "I'm sorry, how rude of me."

"Please, don't apologize." Dr. Burkhart waved her hand in the air. "Choosing which schools to apply for is unnerving. I know it was a hard decision, but I think you've made wise choices."

"Thanks. I'm excited. Now I just need to make it through my last year and a half of high school. Starting a new school is intimidating."

Two

Holding her head high, Katie left the principal's office with her new schedule, locker combination, and a stack of books that gave her an unattractive gait. She read each locker number until she found one-zero-six. Fumbling with the lock, the top three books in the stack slid out of her arms, making a loud *thwack!* as they hit the floor. Katie could feel the eyes of the students on her. If it were a full-sized locker, she would have climbed in and shut the door behind her. Before she could bend down to pick up the books, she heard her voice.

"Are you practicing for the circus, trying to juggle everything?"

Katie looked up to see a mouthful of white teeth smiling at her.

"I'm Maggie, Maggie McKellen. You must be the new student. Your locker is right next to mine." Without asking, she took the schedule out of Katie's hands and looked it over. "We have English Lit together!"

"Oh," Katie began, unsure of how to respond to the bubbly blonde standing before her. "I'm Katie Harrington."

Junior and senior year of high school flew by thanks to Maggie. Katie was drawn to her outgoing personality and they became friends quickly.

Maggie was more interested than Katie was in boys. Katie found them immature, and something about the way they looked at her made her uneasy. She was envious of the popularity Maggie gained by dating the right boys, but locking lips with any one of those pigs from school wasn't worth it as far as Katie was concerned.

Katie's favorite class was Latin, since the medical field still used the dead language. Her teacher, Mrs. Newell, would enter the classroom each day with a cartwheel before clapping her hands and shouting exuberantly, "Who's ready for Latin?" Katie loved studying and absorbing new material. She maintained all As and Bs, giving her the grade point average needed to be accepted to Yale. No one, including Katie, would ever know that the first two years of her high school manuscript were fabricated.

College life was the perfect fit for Katie. Having the independence of making her own schedule, and furthering her career goal, brought her indescribable joy. When it was time to dissect a cadaver that had been donated for science, her heart raced with excitement. *I would've been a brilliant surgeon,* she thought, *but as a nurse, I'll be able to take a break and raise children one day.*

She made friends easily, but didn't enjoy the party scene. She would often join Maggie for coffee. The two had shared a lot since meeting in high school, and were thrilled to be roommates through their college years. However, Maggie was living it up on campus, while Katie was a stick in the mud, always turning down invitations to fraternity parties or a night of dancing in one of the local night clubs.

"I just don't enjoy feeling like a piece of meat in a market," Katie said, rolling her eyes and exhaling a long-suffering sigh. "We need to have shirts made up that reveal if you're willing or not. I mean, do these guys really expect us to be wearing shirts that say, *'Looking for casual sex? Pick me!'* Mine would say, *'Back off, I just want to dance!'*"

"You're such a dork, Katie." Maggie teased. "You can't blame a guy for trying. You're gorgeous!"

"They need to come up with better lines at least. Remember the guy who licked his finger and wiped it on my shirt?"

Maggie laughed. "Yes, what was the line?" She lowered her voice and tried to sound husky, mimicking him, "Hey, baby, why don't you come back to my place, so we can get you out of those wet clothes?"

They were near hysterics by the time they reached the lobby of their dorm. "I'd love to see a guy's reaction if we did that to him!" Katie laughed.

"Can you imagine? I can hear him now . . ."

Katie pretended to listen as Maggie talked, but her attention fell on someone across the room. He was the most stunning man Katie had ever seen. She studied him as he talked to someone, animatedly using his hands to describe something, his dimples sinking deep into his cheeks as he laughed. She let her eyes roam over his muscular body and the way his jeans sat perfectly on his hips. He ran his hand through his thick light brown hair and glanced in her direction. When he caught her gaze, she let her eyes linger on his for a daring moment, drunk from the woozy feeling that swam through her veins. She was unable to smile or look away, until Maggie broke the spell.

"Katie, have you heard a word I've said?"

"Huh? Oh, sorry. Hey, don't look now, but the guy in the navy T-shirt by the window—have you ever seen him before?" Maggie began to turn her head, when Katie caught her by the arm. "I said don't look! You'll make it too obvious."

"How am I supposed to know who you're talking about if I don't look? Besides, the way you've been staring, obvious is an understatement!"

"Okay, just don't . . . be typical Maggie." Katie folded her arms in front of her chest, then quickly unfolded them and shoved her hands into her pockets. She wanted to hide behind the large artificial Ficus tree in the corner, but stood there nervously hoping he wasn't looking when Maggie checked him out.

"Mmm, of course, I've seen him. His name is Branson. He's on the tennis team, and I believe he's a Sigma Alpha."

"I play tennis." Katie smiled mischievously. "Why haven't I seen him before?"

"Because your nose is always in a book! You don't have time for guys . . . or fun for that matter, remember?" Maggie raised the pitch of her voice and mocked her best friend, "I have to concentrate on school."

"Why are we friends?" Katie laughed and bumped Maggie with her hip. "A little flirting never hurt anyone, and besides, it's not like I'm going to fall in love with the guy."

"Hmm, as far as I remember flirting is not part of your life plan. What was it again . . . graduate with honors—four years.

Concentrate on nursing career—four years. Get married on June seventh—"

Katie interrupted. "Hey, don't make fun of me. There's nothing wrong with a game plan."

"You do know that the seventh of June only lands on a Saturday every four years? Have you mapped that out, or are you willing to get married on a Thursday?"

"Actually, it occurs every six years, three times, then not again for another eleven years. And six years from now is perfect."

Maggie's eyes widened in amazement. "I can't believe you know that. Actually, yes, I can believe it. And what if you haven't met anyone, are you just going to grab the closest bachelor on the street, so you can check it off your list?"

"You're ridiculous, Maggie!" Katie laughed, not sure of the answer. What if she didn't find her soul mate? She had always gone by her lists, planning every detail of her life. It was as predictable as the tide chart. "I'd just like a date . . . or two. I mean, jeez, look at him!"

Katie glanced up as he walked past her before exiting the lobby. She could have sworn he had smiled at her, but second guessed herself.

"Well, good luck with that. Maybe you can try the wet clothes line," she giggled. "Are you coming out with us tonight?" Maggie checked herself with a pocket mirror and swept back a strand of curly blond hair.

"No, I've got—"

"To study," she sighed. "Same old story with you. When this semester is over, I'm going to keep you out all night. You've got a lot of catching up to do. It's our senior year—live a little."

"I worked hard to get into the nursing program. If I don't pass finals and the boards, I've got nothing to fall back on." Katie yawned. "But   I was going to say I've got to get some sleep. I'm exhausted."

"Yeah, it was a pretty bad one last night. Same nightmare?"

"Sort of. It was the same scenario . . . chasing a long, black car down the street. But this time there was more. I was being dragged by the hair by someone."

Maggie rested her hand on Katie's arm. "Sounds terrifying. Did you see something on TV?"

"I don't think so." She shrugged. "Anyway, I'd like to get an hour or two of studying in if I can keep my eyes open."

"As much as you study, you'll ace the test. Well, I'm off then. The girls are meeting me for drinks." Maggie stopped and turned. "Never mind the girls. I'm going to stay with you and hit the books, too."

"You're the best friend a girl could have, Mags, but go . . . have a good time tonight."

"Nope. Staying here."

"Seriously, Maggie. I think I'll sleep first, then study. So, unless you've got a thing for watching me sleep—which would creep me out—please go. Besides, someone has to bring me the gossip!"

Later that night, Katie fell asleep after reading the same paragraph over and over again. All she could think about was the guy in the lobby with the most startling blue eyes she'd ever seen and contemplated ways of crossing his path again.

"Are you up for a game of tennis?" Katie asked, her ponytail bouncing along with her.

"Sure, I could use a break." Maggie closed her book, and reached for her tennis shoes and racket.

Once on the court, Katie casually looked around for Branson.

"I don't think he's here." Maggie said, and served the ball across the court. Katie returned it and they volleyed back and forth for several minutes to get warmed up. Katie started the game with her second serve and Maggie scored the first point. "Fifteen-love."

They played a competitive game, but Katie ended up winning the match point in the end. The second game ended quickly, with Maggie scoring all but one point.

"Jeez, that was ugly. One more?" Katie said, breathlessly.

"Yes. My serve." Maggie said as she slammed the ball across the court.

They put everything they had into the game, using backspin to make the ball stop short, hitting it in the opposite direction, making the opponent run across the court to return the ball.

Maggie beamed as she called out, "forty-fifteen!"

Katie won the next two points and shouted "Deuce!"

She readied herself while Maggie served. Using all her strength, she returned it to the opposite corner. Maggie lobbed it just over the net. Katie had to sprint to get to it in time, using her backhand to send Maggie running across the court. Each of them yelled out the score when they had the advantage, and the game seemed to go on and on. When it was finally over, they were dripping wet with sweat.

"Good game, Mags. You played hard today." Katie used her small towel to wipe her forehead dry.

"You beat me twice, but I gave you a run for your money, didn't I?" Maggie beamed.

"I *barely* beat you twice, and I had to recover from the ass-kicking you gave me in the second game."

They took long pulls of their water bottles, packed up their gear and walked toward the gate. Time ticked away in slow motion as Branson and his tennis team walked past them. Katie knew she let herself linger on his eyes a moment too long, but she seemed to be caught in a magnetic force and couldn't pull away. After they passed, she quickly made her way around the corner of the brick building where she was out of sight. Not realizing she'd been holding her breath, she exhaled loudly and leaned against the wall. Her legs were fatigued from the game, and quickly turned to Jell-O as she tried to hold herself together.

"Oh—my—God! He was totally checking you out!" Maggie said, animated.

"He was probably wondering why I was staring at him, I couldn't look away. Good grief, I'm a dork!" Katie slammed her hand against her forehead a little too hard. "And look at me—I'm sweaty and my hair . . . ugh!"

"Trust me, Katie, he wasn't looking at you like you were a dork. The way he was looking at you, made *me* blush!" She giggled.

"Jeez, I can't breathe." Katie grinned as she grabbed her knees and tried to suck in deep breaths.

"Your cheeks are scarlet. You *are* a dork!" Maggie teased. "Let's go."

For the next few weeks, Maggie and Katie were on the tennis court almost every day at the same time, but she only saw Branson twice. It was the same routine, gaze—hold breath—blush until cheeks turn crimson—and chide herself for not having the guts to say hello.

Three

Tuesday afternoon Katie sat down in the lobby with her Synthesis of Nursing Care book and began reading. She and Maggie were supposed to meet for coffee in an hour, but she knew if she read in her room she would lose track of time. It seemed like a good idea at the time, but she was having trouble getting into it with the rush of people coming in and out, causing her to look up in curiosity. Once, the door opened and two girls came through the door talking and laughing about something that was said in class. Another time, it was two guys arguing about a philosophy question. Katie watched as the two of them tried to argue their point all the way through the lobby and into the elevator. *Concentrate, Katie!* She looked at her watch. *Only thirty minutes left to get this chapter in.*

Just when she found her place in the book, the doors flew open again. She tried to force herself to keep her head down, but it was no use. As she looked up, her heart lurched in her chest to see Branson walk in with three of his buddies. Katie felt the heat in her cheeks immediately and quickly lowered her eyes to start reading, hoping he hadn't caught her looking at him. She glanced up, peeking through her eyelashes, to see which way they were going, and was surprised when they gathered across from where she was sitting. *Just keep your head in your book. Don't look at him!*

Every time she glanced up he was already looking at her. She overheard him tell his buddies goodbye and bit down on her bottom lip. *Dang! He's leaving,* she thought. *You should have made a move. Sure, sure. Like what? Walk up to him and introduce myself. "Hi, I'm the girl that's been eye-flirting with you. Are you free on June seventh?"* Katie shook her head before glancing back up to watch his friends walk away. He stayed and seemed to be checking something on his phone.

After reading the same paragraph three times, Katie gave up. Between trying to pretend that she wasn't ogling Branson and trying to convince herself to walk over and say hello, she couldn't concentrate. Katie slammed her book shut.

"Whoa, didn't like that chapter?"

Katie's breath hitched as she looked up to see Branson standing there. She knew he had said something. *What did he say? Who cares, say something! Anything!*

Instead, she laughed nervously in agreement.

"What are you reading?"

For the life of her, she couldn't remember what she was reading. Katie cleared her throat and looked down at the front of her book.

"Synthesis of Nursing Care."

"Sounds riveting," he said sarcastically. "Hi, I'm Branson." He smiled and offered his hand.

"Um, hi . . . I'm Katie." She stood and took his hand with a confidence that surprised her.

They stood there for an awkward moment, neither of them knowing what to say to the other. Branson slid his hands into his blue jeans, while Katie searched for something intelligent to say. She managed to maintain a 3.8 grade point average, but suddenly her brain felt like it had turned to mush. She could feel the warmth creeping up her neck and cheeks and could tell he noticed it. *Deep breaths, Katie. Think of something to say. What's your major? No, that's the typical line. Are you in a fraternity? Um, yeah, hence the Sigma Alpha sweatshirt. Jeez, Katie—this isn't your first conversation with a guy, think! God, those blue eyes* . . . She finally came up with, "I've seen you on the tennis court."

"Yeah, I've seen you play—you're really good. Why aren't you on the team?"

Katie was mortified that he had been watching her without her knowledge. She hoped he hadn't seen her miss the shot that sent her twirling like a ballerina a few days ago. "I don't know. I guess I didn't want it to be something I *had* to do. I just like to play for fun."

"I understand. The coach is brutal. We practice every day. I wish he'd lay off a little, let us actually enjoy our college years."

When Branson laughed his whole face lit up. His eyes reminded Katie of a refreshing swimming pool during the hot summer months and she couldn't believe how attracted she was to him. Her eyes followed the bridge of his nose down toward his mouth, and by the time her eyes made their way to his soft lips, her insides melted.

Gram had convinced her to save herself for marriage, and she had managed to obey that rule for twenty-two years. However, there was no doubt in her mind that she would give herself to him right now if he wanted her.

"Would you like to grab a coffee?" Branson asked.

"I'd love to," Katie answered, suddenly remembering her plans with Maggie. "Do you mind if I text my roommate first?"

Branson waited while Katie typed a quick text:

Rain check on coffee. Explain later.

They talked for hours over coffee before their long walk back to Katie's dorm. "So, you're in the Nursing program?" Branson asked as he zipped up his coat.

"No, basket-weaving, actually. The Nursing book is my fun, on-the-side reading." Katie laughed. "Sorry, you left that one wide open! Yeah, I'm finishing my last year in the Nursing program, how about you?"

"Now I wish I had a smart-ass answer." He smiled. "Business. My father wants me to take over his company, so he can retire."

"What kind of company?"

"It's a document management system company, but we plan to diversify and include computer storage products as well."

"So, you're a techy?" Katie teased. "Quick—favorite line from Star Wars!"

"Do . . . or do not . . . there is no try." Branson gave his best Yoda impression, making Katie giggle. "Wait, how did you know about my obsession with Star Wars?"

"The force is strong with this one." Katie grinned. *Oh God, that was cheesy!*

Branson stopped and turned to face Katie. Her cheeks were rosy from the crisp air, making her mischievous green eyes stand out. "Hmm, should I be worried that you chose to quote Darth Vader, or completely impressed that you can quote it at all?"

"I hope you're impressed." Katie lowered her head, feeling the rush of heat to her cheeks. She desperately wanted him to kiss her, but her lips were frozen and she was sure her nose would run as soon as his lips touched hers, instantly thawing her out. She shivered. "Ooh, I can't wait to get inside where it's warm."

Branson held the door open. "Isn't your coat warm enough?"

"Nothing is warm enough. I don't think I'll ever get used to cold weather. I need to be on a hot beach."

The lobby was crowded with a group watching *Paranormal Activity*. Katie covered her eyes as they walked through the room. "Agh! The preview for that movie scared me for weeks!"

"Really?" He laughed. "What kinds of movies *do* you like?"

"All kinds—even some scary ones like *Friday the 13th* and *Halloween*."

"Those aren't scary!"

"I know, I'm a wuss. I just don't like things with demons or spiritual conflict. However, I do like *Star Wars* and *Lord of the Rings* which are spiritual conflicts—but it's more a battle between good and evil, and evil never wins, of course." *Quit rambling, you sound like a dork!*

"Would it be too soon to invite you over for a movie? I have the boxed set of both of those."

"It probably *is* too soon, but yes, I'd like that." Katie smiled.

After a short drive they arrived at Branson's apartment. She didn't know what to expect—did he have three beer-drinking roommates inside, or would she enter the typical bachelor's sex pad. She imagined walking into his apartment and sitting on a black leather couch, while with a click of a remote, he filled the room with R&B music.

A giggle escaped Katie's lips.

"What's so funny?"

Crap! She thought, trying to think of an answer. "Do you have roommates?" *Oh God, that sounds like I'm hoping he doesn't, so we can have sex.* "Actually, I was just thinking about mine. I was laughing at something she did this morning. I just can't quit laughing about it." *Great, now he'll want to know what she did. Good move, Katie, keep the lies coming—you're doing great!* "I should text her and let her know I'll be home late." *And . . . now you've really made it sound like you want to be gone all night. Crap! Crap! Crap!* "I mean, the movie should take an hour and a half, right? I'll probably beat her home, but I'll text her anyway." *Good recovery,* she sighed, and typed a quick text to Maggie:

Catching a movie. Be home late.

Katie was surprised there were no black leather couches or beer cans lying around. Salvador Dali posters decorating the walls and mismatched furniture confirmed it was a bachelor pad. A stack of books on Architecture was evidence that Branson had a roommate, and Katie wondered if he was home. She walked over to an aquarium and studied the black goldfish with large eyes. "What kind are these?"

"They're Black Moor goldfish. Their names are Voldemort and Saruman."

"Clever."

"You know who they are?"

"Of course—the evil wizards from *Harry Potter* and *Lord of the Rings*."

"Are you kidding me right now?" Branson said as he looked up. "She knows the classics *and* she's beautiful?"

Katie's entire body tensed at his words. She found a seat on the couch and pretended to fix something on her shoe, trying to control the urge to smile like a girl with a mad crush.

Katie had a difficult time concentrating on the movie. She wanted to know everything about Branson from his favorite color to how many children he wanted. Most of all she wanted to know what his lips felt like against hers.

Branson broke the silence. "What kind of music do you like?"

"Hmm?" Katie's heart raced as she tried to get her bearings.

"Sorry, I've seen this movie a hundred times. I asked what kind of music you liked."

Katie scooted around to face him. "That's a hard one—I have a diverse collection—I like classical, opera, folk rock, R & B . . . I guess I like it all, except country. What about you?"

"I have a wide array of tastes too, but I do like country music. I mean, you've gotta love Johnny Cash!"

She nodded in agreement. "He's the exception."

Branson wound his finger around a loose thread from the small pillow next to him. "Where did you grow up?"

"I was born in Vermont, but recently moved to York, Maine. What about you?"

"Born and raised in Austin, Texas, ma'am."

"I thought I detected a Southern accent."

"Southerners do *not* have accents. I have a Texas drawl," he huffed in mock offense.

Katie rolled her eyes. "Okay, Mr. Texas Drawl, what brought you all the way to Connecticut?"

"My father's business brought us to New Hampshire just before I started my junior year of high school, and Yale was the closest and best choice for college."

"That had to be hard—leaving all of your friends in Texas."

"It was at first, but I played sports, so I met people quickly."

Katie smiled and thought, *I could talk to him all night.*

They almost did.

The cessation of music after the movie credits finished, interrupted their conversation. "It's late. I should get you back to your dorm."

As they pulled up to the front of her building, she paused before getting out of the car. "Thank you for the coffee and movie."

"Wait." Branson got out of the car and jogged around to the passenger side, offering a hand to help Katie out. "I enjoyed the evening too." Branson walked her to the door and softly kissed her cheek. He wanted to pin her against the wall and smash his lips onto hers, letting his hands roam over her body, but he restrained himself. Something told him it was important not to rush her. He watched her reaction, and knew he had made the right choice in not pushing her.

A jolt of electricity touched Katie's cheek and coursed throughout her body. Visions of being in his embrace flooded her imagination and brought a heat wave with it. She felt her cheeks begin to warm in reaction and quickly turned toward the door. *Don't crumble yet, at least make it around the corner!*

Before Katie could make it into the elevator, she heard Branson's voice behind her. "Katie!"

She took a deep breath and turned to face him. "Yeah?"

"I forgot to get your number." He pulled out his phone and typed as she called each number. "Maybe we can get in a game of tennis this weekend?"

"Yeah, that sounds fun. Goodnight, Branson."

"Goodnight, Katie."

Katie smiled and stepped onto the awaiting elevator. She waited for it to completely close and begin its ascent before she smiled wildly and danced around the empty gray box.

When she entered her room, Maggie was sitting on her bed with her arms crossed. She looked as if someone had used up all of her shampoo and she was outraged.

"Where have you been?" Maggie asked. Her blond curls bouncing across her shoulders as she stood and tapped her foot. It reminded Katie of a parent waiting on her teenager after missing curfew.

"I was out. Why do you care and what are you doing home so early?"

"I've been calling your cell phone all night. Why haven't you answered?"

"Oh." Katie pulled out her phone and looked at it. Seven missed calls. "I had it on vibrate in my coat pocket, sorry. Is everything okay?"

Maggie's shoulders slumped. "It's over between Ian and me."

Katie sat next to her friend as Maggie told her the details of the night's events. She wrapped an arm around her shoulder, gave it a squeeze. "I'm sorry, Mags."

"I'm surprised at how good I feel about it, actually. He was all wrong for me." She grinned, and her demeanor instantly changed. Katie never would understand how she could change her feelings so quickly. One minute she was sobbing, the next she was laughing and ready to move on to the next thing. "So, where were you tonight?"

Katie looked at her quizzically. "Are you sure you don't want to talk more about *your* evening?"

"Hell no!" Her forehead crinkled, then relaxed. "It's simple. Ian's a slug, who can't keep his eyes from roaming over every tight skirt that passes by, and I deserve better."

"Of course, you deserve better. Besides, you always said Ian was just for fun—you would never marry him."

"I did say that." Maggie sat back on the bed, leaning against the wall. "So . . . where did you go, and with who?" She sat upright and narrowed her eyes. "Please tell me you didn't go to a party without me! What the hell, Katie?"

"I didn't go to a party!" Katie lifted her arms in surrender. "You're not going to believe what I did and with whom." Katie swooned, leaned back against the bed, and began telling Maggie about her evening with Branson.

"You're freaking kidding me?" Maggie shifted on the bed, her eyes wide with wonder. "What did you do? Where did you go? What'd ya talk about? Tell me everything!"

"Whoa! Slow down." Katie couldn't have hidden the wide grin, suddenly cramping her cheeks, if her life depended on it."We talked for a couple of hours at the coffee shop, and then tried to watch a movie in his apartment."

"What do you mean *tried?*" Maggie's face lit up, eager to hear the details.

"Seriously, Maggie! You don't think I would give it up so easily do you?" Actually, she knew she would have, if he'd made a move. He was deliciously handsome, and it took every ounce of will power not to throw herself at him. "We tried to watch the movie, but ended up talking through most of it. A kiss on the cheek when he walked me to the elevator was as far as things got." Katie sighed, falling back onto the bed. "I really like him, Mags. We have a great deal in common and you saw him—he's gorgeous."

Maggie laughed. "Are you going to see him again?"

"I hope so."

Four

Katie was deep into her studies when her phone rang. She didn't recognize the number and let it go to voicemail, so she could finish up and head to lunch with the girls. After packing up her notes and closing her books, she informed Maggie that she was ready to go. After meeting some friends downstairs, they slipped on their scarves and coats, and decided to walk to The Spot for Pepe's pizza. After eating two slices, Katie remembered to check her phone to see if the unknown caller had left a message. She held the phone to her ear and grinned as Branson's voice filled her ear.

"Hi, it's Branson Stone. I was calling to see if you were free tonight for dinner and a movie. My number should be on your caller ID now, so . . . I hope to hear from you soon."

Katie couldn't quit smiling as she thought of a night out with Branson.

"Whoever that was has you grinning from ear to ear—do tell." Alexa Greer rested her elbows on the table and placed her chin on folded hands. She was a bossy, know-it-all that set Katie on edge, to the point she hardly enjoyed the girl's company. She was an attractive girl with a cute, brown pixie cut, but didn't have a personality to match.

Maggie leaned forward and said, "It was him, wasn't it? Branson?"

Katie glared at Maggie for sharing her life with the table. "Yes. He asked me to dinner and a movie tonight." It took all her willpower not to giggle and act like a boy-crazy teenager, instead she said matter-of-factly, "I should be able to go, since I studied this morning."

Alexa's eyes grew wide in disbelief. "Branson Stone asked you out?" she asked, the jealousy clear in her voice and posture.

"Yes, do you know him?" Katie asked.

Alexa sat back in her chair and let the smile fade from her lips. "I don't know him personally, but I've heard he's a real player. A lot of girls throw themselves at him—it's gone to his head."

Maggie whipped her head around to Alexa, looking as if she could burn a hole through her with the power behind her angry eyes. "Well, if that's true, why have *you* been after him for the last two years—attending every tennis match? You don't even play tennis!"

Katie stood and started to put her coat on. "Okay, I'm a grown woman, perfectly capable of discerning a good guy from a player. I'm going out with him again. I really enjoy his company. I mean jeez, it's just a date."

Katie couldn't wait to get back to her room and call Branson in private. She wouldn't dare talk to him with an eavesdropping Alexa within hearing distance. As she and Maggie walked back to the dorm, all she could think about was what she would wear and how she would style her hair. Excitement and nerves played with each other on her insides, and she suddenly wished she hadn't eaten the second slice of pizza.

Branson pulled on a pair of jeans and looked at his grey sweater. He gave it a couple of good shakes, trying to get the wrinkles out, and then slipped it over his head. He thought about Katie. There was something intriguing about her that he couldn't put his finger on. She was beautiful, and kind, but it was her quirky confidence that made him eager to get to know her better. He enjoyed her conversation, and for the first time in his life he had chickened out of kissing a girl. She had given him every chance, and he blew it. He wouldn't make that mistake again.

He let his thoughts wander to the last conversation with his father. *"Dad, you've worked hard to build this company. You can't just let me step in and take over. Let's work together— you're much too young to retire."*

"No, your mother and I want to see the world while we're still young. You're a fine businessman, son, and you'll do an excellent job of filling my shoes. Just don't outshine me too quickly, okay?"

"So, where are you and mom going first?"

"Your mother has always wanted to see Ireland, so we'll start there and travel around Europe. We'll come back to see you on occasion, of course." His dad mussed up Branson's hair, like he had done since he was a kid, and he realized it might be best they didn't work side-by-side after all.

"What about the house? Are you going to sell it?"

"Yes, I figure you'll want a place of your own after graduation." He combed his hair, straightened his tie, and turned to his son. *"You do want the job at PCS, don't you? Would you tell me if there was another dream you wanted to pursue?"*

"Yes, Dad. As long as I have time for an occasional game of tennis, and a few women—I'm all in."

Branson smiled as he thought of his dad. He was constantly combing back his hair and straightening his tie. He was definitely in touch with his inner nerd. He thought about his mom and wondered what on earth she'd seen in his father. She was quiet, sweet, and very athletic, but didn't know a thing about computers, or even how to work the plethora of remotes they kept on the coffee table. She would often call Branson into the living room to change the channel to the Game Show Network for her.

He had been infused with both of their personalities. His mother pushed him into sports and they ran together on the weekends. She was never the type to coddle him, but instead encouraged him to push through cramps and fatigue. Sometimes, he hated running with her, but when it was over he felt a huge sense of accomplishment and was grateful for her drive.

His father was the one who grew his love for technology, math, and classic sci-fi movies. When the new *Star Wars* movies came out in theaters, they saw each of them at the midnight premiere.

He was definitely guided in the direction they both wanted for him, but he hadn't any objections about the career choice.

Branson checked himself in the mirror, grabbed his coat and keys, and let his roommate know he was going out.

Katie walked outside when she saw Branson pull up in a silver car. Branson hopped out and opened the passenger door, gently shutting it after Katie slipped in. "Are you in the mood for sushi?"

"I love sushi."

"Good. I hear Miya's is amazing."

The menu was filled with selections of sushi, sashimi, and spring roll choices. Katie had never seen such a selection and was unsure what to order. *If it comes down to it, I'll just order the second thing on the menu. That's always a safe zone.*

"Do you drink sake? I see they have one called Cherokee Sumac Love Potion." He smiled impishly.

"Somehow, I don't think we need that one." Katie smiled, and then immediately hid her face behind the menu. "Oh God, did I just say that out loud?"

"Yes—yes, you did," Branson laughed heartily. "And I have to agree. How about . . . Okay, they're all named seductively, but the Bonobo juice sounds great. What do you think?"

Katie kept the menu up while she answered. "Yes, that sounds wonderful."

The sake instantly warmed Katie and brought a relaxed confidence with it. "Mmm, this is good. I taste a hint of lime."

"Tell me about your family. Do you have any siblings?" Branson asked before taking another sip of sake.

Katie thought about Gram and smiled. Most girls would have felt robbed without parents, but Katie had the best parent, ally, and comrade in Gram. They often laughed until they were breathless, traveled all over the coastline together, enjoyed operas, symphonies, and not a year passed that they didn't attend the *Nutcracker* ballet for Christmas. She hated the cold, but always looked forward to sipping Wassail by the fire and staying up most of the night retelling stories of their adventures together over the years. She hadn't realized until now how much she missed her, and wondered if Branson would have the chance to meet her.

"My parents were killed in a car accident when I was two. I was raised by my father's mother, Gram." Katie could see the look of remorse on Branson's face and wanted to erase it. "Please, don't look at me like that. Trust me—I've had the most amazing life. Gram was not only a wonderful parent, but she's my best friend, and we've had a great time together. I wouldn't change a thing about my upbringing, except maybe an older brother. I was always so jealous of my girlfriends when their older brothers were so protective of them—giving boyfriends the stink-eye." Katie laughed, and asked Branson about his family.

"My mother is a homemaker, who is never at home. She's involved in everything she can get her hands in. She loves to run—she's completed half a dozen marathons and triathlons. My father is just the opposite, and will tell you that if you see him running it means something is chasing him. I have two older sisters, who are both married. One of whom has a son, Jackson. He's two, mean as a snake, and the cutest kid I've ever seen."

"Do they live close?"

"My sister with the baby, Jennifer, lives about an hour away. We see her once a month or so. My other sister, Laynie, still lives in Texas, so we only see her about four times a year."

"I forgot that you were from Texas. What part?"

"Austin. It's beautiful there, my dad used to take me to the UT football games. I used to wear a huge Longhorn hat to every game when I was a kid—thought for sure I would attend college there. Have you ever been?"

Something flashed in Katie's mind. She envisioned the burnt orange uniforms. She furrowed her brow to dig deeper into the memory, but it ran dry. "I'm not sure, maybe when I was a kid. I vaguely remember watching them play, but it could have been on TV."

"Maybe you and your Gram went when you were younger. She does sound great, if she took you to football games."

"I'll have to ask her. She's never taken me to a football game that I can remember. The symphony, yes. Football . . . not so much."

"We should get going if we want to make the movie on time," Branson said, paying the check and gathering their coats.

Within minutes they were in the car, waiting for the engine to warm enough for the heat to come on. When it did, Katie rubbed her hands together. "Ah, that's more like it."

Branson shuffled through the radio stations, settling on a station playing Lana Del Ray. "This okay?"

"Yeah, I like her. Depressing, but she's got a beautiful voice."

"Tell me something, Katie. Something no one else knows."

"Well, Maggie knows everything about me, but hmm . . . something most people don't know . . . at the risk of sounding like a dork, I've memorized nearly every line of *Les Misérables,* but I've never seen it live."

"Are you serious?" He laughed. "How have you memorized it?"

"BBC. Now, it's your turn."

"I'm wishing I'd chosen a better question. Let's see . . . I was in a commercial once."

"What?" Katie turned in her seat to face him. "Which one? I need to see it."

"I was a baby. It was a formula commercial. Enfamil, I think. You can't even tell it's me, they only show the side of my head. But still, if I'd pursued acting . . ."

Katie giggled. "Yeah, right. I still want to see it."

Shortly after the movie began, Branson slid his hand into Katie's and waited for her reaction. When she gazed up at him with a sweet smile, he relaxed back into his seat and enjoyed the fire that sparked between them.

Branson helped Katie with her coat and was surprised when she took his hand in hers as they walked to the car. "The movie was good," Katie said.

"Yeah, I liked the part when the sweet little woman went all Bruce Lee on the bad guy."

When they reached the car, Branson knew he was going to kiss her before he opened the door. His heart began to race as the nervousness of a first kiss took over. He focused on keeping his fingers from twitching in hers, and cursed the setup of the movie theater parking lot. The only space that had been available when they arrived at the theater now seemed to be on the bordering state, and the walk toward the car seemed to last forever.

"Hurry! Open the door. It's freezing!" Katie released his hand and wiggled in anticipation of a reprieve from the cold air.

Branson opened her door, helping her slide in, and shut it behind her. The timing wasn't right, but the date wasn't over. He wouldn't let the night slip away without a kiss.

Not wanting the date to end, they walked slowly through the dorm. As they arrived at Katie's door, she purposely fumbled for her keys, prolonging their goodbye. Before the key could meet the lock, Branson gently took her chin in his hand, lifting her face toward his.

The anticipation of the moment was nearly too much as Katie's heart slammed against her chest. Branson slowly leaned in and it seemed like his lips would never meet hers, as if each second was stuck in a time warp. Their breath mingled as his lips slowly touched hers, as light and soft as the first snowflakes of winter.

She was surprised that such gentleness could come from someone with such an athletic build, then was caught up in the most soaring, tremendous sensation that swept through her entire body. She instinctively slid her hands up his arms, moaning softly. Branson responded by pulling her body tightly into his. He must have lost footing and stumbled backward, pulling her with him. Thankfully, the hall was narrow and they caught themselves against the opposite wall, instead of tangled up on the floor.

After sharing a nervous laugh, the heat resumed and Katie found herself fervently pursuing his lips again. She pulled away, still breathless and wanting, and broke the spell. "I—I should go . . ." She didn't take her eyes off of him as she backed up. Everything in her wanted to invite him in to explore the raging heat that he sent through her, but instead she slipped inside and shut the door.

Even though she didn't like Alexa, and never trusted anything she said, the word *player* had been put out there, and she wasn't about to find out if that was true tonight.

Five

Prime 16 Tap House was a small restaurant with a long bar and tables arranged against the walls. Branson and Mike found a seat in the crowded pub and ordered burgers and beer. Mike took a swig of the ice cold brew and smiled. "Tell me about this girl that's got you grinning like an idiot."

Mike Burrows was tall and slender. His blond buzz cut nearly matched the color of his pale complexion, and his eyes were gunmetal blue. He and Branson played football together in high school and maintained their friendship through college, although they had taken different career paths and enjoyed separate extracurricular activities.

Branson leaned back in his chair and grinned. "She's amazing."

Mike waited for more details and was surprised when none came. "That's it? That's all you've got to say about her?"

"What do you want to hear? You want me to gush about how beautiful she is?" He took a long sip before continuing, "She's sweet, funny, and gentle—almost an anachronism." He shook his head. "I don't know—there's just something about her, man."

"Sounds like things are getting—" Mike paused as their plates were placed in front of them. "Are you in love with her?"

Branson took a bite of his burger and chewed slowly, processing the question. *Am I in love with her? It's too soon to consider something like that. Lust—yes. Love—doubtful.* "Of course I'm not in love! I've only known her a few weeks. It's too soon—but I do think about her all the time. How are things going with you and Blondie?"

"Jessica? She's ancient history. I thought you knew. Dude, we don't hang out enough." Mike dipped an onion ring into ketchup and took a bite. "I'm interested in someone else."

"Who?"

"You don't know her. We have a class together, and I've been coming up with reasons I need to be on the other side of campus, so I can walk her back to her dorm. Talk about gorgeous—this girl is a knockout."

"Have you asked her out?" Branson asked before taking another bite.

"No." Mike lowered his head in shame. He had always been confident with the ladies, but this girl had him questioning his every move.

Branson shook his head and chuckled. "What happened to Mike Burrows—Womanizer?"

"I'd like to see *your* confidence around this girl. She has these green eyes that—"

"Wait! Green eyes?"

"Yeah," Mike replied slowly.

"Long dark hair?" Branson glowered.

"Shit! Seriously?" Mike didn't even have to say her name. He instantly knew they were speaking of the same girl, and Branson had gotten to her first.

"Please, tell me her name's not Katie." Branson raised one eyebrow as he studied his friend's face.

"Katie Harrington."

Branson's jaw clenched, his fist gripping the glass bottle of Rolling Rock so firmly, he thought it would shatter.

"She hasn't given you the idea that she's available . . . has she?" Branson asked. They hadn't talked about being monogamous, or labeled their relationship as anything, but she didn't seem like the kind of girl who would date more than one guy.

"Nah, she's sweet and she talks to me, but since I never had the guts to ask her out, she never had to tell me she was dating someone." Mike got the server's attention. "Another round, please."

For two months Katie and Branson spent every moment outside of class time together. Each morning she received a sweet text with a quote of the day attached at the end, and every evening ended with a passionate kiss that threatened her propriety.

On Tuesday night, as Katie was studying for her finals in the library, Branson slipped in behind her and set a pumpkin spiced latte on her desk. "Hey! What's this?" Katie beamed. "You can't bring coffee into the library."

"You're not supposed to make out in here either, but it happens a lot. Wanna break another rule?" He grinned nefariously.

"That would be one for the books." Katie laughed and slapped her knee.

"Oh, that was bad." Branson grimaced.

"I know, I know."

"Anyway, I knew you would be up here all night, so I thought a coffee might be a nice treat."

Katie stood and kissed Branson sweetly. "You're the best treat, but thank you for the coffee. Now, if you'll leave me to study, I'll ace my finals and we can celebrate this weekend. Besides, don't you have finals this week also?"

"I do, and I'm studying right over there." He pointed to the cubby across the room where a matching latte awaited him.

"Good. How long will you be here?" Katie knew she had to dig into her books and study hard, but it was comforting to know Branson was there. She hoped they could walk back to the dorm together, so she wouldn't have to walk alone.

"I'll stay long enough to walk you back. It's not safe for a girl as beautiful as you are to be left alone on campus after dark. That creepy old lady from *Paranormal Activity 4* could be lingering in the shadows." His eyes widened for effect.

"Branson!" Katie shivered and rubbed her arms. "You know how terrified I am of those movies."

"Yes, I do." He winked and pulled out her chair for her to sit.

"Thank you. I won't be too long. Let's say no later than eleven thirty?"

"Sounds good, babe. If you want to take a break, just meet me in the Shakespeare section." Branson grinned before kissing the top of her head and walking back to his desk.

Katie watched as he walked away. He was wearing loose jeans, with the design on the pockets, which sat ever-so-nicely on his hips. His navy sweater was snug and showed off his broad shoulders. *Shakespeare section, huh? Jeez, how am I supposed to concentrate with that image in my head?* Katie allowed her thoughts to deviate from her studies and roam into a steamy rendezvous against the bookshelves. She peeked over at Branson, who was reading intently. After a sip of latte, she did the same until she was interrupted by the buzz of her phone. It was a text message:

Hi love. How's it going over there? In the mood for Shakespeare yet?

Katie looked over at a Branson and returned his smile before sending a text back:

Meh. He hasn't offered much help with my finals ;)

Branson stood and walked as he typed:

All work and no play . . .

Katie read the text and watched as he rounded the corner and disappeared. She felt a thrill run up her spine as she contemplated the situation. Looking around the library, her assumption that everyone was looking at her with knowing eyes was erased. She slowly stood and walked toward the row of books that held promise of an exhilarating moment.

Without a word, Branson pulled Katie in close. When his lips found hers, desire took over and her fear of being caught was washed away. Her body ignited as he slid his hands up her waist, over her ribs, and onto her breasts. She twisted her fingers in his hair as their kiss became deeper, and moaned when his thumb grazed across her nipple.

"Shh," Branson smiled.

Katie pulled away and tried to catch her breath. "Sorry, but jeez . . ." She gave him a quick peck on the lips and turned to walk back to her desk.

Katie was vastly aware that she was in a dream state as a thin fog lingered over the ground and snaked through the naked tree branches. The difference between dream and reality was his voice behind her. Branson called out, "Wait up, green eyes!"

The air was chilled and steam exited her mouth and nose as she exhaled. She hated to be cold, but knew warmth would come soon as Branson wrapped his arms around her. She turned, grinning too wide, but unable to hide her excitement. She tried to say hello, but the cold air paralyzed her vocal chords.

Branson wrapped his arms around her, pulling her into him and giving her the warmth and safety she craved. His lips found hers, hungry and forceful, taking more than she was accustom to. During their short time as a couple, he'd been gentle, taming the appetite they both shared. He was a gentleman, taking their journey in measured, attentive steps, respecting her as a lady. His lips tugged against hers, causing her to whimper. Passion swirled through her, mingled with anxiety. Although she enjoyed the heated moment, he was taking more than she was ready to give. His fingers dug into her hips, making the seam on her jeans cut into her flesh.

"You're hurting me, Branson." Katie tried to pull away, but he was strong and greedy. His hands moved to her breasts, mashing them through her sweater. "Please, stop!" She jerked away, pushing against his chest with all the power she could manage.

"Tease!" he answered, wiping the back of his hand across his lips. They were swollen from the aggressive make out session, too swollen.

Katie's eyes roamed over his mouth, lifting slowly up over his nose, and finally to his dark eyes. She stumbled backward, unable to catch herself from falling when she realized it wasn't Branson. "Who are you?" she pleaded, falling . . . falling . . .

falling. Would the ground ever come up to cease the endless decent? "Who are you?" she screamed.

"It's me . . . Maggie." A faded, high-pitched voice echoed through the dark night. "Wake up, Katie. It's okay, it's just a bad dream."

Looking into familiar eyes, Katie sat up and wrapped her arms around Maggie. Sucking in deep breaths, she tried to calm her racing pulse. "I was so scared, Mags. It felt so real."

"What happened? Want to tell me about it?"

"It was Branson . . . and then it wasn't."

"You're shaking, Katie." Maggie turned on the bedside lamp. "Look at me. You're okay. We're in our room and no one is going to hurt you."

"I know, thank you. I'm sorry I woke you . . . again."

"It's okay. I just wish we could figure out why you're riddled with nightmares. Maybe you should see a fortune teller or something?"

She always made me laugh, even when it wasn't intended. "Sure, Mags. A fortune teller. What will she tell me?"

Katie lowered my voice, mimicking her version of a gypsy psychic scammer. "You've been reincarnated into this life. In your past journey on earth, you were a cockroach that everyone tried to stamp out. This is the reason for your terrifying nightmares."

They shared a giggly, four-in-the-morning, sleep deprived laugh. She waited for Maggie to climb back into her bed before shutting the lamp off. "Thanks, Mags. Good night."

"Sweet dreams, friend," she replied, followed by a long, audible yawn.

Six

Celebrations had already begun all over campus by the time Katie finished her last exam Thursday morning. Branson's was in the late afternoon, so Katie had time to enjoy a few beers with Maggie before joining Branson that evening.

As she stepped outside, the air was swirling with little white flakes of snow. The wind bit at her cheeks and nose, causing her to pull her scarf up over them. The sidewalks were blanketed with the sparkling white powder and a thin layer covered the streets, swirling around as the wind blew.

"It's snowing!" Maggie sang as she threw her head back and twirled around.

"Yipee." Katie replied with very little enthusiasm. She hated to be cold, and although it was a beautiful sight to see out of a window, having it land on your head, cheeks, and nose was like having someone stick ice cubes down your shirt as a gag. It wasn't as bad as rain, until it melted inside of your boots and you were left with soaking wet socks and numb toes.

Thankfully, the pub was warm enough to enjoy a cold beer.

"What've you got planned for tonight?" Maggie asked as she tipped the bottle of Killian's Red and took a drink.

"I'm not sure. Maybe we'll end up back here for burgers and beer again." Katie laughed. "What are your plans for Christmas break?"

"My sister and I are going to spend a week on the slopes in Canada, and then we'll be home for Christmas with Mom and Dad. What about you?"

"A week in Canada sounds great, except the frigid temperatures." Katie shivered. "I'll go home to see Gram. Who knows what she'll have planned. I can't wait to take a break from studying, watch Christmas movies, and eat all of Gram's goodies. But two weeks without Branson is going to suck."

"What are Branson's plans? Do you think you'll see him over the holidays?" Maggie grinned, leaning forward as if Katie were about to fill her in on the town gossip.

"I don't know, I guess we'll talk about it tonight. I do hope to see him, though."

After lunch Katie called Gram and talked for an hour. Gram asked her about her exams and college life, and then filled her in on the happenings around York. "I've already got our tickets for the *Nutcracker* this year. You're not too old, now that you're almost a college graduate, are you?" Gram teased. Katie couldn't wait to get home and wrap her arms around her grandmother. She could see Gram's green eyes dancing as she talked, and swore she could smell a hint of her Estee Lauder perfume.

"Of course not. This is a tradition I plan on carrying with my own children one day. I can't wait to see you, Gram."

"Me either, love. It's just not the same here without you. Now tell me more about this boy—what are his plans for the holiday break? I'd love to meet him."

Katie filled Gram in on the most recent dates with Branson. "I don't know what his plans are yet, but I do want you to meet him. He's just wonderful, Gram. He has the most beautiful blue eyes you've ever seen, and dimples that make you come up with funny things to say just to make them appear. He's strong and smart. Did I tell you that he's on the tennis team?"

Katie rambled on telling Gram everything. As she talked, she realized she was beginning to sound like the fisherman who caught the most magnificent fish, but never could reel it in for proof. The story just kept growing until Branson was a perfectly sculptured mythical creature.

She couldn't wait to see Gram and tell her every detail about their dates. He was romantic and thoughtful, always opening doors and pulling out her chair. She thought about him playing a song for her on the guitar for the first time. He began to play a soft tune as Katie watched his fingers strum the strings. He was talented on the guitar and she was impressed . . . and then he began to sing. His rich, smooth voice took her breath and she wondered when she would discover his imperfections.

"Why don't you invite him for the weekend, dear? Let me see this marvelous creature myself."

"That's a great idea. I'll talk to him, and let you know."

"What does he like to eat? I need to make a list."

"Gram, I don't even know if he can make it. I'm sure he'll eat whatever you serve. Don't fuss." Knowing it was a waste of her breath, she had to say it anyway. Gram *would* fuss, she took pride in feeding people. She was generous with her acts of selfless service and hospitality.

"I want him to be comfortable. It's not easy meeting the parents . . . or grandmother!" She chuckled.

God, Katie missed her and couldn't wait to get home. Her brain was pushed to the limit, with all the studying and testing she had done. A break was not only desired, but necessary. "I've gotta run. I'll call as soon as I know something so you can buy way too many snacks." She giggled. "Bye, Gram. See you soon."

Katie sat on the edge of her bed and contemplated a weekend with Branson. She thought of all of the places she wanted to show him. A knock on the door broke her reverie. She opened it to find Branson standing there, smiling. "Come in," she offered.

"Hi." He kissed her softly on the lips. "I just talked with my parents, and my sister is coming in for the weekend with Jackson." He paused, collected his nerves. "I'd like you to meet my family this weekend, if you're able."

"That's hilarious. I just got off the phone with Gram and intended to have you over for the weekend."

Branson laughed. "Well, I would love to, but can you come to my place first, since my sister will be there? She doesn't come home often, and I'd love to see my nephew. We can spend a few days with my family, and then go see yours."

"Of course. I'll just let Gram know that we'll be coming on Monday."

"Perfect. Now let's go play in the snow!"

"Not you, too?"

"What do you mean? Don't you like the snow?"

Katie walked over to the window and watched as the trees were painted silvery-white. "It's beautiful, but I don't see why everyone wants to play in it. You never see anyone running outside to play in the rain, but freeze it and it's a party."

"Oh, no! You're not going to bahumbug Christmas too, are you?"

"I love Christmas. I just don't like to be pelted by frozen water."

"Well, I'm going to change your mind. Let's get you dressed properly, and then we're going to play in the snow."

"No, please, I really don't like to be so cold."

Branson pulled her in close, pressing his body into hers. A gripping current traveled through her and she wasn't sure what the stronger contributing force was—his intense eyes, or firm, well-built body. She longed for the feeling of his lips on hers as he looked at her hungrily. God, he was sexy. He moved teasingly slow, barely brushing his lips across hers and pausing for effect. She tried to pull him in, but he held her arms and resumed the tortuous pleasure by softly planting kisses up her neck and behind her ear. Katie lolled her head back and moaned as the fire spread throughout her body. She was filled with an indescribable desire and felt like her body would detonate, leaving Branson standing there among a pile of ash.

"Are you warm enough to go in the snow with me now?" Branson whispered enticingly into her ear.

"I'm afraid I might catch on fire, actually."

"Good, let's go cool off outside then." He chuckled and pulled away.

"Oh no you don't." Katie pulled on each side of his unzipped jacket until he was close enough to satisfy her. "If I go out there now, I'll melt all the snow and ruin the fun for everyone. You don't want to be responsible for that, do you?"

Branson shook his head and gave her a predatory look. "Where's Maggie?"

"Out." Katie found his lips.

He slipped his arms around her waist and pulled her body close to his, letting her feel how much he wanted her. Her moans were driving him wild and he hoped he could be patient with her and not rush things like a hormone-raged teen. Her body was extraordinary and he couldn't wait to see what it looked like unclothed. As he ran his hand up her small waist and found her breast, she moaned into his mouth again, causing him to nearly lose it.

"God, Katie, I want you."

Katie nodded her head, unable to speak. She had never been so turned on in her life. Branson removed his jacket and tossed it on the back of the chair. Katie ran her hands over the contours of his chest before lifting his blue cotton shirt up over his head. Her hands moved across his bare chest and sculpted abs, memorizing every inch. She traced two fingers over his belly button, down the coarse trail of hair leading to the waistline of his jeans. She felt his body tense under her touch and looked up to see the heat behind his eyes.

"My turn," Branson said as he slowly lifted her thin gray sweater over her head to behold full breasts straining against a gray lace bra. He took her in with his eyes before letting his hands roam over her, greedily trying to unhook the clasp of her bra. Before he could get the last hook undone, he heard the lock on the door being turned.

"Shit! Maggie!" Katie grabbed her sweater and slipped it over her head. Branson retreated to the bathroom with his shirt.

"Hi." Maggie smiled, and then looked at her roommate in surprise. "Oh jeez, is he here?"

"Yeah, he's in the bathroom." Katie nodded her head toward the door. Embarrassed, she kept her eyes focused on the floor, trying to find abstract images in the pale yellow linoleum tiles. "I thought you were going to be out all day?"

"I ran into Ian and it spoiled my fun." She took off her jacket and gloves and plopped herself into the desk chair.

Branson came out of the bathroom looking as if nothing had happened. "Hi, Maggie."

"Hi, Bran—Oh. My. God. I've interrupted," Maggie said. "I'll go watch a movie downstairs, or something. Don't worry—just tie something on the doorknob, so I'll know when it's safe to come back." Maggie eagerly searched for a ribbon.

"Maggie, stop! You didn't interrupt anything. Branson just came up to see if I wanted to play in the snow." Katie straightened her sweater and looked sheepishly at Branson.

"Uh huh, then why is your sweater on inside out?" Maggie smirked. She grabbed her coat and gloves, and placed a black ribbon in Katie's hand before shutting the door behind her.

Katie sighed and plopped down onto her bed. "I'm sorry, but it just feels weird now." She looked up at Branson. "Are you upset?"

"Upset, no. Disappointed, yes. But we'll have other opportunities." One of their roommates was always walking in on them. Branson sat down next to her on the bed and shook his head as he chuckled.

"What's so funny?"

"You're good. You distracted me on purpose, so you wouldn't have to go out in the snow. Now that I know your game, green eyes, it's on."

"But I didn't—" Katie giggled as he lifted her up over his shoulder and threatened to take her outside and throw her in the snow. "Okay! Okay! I'll go. Let me dress in my Eskimo outfit first."

Branson watched Katie's face light up as they played in the snow. She laughed until she was too weak to stand after pummeling Branson with a snowball, and begged him not to seek revenge. They slid down hills on makeshift cardboard sleds, built a miniature snow man, and created snow angels in the thick, white powder before coming back inside.

"That was a blast!" Katie exclaimed. "I had no idea you could have so much fun in frozen water vapor."

"See, that's why you don't know how to have fun in the winter wonderland. It's snow. We made a snowman, not a frozen vapor sculpture."

"Mmm hmm, I guess if I screamed because a tornado was coming, you would say 'it's only a swirling gust of wind—enjoy the ride.'"

Branson pinned her against the wall. "You have a rosy-red nose and pink cheeks. Let's see if I can warm you up." When he pulled away, he rested his forehead on hers and inhaled deeply. "God, I think I love you."

His declaration slipped from his lips without warning. Fearing her reaction, he couldn't look into her eyes. Maybe it was too soon to tell her. *Shit! I said I 'think,' not that I 'do' love her. What the fuck was that?* She pulled away, just as he thought she would. Sliding his eyes closed, he waited for her to question his statement. Instead, her mouth crashed against his, her fingers sliding around the nape of his neck, pulling him closer. For an instant, he understood what she was trying to relay unspoken. Then his hands slipped under her sweater, finding the soft flesh of her small waist, and thinking was no longer an option.

Seven

Katie was thrilled to spend a night out with Branson and some of their friends. She didn't have to worry about studying for an exam or staying out too late for an early morning class the next day. She was free to enjoy an evening out and see what Branson was like around his friends.

"Who knows, you and Mike might hit it off. He's a great guy, and not bad looking either." Katie wiggled her eyebrows at Maggie.

"I hate blind dates."

"It's not a blind date. It's drinks with friends. I'm just saying—he's cute, he's single, and he's really nice. I've given you a head start on Jill, since they're picking us up. If you like him, you better let him know before she sees him." Katie winked. She was in an exceptionally good mood as she brushed her hair once more and looked herself over in the mirror.

Maggie stood facing Katie's closet, looking for something. "Can I borrow your black boots?"

"Of course. I love the black sweater against your blond hair. You look fantastic. Are these jeans okay?"

Maggie turned, looking her up and down. "No, no. You can't wear that." She scrunched her nose. "You're going for hot tonight, not the preppy student look." She flipped through the hangers and pulled out a green dress. "Wear this."

"It's cold outside."

"Wear a coat. Besides, it'll be hot inside."

Katie slipped on the dress, enjoying the sensual feel of the silky fabric against her skin. The brown boots that Maggie set out for her were the perfect compliment. "How's this?"

"You look amazing! I'll bet you twenty bucks Branson stutters when he sees you."

"I hope so," Katie said. She had shaved her legs twice in the shower, in case tonight was the night. "Ready?"

Mike and Branson were waiting downstairs in the lobby. As Katie closed the space between her and Branson, she noticed the way his eyes roamed over her body. She walked with confidence as the dress made her feel feminine and sexy.

"Hi, beautiful." Branson greeted Katie with a kiss before introducing Mike to Maggie. The club was crowded as they walked in and hung their coats on a rack near the door. They found a high top table in the corner and took it before looking around.

"I don't see Jill or Alexa anywhere, do you?" Katie shouted over the noisy crowd.

Maggie shook her head. "They'll probably be late. Let's go ahead and order drinks."

Branson waved over a couple of his friends. "This is Cam and Ryan. This is my girlfriend, Katie, and her friend, Maggie."

Katie smiled. She knew she and Branson were an item, but it was the first time she had heard him address her as his girlfriend. "Hi, nice to meet you."

When the drinks arrived, Mike lifted his beer to make a toast. "Here's to the end of exams and a long winter break!"

Everyone clinked their glasses together in celebration and took a drink. The crowd was electric as the music played and students celebrated. Katie watched as Maggie and Mike shared awkward small talk over the thumping bass.

Jill and Alexa found the table and walked over. "Looks like you guys started without us." Jill said, ogling Mike already. Jill Palermo and Katie met in the Nursing program. She was a pretty blonde with hazel eyes and a flirtatious personality. You either liked her immediately, or were turned off completely.

Maggie watched as Jill flirted with Mike and suddenly felt competitive. "I love this song. Dance with me." Maggie pulled Mike onto the dance floor.

Well, that was easy. Katie thought. She looked at Branson, who must have read her mind since he gave a knowing wink before tipping up his Samuel Adams for a long drink. Katie felt goose bumps rise as his hand rested on her bare knee. She looked out across the dance floor instead of at Branson, knowing that one glance would have them searching for a dark corner.

"I'm going to visit the ladies room." Katie stood. "You're all mine out there as soon as I get back."

When Katie returned, "Adorn" by Miguel was playing. She made her way to the dance floor and motioned for Branson to join her. She moved her body to the music as he finished his beer and began to walk toward her. Without warning, she felt someone grinding behind her and whipped her head around to see who it was. A stranger with dark eyes and a wicked grin pulled her against his body like he had been intimate with her for years.

Katie raised her hands in protest. "Whoa, buddy." She tried to pull away.

"C'mon, our bodies are so compatible," he said, pulling her in and grinding his body against hers.

"I said no—I'm not interested." Her rejection seemed to spur him on as he pulled her in tighter and roamed over her body with his hands. "Don't touch me!" Katie tried to pull away, but he was too strong.

She suddenly felt his body being jerked away from hers, causing her to stumble backwards into another couple. "I'm sorry." She apologized and got her balance before looking around to see what had happened.

A rage came over Branson, like a thick, deep fog as he watched another man force himself on Katie, touching her as she tried to free herself from his grasp. He grabbed the jerk by the arm, pulled him away from Katie and punched him. "Next time a lady says 'no thank you,' back off, prick!"

The guy got up and lunged for Branson, but two of his friends held him back, eventually leading him out of the club.

Katie ran to Branson. "Are you all right?" She noticed him rubbing his knuckles. "I can't believe you punched him!"

"He had his hands all over you," Branson answered, the anger still present in his voice. He watched as the man left the club and his anger receded. He held Katie's chin and smiled. "I'll always fight for you, you're worth fighting for."

Katie kissed his sore knuckles. "Thank you. I feel safe and protected when I'm with you." She looked down. "I'm sorry that ruined our night."

"What? I'm not letting that worm ruin anything." He pulled her in close and began to move as "Ho Hey" by the Lumineers played.

"We can't slow dance to this song, silly!" Katie laughed.

Branson nodded to the DJ as if they had some secret bond and the song instantly changed to "Teardrop" by Mezzanine. Katie laid her head on Branson's chest as she enjoyed the way his arms felt around her. He was strong enough to protect her, yet gentle enough to hold her and make her feel like she was the only woman in the world. She felt tears sting her eyes when the reality of her emotion hit her. She felt alive when she was with Branson, and when she wasn't she thought about him constantly. His eyes disarmed her, his dimples made her giggle, and his body sent an electric current from her toes to the top of her head whenever she came in contact with it.

Her breath hitched in her throat, causing Branson to pull back and look at her. His eyes roamed her face. "What's wrong?"

Katie blinked back the tears that threatened to spill over. She gazed into his eyes for what seemed an eternity before replying. "I—I've fallen in love with you, Branson."

Branson responded with a deep kiss that left Katie balancing on unsteady legs. He felt her wobble and wondered if she had too much to drink already. "Are you all right?"

Katie flashed a crooked smile. "You make my world spin when you kiss me like that."

"You have no idea how much I like making your world spin," he whispered into her ear and kissed her neck.

"Hi, guys!" Maggie and Mike were on the dance floor, interrupting the moment before things got out of hand.

"Hi. Having a good time?" Katie asked.

Maggie grinned and nodded her head. "As soon as this song is over, we're doing a round of shots."

"Not me!" Katie objected.

"Oh, yes, you are. Finals are over and you promised to let me show you how it's done." Maggie grinned.

When the song finished, they were back at the table, shot glass in hand. "Okay, what are we drinking?" Branson asked.

"China White's. Bailey's, Crème de cocoa, and a dash of cinnamon." Mike answered.

On Maggie's count, they all drank and slammed the small glasses onto the table. Maggie looked at Katie and laughed. "It was good though, right?"

Katie grimaced, and then smiled. "Mmm hmm, reminds me of Christmas and hell all at the same time."

Maggie ordered a round of Snake Bites, Branson chose Kamikazis, and Katie attempted to order a drink that she created on the spot. "Bring us something pretty. I like blue. Do you make blue shots?" Katie's words were slurred as she held onto her chair, trying not to slide out of it onto the floor.

"Okay, I think we're done here. We'd like to settle up the tab now." Branson handed the bartender his credit card.

Katie leaned on Branson as they walked to the car and nudged him when she saw Mike and Maggie holding hands. She tried to whisper as she wrapped her arms around Branson's neck, "Maybe she'll go to his place so you . . ." Katie pressed her finger into his chest, "and I . . . can be alone. Or we could go to your place. Is your roommate home?

"As much as I want to be alone with you, it won't be when you're drunk. I want all of your senses on board."

"I'm not drunk, I'm just relaxed." Katie pouted.

"Mmm hmm, I'm sure." Branson kissed the top of Katie's head and helped her into the car.

They arrived safely at her dorm, where he made her drink a glass of water and take two Ibuprofen tablets before putting her to bed. After tucking her in and kissing her forehead, he slipped out and shut the door behind him.

"Please . . . ungh . . ." Maggie flipped on her bedside lamp and rushed to Katie's side of the room. She held her shoulders, trying to soothe her shaking roommate.

"Katie, wake up."

Disoriented, Katie tried to focus on the person looming over her. "Maggie? Shit! Again? I'm sorry. Go back to sleep. I'm okay."

"You sure?"

Katie nodded and wiped the tears from her face with the back of her hand. "I'm sure. It was nothing. Too much alcohol."

"Okay. Goodnight."

Katie hugged her pillow and traced back over her nightmare, trying to figure out who the strange faces belonged to. *I've got to stop watching Criminal Minds and start watching reruns of Andy Griffith or something. This is getting ridiculous. Who the hell is James?*

Eight

"What if they don't like me?" Katie asked as they drove down I-84 toward Branson's home.

He gave Katie's fingers a gentle squeeze. "Are you serious? They're going to love you. Trust me, they're very laid back, and will welcome you with open arms. You do like cats, don't you?" Branson asked, hopeful.

"Oh, yes, I love cats," Katie lied. She'd always been deathly afraid of cats.

"Good, because we have twenty-seven of them . . . indoors." Branson could hardly contain the smile that played at his lips. He remembered Katie's ridiculous fear of cats and couldn't resist teasing her about it now. When he heard her swallow the lump in her throat, he guffawed. "We don't have any cats."

"You're an arse." Katie folded her arms and tried not to laugh.

"So you're British now?" He laughed and squeezed her hand.

"Humph. It's a good thing you're so devastatingly handsome, sir, or else . . ." Katie turned on the radio and found a station playing The xx.

"Devastatingly handsome, huh?" Branson grinned widely, exposing his dimples. Katie wondered how she would keep her hands to herself in the presence of his parents, if he was capable of turning her on with just a smile.

"By the way, you should know that Gram *is* British. She has also won several medals for her shooting skills."

"You jest."

"No, I'm serious, she was born in London."

"And she's an excellent marksman?"

"No," Katie smiled. "I made that up. Payback for your cat tales."

"Pun intended?" Branson laughed.

Three hours later they were winding down a long unpaved driveway enveloped by ancient pine trees. The contrast of the deep green against the white snow was beautiful. The thick shade of the forest eventually thinned, revealing a stunning rustic home of stone, brick, and wood.

"Wow."

"Do you like it? Wait till you see the back." He smiled and turned off the engine. "Ready?" he asked, opening Katie's door and offering his hand.

"Yes." She smiled and checked herself in the reflection of the car window, smoothing a few strands of hair back into place and pinching her cheeks for a little color.

Before he could get his key in the door it flew open and they were greeted by his mother, sister, and little Jackson. "You're here!" his mother sang, before wrapping her arms around her son. "Come in out of the cold."

"Mom, I'd like you to meet Katie. Katie, this is my mother, Celia."

"Hello, Katie. I'm so pleased to meet you." Celia Stone was kind and welcoming. She had short, dark hair, brown eyes, and the same deep dimples as Branson.

"Thank you so much for having me this weekend, Mrs. Stone. It's just lovely here."

"Oh, please, call me Celia." She smiled.

Branson took his eager nephew into his arms and introduced him next. "This little wiggle worm is Jackson, and this is my sister, Jennifer."

"Hi, Katie, it's nice to meet you." She hugged Katie, surprising her, but it had felt good to have his sister's approval so quickly.

"Where's Adam?" Branson asked.

"He couldn't come. One of his clients is angry because their ad ran in the wrong time slot, so he has to fix it—or kiss butt rather."

"You must be starved. I have lunch ready in the kitchen," Celia said, walking ahead.

Following Celia to the kitchen, Katie took in the house, noticing the lodge theme throughout. Large wooden beams crossed the ceiling, framed the cream walls, and lined the doors and windows. As they passed through the living room, Katie felt the warmth radiating from a large stone fireplace and paused to savor the feeling.

Branson put his arms around Katie, hugging her to his body. "Don't tell me my little ice cube is cold?"

Katie tried to wiggle loose. "Agh! Your mom and sister!"

Branson laughed. "What? Do you think I told them you were my tutor—you're here as my girlfriend. Relax."

"I'm shy." Katie batted her eyelashes.

"*You*? Shy?" He laughed. "Since when has Katie Harrington ever been afraid of anything? You'd charge hell with a water pistol."

"Then why are you so dry, sir?" Katie raised one eyebrow and grinned.

"Okay, sassy-mouth, if you want to see my devilish charms—" He pulled her in close and began tickling her.

"Stop! You win!" She laughed breathlessly.

"Are you hungry?"

Katie nodded.

Lunch was served buffet style along a large black slate island. A trio of salads: chicken, tuna, and pasta were offered along with a steaming pot of chicken and sweet potato chowder. Katie filled a bowl and took a small sampling of each of the salads.

"Where's Dad?" Branson asked.

"He's picking up some things from the grocery that I missed when I went out earlier. I had a list and *still* missed three things!" She rolled her eyes and chuckled.

Katie ate every bite of the chowder. "This is delicious."

"Thank you." She raised her eyebrows and grinned at her children. "Cooking's not usually my strong suit. So, Branson tells us you're in nursing school."

"Yes, ma'am."

"Do you have a specialty?"

"I loved my emergency room rotation and the intensive care unit, so hopefully I can find a job in one of those areas."

Jennifer's eyes lit up. "What kinds of things did you see in the ER?"

Katie wondered if they were the type that could handle details, or if she should keep her stories vague. Some of her friends had weak stomachs and always asked her to stop talking about her clinical rotations in front of them.

"Mostly homeless folks that drank themselves to death. I was allowed to attempt resuscitation on five people in one night—three were successful. Others came in for strange things. One had spilled boiling water on her bare feet, another lost his—" Katie stopped short. She'd started rambling about all of the exciting things she had seen in the ER and got carried away. Telling friends at school about these stories was one thing, but this would not make a good first impression with Branson's family.

"What! What did he lose?" Jennifer pressed.

"Sorry, I'm rambling. Branson told me you just ran your first 5K."

"Yes, but you're not getting out of this. You have to tell me what he lost." She smiled.

Katie took in a deep breath. "Okay, he lost his finger."

"How?"

"You don't have a weak stomach, do you?" Katie looked at Branson, pleading with him for a rescue, but he grinned and waved his hand, encouraging her to finish.

"Nope."

"Apparently, he was climbing off of his deck to the pavement below. Some buddies were playing basketball, and instead of taking the stairs he decided to show off and jump down. For some reason he chickened out at the last minute, tried to grab onto the deck to keep from falling, and his wedding ring got stuck." Katie grimaced waiting for the *ooh, gross* comments.

"That's awful, but so cool that you got to see it. Were you able to save it?"

"Yes, they were able to reattach it."

Branson stood and asked Katie if she would like to see the rest of the house. First he took her toward the sunroom off the back of the house. "Do I need my coat?"

"No, it's heated."

The view was spectacular. "You live on the lake? It's so beautiful." Everything but the water was covered in snow, but you could tell the landscaping was perfectly arranged around the path toward the dock. Rolling hills surrounded the water, and Katie imagined sitting in this room every morning with a cup of coffee.

"You should see it in the spring. This is my favorite spot to have a cup of coffee in the morning."

Katie laughed quietly. "I was just thinking how fantastic it would be to watch the sun rise from this spot."

"C'mon." He took Katie's hand and led her through the rest of the main floor. "Dining room . . . office . . . guest bathroom . . . Jennifer and Jackson's room . . . and my parents' room."

Katie studied the pictures on the wall and paused at one of Branson. "Oh my goodness, you were so cute. How old are you here?"

"Four, maybe?" He tugged Katie along toward a staircase leading upstairs, pausing at the bottom. "My sisters' rooms are upstairs. Jennifer is staying in the guest room on this level because of Jackson. Do you want to see? It's just a bunch of purple."

"No, it's okay." It felt intrusive for her to look into his sisters' bedrooms.

Branson led her to the staircase at the far end of the house, past the kitchen and living room. "Okay, so my sisters got the better deal on the view, but *I* got the whole downstairs to myself." He grinned. Katie could see the glimmer of pride in his eyes at his big win over his sisters.

"Wait, if your sister is taking the guest room on the main level, where am I sleeping?" Katie was trying to go back through the house in her mind to see if she had missed another room.

"There are two rooms downstairs, if you'd rather have your own room. I just assumed you would stay with me."

Katie's heart raced. The thought of finally sharing a bed with Branson sent a thrill up her spine, but at the same time she feared the lack of propriety would forever tarnish his parents' opinion of her. "As much as I'd love to spend the weekend in your arms," Katie felt the heat rising to her cheeks and looked down. "I need to take the other room. I couldn't stand the thought of your family knowing we were intimate."

Branson laughed. "Such a proper girl."

"Don't make fun of me." Katie's lips formed a flat line and she wondered how many girls he'd had in his bed. She quickly shook the thought off before hurt feelings turned to anger.

"I'm not making fun of you. I love that you care about my family's opinion. They're very laid back, and they wouldn't think anything of us sharing a bed. But I'll respect your decision." He lifted her chin to look at him. "As long as you'll at least make out with me on the couch before you lock me out."

They shared a nervous laugh before descending down the staircase into a large living area. The walls were darker than upstairs, a sandy-gold color, and the wooden beams carried throughout, like upstairs.

"Whoa, that's a big television," Katie said as she ran her hand across the large leather sofa that faced it. She walked over to the pool table and gave Branson a crooked grin. "You play?"

"I do. Are you trying to entice me to try and beat you?"

"Try you may, but win you won't." She winked.

Branson took a couple of sticks off the rack and handed her one. He racked the balls and asked if she would like to do the honors of breaking.

"Sure, thanks." She leaned over the table, aimed her stick at the cue ball and sent it slamming into the other balls, scattering them across the green felt. Two of the solid balls fell into the pockets, so she lined up another shot. "I call solids." She winked. "Green six, left corner pocket." It glided right in. "Blue two, right pocket." The ball bounced off the corner of the pocket and traveled backward. "Missed it."

"Damn, I was rooting for you. Watching you lean seductively over the table was just fine with me."

Katie smiled at his remark and leaned against the wall. It felt good to be ogled by him. Branson landed one striped ball in a pocket and missed the second shot. "Your turn," he said enthusiastically.

"Hmm, are you throwing the game?"

"Absolutely."

Katie sauntered around the table to where Branson was standing. "I'm feeling a little like a bug in a glass jar." She brushed against him ever-so-slightly and took her next shot. After clearing three more balls, she leaned her pool stick against the table. "Since you've suddenly lost your competitive streak, why don't you show me the rest of the downstairs?"

"Sure, but first . . ." Branson drew her in close and kissed her. Watching her amazing curves as she leaned across the pool table had left him greedy to feel her body against his. Her lips were cool and soft against his, and he took his time enjoying her mouth. He turned so her back was against the wall and pressed his body to hers, cradling her head with his hand. He felt her fingers twist in his hair and nearly came unglued when she wrapped one of her legs around him, pulling him closer.

The hum of the garage door caused Branson to tense. "Great. My dad's home." Branson exhaled sharply and rested his forehead against Katie's, trying to catch his breath. He could see the look of dismay on her face and tried to assure her. "It's fine. The garage is on the main floor. We have a minute or two to catch our breath and then we'll go up."

"My heart is racing, I'm flushed, and I feel dizzy. I'm sure I'll make a great first impression when I woozily say hello and tell him I was overcome by his sexy son."

Branson laughed. "I think that's the best compliment I've ever heard." He gave her a soft peck on the lips and looked into her eyes. "I love you, Katie."

Katie was filled with warmth that slowly traveled from the tip of her toes to the top of her head. She loved him with every atom that made up her being. She paused to let his words wash over her before returning the most important words she'd ever spoken. "I love you, too, Branson."

Phillip Stone was tall. His glasses tried to hide the beautiful blue eyes that matched Branson's. "Hello, Katie, it's very nice to meet you," he said sincerely before pulling his son in for a hug. "Did you all have an easy drive?"

"Yeah, traffic wasn't too bad," Branson answered, and then gave Katie's fingers a gentle squeeze. "By the way, Mom, are there sheets on both beds downstairs?"

"Yes. I wasn't sure—I mean—well, I prepared both rooms not knowing—" Celia was stumbling over her words, trying not to embarrass Katie, but it was too late. Katie was mortified and felt her cheeks begin to flush. The thought of his mother assuming they were intimate made her extremely uncomfortable.

Branson watched Katie's body stiffen and her cheeks turn crimson. He normally would have found it humorous and ribbed her a little, but something made him feel compassion for her situation and reconsider. "Let's see what Jackson's up to, shall we?" He pulled her into the living room where Jackson was watching cartoons and playing with a few toys. "Jen, I'll watch him for a bit if you want to visit with Mom and Dad."

"Thanks, I could use a cup of coffee."

Branson was great with Jackson. He played with him on the floor, running a toy truck up the side of Jackson's leg, causing the little boy to giggle and squeal, "Again! Again!" After a dozen truck rides up his leg, Jackson walked over to Katie and drove his small red truck over her arm.

She laughed and played along like it was the most ticklish sensation she had ever experienced. Jackson laughed and repeated the process several times before climbing up on the couch and leaning against her. He tipped his Sippy cup to drink the last few drops of his juice and concentrated on the television show.

"Are you all right with that?" Branson asked.

"Yes, he's such a sweet boy." Katie ran her hand across the top of his fine brown hair.

"I've never seen him cuddle up to someone he's just met. He's usually climbing all over them, digging his sticky fingers through their hair." He smiled and sat down on the other side of Jackson. "You movin' in on my territory, little man?"

Nine

A too-large bite of overcooked roast was being wrestled between Katie's teeth, while she soaked in the atmosphere around the dinner table. Conversation flowed freely and Mr. and Mrs. Stone took turns embarrassing Branson with stories of his childhood.

"You're the first girl Branson has brought home from college," Celia said, lifting her glass of Pinot to her lips.

"Mom!" Branson scolded.

"What? It's true. We never got to meet anyone. The last girl you brought home was Kayla, and that was senior prom."

"Her name was Kyla, and sometimes a guy just wants to come home and relax. Now, if you're done with the stories of how I used to run through the house in my cape and red underwear, I think we'll go downstairs and watch a movie."

"All right, son," Celia laughed. "Goodnight, Katie."

"Goodnight, everyone." Katie stood. "By the way, there was a guy on campus seen running around with nothing but a cape and red underwear . . . you don't think . . ." Katie laughed and braced herself for the incoming retaliation from Branson. He picked her up, effortlessly tossed her over his shoulder, and started out of the room.

"Agh! Put me down, you barbarian!" Katie giggled, enjoying his playfulness.

Branson hurried through the living room and carefully descended the staircase leading to the basement. He set her down when they reached the bottom and stole a kiss before taking her suitcase to the guest room. "So, here is your room. The bathroom is through those doors."

Katie walked through the door, examining the tastefully decorated room. The comforter was olive green and brick red plaid which instantly made her feel like she was in a cozy cabin. A claw foot tub sat in the corner of the bathroom. "Oh, I love that tub."

"You can take a soak anytime you like."

"So, where's your room? I'm dying to see what kind of posters you have on your walls."

Branson led her into a large bedroom with caramel colored walls and a large four poster bed crafted out of pine logs. The room was masculine and revealed no evidence that a teen ever lived there. "Where are your posters?"

He sighed and led Katie to a reading nook where his stereo and gaming system were kept. "Here."

Katie giggled when she saw the mix that decorated his walls. There was one of Freddie Kruger, a blonde in a pink string bikini, one of the Dallas Cowboy cheerleaders, and finally Darth Vader. "Classic. I might have to sew a sweater on that poor girl in the bikini, though. She must be freezing."

He threw his head back and laughed loudly at the thought of his poster wearing a sweater. "Don't you dare!"

"You better sleep with one eye open tonight," she teased.

"Are you up for a movie?" he asked.

"I'd love to watch a movie. Can I slip into my pajamas first?"

She was glad he wasn't too tired. She only had a few nights with him before they left for her house. The plan was to spend a few days with his family, and then a few days with hers. He would drive with her to York, then go back to spend Christmas with his family, and pick her up on the way back to school after Christmas break.

Branson gave her a predatory look. "Need any help?"

She searched for something smart-mouthed to say, but instead shook her head and closed the door.

Katie came out in her red flannel pajamas. They were warm, comfortable, and presentable in case she wanted to go upstairs in them. The look on Branson's face when she came out nearly sent her into hysterics. He must have expected her to wear something more revealing.

"Well, aren't you . . . warm and cozy."

"Yes, I am. These are my favorite pajamas. Just be glad I didn't bring my long flannel nightgown with the unicorns." She laughed.

"You're not serious?"

"No. But I do love these pjs, and I can wear them in the sunroom tomorrow when we watch the sun rise with a cup of coffee."

"Ugh. I was looking forward to sleeping in tomorrow. Let's wait until Sunday morning to do that. It'll be a great way to end our stay here."

"We'll see. Show me those dimples one more time and I might be talked into it," Katie said, plopping down next to him. He was wearing a pair of plaid pajama bottoms and a black T-shirt that made his eyes change from sapphire blue to a darker navy.

"If that's what turns you on, I can smile all night." He grinned, answering her request.

His smile made her stomach flip-flop. As he leaned in to kiss her, she felt her breath hitch. She had felt his lips on hers hundreds of times over the last few months, but the hunger in his aggressive kiss had her pulse racing and butterflies slamming against her chest. She could feel and hear her heart beating loudly in her ears and wondered if he could hear it too.

"It's so quiet."

With the click of a button, the stereo came on, filling the room with the haunting, seductive music of Mazzy Star's "Fade Into You." He pulled Katie into his lap with ease and gazed into her eyes.

"Hmm, your green eyes against these red pajamas remind me of Christmas." His lips found hers before they traveled down her neck. He found the spot behind her ear that caused her to moan and lingered there, letting his hot breath wash over her. She tilted her head back, giving him more access, and closed her eyes. "I'm not waiting until Christmas to unwrap you," he whispered.

Katie felt herself spinning out of control. Between the music and rapture of Branson's touch, she was quickly slipping into a state of euphoria. "Are you sure no one will come down here?"

"I'm sure." His voice was filled with desire.

Katie unbuttoned the top button of her flannel pajama top. Before she could reach the next one, Branson's fingers covered hers. "Let me," he said. She watched his face as he finished the buttons and slowly slid the fabric over her shoulders. He had her nerve endings tingling as he grazed her shoulder with his lips while removing her top. He kissed her deeply as he unfastened the single hook on the front of her bra, and pulled away to look at her. She inhaled sharply as his hand found one breast and then the other. Katie raised his shirt over his head and let it fall behind him. Her hands outlined his chest and shoulders, before moving on to the ripples in his strong arms.

"You're so beautiful, Katie." Branson scooped her up into his arms and carried her back to his bedroom. When he set her down on her unsteady feet, he tugged at the silk ribbon waistband, releasing the knot and letting her pajama bottoms fall to the floor. Katie stepped out of them and reached for Branson's bare skin. She traced two fingers slowly down his sculpted abs until she reached the waistband of his pants. His body tensed and a wave of heat coursed through her.

Branson struggled to control his adrenaline as Katie's fingertips swept across his skin. The feel of her soft touch sent shockwaves through his body. He'd never been so turned on, and had to resist the urge to speed things up. He lifted Katie in his arms and gently laid her on the bed, guiding her head down onto a pillow before trailing soft kisses down her neck. His mouth lingered on her breasts, taking his time with each one, while Katie arched her back and whimpered with pleasure. He slowly made his way down her stomach, ravishing her smooth skin with his hands and lips.

Katie wanted to let go and enjoy the moment, but in the back of her mind she could hear her subconscious scolding her. She had been taught to save something so intimate for marriage. She had only known Branson for a few months, and although she was certain he loved her, marriage wasn't something either of them was ready for at this point in their relationship. But with the music encouraging her to give him everything, and the hot breath of his lips caressing her skin, it was impossible to stop. It felt so damn good to be touched by him.

Branson sat up to look at her. "Are you okay?"

"Yes."

"You're shaking. Are you cold?"

Katie was suddenly self-conscious and closed her eyes to hide from his gaze. "I'm not cold, I'm just a little nervous."

"I promise you, we're alone."

"I know." The humiliation was almost unbearable. "I've just never . . . well . . . you're the first—" Katie scrunched her eyes closed again, felt for a small throw pillow to grab, and covered her face with it.

Branson pulled the pillow off of her. "You can trust me." He kissed her softly. "I love you and I'm here to stay."

"I love you, too," she answered him in a whisper.

Branson brushed his lips across hers, kissing each side of her mouth before taking the fullness of her lips. He slowly made his way back down, savoring the small dip at the base of her neck. Traveling down her stomach, he enjoyed her response as he reached just below her belly button. He slipped his fingers under the waistband of her satin panties and pulled them down her legs, over her knees, and off her feet. He traveled the lines of her inner thighs with his hands and lips, feeling her squirm beneath him.

"Branson," she pleaded.

"Relax, babe," he whispered, while guiding her legs apart. He slid one finger into her opening, and moaned when he felt how ready she was. He moved his fingers expertly, bringing her to the brink of orgasm.

"Oh my God, Branson!"

Branson rolled off the bed and removed his boxers before pulling a foil packet out of his nightstand drawer and sliding the condom on. He positioned himself over Katie, spreading her legs with his knees as he kissed her, and guided himself into her. He groaned as he worked his way into her, "You feel so good, baby."

Katie felt every inch as he pushed inside of her. The feeling was exquisite. He was gentle and careful, letting her body adjust to having him inside her. Katie justified her feelings against the notion that she should've waited. Everything felt right and natural. Although it was her first time, there was a familiarity to their lovemaking, as if it were meant to be. She arched her back with pleasure every time he moved, and gripped his arms, her fingers digging into his triceps. The rhythm began gradually as they enjoyed kissing and experiencing their first time together. Whimpering with each thrust, the frenzy began building deep inside of her. She wrapped her legs around his back to pull him in closer. Branson laced his fingers in hers, guiding her hands over her head, and thrust deeper into her, accelerating the pace.

"God, Katie," Branson growled into her ear.

His words mixed with the hot breath caressing her ear sent her over the edge. She cried out his name as a powerful orgasm coursed through her body.

Branson gripped the headboard firmly with his right hand as he thrust into her one last time, letting out a primitive groan with his release.

Katie could hear Branson breathing heavily as he rested his forehead on the pillow next to her ear. She felt his body tense each time she throbbed around his fullness inside of her. As she caught her breath, she wondered if he enjoyed her as much as she had enjoyed him.

"I'll be right back." Branson kissed her before rolling off and heading into the bathroom.

Katie pulled the covers up around her and sank deeper into the pillow. The aftershocks were still reverberating through her body.

When Branson returned, he slipped in beside Katie and kissed her forehead. "Are you all right?"

"Mmm hmm."

"What are you thinking?"

"I was just wondering—" Katie hesitated. "Was I okay? I mean, I know I have a lot to learn—"

Branson propped himself up on one elbow and laid a finger over her lips. "Baby, you were amazing."

"Can we do it again?" Katie swirled a finger around his chest playfully.

And they did, again and again.

Sunday morning was spent watching the sun rise over the lake with a cup of coffee just like Branson had promised. "It's just beautiful, isn't it?"

"Yes. I'm looking forward to meeting your Gram. As many stories as I've heard, I feel like I already know her."

"You're going to love her. She's so fun to be around. You'll have to sleep in the guest room though, I don't have the basement to myself, and she wouldn't approve of you violating her granddaughter." Katie giggled.

"Hey, I'm innocent here. Will she accuse me if you're caught sneaking into my room?" He raised one eyebrow and flashed a crooked smile.

Bright-eyed with hair sticking up in every direction, Jackson came running into the sunroom with a Sippy cup full of milk. He reached for Branson, who pulled him up into his lap and complemented his fire truck pajamas. "These are cool, little man." Never taking his lips off of his cup, Jackson pointed to the truck with a ladder in response. He leaned his head back, resting against Branson's chest, and finished his milk.

Katie sipped her coffee and watched the two of them together. He was so good with his nephew—fun, gentle, and loving. The glimmer of pride in his eyes when he smoothed Jackson's hair filled Katie with wonderment. *He'll be a wonderful father one day.*

Jennifer stumbled into the sunroom with a cup of coffee. She looked as if she could have used a few more hours of sleep. "Jackson wiggled and kicked all night. Why are you two up so early?"

"I promised Katie we would watch the sun rise at least once before we left."

"My brother the romantic." Jennifer smirked. "When did that happen?"

Katie enjoyed the playful banter between them. She had never known what it was like to grow up with siblings and missed the fighting, playing, sharing of secrets, and everything else that came with a brother or sister.

"Good morning." Celia entered with a carafe and refilled Katie's mug. "Katie, I so enjoyed getting to know you. I hope you will come back. Winters are harsh, but spring is beautiful, summers are spent on the water, and autumn is my favorite— you can't imagine the colors that are displayed across the mountains. Branson, promise you'll bring her back after graduation."

"If she hasn't grown bored of me by then, I promise," Branson answered, flashing Katie a wink.

Katie looked down at her mug, afraid she was blushing. *Bored with you, Branson Stone? I don't think so. I'm indubitably in love with you.* She sipped her coffee, and listened as the three of them reminisced about their time together swimming, skiing, and boating on the lake. Phillip joined the conversation and added a few fishing stories before ending the fun.

"What time are you and Katie planning on taking off, son? The Weather Channel said more snow is on the way by late afternoon. You'll need to get ahead of it."

"Oh. We were planning on going after lunch. Do we need to go earlier?"

"I think you'll be okay if you're out of here by one o'clock. It should only take about forty-five minutes, but you'll want to allow a little extra time for possible traffic."

Katie loved the feel of New Hampshire. It was crowded but friendly, and full of little mom-and-pop restaurants. She was certain the hiking trails were excellent, but it was too cold and dangerous in December. She hoped she would have the chance to come back in the spring.

Ten

Two hours later Katie and Branson stepped out of the car in her driveway. Branson rubbed his neck muscles. "That was a little tense, huh?" The traffic had been horrible due to the heavy snowfall, and they had driven most of the way in silence due to the stress of the drive and the impending meeting with Katie's only living relative. Branson popped the trunk to get the luggage, but Katie quickly shut it. "Let's get it later. I can't wait to see Gram, and introduce the two of you." She took Branson's hand and skipped up the path toward the house. The sight of the large white house with black shutters and roof against the white snow made Katie's heart soar. She was home.

When they stepped through the front door, Katie called out for Gram.

"Oh my heavens! Is that my little Katie-girl?" Gram raced around the corner to find Katie grinning from ear to ear.

"Gram!" Katie bounded into her grandmother's arms and squeezed her tight. She inhaled the soft, comforting scent of her perfume. Katie had copied Gram's habit of lightly dabbing one dot of perfume behind each ear. *She remembered watching her get ready for the day and listening to her instructions. "You are beautiful and will never need makeup, but when you do apply it, do it tastefully—applying as little as possible for a natural look. When you walk into a room you want people to notice your beautiful eyes, not your beautiful makeup. Also, perfume should be added lightly and never overpowering. Just add a tiny dab behind each ear."*

"I'm delighted beyond words to see you, my dear." She looked Katie over before turning her attention to Branson. "Oh how rude of me, you must be Branson. I'm Elizabeth Harrington, but all of Katie's friends call me Gram." She offered her hand for a shake.

"I'm pleased to finally meet you, Gram. Katie speaks of you often." Branson was sure he had never seen Katie so happy. Her entire persona changed when she saw Gram, and watching her he now knew what she had been like as a child. It was obvious from the stories that she adored her grandmother, but seeing the two of them together, he realized their bond was exceptionally profound and unbreakable.

Gram led them through the house to the kitchen where she had a pot of water ready for tea, along with shortbread cookies. Branson looked around and realized there were no masculine touches anywhere, which was completely opposite of his family's rustic home in New Hampshire. Katie's house was light and had a beach feel to it, making him forget that it was winter and snowing outside.

Katie handed him a cup of tea. "I've never seen you drink tea, but will you join us?" He nodded, and thanked her for the cup. "Would you like honey, milk, or lemon?"

"I have no idea. I'll just try it the way you fix yours."

Katie added a dab of honey to his cup and placed a few cookies on his plate. "Gram makes these cookies every

Christmas. They're my favorite." She waited for him to try a bite, eagerly awaiting his reaction. When he agreed they were the best he'd ever tasted, she enjoyed her tea. "Gram, where's the tree? You haven't decorated a stitch."

"I wanted to wait for you. I thought it would be nice to do it together like we have every year." She smiled and turned to Branson. "Tell me everything about yourself. Katie tells me you're studying business?"

Branson answered her questions about his family, future goals, and his version of how he and Katie met. "I missed my four o'clock class so I could meet her. I'd seen her on the tennis court, but never could find the chance to introduce myself. This particular day she was sitting in the lobby of her dorm. I have to admit she's the most beautiful girl I'd ever seen, and I lost my nerve. I stood there, like an idiot, talking to a couple of buddies until I talked myself into saying hello. Normally I'd describe myself as a fairly confident man, but Katie had me turned upside down."

Katie and Gram shared another cup of tea as Branson retrieved the luggage out of the car. They got caught up on all of the town gossip and made plans to give Branson a glimpse into the wonderful world of the Harrington's during the Christmas season.

"He seems like a wonderful young man, dear. He can't take his eyes off of you—I know a man in love when I see one. How do you feel about him?"

"I love him, Gram. He's kind, gentle, funny. You should see him with his nephew—and have you seen his dimples? He's one of the best on the tennis team, and he likes to run and hike and . . . oh, listen to me ramble on. I'm so glad to be home! When can we put up the tree? Are you going to make Wassail?"

Gram laughed. "Yes, he's very handsome, we can put the tree up whenever you feel up to it, and I'll make Wassail tomorrow. Oh, Katie, it's so good to have you home!"

Katie showed Branson where he would be sleeping, and then gave him a tour of the house. "You've seen the kitchen, here's the library." She took his hand, leading him down the hall to the living room, and walked to the large picture window facing the sea.

"Wow. What an amazing view. The sea looks so . . . angry." He watched as the water threw itself against the rocks below, spewing white foam up the side of the cliff.

"I'm sure it *is* angry, because it's so cold." Katie folded her arms and rubbed them up and down with her hands.

Branson stood behind her, wrapping his arms around her. "You and the sea— your eyes are the same color as the water and neither of you like the cold air. If I believed in that kind of nonsense I'd be really weirded-out right now."

"Weirded-out? You go to Yale, and that's what you come up with?" Katie giggled. "I'm trading you in for someone who speaks proper English." Katie peeked around to make sure Gram wasn't behind them before playfully planting a kiss on the corner of his mouth. "See that railing on the cliff over there? That's my favorite spot. Sometimes I spend hours leaning against the railing, staring at the sea. It's glorious, terrifying, and peaceful all at once."

Continuing through the house, she showed him her room and the recreation room, lingering at the pool table. "If you want a re-match just let me know." She smiled provocatively, slowly running her hand along the smooth wood edging the table.

"You better watch it, babe. You don't want your grandmother to shoot me, do you?"

"Why would she shoot you?" Katie grinned and feigned naïvety.

"For violating you right here on this pool table, if you keep looking at me like that." His eyes darkened as he gave her a predatory look.

The familiar stir crept through her, settling in her belly, as she roamed over his face and body. The way his jeans hung on his hips—damn, he was sexy. Katie shouted down the hallway toward the kitchen, "Gram, I'm going to show Branson the wine cellar and pick out a bottle for dinner. Do you have a preference?"

"No, dear, just pick what you like."

Katie led Branson downstairs to the stone-walled cellar. It was always kept at a cooler temperature. She usually dreaded going down there, but she was burning up inside, and only one thing could extinguish it. She pulled Branson with her to the farthest wall and gazed into his eyes. "Kiss me," she commanded.

Branson pinned her arms over her head, not daring to let her touch him. He hadn't been in her grandmother's house an hour and he was already considering breaking her rules. "God, Katie, what are you trying to do, get me killed?"

She pressed her hips into him, causing him to moan into her mouth and release her arms to gently fall down by her sides. "I can't help myself. You're so damn irresistible when you look at me like that."

Branson's desire for her grew stronger than his common sense as he succumbed to her persuasion. He kissed her deeply, making love to her mouth as he caressed her breasts through her sweater. He stopped abruptly and pulled away when he heard Gram call down from the top of the steps.

"Go ahead and grab a bottle of sherry for me, would you, dear? I need it for a recipe."

Katie exhaled the breath she had been holding. "Yes, ma'am." Leaning against the wall, she took a few deep breaths in and out, trying to rid the mounting frustration. She glanced at Branson, who seemed to be coming out of a state of panic. "Sorry."

"If you see my heart anywhere, let me know. I believe it jumped out of my chest." He laughed uncomfortably.

"Ugh." She pecked him on the cheek. "To be continued."

Three magical days quickly passed with the two people Katie loved most. Gram went out of her way to make Branson feel welcome. They trimmed the tree, filled their bellies with seasonal treats, sipped wassail by the fire, and watched the traditional classics *Christmas Vacation* and *A Charlie Brown Christmas*. Katie felt perfectly content thinking about the past week. She was at the peak of happiness and couldn't imagine there was room in her heart for any more joy—she was filled to the top.

Gram, Katie, and Branson were in the dining room, sipping the last of their wine as they talked. Branson was telling of his childhood in Texas and how his plans to attend the University of Texas to pursue an architecture degree had changed when they moved to New Hampshire. "My father's idea was a hit and he accepted a job with SLS, now PCS."

"What does PCS stand for?" Gram asked.

"It actually stands for Personal Computer Storage, but my father calls it Phillip and Celia Stone. Celia is my mother's name."

"So you wanted to be an architect—what changed your mind?"

"I went to work for my dad that summer and loved it. I was hired for the packaging department, but it wasn't long before they realized I was good at math, and I was promoted to the business side of the company. My love for business outweighed my fantasy of becoming a famous architect, which most likely wouldn't have worked out well for me." Branson laughed. "I love art and studying structures, but I wasn't gifted with an artistic hand."

Katie stifled the naughty response that played at her tongue and asked Gram about their time in Texas. "When were we in Texas last, Gram? I have vague memories of watching UT football games. I remember seeing orange uniforms, and those ridiculous Longhorn hats. Did we go to a game? I thought you hated football?"

Gram managed a smile as she shifted in her seat. *Damn! He had to be from Texas. How could she have memories of a UT football game? I remember it was Daniel's favorite team, but he surely didn't take her to a game. Maybe she remembers him watching them play on television? What if Branson jogs more of her memories? I can't let that happen. I'll have to think of something. I really liked him for her, too. Oh, Katie, I'm sorry, my angel, but I've worked too hard to protect you from your past. I can't let some boy come in and ruin everything. You'll get over him, and find someone else to love. You're stronger than you think. I am so very sorry.* "Oh dear, I forgot to turn off the oven. Please, excuse me."

Katie cleared the dishes from the table and found Gram in the kitchen in a daze. She had a melancholy expression on her face. "Are you all right, Gram?"

"Yes. I was just—it's nothing dear."

"I know you too well, there's something wrong. Please, tell me what it is. There have never been secrets between us."

"I don't want to spoil your last day here. Can't we just talk about it by phone next week?"

"No, tell me what's going on. Are you ill?"

"I'm just fine, but I'm not so sure about Branson."

Katie cocked her head to the side curiously. "He seems fine to me."

"Listening to him talk about Texas and his dream to be an architect, his true personality shone through, and I saw something that I can't quite put a finger on."

"What do you mean?"

"Well, love, I'm not positive . . . but he seems ill-contented. I've been around a long time and I've seen that look before. He's going through the motions for his father's sake, but his passion is in architecture. I have no doubt that he loves you . . . as much as he is capable of loving someone."

"What on earth is *that* supposed to mean?" Katie hadn't remembered ever getting angry with Gram, but a storm was brewing inside of her, listening to her imply that Branson didn't love her.

"Tell me, have the two of you been intimate?"

"*Gram!*" Katie was astonished that she would ask her such a thing.

"I didn't think so. It usually changes the way a man looks at a woman, and I don't see him looking at you in that way. Thank goodness you haven't slept with him—if you had I'd be certain in my assessment of his lack of feelings for you. But now that you've assured me it hasn't happened, I'm sure I was wrong. He'll look at you differently once you've consummated the relationship—which will be after your married, young lady," she said in a firm voice, and then winked. *Oh God, that was the hardest thing I've ever had to do. This is the second time I've lied to and manipulated my sweet Katie. She'll be broken-hearted, but it's for her best interest.*

Katie's shoulders slumped slightly as she walked out of the room. *How could Gram possibly know so much? Maybe she's wrong about the way he looks at me?* She rubbed her hands up and down, trying to relieve the shiver that ran through her body, leaving a trail of goose bumps. Her mind traveled to their silent two hour drive and wondered if, instead of being stressed over the weather and traffic, he really had been rethinking things. She'd heard Gram tell her during some of their conversations about boys, *"Why buy the milk if you can get it for free? Never give yourself away, Katie, dear." How could I have let myself fall so hard for someone who doesn't feel the same about me? He took me home to meet his family—was it all a set up just to get me in bed?* Between the effects of the wine and the impending doom that threatened her core, she couldn't think straight. She wrapped her arms around herself, holding tightly, so the imminent sobs wouldn't escape in front of Branson. She wouldn't give him the satisfaction of seeing her cry over him.

"I'm going to bed," she informed the air as she slipped down the hallway toward her room. Once her head was safely buried into her pillow, she cried herself to sleep.

Eleven

Branson sat alone at the dining room table waiting for Katie to return. He grew fidgety and traced the fleur-de-lis pattern on the tablecloth with his finger.

Gram returned without Katie and busied herself wiping down the table. "Where's Katie?"

"I don't know, she was with you, wasn't she?"

"She was. She must've gone on to bed. She did mention having a headache." Another lie in the books. She justified it by telling herself it was for Katie's best interest. "I'm glad to have a moment alone with you, Branson. We should talk about you and Katie." Branson immediately knew this wasn't going to be a pleasant conversation by the way Gram was looking at him.

"I had no idea she was feeling bad. I should see if I can get her anything."

"Just let her rest. I want to talk to you about something serious."

"Okay," he said cautiously. He hadn't seen this side of Gram, and wondered if she had known he snuck into Katie's room each night. *Too bad, we're twenty-two years old—grownups—and very much in love. I have every intention of marrying Katie and spending the rest of my life with her.*

Branson braced himself for the conversation. He knew he loved Katie, but had never actually entertained the idea of marriage. However, thinking about it now, he was sure he wanted to spend his life with her. He wanted to be the one to warm her shivering body when she was cold, make love to her each night, watch the sun rise with a cup of coffee every morning, and—yes, he wanted her to be the mother of his children.

"Branson, you're a sweet young man. It hurts me to break your heart like this." Gram folded her hands in front of her and rested them on the table. "Katie is a naïve girl who has always been in love with love. I have no doubt that she loves you as much as she is capable of, but—"

Branson slammed his fist on the table, interrupting her speech. "You're good, but I can see right through your scheme. I know for a fact that Katie loves me completely and perfectly, the same as I love her. I don't understand why you'd want to break us apart."

"Okay," she said slowly, re-thinking her game plan. "Let me just shoot straight with you then. You're no good for my granddaughter. If you love her as much as you claim, you'll leave here before she awakes and never cross her path again."

"Who are you to tell me I'm no good for her? You've known me three days. You cannot, and will not, separate me from her." Branson could feel the heat in his cheeks and neck from the rising anger.

"How much will it take? Name your price." Gram pulled out her checkbook and readied her pen. "Surely you could use a new car or a sporty new motorcycle—a red Ducati maybe?"

Branson slowly rose from his seat, not taking his eyes off Gram. He spoke slowly and deliberately. "I won't let you do this. I love Katie more than I have ever loved anything, or anyone, in my life. She will be my wife, lover, best friend, and mother of our children—and there's not a damn thing you can do about it." He turned to leave the room.

"Wait! Please." Gram was uncertain of her next move. She had tried everything in her power to break their bond for Katie's own good, but to no avail. The only option left was to leave the situation to chance, hoping no more memories would surface. "You've convinced me that you *do* love her. I didn't see it at first, but now I do." She lowered her head, unable to look him in the eyes. "I only want the best for my granddaughter, you can't blame me for that. Please, forgive me."

Branson wasn't even close to coming down from the rage that had built inside of him. He couldn't calm down enough to speak, so he nodded his head, smiled weakly, and left the dining room.

Without knocking, he quietly opened Katie's door and shut it behind him. He slipped into bed beside her, fully dressed, and guided her head on his chest. *She can stick her stupid rules—*

Katie stirred and sat up. "What are you doing?"

"I have no idea what Gram told you, but she just did a number on me, trying to convince me you didn't love me. She even tried to pay me to leave you."

"Branson, get out." Katie instinctively held her stomach to keep the stream of sobs from erupting again.

"No." He pulled the small gold chain on the bedside lamp, filling the room with a soft glow. "Look at me, Katie." Branson gently took her chin in his hand, turning her to face him. "I love you with every fiber of my being. Do you feel the same about me, or not?"

As hard as she pressed her arm into her stomach, it wasn't enough to keep a sob from escaping. She couldn't find her voice to answer him, so she nodded her head. Branson pulled her tightly to his chest and stroked her hair. "I'll never understand your relationship with her, but I do know she loves you enough to do anything in her power to protect you. One day, you'll believe the same of me." He kissed the top of her head and eased his head down onto the pillow. "I'm staying here tonight. Goodnight, my love."

Katie popped her head up. "All night? You can't."

"Watch me."

Katie lay there worrying what Gram would say or do, then she recalled their conversation in the kitchen earlier and thought, *She already knew we were intimate, she played me. Why on earth . . . ? Well, I'll just have to think about that later. Right now, I just want to concentrate on the man I love. The only one brave enough to stand up to Elizabeth Harrington.*

Katie slid out of bed and locked the door. She walked over to the side of the bed where Branson was laying. "Get up."

"I'm staying."

"I know. Get up."

He did as she commanded and was rewarded with a passionate kiss conveying the depth of her need for him. Branson's body immediately stirred in response to her hands moving over his chest and arms, lingering over every muscle as if she was savoring him. His hands intuitively moved across her lower back, up to her shoulders and arms, feeling goose bumps rise. "Are you cold?"

"No." She smiled.

He kissed her slowly, wanting to take his time savoring her exquisite body. Methodically, she unbuttoned his shirt before sliding it off, letting it float to the floor. She slowly moved her hands over his chest, as if discovering him for the very first time. She traced over each ripple on his firm stomach before slowly following the trail of dark hair past his navel to his waist band. His body tensed at her soft touch and he groaned softly, allowing her to free him from his jeans. A mischievous grin played on his lips as she slid his pants the rest of the way down with her foot, never breaking their heated gaze. Katie had gone to bed in a long, cotton T-shirt that he slipped over her head prior to stepping back to admire her beauty.

"I love you," he said, before guiding her onto the bed. He traced every inch of her body with his hands, feeling her writhe beneath him, his own body threatening to explode with each of her soft moans. She reached for him, but he took her wrists and held them over her head, running the back of his free hand down the inside of her left arm. Her breasts were rising and falling with each deep breath she took, and when he took one nipple in his mouth, she closed her eyes and softly bit down on her bottom lip.

Katie was reeling from his expert touch. Her body quivered beneath him as she moaned in undulated pleasure. "Branson," she pleaded. "Please!" As soon as he released her arms, she pulled him down to her. She found his lips and conveyed her ravenous desire for him with her mouth and hands.

Branson fought with himself for control of his desire as her soft hands roamed over him. The intensity behind her desire-filled green eyes drove him wild and he couldn't wait any longer. He wrapped her in his arms as they made love, holding her tightly to him while shockwave after shockwave reverberated through their bodies.

Katie felt an overwhelming amount of emotion rip through her, causing tears to spill over her lashes. She couldn't believe she was crying after experiencing something so perfect and wonderful. With Branson's fingers laced in hers, she tried to turn her head to the side to wipe the tears on the pillow before she was caught.

"Hey," he said, "What's wrong?"

The simple question opened the floodgate and more tears spilled from her eyes. "I have no idea why I'm crying. I'm just overwhelmed, I guess. I love you, Branson William Stone."

Branson looked into her moist eyes and smiled. Her words made him feel good all over. He thought about sitting at the table with Gram just an hour ago, and how bad it felt thinking he and Katie were finished. Now, he held her in his arms after the most intense lovemaking of his life. She was so delicate beneath him and he felt a vast need to comfort and protect her. "And I love you, Katie Rose Harrington."

Thursday morning arrived unwelcomed, and Katie frowned in sadness. "Call me when you get there."

"I will." Branson enfolded Katie in his arms. "Have a great Christmas."

"Please, be careful." Katie's Christmas present from him sparkled on her wrist. The tiny diamonds were dazzling in the hint of sun peeking through the gray clouds. It was beautiful and dainty. She'd told him how much she loved it, and then giggling, proclaimed, *"A tennis bracelet from my tennis player!"*

Christmas with Gram was just as Katie imagined it would be. After a long talk, and deep, heartfelt apology from Gram, they were able to enjoy the rest of their time together. Gram got tickets for the *Nutcracker* ballet. The seats were superb. They stayed up late each night, talking and laughing.

"Remember when we were sitting in the airport talking about the French lady? You said 'French is such a beautiful language' and I agreed, but said my favorite is Italian. And then the guy next to me lowered his newspaper and chimed in, 'I like Thousand Island.'" Katie and Gram laughed until their vision was blurred with tears.

"Yes, we laughed so hard. That poor man, trying to make conversation, and all we could do was laugh 'til we nearly wet ourselves."

Katie recalled memory after memory until their sides ached from laughing. "Okay, last one. Remember when I was learning how to cook and begged you to let me make the spaghetti sauce? I stirred too vigorously and spilled some onto the stove. You walked over, looked at the mess, and took the spoon away from me. I thought you were going to be so mad, but you slapped the spoon on top of the sauce, making it splatter everywhere and said—"

Gram broke in and finished, "If you wanted to learn how to slop it out of the pan, all you had to do was ask. I'll show you how to properly slop!"

"Jeez, we've had some great times, haven't we?" Katie wiped the tears of laughter from her eyes and tried to catch her breath.

"We sure have, Katie-girl." Gram stood. "I'll make some tea, while you pick a movie."

Although Katie was enjoying her time with Gram, her heart ached for Branson. She read his text after slipping into bed that night.

Missing U terribly. Hope U R having a good time with Gram. I love you green eyes! xoxo

Katie smiled and texted back:

Gram & I are having a blast. I love U!

Two weeks at home passed quickly. Gram wanted to fill their last day together with fun memories. They sipped cappuccino while shopping at the mall, and watched a little boy trying to reach money in the fountain. He leaned and stretched his arm until his face lit up with his success. He must have lost his balance, because a second later he fell in. Once Katie saw that he was okay, just angry and embarrassed from his escapade, she and Gram laughed until they could hardly stand.

After picking up a few items for Katie's dorm, they lunched at Weathervane and enjoyed twin lobster tails with a glass of Bordeaux. Gram asked, "How serious are things with you and Branson?"

"Very. Do you really want to argue on our last day together, Gram?"

"No, I'm not going to interfere again. I just wanted to indulge in some girl-talk." Gram smiled.

"All right," Katie said, cautiously. Her trust in Gram had diminished slightly, after learning of the level of manipulation she tried to inflict on her and Branson. "What do you want to know?"

"I guess I just want to know what your plans are after graduation."

"I really haven't gotten that far in my planning, but I assume I'll come home and find a job close by." Katie sipped her wine and thought about the question a bit further. "Oh, unless you were planning on me finding a place of my own. I could find an apartment."

"No, no! Of course, you're welcome to live at home. It's your home too, Katie, and it always will be."

"It's settled then. Hopefully, I can find a job at York Hospital, but I'll put in resumes in the surrounding counties, too."

After lunch, they baked cookies for Katie to take back with her, packed up her stuff, and got into their pajamas. Katie made popcorn while Gram poured two cups of steaming wassail, then they settled in for the annual tradition of watching *Gone with the Wind.*

Late that night, Katie slipped under the soft, cool sheets and snuggled in before reading a text from Branson:

Tomorrow can't come soon enough. xoxo

Katie swooned as she thought of wrapping herself in his strong arms. It was late, and she was sure he would already be asleep, but she sent a reply just in case:

I can't wait to see you! xoxo

Twelve

Katie leaned against the counter, trying to absorb Branson's words.

"I have to go to New Hampshire. My father's plans can't be put on hold—they've already bought airline tickets," Branson said. "There's no one else to run the company."

Katie was unsure of what to do. She couldn't bear the thought of being away from Branson, but Gram was all alone and expected her to come home after graduation. "What about *my* home and Gram?"

"*I* want to be your home, Katie. Just give it a try. You don't take your boards for another month—come with me until then. If you want to go back to Maine after that, then I'll respect your decision and we'll make it work somehow."

Katie found an empty chair and sat down. She was surrounded by boxes filled with their belongings, ready to be moved out. Branson and Katie had found an apartment off campus to share their last semester of school. Maggie had met someone from Kennebunkport over the break and didn't seem to mind Katie's absence in her life. Graduation came and went without incident, forcing Katie to make some difficult decisions. Gram always talked excitedly about Katie returning home and working at the local hospital. She couldn't wait to have her back to share tea, conversation, and late-night giggling.

Branson squatted down in front of her. "Why are you struggling with this decision? What are you afraid of?"

She thought for a moment before answering. "I'm worried about Gram being alone. I'm also worried about losing myself. I'm worried about finding a job in a town I know nothing about . . ." Katie rested her elbows on her knees and lowered her head into her hands. The more she talked, the greater her fear of the unknown grew.

"Baby, I won't let you lose yourself, and you'll have at least two months before you're licensed and ready to look for a job. I'll get you acquainted with the town before then." He gave her knees a gentle squeeze. "Gram will be just fine. She's been without you for four years, with you only visiting every now and then. You'll be able to see her every day if you want—it's only a forty minute drive."

"True . . ."

"Tell you what, why don't you give her a call and feel her out. She might surprise you." Branson knew what she would say, he had already talked to her about his plan to ask Katie to move in with him. Although she was not happy about the idea, Branson had finally convinced her.

"All right," Katie agreed, and phoned Gram to tell her the plan. Surprisingly, Gram was compliant and encouraged her to follow her heart.

"I won't be here forever, Katie-girl. You're a grown woman now. It's right for you to move on and find your life.

I'm only a half hour, or so, away. When you're settled, I'll come for a visit, okay?"

"I'd love that! Thank you for being so supportive. I love you so much, Gram."

"You won't understand the depth of love I have for you angel—until you have a daughter of your own one day."

The thought of a child made Katie smile. She pictured a little girl with dark hair, Branson's blue eyes, and deep dimples. Once she had Gram's blessing, she relaxed and enjoyed the thought of finding a home to share with Branson.

Branson grinned and kissed Katie hard on the lips. "Let's celebrate." He found two plastic cups and half bottle of wine in the fridge.

"Will we always live this lavishly, Mr. Stone?" Katie giggled.

"Only the best for you, Miss Harrington." He laughed and raised his red Solo cup. "To us."

Katie tapped her cup against his and felt the crisp white wine coat her throat. She had been working all day and didn't realize how thirsty she was. "Mmm, more please."

After finishing off the wine, they packed the rest of the boxes and ordered Chinese takeout for dinner.

Branson dipped his chopsticks into the Chicken Lo Mein, and swirled them around as if searching for treasure. "What do you think? Should we move into my parents' home, or find our own place?"

"Your parents' home is amazing—great location, breathtaking view. I just don't know if I would ever feel like more than a visitor there. I want to cook you meals, and run through the house naked if I want to. I'm not sure I'll feel comfortable doing that there."

Branson laughed at the thought and shook his head. "I can't wait to see that. Well, at least we'll have a place to stay until we find a place of our own, so you'll have some time to make up your mind." He took a bite and thought of living in that house with Katie. It was much too big for the two of them, but when they filled it with children it would be perfect. He wasn't sure they would ever find a place more perfect to raise their family. The house was right on the lake, and he envisioned someday teaching his son to water ski and fish. *I'll have to put a wrought iron fence around the pool until the kids are older.*

Katie watched Branson's face as he seemed to be mulling something over. "What's got you so deep in thought?"

"Honestly?" Branson smiled, a little embarrassed.

"No, make up something so far out I would never believe you." She smirked.

"Smart-ass! I was actually thinking about teaching our son to fish on the lake." He glanced at her, fully expecting her to laugh.

"Are you expecting?"

"Not yet, but I'm crossing my fingers." He stood, kissed Katie on the tip of the nose, and went to the kitchen for water. He set a cup down in front of her and asked, "Do you want children?"

"Yes, very much. But not immediately. I'd like to live life a little—enjoy some things that we won't be able to when we're parents. Wouldn't you like to travel, ride roller coasters, and—"

"Run through the house naked?" Branson grinned. "Yes, absolutely. I just wanted to make sure you wanted them."

"Yes, I want three—maybe four. Two boys and two girls."

"Four kids. Hmm, we'll need a big house." Branson winked. He was pushing hard for the house on the lake.

Branson drove down I-84, while Katie flipped through the radio stations. She found a station playing Colby Caillat and started tapping her fingers on her leg. "I love this song!"

She began to sing along, *"But what am I gonna say . . . when you make me feel this way? I just mmmmm. And it starts in my toes . . . makes me crinkle my nose . . ."*

Branson laughed to himself and listened to her sing out of tune.

"Hey, you missed your exit. Weren't we supposed to take I-290?" Katie asked.

"Oh, you're right. Darn, I guess we'll just have to drive up to York and see Gram." He smiled and searched her face that lit up as soon as she realized what he said.

"Thank you! Does she know we're coming?"

Branson nodded. "Of course, do you think I would try to surprise that woman?"

Gram was working in the garden when they arrived. She hugged them both and led them inside. She always had something cooking on the stove, and the smell of butter filled the house.

"Lobster?" Katie asked.

"Your favorite—with parsley roasted red potatoes." Gram served lunch in the sunroom and they feasted on the delicious, tender lobster. Katie savored each buttery bite.

Branson finished his glass of Riesling and wiped the buttery remains from his mouth with his napkin.

Gram stood and began clearing plates. "Let me help," Katie said, carrying dishes to the sink.

"Thanks. I'll need a few moments to finish up dessert. You go and sit with Branson."

"I can help with dessert." Katie protested. "Tell me what to do."

"Oh no you don't. I just cleaned this kitchen. We're all safer letting me do it!" Gram laughed.

"Hmph." Katie crossed her arms, feigning hurt feelings. "There was something wrong with the mixer!" Katie recalled the last time she had helped make dessert. She was in charge of making Chantilly cream for the strawberry shortcake. When the stiff peaks began to form, Katie was so pleased with herself she lifted the beaters out of the bowl, forgetting to shut it off beforehand. The kitchen was splattered with white sticky foam and Gram was kind enough to laugh, instead of cry, when she saw the mess.

She joined Branson at the table and started to take a seat. He stood and said, "Will you show me your favorite spot to watch the sea?"

"Sure. We'll be right back, Gram. Leave the dishes in the sink for me. You cooked, I'll clean up."

Katie took Branson's hand and led him around the back of the house to the farthest corner of the yard. They walked along the stone path toward the edge of the steepest cliff that was safeguarded by a metal hand railing. Katie inhaled the sweet, salty familiar smell of the ocean. "Isn't it just glorious?" She leaned over the railing, letting the wind sweep her hair away from her face.

Branson took her hands and turned her to face him. "It's an enchanting spot. I know how much you love it here, and that's why I chose it."

Katie looked puzzled. He didn't choose this place—it was hers. He had only seen it through the window last winter. He seemed nervous, and she began to worry that he had terrible news for her. "Katie, you have captivated my heart and soul. I wanted to bring you to your favorite spot to tell you that I love you."

"I love you, too, babe. Why are you so serious? Is everything all right?"

"Yes, just listen to me, Katie . . ." he started and paused before clearing his throat. He flashed a nervous smile before starting again. "I love you and I want to spend the rest of my life with you. When I look into your eyes, I see our future. I see two little girls, with green eyes the color of the raging sea, hanging onto your leg and asking you to brush their hair. I see two rambunctious boys out back fishing and skiing. I can't imagine a life without you. I want to wake up every morning knowing that you are in bed beside me, and fall asleep each night holding you in my arms."

Katie felt tears stinging her eyes. She listened to the words he was speaking and let his blue eyes take her into their future. As the tears spilled down her cheeks, she watched him lower to one knee and pull out the most exquisite ring.

"Katie Rose Harrington, will you marry me?"

She looked into his amazing blue eyes that were accented by long dark eyelashes. His dimples sank deep into his cheeks and her heart melted. His smile tugged at something deep inside of her that made her want to giggle and kiss him at the same time.

"Yes! Of course, I will marry you!" She dropped down to her knees and threw her arms around his neck.

Branson slipped the large square diamond ring out of the black velvet box and onto her finger. "Good, it fits."

"It's just beautiful. I love you so much." She kissed him with every bit of passion inside of her, wanting to express the depth of her love and happiness.

When they finally pulled away, Branson helped her to her feet. Holding her in his arms, they watched the waves roll in and crash into the rocks. "C'mon." He held her hand and led her back toward the house. "Let's tell Gram."

"She doesn't know?" Katie was surprised.

"No. Some things are just for you and me."

Thirteen

2001 Mountain Retreat Road was different than the last time she had been there. Everything was in full bloom and the landscaping was lovely. The first thing they did was run around to the backyard and look at the lake. After unpacking the necessities, they ordered takeout and cuddled on the couch in front of the television.

"It feels different. Don't you think so?"

"There aren't any personal touches—Mom and Dad packed everything up in case we decided to list it and find something else. Or, if I buy it—we might like to add our own stuff."

"I like all the furniture, but I can't sleep in there." Katie pointed toward the master bedroom. "Not in your parents' bed. We'd have to get our own bedroom furniture."

"Of course." Branson crinkled his nose. "I couldn't do some of the things I plan on doing to you in *that* bed."

Katie giggled. "It's settled then. You can teach your son to fish right out there someday."

Branson kissed her firmly and quickly on the lips before planting more kisses all over her face. "Thank you. We're going to be so happy here."

"So, when are we going furniture shopping? I can't wait to find out about the things you plan on doing to me in our new bed." Katie smiled.

"Tomorrow sounds good to me. For now, we have my room downstairs." Branson smiled. "Or the pool table." He lifted Katie up over his shoulder and carried her downstairs as she giggled and barely tried to wriggle free.

Katie was vaguely aware that she was in a dream state. *The air was thick with an eerie fog that didn't make sense being inside of the apartment she stood in. Maybe it's smoke? She looked around the room, not recognizing any of the furniture, or people, in the room. Their faces were blurry as she tried to focus. She walked around them, but no one acknowledged her presence. She was sure she recognized them, but wasn't sure how or why. Someone was crying behind her, causing her to run to where the girl was lying. Her legs were heavy and way too slow as she finally made her way to the battered girl. "Ally!" she screamed. "Ally! Can you hear me? Wake up!"*

Katie opened her eyes to find someone shaking her shoulders. "Katie! Wake up."

Her eyes tried to focus on the man in front of her. "Branson?" Her body trembled as he rubbed her arms.

"It's okay, baby, you were having a bad dream."

Inhaling deep, cleansing breaths, she lowered her heart rate and minimized the shakes. "It was the strangest dream . . ." She racked her brain to find the faces and make sense. "I don't know why I would dream such a thing. I could swear I knew the people in the dream, but I can't place how I know them or who they are."

"You were screaming for someone named Ally. Who's that?"

Katie brushed a strand of hair from her face and tucked it behind her ear. Her forehead was beaded with sweat. "I don't know? I've never known anyone named Ally."

Branson pulled her over onto his chest and wrapped his arms around her. "You're okay, now. See if you can fall back asleep." He stroked her back and shoulders until he felt her body relax.

Branson awoke to the tantalizing aroma of freshly brewed coffee. He stretched his arms over his head and rubbed his eyes before opening them to Katie standing beside the bed. "Good morning, beautiful. Why didn't you wake me when you got up?"

"I couldn't sleep, so I awoke early and watched the news. There's some disturbing stuff going on in our world—I had no idea. I've always hated watching the news because of all the crime and sadness. It's freaking dangerous out there. I feel like we're in our own little world way out here and nothing ugly can touch us. I mean, we *are* on Pleasant Lake."

Branson sat up and kissed Katie before taking the mug of coffee. "Mmm, it's good, thank you." He patted the spot next to him and Katie slid in, resting her back against the headboard. "So, you couldn't sleep last night?"

Katie shook her head. "No, I dozed, but those faces haunted me all night. I just had to walk around." Her face lit up. "I can't wait to go furniture shopping today!"

"You're pretty wound up for someone who didn't sleep much last night. How much coffee have you had?"

Katie smirked. "Only two cups—this makes three. But that's not why I'm jazzed. This place is incredible, you're incredible, last night was . . ." She blushed. "I'm just happy."

He planted a soft kiss on her forehead. "Are you looking forward to the engagement party Saturday night?"

"Mmm." She blew the steam off the top of her mug and took a sip. "Maggie knows how to throw a party. Should be a lot of fun. I'm sure I'm not as excited as you, though," she said, sarcasm dripping from her lips.

The sound of glass breaking shook Katie out of her trance. When she looked up, she realized everyone was looking in her direction. Her legs were wet from the full glass of Chardonnay that splashed up when she dropped her wine glass.

Everything seemed to be happening in slow motion. She let her gaze linger on her fiancé who began walking toward her with a look of concern on his face. He was wearing a white oxford shirt with the khaki pants she found incredibly sexy on him. His face and arms were lightly bronzed from the summer sun and his short brown hair had lightened a shade.

By the time he made it to her, time caught up and everyone seemed to appear normal again.

"Are you okay? What happened? Are you cut?" Branson asked, looking over her legs.

"I'm fine. The glass just slipped out of my hands—I can't believe I made such a mess."

"You looked upset, are you sure you're okay?"

"Of course. I'm just embarrassed that I caused a scene. Maggie worked so hard to make this night perfect."

"Did I hear my name?" Maggie appeared, smiling.

"I'm sorry, Mag—"

"Stop. This is so not a big deal." Maggie pulled out a cloth and handed it to Katie for her legs. "Thankfully it was white wine—a *Carrie* reenactment might have been too much entertainment for this group!" She laughed. Within seconds, she returned with a small broom and dustpan, swept up the shattered glass, and disappeared as fast as she had appeared.

Maggie was an effervescent ball of energy, prancing around the party, ensuring everyone was having a good time. Her strawberry blond curls bounced around her shoulders as she refilled champagne flutes and checked the food tables.

The catering company kept busy stocking the party with wine and beer. The guests devoured the shrimp cocktail, which ran out early forcing them to survive on a menu of stuffed mushrooms and prosciutto-wrapped melon, among other beautifully presented hors d' oeuvres.

After everyone was gone, Katie found herself sitting in Branson's lap with a blanket wrapped around her shoulders. The cool May night air was beginning to leave dew on everything it touched.

"Did you have a good time?" Branson kissed her cheek before bringing the glass bottle of Rolling Rock to his lips, tipping it up to finish it off.

"I did, what a perfect night," she sighed, leaning her head on Branson's shoulder. "I've never been happier."

"I'm glad. I've been a nervous wreck these past two weeks."

Katie turned to look into his clear blue eyes. "Did you doubt that I'd say yes?" She giggled.

"I guess there's always that bit of doubt." Branson tucked a strand of dark brown hair behind her ear. "You're quite a catch, Katie. I'm a very lucky man." He smiled and kissed her softly.

"You're quite a catch, too, Branson Stone. Now, take me to bed, my handsome fiancé."

"Already bossing me around and we're not even married." He smirked, lifting her up into his arms and carrying her into the house.

Katie used her foot to shut the back door. She sensed the playful mood radiating from Branson and giggled when he tossed her onto the bed. She quickly tried to scoot away from him as he crawled toward her like a predator hunting its prey. "I'm not *that* easy," she cackled, and tried to roll off the bed.

Branson grabbed her by the ankles and pulled her toward him. "No, but I know your weaknesses." He let his fingers dance across her ribs, causing her to wiggle and laugh until she was rendered breathless.

"Agh!" Katie laughed. "Okay . . . you win! Have your way with me, clever beast!"

Each time they made love, Katie was overwhelmed with a feeling she couldn't describe. It was deeper than lust, stronger than love, and more powerful than anything she had ever experienced. She was perfectly and completely addicted to Branson.

As she lay spent, Katie studied the man lying next to her. She watched his muscular chest rise and fall with each breath, and traced her fingers gently across his sculpted shoulders and arms. *I can't imagine being any happier than I am, right now,* she thought. He was gentle, but strong, kind but protective. He was smart and successful, knew how to make her laugh until she cried, and a magnificent lover. She had everything she'd ever wanted and fell asleep smiling.

Katie woke up in the middle of the night after another nightmare. She felt Branson pull her backside into him and wrap his arms around her trembling body.

"You're okay, I'm here," he whispered, holding her close to him as she softly cried herself back to sleep.

As the warm buttery glow of sun filled the room, Katie stirred. She snuggled deeper under the covers, trying to make sleep come again, but it was no use. Flashes of the nightmare that had kept her awake most of the night invaded her thoughts. She tried to recall the entire dream, but could only remember pieces. She was running down the street chasing a long black car, screaming for it to stop. It was carrying something precious, though she didn't know what.

She rubbed her eyes and stretched her arms over her head, feeling the pull of each muscle as she prepared herself to get out of bed and start the day. Another flash of the nightmare caused Katie to pause. This time she was watching a little girl hold onto one of the posts that lined the steps of a front porch. The little girl had long brown hair and green eyes. She was crying and begging the people in the dream not to take her away. She was wearing a lavender dress with tiny purple and green flowers. *Brown hair . . . green eyes.* Katie ran her hand through her hair and sat up in bed. *Is the little girl supposed to be me? Why would I dream something like that?*

"Good morning, love," Branson said as he rubbed his forehead. He looked over at Katie, who was sitting up with a confused look on her face. "Another bad dream?"

"I can't figure out why I keep having the same dream. It makes no sense."

"Maybe you're stressed out with work?"

"I don't think so, I love my job. Why would an ER nurse have dreams about a little girl being taken away? Or chasing after a black car? How does that relate to broken bones and Code Reds?"

"Something from your past?"

"I don't think so, I've never been kidnapped—and the black car—we never owned a black car. Gram always drove a white Lincoln. Actually, she had a pale yellow one once, but never black."

"Maybe it's time you see someone. You've got to get this under control, so you can get a good night's sleep again."

"I know. I'll call tomorrow. Right now, I need to get ready for work." Katie slipped out of bed and headed toward the bathroom.

Branson watched her lean, graceful, nude body as she walked toward the bathroom. She had never been modest, and had no reason to be with that figure. His own body stirred with desire as he watched her long brown hair sweep across her back and decided to join her in the shower.

"Room for one more?" He smiled and stepped into the large tiled shower. Her hair was jet black when it was wet and her green eyes sparkled when she looked at him, revealing desire. He took his time with her, savoring every inch of her gorgeous body and watching her writhe beneath his touch. He loved pleasing her. "You are so beautiful, Katie," he whispered in her ear, making love to her until she cried out his name.

Branson took the shampoo from Katie. "Let me." He poured a small amount into his hand, working her hair into a thick lather. Carefully, he tilted her head back into the water and rinsed the suds out.

"My turn." Katie massaged his head with shampoo and giggled when he acted like the feeling was better than sex.

"I have to work late tonight, babe." Branson buttoned his shirt and grabbed a tie off the rack. "There's a big deal on the table and the board is having a dinner meeting at six."

Branson had inherited his father's company when he graduated from college. He was the baby of the family with two older sisters that tried to coddle him through life. He was compassionate, charming, and had the biggest blue eyes and deep dimples. He learned at an early age he had the power to melt their hearts and make them give him anything he wanted. He never had to deal with problems, having them around to protect him, and he was made to believe he could do, be, and have anything in life. His father often scolded his sisters for babying him so much. *"You'll make him lazy. He'll never know how to deal with the real world and face problems that come his way."* His father was wrong. Branson worked hard to prove himself, and graduated with honors.

Katie kissed him and straightened his tie. "My handsome fiancé, how will I make it through the day without you?"

"I hope you'll think of me often—well, maybe not while you're setting a broken bone, or something gross." He flashed a crooked grin. "See you tonight."

"We've got to set a date. My parents are harassing the moose stew out of me."

Katie giggled and tickled his ribs. "When did you eat moose stew?"

Branson held both of her arms with one hand and tickled her until she was breathless. "Stop! I give!"

"I was thinking this fall might be nice. Do you want a big church wedding, or something outside?"

"I don't care. Believe it or not, I wasn't one of those girls that fantasized about her wedding day since she was little. I do want Gram, your family, and our close friends there." She rolled her eyes. "Oh, and I suppose it would be helpful if *you* were there." Katie laughed and ran through the house after seeing the look on Branson's face. If he caught her, he would tickle her, making her beg for mercy. She was on the opposite side of the dining room table, trying to predict his next move. He lunged to the left, so she lunged right and tried to run, but he caught her. "You tricked me!"

Instead of tickling her, he held her against the wall and pinned her arms. "I'll tickle you all morning until you set a date." He teasingly let his hand hover over her ribs.

"Okay!" She giggled. "Second Saturday in October. Now let me loose!"

Katie grabbed a couple of granola bars and bottles of water for a morning hike. They didn't plan on going far, maybe just an hour or two in the great outdoors before furniture shopping. As they climbed through the vast woods, listening to the wind whistle a happy tune through the tree branches, Katie was at peace. The emergency room was exciting, fast-paced, and made her feel like she was doing something good. She was able to ease pain, repair wounds, and reduce fear. But the sounds and smells of the forest brought her an indescribable serenity.

Branson led the way off the trail and higher uphill. "I want to show you something." Katie followed him, pulling branches out of the way and stepping over rocks. The woods began to thin until they were finally at the top, overlooking the surrounding mountains.

Branson sat down on a large, flat, rock, and took a drink of water before passing it to Katie. The quick hike had made him hot, so he pulled off his shirt and looked around at the beauty that surrounded them. He pulled out his guitar, remembering all the times he had come to that spot to play a tune and listen to the birds and trees respond with a song of their own.

Katie watched as the ripples on his arms and chest moved with each stroke of the guitar. He was magnificent as he sat there strumming. Branson looked up, smiled broadly enough to flash those dimples that drove her wild, and said, "I wrote this for you."

"The sun may set . . . and the song may end . . ." His voice was smooth and sexy and sounded a lot like Sting. *"The pearl may lose its luster . . . and the broken wheel may not mend . . . but as long as I feel your embrace . . . and the sweet rapture of your touch, happiness will never fade . . ."* Branson looked at Katie for a moment before looking back down at his fingers as they strummed across the strands of the guitar. *". . . and I will not want for anything else."*

Katie clapped. "That was beautiful," she whispered.

"Thanks. I'm not finished with the song yet." He set his guitar down and sat down next to her. "I used to come up here all the time to get away. A lot of teen angst, I guess." He took Katie's hand in his and kissed her fingers.

"It's absolutely breathtaking."

"See that rock protruding from the side of the mountain over there?"

Katie followed with her eyes as he pointed. She roamed the side of the mountain until she saw the rock. "Yes, I see it."

"It looks like a man's face, doesn't it? The profile—see the nose and chin? The eye sockets curve in, along with the mouth. See it?"

"I do! Wow, it looks like someone carved it."

"But they didn't—it's all natural. I used to sit out here for hours finding faces in the rocks and clouds."

"Well, now you've just given away your secret hiding place. When you're mad at me, I'll know where to find you." Katie smiled.

"I can't imagine being mad at you. I actually had other things in mind for this spot. Picnics . . ." He kissed Katie's neck. "Reading . . ." Katie closed her eyes, enjoying the thrill that ran up her spine as his hot breath tickled the back of her ear. She felt his hand slowly slide up her leg, making his intentions clear.

Katie giggled. "I can hear us on the *Newlywed Game* when they ask us to name the craziest place we've ever made love."

Branson's eyes darkened and he smiled mischievously. "On the edge of a cliff."

Katie was exhausted. Three twelve hour shifts in a row always took their toll on her mind and body, and she exhaled with pleasure as she sank into the soft leather couch next to Branson.

"Hard day, babe?"

"Oh my goodness. Five people were brought in from a horrible car accident—we were understaffed and ill-prepared for how bad it was. Thankfully, everyone is going to be all right, but it was a little overwhelming."

"I'm sorry. How about a glass of wine and a movie?"

"That sounds wonderful."

Katie sipped her wine while Branson found a movie and slipped it into the player. He pulled her legs into his lap and rubbed her calves. "Oh that feels so good." Halfway through the movie she was sound asleep.

"C'mon, babe, time for bed." Branson carried her back to the bedroom, pulled back the covers, and gently slid her in.

"Thank you," Katie mumbled groggily. "So tired."

Branson shut the bedroom door behind him, so the sound of the television wouldn't wake her. She had been so tired the last few weeks, he began to worry. *Maybe she needs to cut back to part time. She doesn't need to work, I don't know why she feels like she has to. I know she loves it, but it's wearing her out. It's probably the cause of her nightmares, too.* Branson stopped the movie, since he was having trouble focusing and started flipping through the channels. He thought about how little Katie had been eating and wondered if that was the reason for her exhaustion. He would insist on her being seen by a doctor in the morning, just in case. His reverie was broken by Katie's screams.

"Katie! Wake up, honey." He gently shook her shoulders until she opened her eyes. A look of panic washed over her face. Or was it pain? "It's all right, my love. It was just a dream."

Katie tried to speak, but her throat was dry. After clearing it, she tried again. "I was a little girl, holding onto the front porch post. Someone with dark glasses grabbed me and put me into a long black car. The dream shifted and I was back on the porch—suddenly chasing the black car down the street. I was screaming for my baby—our son. It was terrible, Branson." Katie buried her head into his chest and cried.

"It was just a dream, babe." He held her tightly while stroking her hair.

Katie suddenly pulled away and grimaced. A sharp pain shot through her abdomen, causing her to double over and groan. She felt a gush of warm liquid between her legs and ran to the bathroom. Branson was right behind her, but she shut and locked the door to keep him out.

"What is it? Are you okay?" He could hear that she was in pain. "Katie! Talk to me!"

It took her a moment before she had the strength to speak. "I don't know what's happening. I guess I've started my period, but it hurts . . ." She cried out. "Really bad!"

"Has it ever hurt like that before?"

"No."

"Unlock the door."

"I can't reach it. Just leave me for a minute. Maybe it will stop in a—" She groaned in pain again. "Ow!"

Branson found the key above the bedroom door and worked the bathroom lock. He found Katie on the floor, all the color drained from her face and skin. Her nightgown was soaked in blood. After calling an ambulance, he changed her clothes, and wrapped a blanket around her shoulders, rocking her gently in his arms. "It's going to be all right," he repeated mechanically until the sound of sirens broke his trance.

Fourteen

Katie lay on her side, hugging the thin sheet that covered her as she waited for the doctor to come in. Branson sat on the edge of the stretcher, held her hand, and methodically stroked his thumb across the back of her knuckles.

"Miss Harrington, I'm Dr. Elson." The blonde smiled tenderly as she walked into the room.

Katie braced herself for the worst. *It's cancer—I'm going to die.*

"I'm sorry, but you've had a miscarriage."

Katie sat up in alarm. "But I'm not pregnant."

Dr. Elson moved closer to Katie's bed and rested her hand on Katie's. "The blood test confirmed that you were pregnant, and the ultrasound shows that your uterus is clear, so a D & C won't be necessary. I am so very sorry." She turned to address Branson. "Here are the discharge papers. If she develops a fever, please, bring her back. You can give her Ibuprofen for pain, but no Aspirin. You're free to go when you're ready."

Katie was in shock. *How could I have been pregnant? We always use birth control. Except for the one time, but . . .* She was suddenly hit with an overwhelming emotional pain. *I was pregnant? I lost our baby?* All it took was one look at Branson to bring the all-consuming, body-shaking sobs.

Branson was by her side in an instant, holding her to his chest. "It's okay."

"I . . . lost our . . . baby." She sucked in small, tight breaths.

"Shh, I've got you." He held her in his arms and let her release the pain of their loss until she was too exhausted to cry any more. When he thought she was okay, he slipped out to ask the doctor some questions.

"Excuse me," Branson said as he approached Dr. Elson in the hallway. "Could this be the reason she's been so tired and weak? She hasn't been eating or sleeping well, and . . . will we be able to get pregnant again?"

"Yes to all of the above. She'll need to rest and heal, and she may go through a grieving process, even though this wasn't a planned pregnancy."

Light suddenly flooded the room burning Katie's puffy, sore eyes. "Agh! Shut the curtains."

"No. You've been in here for three days. It's time to get up." Branson proceeded to pull back all of the curtains in the room before sitting on the side of the bed and holding out a glass of orange juice. "Drink it," he commanded.

Katie took the cup and slowly took a sip before passing it back.

"Oh no you don't. Drink every drop." He felt a little more like a father than a fiancé at the moment, but nothing else had worked. He had allowed her to cry and starve herself long enough, and now he wanted her back.

Katie reluctantly took the cup, drank all of the juice and gave it back to him. "Satisfied?" she said sulkily.

"Now then, I've got a bath ready for you—let's go."

Katie slipped into the warm bath, allowing the silky water to soothe her stiff muscles. Her hair was tangled and unkempt against her head. Branson gently soaped her shoulders and arms before washing and conditioning her hair. As the soap trickled down her arms, rinsing away the grime of three days in bed, it also took with it the heavy feeling of sorrow. Slowly, Katie came back to life. "Thank you," she whispered.

"My pleasure." Branson held a fluffy white towel for her to step into and wrapped her up in his arms. "I know you're going to be sad for a while—I am too. But I need you to be all right. I miss you. Let's get through this together."

Katie nodded her head. "I'm okay, I just didn't realize . . . how can you love something so much, when you didn't even know it existed in the first place?" She dried herself off and slipped on a robe.

Branson knew exactly what she meant, but he needed to be strong for her. "Let's get out of here and go see a movie."

"Okay." Katie blew her hair dry and tied it back into a low ponytail, slipping into her favorite jeans.

Midway through the movie, Katie began to relax and feel human again. Branson had chosen a romantic comedy, and she was surprised the first time laughter erupted from her. After that, she sipped on her soda and indulged in the healing laughter often. She noticed Branson watching her every now and then, and wondered how he was doing. They hadn't talked after that night in the emergency room. She had retreated emotionally and physically from him and the rest of the world for the past three days. She reached over and rested her hand on his leg, giving him a reassuring smile when he looked at her. With that look, they both said all that was needed without uttering a word. Everything was going to be fine.

After the movie, they drove toward Millstone restaurant. A red Toyota Camry cut in front of them causing Branson to slam on the breaks. Katie thought, *Jerk! If I'd been driving, I would have rammed you right into that eighteen wheeler!* She was horrified at her sudden rage. *Where did that come from?*

Branson ordered a steak with a coffee-marsala reduction and insisted Katie order her favorite, the lobster. *I'll order whatever I please. Maybe I'm in the mood for red meat tonight.* Again she was surprised. She smiled sweetly. "That sounds wonderful." *What's wrong with me?*

Planning the wedding lifted Katie's spirits. Spending time with Gram and Maggie over flowers, cake, and dresses took her mind off the sorrow that grabbed at her chest every now and then. She was reminded of an old saying about choosing which emotion to feed. She could either focus on her loss, or focus on her future. Spending the day at the bridal shop with Gram and Maggie would be much better if she chose to focus on future.

Katie tried on several dresses before finding 'the one'. It was beautiful, romantic, and classic. Made from raw silk, the strapless beaded bodice hugged her curves until it swept into a full ball gown skirt. She paired it with a simple veil that trailed a few inches longer than her train.

With Maggie there, offering her expertise, it had been easy to choose flowers—orange roses with green foxtail fern and little reddish-orange berries.

The cake tasting had been the highlight of the day. The three of them spent two hours tasting cake, and laughing.

"I don't know. The lemon is light and fresh, but the Italian Cream is rich and delicious. Which is your favorite?" Katie looked to Maggie and then Gram.

"At the moment, I don't ever want to see cake again." Gram rubbed her belly.

"I liked them both, but I think the Italian Cream will go best with your dinner menu," Maggie said.

"This has been the best day. Thank you both." Katie had been on a roller coaster of emotions. She had needed this more than she knew. She was eager to get home to Branson and make up for the lifeless mannequin she'd been toward him the past few weeks.

Katie wrenched upright in bed. Her breathing was heavy, her forehead and chest wet with perspiration, and tears trailed down her cheeks.

Branson sat up with her, trying to calm her down. "You're all right, it was just a nightmare."

"I'm sorry for waking you, go back to sleep. I'm going to the living room for a bit, and then I'll come back to bed." She quietly made her way to the kitchen, fixed a cup of tea, and sat down to process the nightmare. *What was that? Who are these people?* She concentrated on the three men and their features, trying to pull more out of her subconscious. *God, I'm going crazy! I keep having these nightmares that don't make sense, and the bouts of rage . . . what's happening?*

She laid her head in her hands and tried to dig deep. Branson entered the kitchen, interrupting her excavation, and sat down across from her. "Babe, I think you need to see someone about these nightmares. I know you've been through so much, maybe you need some grief counseling?"

"No, I'm fine."

"You're not fine, Katie. I'll go with you if you want, but—"

"Jeez!" Katie interrupted. "Quit nagging me like an old—" She stopped short. "I'm sorry, babe. I don't know why I've been so snappy. I just can't make sense of these nightmares—they have nothing to do with me. They say if someone is chasing you in your dream, it's because you're under a lot of stress. If you lose your teeth it's because you're self-conscious about an upcoming speech or presentation. But how do you explain the strange faces of men and a battered girl on the floor?" Katie wished she hadn't told him about that nightmare in particular. He would assume she was crazy for certain now.

Branson shrugged his shoulders. He desperately wished he could help her. What had happened to the woman he'd fallen in love with? Happy, sweet, passionate, and lively Katie had been replaced with a discontented shell. She resembled Katie physically, but her spirit had been replaced. He would do whatever it took to bring her back.

On Tuesday, Katie had an appointment with Dr. Bailey Windsor. She walked up to the receptionist at the Windsor Center and gave her name. She smiled and waited for the lady behind the desk to find her on the computer screen. The receptionist had short dark hair, reading glasses and a sweater tied around her shoulders. She was sitting up straight, as if trying to balance a stack of books on her head. *She's trying too hard*, Katie thought.

"Yes, I've got you down. Please, take a seat and she will be ready for you in a moment."

Katie took a seat in the lobby and picked up a magazine. She had only enough time to flip through the first few pages before her name was called and she saw Dr. Windsor standing in the doorway of her office. Her long auburn hair was pulled back into a low ponytail that lay against her navy pantsuit. She had brown eyes and a few small freckles across her nose. "Hi, Katie, I'm Bailey Windsor." She led Katie into her office. "You can sit here, or we can sit over there on the sofa—whichever is more comfortable."

"Thank you for seeing me." Katie took a seat and sank deep into the dark brown leather chair.

Dr. Windsor took a seat in a wing-back chair across from her. "So, what brings you in today?"

"This might sound silly, and I'm not sure it will do any good for me to be here, but I'm not sleeping well. I keep having these recurring nightmares. I'd like to know why." Katie wrinkled her brow and felt a frown form on her mouth. "Also," she hesitated, not sure she should divulge any more information. She wasn't comfortable sharing such intimate details about her life. But Dr. Windsor was a professional—sworn by oath not to share any information about her patients. *This should be a safe place. Relax, Katie. Just tell her everything and let's get this stuff out.* "I've been having these . . . pictures that flash through my mind—like memories, but they're not memories. It's not anything that has ever happened to me—it's places that I've never been, people I don't know—but these pictures are portrayed in my mind like lost memories." Katie exhaled, realizing she hadn't remembered to breathe. "It's really bizarre and confusing. Am I losing my mind or something?" Katie chuckled, trying to make it seem like a joke, but inside she was worried that something might actually be wrong.

Bailey scribbled a few things in her notepad before looking up. "No, Katie, you're not losing your mind. Are you experiencing any high levels of stress—a new job, moving? Stress can come from good as well as bad."

"I—" Katie looked down at her hands as she twisted her fingers. "I recently experienced a miscarriage, but the nightmares began before that happened."

"I'm so sorry for your loss. You said the nightmares began before this?"

Katie nodded her head. "Off and on for a few years now, but they've become more frequent."

Dr. Windsor set her notepad on her lap and looked up at Katie. "I have a few ideas that I'd like to try—see if these are actual memories, or something caused by stress. First, have you ever had a severe head trauma?"

"No."

"Okay, get comfortable. I'm going to ask you a few questions. Try to answer quickly, the first thing that comes to mind."

Bailey Windsor went through a series of questions, and once she felt like Katie was comfortable she continued with harder ones, having Katie look up and to the left as she answered, and then to the right.

Katie felt like the whole experience was a bit hokey, but she participated and did exactly what the doctor asked. When the session was over, she made an appointment for another visit. Nothing was accomplished, but she felt extremely relaxed. Wasting a day at home on the couch wasn't an option Katie cared to entertain, so she drove toward the Bean, hoping a cup of coffee would stir her back to life. With a steaming cup of latte in hand, she pulled out of the parking lot and took a left toward her favorite boutique. Katie was trying to get into the turning lane, but the car next to her wouldn't let her over. *I'll run your ass off the road!* Katie thought as she pushed her way in front of the car. She waved a sarcastic "thank you" in the rearview mirror. *Jeez, what's wrong with me?*

Fifteen

"Have a great day!" The two sisters that owned Navy & White waved as Katie walked out of their shop.

Katie found several cute things—a navy polo dress, a navy and white striped hooded shirt, a pair of boat shoes, and a pair of sliver studded earrings. As she walked to her car, fishing for her keys deep in her purse, someone bumped into her, causing one of her bags to drop.

"I'm sorry." The man handed her the dropped bag.

"Thank you, I wasn't watching where—" Katie got a quick look at the tall blond before he turned away. She thought the interaction was strange as he hurried off before she could finish her apology. Finding her keys, she unlocked the trunk and set the bags inside. Before she started the engine it dawned on her that she might have been robbed. *Shit!* She searched her purse for her wallet and discovered it wasn't there. After calling both credit card companies to cancel future purchases, she dialed the police and tried to give a description of her robber. She sat in her car for a moment, angry that he had done this to her—and was aggravated after realizing she would have to replace her driver's license, too.

Katie suddenly snapped out of a trance, wondering how long she had been sitting there. The clock answered by showing that thirty minutes had passed. *What happened? That was more than a daydream—crap, I AM going crazy!*

The following week Katie entered Dr. Windsor's office and sat on the couch.

"Hi, Katie. How was last week?"

"The flashes are getting worse. Also . . ." Katie lowered her head, ashamed. "I've been having spurts of rage. Not outwardly, but in my head. I'm cursing people on the road, thinking ugly things about people I pass on the street or in the grocery. This isn't me—we've got to get this figured out. I'm going out of my mind."

"We will." Bailey Windsor leaned forward and set her pad of paper on the side table. "I'd like to hypnotize you, Katie. How would you feel about that?"

"I don't know, it sounds a little frightening."

"There is absolutely nothing to fear. It's like dozing off for a nap. I'll ask you a few questions, and then you'll wake up."

Katie hesitated for a moment, contemplating the pros and cons. She was afraid of someone getting inside her head, but at the same time she was ready to have her life back and have answers. "Okay, let's do it."

Ten minutes later, Katie was under. Dr. Windsor spoke softly and calmly. "Katie, you're completely safe and relaxed.

I'd like to ask you about your earliest childhood memory. Can you tell me the last thing you remember about being a little girl? Where are you? Who is with you?"

Katie's voice was hollow and far away when she answered. "I'm holding my doll, Ashley. I'm brushing her hair. No! Don't let them take me! Please! No!" Her body began to tremble and tears flowed down her cheeks.

"It's okay, Katie. You're safe. No one is going to take you. Who do you see?"

"A woman. She's trying to take me, but I don't know her. No! Please! I won't let go of the post. She's prying my hands loose. Ashley! Ashley!" Katie began screaming.

"Katie, I'm going to wake you up on the count of three. One . . . two . . . three."

Katie opened her eyes and wiped the tears from her face. "What happened? Did I say anything helpful? Why am I crying?"

"You said someone was taking you away. A woman was prying your hands from the post you were holding onto. Then you started screaming for Ashley. You were upset, so I woke you up." Dr. Windsor handed Katie a box of tissues. "Does any of this mean anything to you?"

"No. It's the dream, but none of that ever happened to me. I've never had a doll named Ashley, and no one ever kidnapped me."

Bailey Windsor jotted a few things in her notebook. "Let's try again in a week." She looked up at Katie. "Sometimes hypnosis can bring out buried memories. If you have any other flashes, either call me or write them down for our next visit."

Katie sat on the back deck enjoying a glass of wine. It was a warm, breezy afternoon in July. She planned on drinking the entire bottle as an emptiness took over like a pit in her very core, threatening to eat away every ounce of who she was—or who she thought she was. She had always been a happy, carefree woman, but the pull of depression was so strong she couldn't fight it and decided to give in, helping it along with the numbing effects of the alcohol. When she finished her second glass of Chardonnay and reached for the bottle to pour another, tiny flashes of what seemed like dreams flooded her mind. They came in waves, like jolts from a form of shock therapy, only they were painless—at first.

Katie left her glass on the table, retrieved her keys, and drove down I-89. Deep in thought, she exceeded the speed limit, driving faster and faster. After setting the cruise control to help maintain a safer speed, she merged onto I-93 and let her thoughts wander. *It can't be true! There has to be another explanation. Gram will know, she'll help make sense of all this.*

The lines on the road became blurry from the tears that rushed from her eyes. She tried to blink them away and focus on the road when she heard tires screeching and a horn blowing. Katie screamed when she saw that she had veered into oncoming traffic. After bringing her car back into its own lane, she pulled over on the shoulder. She sat there for at least thirty minutes, letting the tears flow along with fresh new memories of her past. Her mind was flooded with faces and names. She vaguely remembered her horrible foster parents, the cruelty they inflicted on her and . . . Katie racked her brain to remember the girl's name that she shared a room with. *Amy? Abby? Ally! Her name was Ally.*

Ally's name brought with it a floodgate of memories. She remembered being torn from her parents' home—begging the strange man and woman not to take her away. Katie held her hand tightly over her chest, fearing her heart may break all over again. As the memories swiftly came back, it was like watching a movie.

Sixteen

Sixteen years ago . . .

"Please, don't let them take me away!" Katie cried, holding onto one of the white posts that lined the front porch steps. The chipping paint felt rough on her little hands, but she held on as tight as she could. Strong hands pried each finger and finally carried her away from the only home she had ever known.

"Ashley! Ashley!" Katie screamed and reached for her ragged doll that lay on the third step of the porch. A tall man in a dark collared shirt walked over, picked up the doll, and handed it to a sobbing Katie, who wilted in defeat. She hugged her ragged doll to her chest and whispered, while stroking its long silky blond hair, "Don't worry, Ashley, I won't let anything happen to you."

As the long black car pulled away, Katie tried to swallow the growing lump in her throat. Warm tears stung her eyes, but she refused to let any more fall. No one would see her weak side, her broken heart, or her fear ever again. Six was much too young to worry about such things, but Katie had never really been given the luxury of childhood. If she wasn't holding her mother's hair while she vomited, or fetching another beer for her father, she was hiding from the plethora of drug-induced zombies that her parents referred to as friends. After one of her father's friends put his cigarette out on the top of her head, she knew it was best to stay in her closet with the door shut and keep very quiet.

When the car came to a stop, Katie looked out of the window. Her new home was a red brick single-story home lined with large trees and a wood-fenced back yard. It didn't appear to be anything like her parents' home—a rundown double-wide with stained carpets, peeling wallpaper, and garbage everywhere. If you wanted to watch television at Katie's house, you either had to sit on the floor, or dig out a spot on the sofa to sit down, which was never worth it to Katie.

The new house looked acceptable from the outside. She wondered what awaited her on the inside. One of the strangers—a lady wearing a cream blouse, who sat in the backseat with Katie during the ride—rang the doorbell. Someone, a lady it seemed, opened the door and greeted the two strangers before addressing Katie. "Well, hello there." She smiled and tried to make eye contact with Katie, who was still hiding behind the lady in the cream blouse. Katie's body was paralyzed and her muscles ached from the continuous trembling. Her teeth were clenched together, and she was sure if she tried to speak, they would chatter.

Katie peeked around one of the men and glanced at the strange lady. She was thin with bleach-blond hair that fell loosely around a floral blouse. She wore a shimmering bubble gum pink grin that stretched across her pretty face. Katie found an ounce of confidence as she crept out from behind the men and spoke so quietly it was almost a whisper. "Hi," she said, immediately lowering her head and twisting the hem of her lavender floral dress between her fingers.

"Come on in, Katie." The lady led her into the house and shut the door behind them. "This is your new home. I think you'll like it here. I'll show you to your room." Katie followed the lady down the hall, taking in her surroundings as they walked. "I'm Maxine Higgins, you can call me Maxine."

They reached the door to Katie's new room and stepped inside. The walls were white with purple checked curtains that matched the comforters on the twin beds. Katie didn't see any toys in the room, but it was very clean. *Maybe the toys are kept in the closet?* Katie's eyes darted to the closet door, eager to peek inside. "Miss Maxine, is one of the beds for me and one for Ashley?"

"Who is Ashley, dear?"

"My doll." Katie held up her doll.

"Oh my!" Maxine scrunched her nose up and took the doll. "She needs a bath."

Katie grabbed for Ashley.

"Don't worry, I won't hurt her. We'll get you both cleaned up before Ally gets home."

Katie looked up, puzzled.

"The other bed is for Ally. You'll meet her after school. She's in third grade, only three years older than you."

Katie was left to soak in a tub while Maxine cleaned the doll. "Here's soap and a washcloth. Make sure you scrub everywhere. I'll be right back and we'll wash your hair."

"I can wash my own hair," Katie insisted.

"Okay, but I'm going to check to make sure you've done a proper job."

Katie couldn't remember anyone washing her hair for her. She was six years old, and had been taking care of herself, as well as her parents, for as long as she could remember. She groaned as Maxine guided her head back under the running bathtub faucet.

"When you learn how to do it right, I'll let you wash it yourself." Maxine pulled the plug from the drain and handed Katie a towel. "I've laid clothes out on your bed. You can wait there until Ally gets home."

Katie wasn't sure what to expect when she heard her new foster sister arrive home from school. Was she a nice girl? Would they get along, or fight like the siblings she knew in her trailer park. She remembered watching in horror as Trevor chased his younger sister, Angel, down the street with a steak knife. She had eaten the last piece of cake and he was going to make her pay. An older man walking his poodle pulled Trevor off of his sister right before he carved an X on the back of her right hand.

Katie listened as Maxine and Ally talked. She couldn't make out words, only the tone of their voices as they spoke. Katie stiffened when the bedroom door flung open, and Ally stood there with a smug look on her face.

"So, you're the baby I'm going to be responsible for, huh?"

Katie sat still on the bed and let her eyes roam over Ally's face. Her blond hair was pulled back in a high ponytail, revealing grey-blue eyes. "I'm not a baby," Katie protested. "I'm six."

"Well, I'm nine, so you'll follow *my* rules." Ally flung herself back onto her bed, folding her arms behind her head. "You're going to hate it here."

"It seems nice."

Ally whipped her head around to face Katie. "You haven't met Rick. He's evil. And Maxine . . . don't cross her." She got up and sat on the edge of Katie's bed, causing her to flinch and scoot back against the wall.

Ally noticed her fear and said, "I'm not going to hurt you." Once Katie relaxed, she went over the rules of the house—rules she had learned the hard way.

Seventeen

On Katie's second day in the Higgins home, the real Maxine was revealed to Katie. She had put on a show in front of the two social workers the day Katie arrived. Maxine sang Ally's name as she called her into the bathroom to pick up the hairbrush she left out on the counter. Before Ally could put it away, Maxine spanked her with it until it broke in half.

"You can share my brush," Katie said, laying a hand on Ally's back as she cried.

Maxine was a clean freak. Everything had to be spotless, and there was no leniency. The same week, Katie left her toothpaste on the counter instead of putting it back in the top drawer. Maxine emptied every drawer onto the bathroom floor and screamed, "If you want to live like a pig—do it right." She stormed out and down the hall after commanding Katie to clean everything up.

Later that day, Katie made the mistake of leaving her shoes by the front door. She had taken them off so she wouldn't track grass into the house. The way Maxine looked at her sent a chill up her spine. She grabbed Katie's shoes and threw them at her. "You'll never be worth anything. You'll live just like your parents did—in drugs and filth. I thought I could help, but it's useless. No one can help you."

Rick pulled Katie into his lap to join him in the recliner. She braced herself as his scruffy beard grazed across her cheek. His T-shirt, hugging tight against his large belly was damp with sweat and freshly spilled beer. He smelled of diesel, fresh off a job as a long-haul trucker. Katie's stomach churned as she sucked in shallow breaths, trying not to gag. It was only a matter of time before he had a good buzz going and the shouting would begin. If he had a nice side to him, Katie never saw it.

On Ally's twelfth birthday, Rick came home to join the small celebration. His eyes were already bloodshot and the familiar crazed look was displayed across his face. Maxine yelled, calling him things that would have made Katie and Ally giggle, if they weren't so terrified of what might happen.

"You're a skinny little tramp and you wear too much makeup. You remind me of Lady Elaine Fairchild."

"Who the hell is that?"

"You know," He laughed. "The puppet on *Mr. Rogers Neighborhood.*"

"You big, fat drunk. Look at you! You come into this house reeking of beer and . . . stink. You're a slob."

"Don't you talk to me like that in my house, woman! I'll put you back on the street where I found you."

That must have been the magical line, because it sent Maxine running to her room, slamming the door behind her.

Rick's eyes glazed over as he looked at Ally. Katie stood close enough that she could feel Ally vibrating with fear. Her fingers were clenched and she seemed poised to run. She was terrified, and Katie didn't understand why.

He leaned in, his face inches from hers and said, "Stand up."

Ally obeyed, her eyes filling with tears as she stood. Rick took her hand and spun her around slowly. "Look at this body. You're developing into a fine-looking woman."

Katie instinctively went to the fridge and pulled out a can of Miller Light. "Here you go, Rick. I think your wrestling show is about to start."

Rick took the can of beer, popped the top, and finished it in one guzzle. He smashed it flat on the kitchen table, and boasted a proud grin. "Come, keep your old man company." He started toward the living room, waving the girls to follow.

"Be right there, I just need to use the restroom first." Ally called out. She took Katie by the hand, bringing her with her, and locked the door. "Thank you."

"He's so weird," Katie remarked. "Do you think he'll pass out before he comes looking for us?"

"I think so. He was pretty wasted."

Katie and Ally fell slept huddled on the bathroom floor that night.

If it weren't for Ally Perkins, Katie would have shriveled up and died in that house. Ally kept her laughing with her silly jokes and funny faces. Ally changed over the years, and age fourteen seemed to be her breaking point. She was unaffected by Maxine's comments, and Katie wished she possessed her confidence. Negative comments were unleashed daily about how worthless they were and how they would never amount to anything.

Ally comforted Katie and told her lengthy, detailed stories about what their life would be like when they were older and on their own. *"We'll be models and actresses. We're definitely pretty enough."* They plotted their escape each night as they lay in bed whispering.

Growing up in the Higgins house was dismal. The loneliness wasn't so bad. Even though it left a hollow pit in Katie's stomach, she could live with it. She could even listen to the degrading comments and stick them in a separate compartment in her brain that protected her heart from the venomous words. It was the lack of love that affected Katie the most, threatening to push her over the edge into a pit of depression so deep no one would be able to pull her out.

As the years passed, Katie and Ally became very close. Ally let her golden hair grow long and she encouraged Katie to do the same. "I wish your hair was blond, but at least it's long like mine," Ally said as she brushed and braided Katie's dark brown hair. "I watched a video on how to do makeup. I'll show you, but we'll have to choose different colors for your green eyes. I only learned how to do brown eyes."

"That'd be great," Katie beamed. "I wish I was as pretty as you."

Ally walked around to face her. "You're beautiful, Katie. Don't let anyone tell you differently."

It was clear that Ally was the leader of their two-person group. Katie was glad to follow her anywhere and do anything she asked. They got into trouble on a regular basis because of Ally's schemes, but it was always worth it to Katie when nighttime came and they could giggle about what they had done.

Ally had come up with the idea to place a piece of raw shrimp behind the refrigerator one night as Maxine was cooking and see how long it took her to find it. After three days, the smell became unbearable and the culprit was found. The girls imagined they were paid actresses pretending they knew nothing of the shrimp fiasco. They held straight faces as they brushed their teeth and got ready for bed, and didn't relax until they were sure Maxine was out of earshot.

"Did you see her face?" Katie giggled.

"Yes, I thought she was going to tear the whole house apart to find out where the smell was coming from. That was great!"

"I can't believe we got away with it. I thought we'd get a beating for sure."

Each Saturday night, Rick would come home from a week on the road and consume his usual amount of beer. Katie and Ally were always in their rooms when they heard the screaming match begin.

"Here they go." Katie shrugged her shoulders and turned up the radio.

The sound of glass shattering had them both sitting up in alert, and wondering what to do.

"What was that?" Katie asked. "Should we make sure they're all right?"

"I'm not going out there." Ally's arms were folded across her chest as she stared at the ceiling.

"They don't normally break things. What if someone's hurt?"

"Who gives a shit, Katie?"

The sound of the front door slamming interrupted their conversation and had the girls scooting out of bed to see if Rick had left. Ally opened the bedroom door an inch at a time, trying not to make a sound, and slipped into the hallway. Katie stuck to Ally as they peered into the living room to see it was empty.

Ally sighed, "Good, he's gone."

Katie tiptoed behind Ally back to their room. Before she could get inside she was jerked backward by her hair. "Ow!" she cried, "let me go!"

Ally beat her fists into Rick, trying to make him release Katie. He did, and then back-handed Ally so hard, it looked like she had been shot out of a circus cannon. It took Katie a moment to gather herself after Rick stormed out of the house. She crawled over to Ally and gently shook her shoulder, but she wouldn't wake.

"Ally, please wake up!" Katie trembled as the tears flowed down her cheeks. She took Ally's head in her lap and sat there wondering what to do next. As the crying turned to weeping, Katie's body began to shake.

Ally groaned and pressed a hand to the back of her head. "Stop shaking me, Katie, jeez!"

"Thank God, you're all right! I didn't know what to do."

"Is he gone?" she asked, sitting up and looking around.

"Yeah."

Katie knew that Ally had saved her from something too horrific to wrap her mind around, and she loved her as much as any sister could love another. Blood-related or not.

Eighteen

"I have a plan to get us out of here, are you in?" Ally asked one night as they lay in their beds.

"I guess . . ." Katie said, not sure what Ally had in mind. Some of her ideas were ridiculous and never made it off the planning table. "What are you thinking?"

"We're going to California." Ally beamed.

"California? What's in California? How are we getting—"

"Jeez, Katie, this isn't twenty questions. I'll tell you what's in California—acting and modeling jobs!"

"Are we old enough?" Katie asked.

"Of course. Garrison says we're at the 'prime' age." Ally held her hands up and made quotation marks over her head. "I've set it all up. We're going to pack light—just the essentials—and meet Garrison Thursday at three a.m. in the park."

"Who's Garrison?"

"He's a guy I met the other night when I snuck out. You should've come out with me. I had to convince him to take you with us."

"Weren't you scared out there in the middle of the night?" Katie hugged her comforter to her chest.

"Me? I'm not afraid of anything." Ally sat up in her bed and faced Katie. "You've gotta grow up, Katie. We can't stay here. We have to make our own way. You want to be a doctor, don't you?"

Katie nodded her head. "Yes."

"Well, if you stay here you'll become Maxine's maid, if Rick doesn't have his way with you first. Or kill you."

"What are we going to do when we get there?"

"I've got it all taken care of." Ally's face portrayed a confidence that made Katie believe her.

Katie's mind was flooded with questions and apprehension, but anything would be better than living with the Higgins. She let her mind wander back to a few months ago. She lay on her bathroom floor, willing herself to die from the brutal beating Rick had given her with the buckle side of his belt. Large purple welts covered the backs of her legs and some of them had bled. When death didn't come, but the pain throbbed until life was unbearable, she raided the medicine cabinet and swallowed the entire contents of the first bottle of pills she found.

As she lay there waiting for the peace of death to come, she wondered if she would go to hell for taking her own life. *I AM in hell. What would be the difference?* She sat up, trying to present herself in a more dramatic position when her body was found. *They'll be sorry when they find me. I wonder if the police will come and investigate. They'll put Rick and Maxine away forever, and Ally will be free from this hell. Ally! What will she do once I'm dead? She'll be heartbroken . . . and all alone. What if the police don't put Maxine and Rick away and she's left to take all the beatings? Oh no, what have I done?* Katie pulled herself up and took the empty bottle off the counter to read the label. *I'll just call poison control and see what I should do.* When she read the label on the bottle she exhaled a breath of relief and then chided herself for being so stupid. *Aspirin*!

Thursday seemed to tick by at a turtle's pace. Katie thought she would lose her sanity before three a.m. arrived and they began their adventure to California. Trying not to arouse suspicion, they finished dinner, helped Maxine clean the kitchen, and headed to their room to finish homework.

"We can't pack until Maxine goes to bed, but do you have an idea of what you're bringing?" Ally asked.

"Yes, I think so. How many shirts are you bringing?"

"He said whatever we can fit in a small duffle. There's not a lot of room for bags. I think I can fit three shirts, an extra pair of jeans, socks, underwear, and toiletries."

The door to Maxine's room shut at exactly eleven forty-five. Ally and Katie quietly gathered their things and packed the two small duffels before tiptoeing down the hall to the bathroom for toiletries. Returning to the room, Ally pulled out a wad of cash from under her mattress and tucked it in her bag between her folded jeans.

"Where did you get that?" Katie asked.

"I took it out of Rick's wallet," Ally grinned, proud of herself.

"He'll kill you when he finds out."

"He won't be able to find me, Katie. We'll be long gone before he even realizes it's missing."

"You're right." Katie twisted a strand of hair around her finger until the lack of circulation made the tip pulse. "I'm nervous, Ally. Are you sure we're doing the right thing?"

"Yes, I'm sure. We're starting our lives tonight. You'll be a wonderful surgeon one day, and I'll be a famous actress. You'll see, Katie, everything is going to be just perfect. Garrison promised that he would help us out—he already has jobs lined up for us and a place to stay. He has connections in California."

Katie stuffed her ragged doll into her bag, ignoring Ally's scolding face. "I'm bringing her." She felt the surge of confidence soar through her and decided from this moment on she would no longer be a timid little girl. From now on, she was Katie Rose Harrington, rising surgeon.

Ally and Garrison were obviously arguing. Katie tried to listen in on the conversation while sitting on one of the swings at the park. She looked over Garrison Ford, trying to form an opinion of him. He appeared to be only a few years older than they were—sixteen or seventeen. He had messy blond hair, blue eyes, and wore a black leather jacket. She watched him flick his cigarette butt across the parking lot, using his thumb and forefinger. His tone changed, causing Katie to sit straighter while she listened. He was scolding Ally. "This is all you could get? Forty bucks won't even be enough for gas."

"It's all he had. I'm sorry."

"You were supposed to bring at least twice this much."

"He would've killed me, Garrison. You don't know how mean he is."

"Well, I don't know what we're gonna do. Seth's coming too, hopefully he has some cash." Garrison shook his head and leaned against the white Ford Mustang. "At least money won't be an issue for long," he mumbled under his breath.

"Who's Seth? You didn't say anything about anyone else coming."

"He's fine. Just be cool, and don't give me a reason to leave you both behind."

Seth walked up in a black jacket and jeans. He was obviously older than all of them, in his twenties, Katie assumed. He had black eyes and black hair and reminded her of the bad guy from a movie she'd seen recently. He gave her the creeps. She rubbed her hands up and down over her arms, trying to rid the goose bumps.

Katie strained to hear what Garrison and Seth were talking about, but their muffled whispers came through in chunks that didn't make sense. "James . . . that one . . . pissed . . ." She casually got off the swing and inched her way closer, pretending to look for a dropped earring and heard Garrison say, "What was I supposed to do? Besides, I should get a bonus for bringing two."

Ally lifted Katie up by the arm. "What are you doing?"

Once the informal introductions were made, they were on their way. Assuming the police would be looking for them, they drove at night and pulled off on undeveloped dead end streets to sleep during the day. Katie and Ally were mostly quiet during the three day trip, listening to the radio and conversations coming from the guys in the front seat. Everyone was exhausted and hungry, which caused their tempers to be on edge. They arrived in California around two in the morning, following the directions Garrison read from a slip of paper as Seth drove.

They finally pulled into an apartment complex that looked as if it might be condemned.

Katie leaned over, whispering in Ally's ear. "I hope he took a wrong turn. This place is creepy."

"I don't even care," Ally said before yawning. "I just want to stretch my legs and lie down somewhere—anywhere."

Katie could barely carry herself up the stairs leading to the apartment, let alone her small duffel bag. She was exhausted from being cramped in the backseat for three days with minimal food and drink. The best meal she had on the trip was a small order of French fries that she choked down.

They entered the dark apartment and set their bags down by the door. Katie was led to a twin mattress on the floor of the living room and fell onto it gratefully, allowing the veil of sleep to wash over her.

The smell of strong cologne mixed with something that burned Katie's nose woke her up. She blinked her eyes open, trying to figure out where she was, but it was too dark. A fresh wave of the burning filled her nose and she discovered it was a cloud of cigarette smoke being blown directly into her face. Katie coughed and turned her head into her pillow, trying to suck in a breath of fresh air. Her muscles tensed at the sudden foreboding.

"Oh, did I wake you, princess?" A gruff, sarcastic voice filled her ears and sent a chill down her spine.

"What—where am I?" she cried.

"Heaven," the man replied before injecting something into her arm. Katie tried to break free, but the full weight of him was pinning her down and holding her arms. The drug swam through her veins, causing the walls to breathe in and out as if they were alive. Katie's body felt warm and spongy as she lay on the mattress on the floor. She knew she needed to get out of there, away from the people in the room, but she couldn't move. She lifted her arm up into the air, as if it would somehow be the leader, commanding the rest of her body to follow. Her arm dangled in the air alone and the rest of her body just watched as it fell back down onto the mattress defeated. The people around her looked like something out of a comic book and she smiled as she watched their lips curl up and around past their ears. She tried to focus on her surroundings—figure out where she was—but everything started to get hazy and she slipped into a deep, dreamless sleep.

The room was suddenly cold, causing Katie to reach for cover, only to realize her arms wouldn't obey. She squinted, trying to make out the shadow hovering over her. The face contorted from a human to a large orange dinosaur she had seen on a children's television program, causing her to laugh. She began to sing the song that he sang every day before a large white sheepdog pranced in, knocked him down playfully, and covered his face with kisses. *"One-two, here's a clue. Three-four, he's never a bore. Five-six, he kisses with licks. Nine-ten, it's my best dog Ben!"* Katie smiled and said, "Where's Ben?" before closing her eyes, trying to make the room quit spinning.

When she opened them again, the shadowy figure's face was much too close to hers. She tried to focus on his features, but his face danced around like a strobe light. She tried to grab his head and steady it, but her arms were heavy as lead and felt like the flesh was melting off her bones. She barely grazed his chest and felt her arms fall down next to her body.

She lay there, suddenly realizing she was naked and cold, and pleaded with the stranger to get away from her. His mouth was abruptly on hers, his tongue forcing its way between her lips, and she was powerless to stop him due to the drugs that swam through her veins.

"Please . . . stop." Katie slurred and tried to free herself from underneath the shadow. "I'm only thirteen . . ."

The shadow ignored her pleas and proceeded to rob her of her innocence until she passed out from the mixture of drugs, pain, and shock. Katie fell in and out of consciousness as the horrific event seemed to go on for hours. She concentrated on one specific feeling—the worst one—a feeling of sandpaper scraping inside of her.

When the traumatic event was finally over, hot tears slipped down her temples into her hair as she wept before slipping back into the darkness.

Nineteen

Sunlight breached the dark curtains, causing Katie to stir. It was an effort to open her eyes. The rank smell of alcohol, cigarette smoke, and cheap cologne filled her nose. She tried to swallow the lump in her throat, but it felt scorched and dry, as if someone had stuffed cotton balls down her trachea. With every heartbeat her head pounded in an offbeat rhythm as if someone were learning to play the drums for the first time. As she tried to remember where she was, she was instantly filled with terror. Trying to be as quiet as possible, she lifted herself up onto her elbows and looked around. Katie felt like she was hit by a truck. Each time she moved the pain reminded her of what had happened. She let a slight groan escape her lips, looking around to see if anyone had heard her. Three males were asleep in the small, dingy apartment. Two were on old, beat-up couches and the other was slumped over in a tan recliner while the remains of a beer can dripped slowly onto the arm of the chair.

A guy with black hair and a goatee slept on one of the couches with one tattoo-covered arm dangling. Her eyes roamed to the guy in the recliner, who would surely have a crick in his neck when he woke up. He was short, stocky and had thick brown hair. Finally, she came to the last person on the other couch and her heart raced in panic. It was the shadow that hovered over her just a few hours ago, causing so much agony. She studied his features, beginning with his messy blond hair . . . *Garrison! But why—how could he?—"*

Katie cupped a hand over her mouth to stifle the sob that threatened to escape. She slowly sat up and let the pain settle before she wobbled to a standing position. She looked around for her clothes and found them in a pile next to the mattress. While slipping on her underclothes, she noticed the dried blood stains on her legs and mattress. Silent tears spilled down her cheeks and her chest heaved violently as she held back the sobs that threatened to give her away. Katie quietly dressed and stood to sneak out of hell.

Where's Ally? Did she leave me here, or is she looking for me? How could she let Garrison do this? Did he hurt her too? Katie tried to remember what happened last night as they arrived at the apartment. The last thing she remembered was parking, but couldn't remember getting out of the car. Looking over each of the men sleeping, Katie wondered how she could make it through the front door without waking them. She looked down the hall and knew she should look for Ally before leaving, but the desperation to escape was overpowering. *I'll come back for you, Ally. I'll get the police and come back for you.*

Each step she took seemed to last five minutes. Being very careful not to make any noise, Katie reached the front door and slowly unlocked the deadbolt. She held her hand over the lock as her fingers slowly turned it to the left. *Just a little more—I'm almost out, and then I can run as fast as I can for help.* Katie exhaled slowly as she felt the lock give and put her right hand over the knob. Slowly, she turned the knob all the way to the left and pulled the door toward her. *Click-click-click,* she heard the hinges of the door creak with every move. She decided to just go for it and make one quick movement before fleeing out the door and making a run for it.

As she stepped out into the sunlight and readied her feet for the fastest run ever, she was jerked backwards by the swift and painful pull of her hair. "Where do you think you're going, princess?" The man with the goatee still had her by the hair as he turned her to face him, flashing the most evil grin Katie ever witnessed.

Katie couldn't speak, her eyes were wide with terror and she felt her legs start to tremble. She wanted to scream for Ally, but was frozen in fear. Her chance to escape was fleeting, and desperation took over. "Please, let me go. I don't want this."

Garrison handed her a cup. "Here, drink this."

Katie looked at the man she had trusted for the last four days. He promised to take care of her and Ally, finding them jobs and take them away from the hell they were living in. Instead, he took her further into the pit. With all the hatred she could muster, she looked directly in his eyes, "You're a pig from hell!"

Katie braced herself as Garrison lunged toward her, threatening to hit her, but he stopped short and laughed.

"Where's Ally?" Katie asked.

"She's in the back bedroom. I'll take you to her if you'll stop being such a bitch and have a drink."

"No. Just take me to her, or I'll start screaming."

"You start screaming and you'll find yourself in a really bad situation, princess." Garrison stepped close, grabbing Katie's cheeks between his fingers. "You think you had it bad back home? You haven't seen nuthin'. Now, take this drink, or James will hold you down and I'll pour it in."

Katie glanced at the man with the goatee, assuming it was James, and took the drink, which turned out to be orange juice. She let the cool liquid coat her throat and quench the scorched, dry burning.

"Good girl," Garrison said as he led Katie down the hall toward Ally.

"Ally!" Katie cried and wrapped her arms around Ally's neck. She seemed happy about something—too happy to know about what happened the night before. "Ally, are you okay? We need to get out of here. I want to go home."

Ally sat up and smiled. She seemed to be drugged and her speech was slurred. "No, Katie, we're staying here. We'll have to do some things we don't want to do, but we can make a lot of money—enough money to put you through medical school." She stroked Katie's hair and smiled before falling back onto her pillow. "Trust me, Katie, and do what you're told."

Katie couldn't believe what she had just heard. How could Ally do this to her? She trusted Ally with her life, looked up to her as a big sister . . . how could she betray her like this?

Katie rubbed her temples and tried to remember any clues from the night before. Did the apartments have other tenants or was it abandoned? From the inside it looked like it hadn't been occupied in years. *Think, Katie!* And then her mind started to get fuzzy. The squishy feeling that she had experienced the previous night started to sweep through her limbs again.

"You drugged the juice . . ." She slurred. Katie concentrated all of her fear, anger, and the confusion over

Ally's treachery into her core and flew into James. She envisioned smashing his nose with her fists and ripping that smug goatee right off of his face, and did manage to get one weak punch into his stomach before Garrison grabbed her from behind, holding her arms down at her sides. Katie never saw James's fist coming at her, she only felt the excruciating pain that brought dancing white specs to her eyes. Instinctively, she held her hand over her nose and felt the warm, sticky liquid spilling between her fingers.

She felt every punch inflicted on her body as she lay in a small heap on the coarse beige carpet. Each sob racked her body with agonizing pain. She realized she would never escape— medical school was not in her future. She was in hell all over again and would remain there until she had the courage to take her own life.

She felt someone slide their hands under her and lift her up, then tossing her onto the mattress where her nightmare had begun. "Why are you doing this to me?" Katie cried. Her words slurred along at the same pace as the drugs that coursed through her veins.

Katie was aware of at least five days passing, but it could have been more. As she lay on the mattress feigning unconsciousness, she planned her escape and let her mind fill with an uncontrollable loathing. Three things she knew for certain. One, she would hate Ally with every fiber of her being until the day she died. Two, you couldn't die from being raped repeatedly . . . no matter how desperately you begged for death. And three, she would do whatever she needed to do—use anyone she could—to escape.

A cell phone buzzed behind her and she strained to listen, remembering to control her breathing to maintain her ruse.

James answered, "Speak to me." After a pause, he said, "Good. I'll be in touch."

Katie wasn't certain, but she assumed he hung up and dialed someone new. When he spoke again, his tone was more authoritative. "I need you in Casa Grande, Arizona . . . yes . . . and don't screw it up. If the cops . . . you better." He slammed his phone shut and opened the door to the refrigerator. Katie heard the air pressure release from a fresh beer and James's throat taking the liquid down in gulps. She remained still and processed what she had gathered from his one-sided phone conversation.

James was the man in charge and Garrison and Chase were his goons. They never collected more than one girl from the same town for some reason. She supposed that was the reason Garrison was worried the night they left Texas.

James finally slipped out of the apartment, leaving the girls with Chase. Chase Morris seemed to be the mellower one of the group. Katie hadn't heard him speak more than a sentence or two. As soon as she heard the door shut, she opened her eyes and studied the stocky fellow. His thick greasy hair sat atop his head, like a mop dipped in mud.

How will I get past him? Think! I've got to get him out of this room, so I can get through the front door. "Um, can I take a shower? I'm feeling really grungy."

"I'm not supposed to take my eyes off of you," Chase answered flatly. "Sorry, no shower until they get back."

"You don't have to take your eyes off of me," she thought it through before she said it. "Do you want to come with me?" Katie tried to give a flirtatious smile, and hoped he couldn't see her lips quivering. She tried to hold his gaze, but the awkwardness was too much, so she looked down at her foot tapping nervously.

Chase grinned widely and stood. "You don't have to ask me twice." He gestured toward the hall, encouraging her to lead the way.

Katie's insides were shaking, like she had guzzled three energy drinks. She feared she would vomit and mess up her spur of the moment plan. *This has to work. Calm down—focus and don't screw it up!*

Katie remembered all the times she and Ally pretended to be famous actresses playing a difficult part. She swallowed hard, took in a deep breath, and took on the role of her favorite soap opera character. After turning on the shower, she laid her hand on Chase's chest. Knowing that she needed to gain his trust, she tried to be sexy and slide her hand around, but instead it mimicked someone rubbing sunscreen over a T-shirt. He must not have cared as he pulled her in and hungrily explored her mouth with his tongue. Katie grimaced as she tasted the mix of beer and tobacco, wondering if he had ever used a toothbrush. She reminded herself, *I am Claire De Luna from Sands of Time.*

Katie clumsily pulled off his shirt and began unbuttoning his jeans. In a matter of minutes she had him undressed and raring to go.

"I knew you'd come around." He grinned, unbuttoning her jeans. "A body like this was made for sex."

"Mmm hmm." Katie's smile was weak and pathetic, as she tried not to cry. Letting her eyes fall on his arousal, her breath caught as a wave of panic invaded her chest. *I've got to get out of here!* "Hold that thought." She pretended to be breathless with desire. "Make sure the water is hot while I grab a couple of towels."

Katie turned to go and waited for Chase to grab her arm. Her eyebrows creased, waiting for the impending failure of her plan. She made it out into the hall, opened and shut a closet door, and yelled out, "Here I come. I hope you're ready." As soon as she got the last word out, she ran to the door leading out of the apartment, toward any chance of freedom. She managed to twist the lock on the doorknob and reached for the bolt lock when she saw Chase running towards her. Deep-frenzied rage was portrayed on his face—and if he reached her, she was sure he would kill her.

Katie jerked open the door and convinced her wobbly legs to move forward. She felt like she was stuck in a dream and had to command each leg to take a step forward. *Right leg—go! Left leg—go!* She felt herself being tugged back toward the door, but jerked herself loose, taking off running as fast as she could without looking back. She felt sure he wouldn't chase her into the street naked, but the past week's events proved her rationale was flimsy.

When she couldn't run any farther, Katie found refuge at a boarded up gas station. She found a bathroom attached to the back of the building and was relieved to find it unlocked. The water was turned off, but at least she was hidden from the world and could gather her breath along with her thoughts.

Staring at her reflection in the mirror, she reminded herself, *I will survive this. You just wait and see. This is not the end of me.* Katie held tightly to the rim of the porcelain sink fighting the black cloud of despair threatening to take over. She slowly slid to the floor, hugged her knees to her chest, letting the air-sucking sobs flow out of her until her tear ducts ran dry and hiccups took over. She was too tired to contemplate what her next move would be, so she fell asleep on the dirty floor of the bathroom.

Twenty

Nearby sirens startled Katie out of her deep sleep. The room had grown dark and it took her a few minutes to remember where she was. Courage abandoned her temporarily as she hugged her knees to her chest, seeking comfort. After her eyes adjusted to the small room, she stood and peered out into the warm, dark air. Braving the empty parking lot, Katie wandered into a new neighborhood still under construction. The only light came from an almost full moon. She looked around at the cookie-cutter homes absent of life and light, and noticed there weren't any cars in the driveways or on the street. She broke into a home that was almost finished and spent a few hours thinking of her next move. She was frightened, lonely, and her stomach panged with hunger while she sat in front of the empty stone fireplace pretending to warm her hands. *I'll worry about what to do next tomorrow. For now, I'm thankful to be alive and free.*

Over the next few days, Katie found enough food to keep her alive, pocketing half-eaten packages of peanut butter crackers or a few French fries that had been tossed in the trash bins, and she only traveled around at night. Her mind wandered to Ally and the others. She thought about making an anonymous call to the police, but didn't know where to go or who to turn to for help. *What would I say? "Hey, my sister and I were kidnapped by some guys—well, not kidnapped really—we ran away from our foster home and agreed to go with these strangers. But when they raped us, I escaped. Yes, I left my sister there—she was cool with the whole thing. I wasn't. I'd rather live in an abandoned house, while I slowly starve to death, than go back to that hell." I have to figure something else out.* Katie's mind raced trying to find a solution.

She crept back into the house through a loose board that acted as a makeshift back door, paying attention not to nick herself on the rusty nail again. As she curled up, ignoring the sound of her rumbling stomach, she drifted into a deep sleep and dreamed of being warm, comfortable, and very full.

A strange noise outside roused Katie to sit up and concentrate on where it came from. The strange noise rattled through the silence as she let her eyes adjust to the darkness of the bedroom. She had managed to steal a blanket off a clothesline the night before and pulled it up to her chin. She heard the sound of shoes shuffling on carpet and held her breath, afraid the noise would give away her location. She tried to convince herself that it was just some kids trying to vandalize the place and if she could just make it into the closet they would never see her. Katie stood on shaky legs, hugged the blanket as if it were her only security, and climbed into the closet. She crouched down in the far corner and pulled the door almost closed, avoiding the sound of the closing latch by leaving it cracked.

Barely audible footsteps traveled through the living room and first bedroom. When they entered the bedroom that Katie was in, her heart began to thud against her chest so rapidly she feared it would burst. She took in tiny wisps of air through her nose at the same rate as her heartbeat. It wasn't enough air to satisfy her hungry lungs and they started to burn.

"You're sure you saw her come in here?" A male voice whispered.

Oh God! James! The sudden intake of air whistled slightly against Katie's lips and she desperately hoped it was soft enough to go unheard.

James's maniacal laugh filled Katie with an indescribable terror that coursed through her trembling body, like flames chasing the source of oxygen. She swallowed back the sob that threatened her throat and tried to remain still, but the door was suddenly jerked open, giving Katie a glimpse of the demons eager to take her back to the hell she thought she had escaped.

All hope abandoned her as she hugged her knees tightly to her chest and buried her face. She knew she wouldn't die—he was too angry to be compassionate. No, he was going to make her suffer.

James gritted his teeth as he spoke to Chase. "Make it quick and don't mark her up too badly. I'll wait outside." James lit his cigarette, inhaled deeply, and shut the door behind him.

Any pain that was previously inflicted didn't come close in comparison to what she experienced that night. Without the numbing effects of the drugs, she felt the depth of pain inflicted on her, wincing as Chase forced himself inside. She turned her head, so he wouldn't have the satisfaction of seeing her cry, but he grabbed her by the hair and forced her to face him. Katie slipped into a protective shell, allowing her mind to close off all truth and feeling. When it was over and she found herself in the fetal position in the backseat, something took over and brought with it a life-sucking sensation . . . defeat.

Twenty-One

Katie adjusted to her new life over the next few months. She became good at what she had become and found ways to use her gift to get things she wanted. And she would do whatever she needed to do—use anyone she could—to get out of this life.

Katie glanced at her reflection in the mirror. *You'll never be more than a drug addict's kid and whore.* Katie shook her head at the pale, emaciated figure staring back at her. Her long hair had lost its luster and now resembled her ragged doll's hair—dull and brown. *Okay, let's get this over with.* She opened the door to the bathroom, walked over to the bed, and greeted the stranger with a seductive smile.

Businessmen were always quick, skipping lunch to feed other hungers. Left alone in the hotel room, Katie filled the tub and tried to soak away the filth and depression that was creeping in on her, like a slithering snake. She felt a deep, magnetic pull to sink below the water and never come back up. Instead, she dried off, slipped back into her dress, and left the room.

Katie braced herself when James shook a wad of cash in her face. "What's this?"

The familiar feeling of impending doom filled her, but she put on her best poker face. "Looks like money to me. Where'd you get it?"

"Under the carpet in your room. You stealing from me?"

Katie knew not to cross James Durand. His black eyes were the window to his poisonous soul, and just looking at him made her tremble. How could she explain the money without provoking his wrath? Her mind played out every scenario and she settled on the last idea that came to her . . . the truth.

"I've been charging clients fifty dollars more than we originally agreed on, so I could put money aside for medical school." Katie's eyes measured James's reaction. Obviously, the truth wasn't the way to go.

Ally leaned against the door frame and exhaled a cloud of smoke from her Marlboro light. "Not one of them has complained." She took another drag and rested a shaky hand on her hip. Still trying to play the role of big sister, she attempted to extinguish the mounting wrath of their cruel pimp.

"I've got this." Katie narrowed her eyes at the one who had gotten her into this mess. Ally had tried to mend things, in her own way. Sneaking trinkets into Katie's room, leaving her lengthy notes of apology, and promising to get them out as soon as she saved up enough money. But Ally hadn't saved a penny, and when she did it was used for drugs. Katie was on her own. Any sisterly love that had been shared between them was lost.

The back of James's hand flew across Katie's cheek, knocking her against the wall. Her eye felt like it was exploding in its socket as she held onto the wall and cried out. "What the hell was that?"

James swung her around to face him and took her chin in his hand. "You don't have anything, do you understand? If you need clothes, I buy them. If you need food, I feed you. Don't ever hide money from me again." He let go of her chin and inhaled deeply. "I'm not going to kill you, since you are my most requested girl, but I *am* going to make sure you know who's in charge here, and that you are never tempted to steal from me again."

Ally jerked back as James walked with purpose toward the door. He kicked it shut, rattling the single framed poster on the wall. Eager to reinforce his authority over Katie, he shoved the wad of cash in his back pocket and rushed across the room to where she stood.

Katie lay in a small pool of her own blood after the brutal beating. Each sob racked her body with agonizing pain. She realized as she lay there on the floor, she would never escape. Medical school would not be in her future. She was in hell and would remain there until she had the courage to take her own life.

Twenty-Two

Elizabeth Harrington sat in the dark paneled library with a cup of Yorkshire tea. She ran her finger across the top of the fine bone china cup and tried to think of a way to make her plan work. She was a slim, elegant woman with a regal bearing that commanded respect. *It will work . . . it must.*

Elizabeth's tea had grown cold as she let her mind wander. *How could I not have known that she existed? I was wrong to cut all ties with Daniel—he was my only son. But what was I to do? Let him continue to steal from me to support his drug habit? I thought a little tough love would clean him up, how was I to know he would drug himself to death? And how could he bring a child into that kind of life? Bloody hell, what was he thinking! She would've been better off dropped at my doorstep. He could have given her to me—at least she would've had a chance at a decent life. Her entire life has been a living hell—escaping one pit just to fall into the next. I have to do something to save her. I've never even met her, but I love her so much already. Oh God, how did we get into this mess? I gave you everything, son. I wanted you to have a full life and have every chance at happiness. But somehow, I failed you miserably. I*

*promise you, I will help your daughter. I'll get her out of this
mess and give her a chance at a good life. I failed you . . . I
won't fail little Katie.*

Daniel was fourteen when his late father, Charles, was
transferred to the states because of his job. Daniel was a good
boy—involved in soccer and a garage band with five of his best
buddies—but the move from England was hard on him. A
British kid with a heavy accent, trying to fit in with Texans. He
dropped the soccer team after getting beat up by two of the
boys, and his guitar was used to hang his clothes on.

Charles wasn't around enough to see their son sinking into a
pit. Elizabeth saw it, and tried everything to help him,
reassuring him that it would pass and he would find friends.
When he did find that group of friends, she couldn't pull him
away from them, although she was certain they were bad news.
*Just let him get back on his feet, and then we'll find a better
group for him to be involved in,* she thought.

Before the end of his junior year, Daniel was addicted to
heroin. Elizabeth and Charles tried getting him help. He was
admitted to a rehab clinic twice. They even moved forty
minutes away so he could have a fresh start, but the pull of
drugs was a force Daniel couldn't—or wouldn't—turn away
from. By the time he was eighteen, Elizabeth was afraid of him
and did nothing to cross him.

The following year was most difficult for Elizabeth. Charles
died suddenly of a heart attack, and Daniel spiraled out of
control. He was dangerous, and she feared for her life each time
she tried to deny him drug money.

With Charles's death so fresh, Elizabeth was angry. Daniel
hadn't given a damn about his father's death, or her feelings.

She locked her son out of the house with a note on the front door.

> There will be no more money or warm bed for you until you're clean.
> Green Leaf Rehab Center is waiting for your arrival.
> Once you complete the program, this will be your home again.
> I love you, Daniel. Please get the help you need,
> Mother

Daniel had broken into the house while she was asleep, stuffed as many valuables as he could carry into a pillowcase, and set the house on fire. Smoke alarms alerted Elizabeth in time for her to get out unharmed, but the entire west wing of the house had to be torn down and rebuilt. Elizabeth didn't care about the house or the antiques that were pawned. She'd said, *"Things can be replaced, houses can be rebuilt. I just can't believe that the boy I love with all of my heart and soul, the child that I gave life to—would try to extinguish mine."*

Elizabeth set her cup on the side table and dialed Pete Savalli. Though she had been in the states for the past twenty-two years, she maintained a musical British accent from her London upbringing. "Pete, love, it's Liz. I understand you found Daniel's daughter?"

"Yes, I did." He let out a breath through gritted teeth. "It's not good, Liz. She's on the streets . . ." Pete found it difficult to give her any more details of the situation her granddaughter was in.

"Oh God, how could this have happened?"

"Let's discuss it more in person. I can be there in a couple of hours."

Elizabeth took a deep breath before opening the front door. She knew it would be difficult to see Pete. Had it really been fifteen years? She pinched her cheeks once more to add a little color, and swung open the door to greet the man that still held her heart. Age had been kind to him, the touches of grey enhancing his masculine jaw line and framing his dangerous dark eyes. They had remained friends and kept in loose contact through telephone. She knew he had a family, and wouldn't hint at destroying it, but it was surreal to have him there, close to her.

"It's so good to see you again, Liz." Pete kissed her cheek.

"Yes—" Elizabeth's voice cracked. "Please, come in."

They sat in the kitchen and discussed a plan to remove Katie from the streets. "I know it will work, Pete—it has to." Elizabeth said, bright-eyed.

Pete stood and refilled both cups of hot tea. He added a touch of honey to Elizabeth's cup and handed it to her. "I think it will, Liz, but don't get your hopes up. She's grown up in a world that you can't begin to understand. She may not want your help. I hate to be the one to verbalize this, but you have to be prepared—she may not want anything to do with you."

Pete looked at her poignantly. He knew her hopes were high, and he was sure she couldn't handle another disappointment so soon after learning her only son died from a drug overdose. He had held her for hours while she cried over her son's bad choices, feeling her shoulders shake beneath his arms—it was a feeling that would haunt him forever. He once thought he had lost her friendship for good, offering his opinion on how to deal with Daniel. He had suggested—insisted actually—that she cut ties with her son. *"They call it tough love. You are financially and emotionally supporting his addiction. It's the same as buying the drugs and giving them to him yourself. You have to step back and make him grow up."*

"I have to try, Pete. I owe her the chance. I owe it to Daniel."

"You were a good mother, Liz. You did everything in your power to give Daniel a good home. Daniel made some bad choices and got sucked in too deep for you to pull him out. You've got to quit blaming yourself for his death."

"I know, and I hear you. But my heart refuses to listen. It's shattered and the only way to patch it up is to help that poor girl. She never had a chance, and I have the resources to give her that chance. Daniel's death is—well if he hadn't died, I never would have known she existed. It's nothing short of a miracle that you were able to follow the trail and find her."

"Nothing is impossible for the Savalli's, it's the one perk—" Pete's voice faltered. Bringing up his family wasn't a good idea. It's what ripped them apart fifty-five years ago.

Twenty-Three

The July evening was airless, but pleasant, as Katie leaned against a lamp post on Sonoma Boulevard. She displayed her flirtiest smile as a black, convertible Porsche Boxster slowed in front of her. *Damn, that's a nice car.* Katie gave the other girls an admonishing look as she approached the car that was now pulled to a stop against the curb. She leaned over the window, making sure her cleavage was showing just enough to entice. "Hi there, looking for some company tonight?" Katie asked as she looked over the fine red leather interior of the car. She didn't care what the stranger looked like—she just knew she wanted to drive away in this spectacular car. She would make sure he was a repeat customer, so she could enjoy an occasional spin in such an elegant machine.

Katie had learned to use her body to please men. She enjoyed the control she possessed over their bodies. She could easily arouse a man with a look or kiss and have them begging and promising her the world if she would quench their unbearable hunger. She decided men were desperate fools, who would do anything for her—except what she wanted and needed most—escape from a controlling and dangerous pimp.

"Yeah, I'm looking for some company tonight. Hop in," the stranger replied, breaking Katie's reverie.

Pete Savalli was certain the girl sliding into the passenger seat was Katie. He only had to study the photographs once before the empty green eyes haunted his sleep. She was just a girl. Her large almond shaped eyes were similar to Elizabeth's, but darker. Where Elizabeth's eyes sparkled with life, this young girl's eyes revealed pain.

"Nice car," Katie said. The seat was cool and soft on her back and legs and the smell of new leather filled her nose. Her eyes skimmed over the plethora of buttons below the navigation screen and she fought the urge to push every one.

"Want to find some music?" Pete asked.

"Uh, no. I'm okay." Katie stuttered.

Pete pushed a button, turning on the radio and showed Katie how to browse through the channels and genres. The kind gesture spiked Katie's curiosity and she finally looked at the strangers face. He was a handsome older man. He looked to be in his fifties. Shades of gray streaked his dark hair that swirled around his face from the wind. He was wearing jeans and a tight charcoal T-shirt. Katie let her eyes roam over his muscular chest and arms. *He takes good care of himself. I wonder what he does for a living.* Katie flipped through the stations and landed on "Crash Into Me" by Dave Matthews. She relaxed back into her seat and let her eyes close. "What's your name?"

"Pete. What's yours?"

"Katie. You seem nervous, Pete. Is this a new experience for you?"

"Uh, yes. Definitely a new experience." Pete gripped the steering wheel and looked at the navigation system, revealing his next turn.

"I'll be gentle with you." Katie grinned and watched his body tense from her words.

Katie found herself talking nonstop on the long drive. She hadn't held a decent conversation with anyone in so long and found it refreshing to talk about anything other than drugs, money, and sex.

"Have you been to an Opera?" Katie asked.

"Yes, several. You?"

"No." Katie frowned. "But I want to see *Madame Butterfly* one day."

Talking to Pete distracted her during the drive, making her feel like a normal girl. She hadn't realized that they had been driving for nearly forty-five minutes when the GPS instructed them of their arrival on the left.

When the car pulled into a long gated driveway, Katie was filled with uneasiness. "Is this your home? You can't take me home—I'm not a pet—take me to a hotel!" Katie scowled. One rule she always followed was to never get personal with a client. She had gotten her hopes up too many times that one would fall in love with her and help her escape, only to be disappointed, and usually beaten for staying gone too long. Home was definitely personal.

"Don't worry, it's not *my* house."

Katie sensed something was off, but she wasn't sure what. He looked nervous, and she let her mind decide on the reason. *He's probably one of those serial killers who want to clean up the dirty streets. He's going to take me into the basement and chop me into pieces!* Katie felt panicked as she thought of all the tortuous ways he was going to kill her. *Whatever, Katie, you'd be better off dead anyway. You're always begging for your clients to help you flee the hell you're living in, well here it is—death.*

Katie tried to calm her racing heart by taking deep breaths. She welcomed the peacefulness of death, but couldn't prevent the fear from slinking through her spine causing her to tremble.

"What's wrong?" Pete asked with a concerned look.

"You're one of those serial killers that prey on prostitutes!" Katie pointed her finger at Pete.

"*What?* Why do you think I'm going to kill you?" Pete tried to stifle the smile that played at his lips.

Katie studied his face and wondered what she had done to be so inauspicious. *I finally find a client that I like and he's planning on killing me. Seriously? Who on earth is that unlucky?*

"First of all, your car, clothes, and I assume house are perfect—a dead giveaway that you're a control freak and probably have a serious case of OCD. You're too rich to have to buy a woman's company, which means you only have one agenda—to rid the world of as much dirt as you can. You *will* get caught, you know, and you'll get the electric chair!" Katie found herself rambling due to her increasing fear, not so much of death but pain. "Not that I care if you kill me. What've I got—?"

"Whoa!" Pete put his hand up. "I'm not going to kill you. I'm curious though, why do you welcome death so willingly?"

"Are you serious right now? I'm sold to strangers for money that I'll *never* see. I'm completely controlled by the most evil man I've ever known, and will never be happy, or free, to do what *I* want to do. Once you wake up in a pool of your own blood, unable to open your eyes because they're swollen shut, you start to feel a little defeated." The sarcasm oozed out of Katie's mouth like lava. "Anything is better than this . . . even death." Katie sat stunned over the fact that she'd just poured out her soul to a stranger. Looking down, she traced the floor mat with her eyes.

Pete's gut ached, like he had just been sucker punched. He wanted to pull this beautiful, fragile girl into his chest and tell her everything was going to be okay. He wanted to tell her that the life she had been forced into would soon be over and she would know what freedom felt like. He had never known anyone who loved as deeply as Elizabeth did—with her entire being, no holding back. If anyone had a chance at helping this girl, it was Elizabeth.

Pete exhaled slowly. "There's no need to fear me, Katie. I don't have obsessive-compulsive disorder. And you're right, I've never paid for a date. I was asked to find you and deliver you to a dear friend of mine. We'll stay here tonight, and fly out in the morning. Once we arrive, you will have all the answers you need—and there is no death involved, I promise."

"Wait! What do you mean you picked me up for someone else? That's not my game, mister—I know I don't have any control over my life, but I *do* get to choose who I go home with. I am *not* walking through those doors. Take me back, right now!" Katie folded her arms in front of her chest.

"No, no. It's not a male friend, it's—"

Katie cut him off. "Holy shit! A wife of one of my clients? You can't throw me to the wolves!" The worry lines reappeared over Katie's eyebrows. "Please, take me back."

Pete's heart sank as he searched Katie's green eyes. She couldn't have been more than sixteen. "It's not an angry wife, it's your grandmother."

Katie looked at him in disbelief. She thought she knew what evil men looked like, but she had never witnessed anyone as evil as Pete. How could he play on her fears, pretend to be concerned, and then lie just to get her into that house where an angry—and probably violent—wife of one of her clients lived. "I don't have a grandmother." Katie's words came out staccato. "My grandparents on both sides are dead. Who the hell do you think you are?" Katie got out of the car and started walking down the driveway toward the street.

Pete slammed his fists on the steering wheel before climbing out of the car and catching up to Katie. "Stop. Where are you going to go? Back to that hell?"

Katie whirled around to glare at Pete. "Who are you *really*? Do you work for James? Did he put you up to this? Or did the Higgins send you—?"

"Whoa! Stop blabbering like a fool. I told you who I was and who sent me. I don't know James, but I do know all about the Higgins and you no longer have to worry about them—they've been taken care of."

"You killed them?" Katie questioned matter-of-factly.

"You don't seem too brokenhearted about it." Pete wondered what kind of hell a young girl would have to go through to not flinch after learning of a murder. He had seen plenty, and had become immune to any feelings associated with death, but he was a man that had grown up seeing death all around him. "No, I didn't kill them. They're alive and well. Actually, I wouldn't say they're well, but they *are* alive. The police should be finding evidence of meth production and distribution right about . . ." Pete looked at his watch and smiled, "now."

"Nice." Katie nodded her head. "So, you're what—a crooked cop? Oh, I know! You're mafia."

"There's no such thing as the mafia, kid. You've got quite an imagination. I'm not a crooked cop either, just a guy helping a good friend."

Katie rested her fists on her hips. "No such thing as the mafia, whatever. I happen to know for a fact that—"

"Shh." Pete held a finger to his lips, making her feel like she was in on a big secret.

"James won't go for me being gone overnight. He'll kill me this time. I know he will."

Pete scowled. "You don't have to worry about James anymore. You don't ever have to go back there. You have a grandmother that loves you and wants you to have a happy life. Of course, it's your choice—I'll take you back if you prefer. But I should tell you, she's a magnificent lady, full of life and love."

"I don't know, I'm scared." Katie chewed on her fingernails. "James will find me. He has connections and he always finds me. When he does—death would be a kindness compared to what he did last time."

Pete knew he couldn't say or do anything to make her trust him, but he had to try. "I know you don't have any reason to trust me, so you're just going to have to trust your gut. If you say things are so bad with James, sounds to me like your alternatives couldn't get much worse." He shrugged his shoulders and waited for her decision.

"Okay, I'll go with you. But if things don't work out, I'm on my own—I'll *never* come back to California."

Katie followed Pete to the front door of a massive European style home.

"Good evening, please, come in." A lady with shoulder length auburn hair smiled. They stood in a large foyer with white marble floors and a table that held a massive bouquet of flowers. "I've got rooms ready for both of you upstairs. Would you like something to eat first? I've prepared sandwiches in the kitchen."

"No thanks, I'm fine," Katie answered. Her stomach growled loudly in defiance, causing the lady to smile.

"C'mon, follow me. I'd hate for those sandwiches to go to waste. Pete's always hungry, too."

Katie quickly devoured a ham and cheese sub sandwich and washed it down with a glass of sweet tea. After being shown to her room, the kind lady laid out a pair of pajamas for her to wear and a towel in case she wanted to shower. "Thanks," Katie said, not able to look at the lady when she spoke. She felt completely out of her element, and wondered what the lady knew about her.

Sleep did not come easily for Katie that night. The room was larger than any hotel room she had ever seen and she felt lost in the massive king-sized bed. It was the most comfortable mattress she had ever laid on, but she was terrified James would find her in the middle of the night, or a dangerous prank would be inflicted on her as soon as she closed her eyes. Instead, she lay in bed all night wondering what her grandmother was like and why—if she was such a wonderful, generous woman—didn't she rescue her years ago.

Twenty-Four

It took half an hour for Pete to convince Katie to board the small Cessna jet awaiting them. She took one step up, and then climbed back down. She paced the parking lot, ranting off reasons why she wasn't going to get on that rubber-band toy he called an airplane.

"It doesn't look safe." *You don't even know what safe is.* "We could crash." *You might be shot before we board, kid!* "How do you expect me to trust that you're really taking me to my grandmother?"

This one got him. "You have no reason to trust me, I understand." He pulled out his phone and found Elizabeth's contact information. "Here is where I'm taking you. York, Maine. See the contact information? I don't know much about human trafficking, but you have to agree the name Elizabeth Harrington doesn't sound like someone who would hurt you, does it?"

Katie studied the name and address. She considered the fact that Pete could have easily conjured up a phony name and address. He could have made up the entire story, gaining her trust, when in reality he was going to sell her to someone in another country. She would be used as a sex slave, or worse. But what did she have to lose? She was already in hell, and unless they had different levels of severity, it couldn't get much worse.

She took each step hesitantly, convincing herself as she ascended the staircase that she was strong. She could handle anything that came her way.

Four leather seats were available to choose from, and Katie chose the one facing the cockpit door. She couldn't imagine the feeling of flying backwards—she wasn't crazy about the idea of being in the air at all. Pete took the seat adjacent to hers.

A lady dressed in a navy blue suit walked up, flashing a cheerful smile. "Can I get you something to drink before we take off?"

"I'll have a Scotch on the rocks, please," Pete answered.

"And I'll have a vodka and orange juice," Katie replied.

Pete sat up in his seat and held his hand up for the airline attendant to wait. "Whoa, how old are you?"

"How old do I look?"

"Not old enough to drink. You're about sixteen-seventeen, right?"

Katie nodded her head and frowned.

"She'll have a Coke, thank you."

"Jeez, this is going to be a fun ride. Eight hours in a tube with you and a soda." Katie folded her arms across her chest and slumped down in her seat.

Pete dug in his bag and pulled out an iPod. "Here, it might not be the kind of music you like, but it's better than an eight hour conversation with me."

Katie smiled.

The iPod didn't get any use on the flight. Instead Katie and Pete talked. He led her down the path of telling him everything about her and Ally's plan to run away and become actresses or models. She had spared him the harsh details, although he still had to swallow back the bile that threatened his throat with the smallest of details. Her story included detailed descriptions of James, Chase, Garrison, and Seth. By the end of the flight Pete felt like he personally knew each person Katie spoke of. He made mental notes of everything she told him.

When she fell asleep, Pete was amazed at how her face changed. Awake, she had a harsh tone and painful eyes. Her face portrayed someone who was ten years older and had experienced enough life for a forty-year old. But when she slept, her face was relaxed and soft. She looked like the typical teenager. Watching her sleep, his heart shattered into a million pieces. At that moment he knew what he had to do.

After the flight, Pete and Katie pulled up in front of a large white house. Katie took in her surroundings, noticing the grandeur of the home. A warm breeze rustled the lush green trees in the front yard, and sent a whiff of salty sea air under her nose. She followed Pete on the winding cobblestone path surrounded by well-manicured greenery and clusters of white rose bushes toward the front door. Pete rang the bell and Katie shoved her hands deep into her jacket pockets. She wondered what her grandmother looked like. Would she be in a wheel chair with an oxygen tank in her lap?

The door swung open and Katie was surprised to see a woman that looked to be in her forties. She quickly did the math in her head, and decided that if this was her grandmother, she must have given birth as a child, or had a lot of work done to hang onto youth.

"Good evening, I'm Jane. Please, come in, Mrs. Harrington is expecting you." The lady smiled. Katie's eyes took in everything as she followed the lady down the hall. The home was luxurious and clean. Oil paintings hung on cream walls and everything was trimmed in the same wood that was beneath her feet. She saw a glimpse of the ocean, which took her breath, through the glass wall in the living room. Jane opened a door, encouraging Katie to go in. "Please, take a seat and Mrs. Harrington will be with you shortly. Mr. Savalli, please, come with me."

Katie slowly walked into the room and let her fingers glide over the bookshelves that lined the walls. She didn't dare venture into the middle of the room, leaving the stability of the walls, but instead read some of the titles. The shelves contained all the classics—the Brontë sisters, Austen, Dickens, Twain, Salinger, Steinbeck. Tugging at the bottom of her tight black skirt, she realized she didn't belong here. Letting her gaze roam the dark, wood-paneled room, she lingered on the massive oil paintings that were illuminated by their own individual lamps. Her eyes fell on one that held her gaze and curiosity. There was a familiarity to him—his eyes matched hers.

"Pete!" Elizabeth wrapped her arms around his neck, giving him a quick squeeze before backing up to look at him. "How does she look? Are you certain it's the right girl—Daniel's daughter?"

"Yes, it's her."

"I can't thank you enough for what you've done, Pete. I'd like to spend the next few days with her, but will you come for dinner soon?"

"I would like that." Pete kissed Elizabeth's hand and turned to leave.

"Pete—" Elizabeth called out, regretting it as soon as she did. She knew she couldn't get involved with Pete Savalli again. She had made the decision to break their engagement over fifty years ago. After learning of his deep family ties within the mafia, she nearly died of a broken heart. Charles Harrington had come into her life just in time to save her. He was supposed to tutor and help her pass the last three classes in order to receive a Bachelor of Science degree in Journalism. He wasn't hired to make her laugh, but he did. She wasn't supposed to make him fall in love with her, but she did.

Pete turned and waited for whatever Elizabeth had to say. She had aged beautifully, her green eyes still sparkled with the vivacity of a young woman.

"I—I've missed you. I *do* hope you'll come for dinner."

Pete smiled, holding back the urge to take her in his arms and kiss her.

Elizabeth Harrington put her hand over her mouth to stifle the sob that threatened to escape when she saw Katie. "You look so much like him."

Katie was frozen in her spot, not knowing what to do, or say, to the woman that stood inches from her. She tried to say hello, or at least smile, but remained paralyzed with anxiety.

"You must be frightened with all that's happened over the past few hours. Would you like something to drink?"

Katie shook her head and held onto the side of the high back chair next to her as she studied her newfound grandmother. She was a lovely woman with a kind smile. She had a petite frame, but her regal demeanor made her appear tall and in control. When she spoke, it was so proper and laced with a touch of an English accent.

"Let's sit." Elizabeth took the chair across from Katie and waited for her to sit down. "We have a lot to talk about."

When Katie finally got over her nerves and was ready to talk, she was filled with questions. Her words came out slightly louder than a whisper. "My parents told me I didn't have any grandparents."

"Your father and I had a falling out." Elizabeth's shoulders slumped forward as she recalled their argument—the last time she saw her son alive. "Daniel, your father, sank into a drug-induced pit so deep I couldn't reach him. Things got so bad, I had to let him go. I thought he would see the error of his ways and want to get off the drugs and come home, but he never did. The last time I saw him was eighteen years ago. I didn't even know you existed until after your parents' death. I've been looking for you since." Elizabeth wiped a tear from her cheek and looked at Katie. "How old are you, dear?"

"Almost sixteen." Katie answered while twisting a strand of hair around her index finger. She looked at the clock against the wall when it struck ten o'clock. *James is going to be so pissed.* A chill ran up her spine thinking about the crazed look on James's face when she hadn't come back, and then she thought about what he would do to her if he ever found her. "Mrs. Harrington?"

"Please, call me Elizabeth. Or you could call me . . . Gram. I always thought my grandchildren would call me that."

"Gram," Katie looked down and smiled shyly. It felt good, but weird.

"I can't keep my eyes open." She was beyond exhausted and her insides were twisted up tightly. She needed a reprieve from the emotional overload.

Elizabeth resisted the urge to take Katie's chin in her hand. She wanted to take away all the pain and self-hate out of Katie, but knew she wasn't ready for someone to pour love and compliments into her. *It will take time. Time I am willing to spend. For every cruelty inflicted on this poor child, I will triple the love and kindness.* "Oh dear, I'm sure you *are* tired. I'll show you to your room." Gram showed Katie where the kitchen was as they walked down the hall toward the bedroom. "Katie, I know you've had a very hard life so far, and I'm so sorry I couldn't save you from any of it. But I promise you this—I'll do everything in my power to make sure you have a full, happy life here with me, if you'll stay."

Katie's insides were trembling as tears welled up in her eyes. "Here's your room. The door on the left is a closet, and the one on the right is the bathroom. Get some sleep and we can get to know each other more tomorrow."

Katie stood on the dark hardwood floor in the middle of the bedroom. The room was decorated with an English-country theme. White walls were held up by dark wooden beams and lined with oil paintings of the French countryside. A white cotton robe lay on the end of the bed with a pair of folded pink silk pajamas. Katie ran her hand across the cream comforter before sitting down and studying the rest of the room. *Is she serious about letting me stay here? I've wanted out for so long, I can't believe this is real! I'm not sure I can be who she wants me to be. Well, at least for tonight, I am going to enjoy sleeping in this bed.*

A soft knock on the door broke Katie's daydream. She opened it to find her grandmother in her pajamas and robe. "I took the liberty of buying you a few things. Everything in the closet and drawers is yours. Your bathroom is fully stocked with towels, shampoo, toothbrush and paste—I think I remembered everything. If you need anything else, we can pick it up tomorrow. Will you be all right sleeping in here tonight? My room is just down the hall on the left if you need me."

"Yes, thank you. I've never slept in a bedroom this nice before. Hell—it'll just be nice to have the mattress off of the floor actually!" Katie laughed nervously. "Oh, sorry."

"It's okay, dear. I don't want you to try to be someone you're not. This is your home, now. It's going to be a hard adjustment at first, but we'll find our groove and it'll get easier." Elizabeth clasped her hands together and smiled. "I'm just so glad you're finally here, Katie."

Fatigue did not encourage sleep to come easy for Katie. She lay awake wondering what all of this meant. *I have a grandmother—okay. She wants me to live with her in this beautiful house. What else does she want? Life has never been easy for me, why should it be now? Well, why shouldn't it? Other kids have families and live in houses with real bedrooms and food in their stomachs. She asked me to call her Gram— said that she always wanted her grandkids to call her that one day. Maybe she needs me as much as I need her? I want to make this work. I'll try to watch my language and practice better manners. I won't know how to carry myself around Gram's friends or what to talk about with them.* Katie frowned and turned over in bed. *Go to sleep!*

Katie sat up in alarm as she heard a light tap on her door. *He found me!* She looked around the room for a place to hide.

"Are you awake?"

Gram's voice came through the door, calming Katie's nerves a bit. She pulled back the covers, slipped the thick cotton robe over her silky pajamas and opened the door.

"I'm sorry to wake you. I just couldn't stand to wait one more minute. I had to see that you were still here and all right," Gram said. She was fully dressed in a plum blouse and tan slacks.

"What time is it?"

"A little after noon. Are you hungry?"

"Noon? I can't believe I slept so long. I'm sorry."

"No need to apologize. You must have been exhausted. I'll give you time to shower and dress before lunch. Do you eat meat?"

Katie smiled. "Yes." She shut the door and found a pair of jeans and T-shirt to lay on the bed, then took a shower.

Twenty-Five

Pete was waiting in Garrison Ford's apartment. After unscrewing all but one light bulb, he sat in the tan recliner facing the door.

With the click of a lock and turn of the knob, Garrison entered the unlit space alone. Pete studied the man's outline, making sure he was Garrison Ford, and waited for him to try each light unsuccessfully. Once he shut the door and walked toward the kitchen, Pete flicked on the lamp beside him.

Garrison jumped back, noticeably shaken, and demanded, "Who the hell are you and how did you get in here?" He started to pull something out of his jacket when he saw the gun in Pete's hand. "Whoa." He lifted his hands. "What do you want?"

"I'm here as a favor for someone." Pete's voice remained calm and collected as he twisted the silencer onto the end of the pistol.

"A favor . . . who sent you?" Garrison backed up until he felt the wall behind him.

"You'll get your answers, in time."

"Listen, I can get whatever you need. Girls . . . drugs . . . money—" His legs threatened to give out.

"Why don't you take a seat?" Pete nodded to the chair adjacent to him. "I've poured us a drink."

Garrison's eyes darted toward the drink then back at Pete. He walked to the chair, his legs unsteady, like a fawn learning to walk. Beads of sweat gathered on his blanched forehead. He took a seat and looked at Pete.

"Drink." Pete held up his own glass of Crown Royal and took a swallow.

He had trouble gripping the glass, slippery with condensation. His hands trembled, causing the ice to clink together until he brought it to his lips. Consuming the drink in one gulp, he slammed the glass back down on the side table and scrunched his face, biting back the bitter aftertaste. "What's this about?" he asked, emboldened by the effects of the alcohol.

Pete was in front of him within seconds. Before Garrison could flinch, he landed a right hook across his nose, knocking him backwards onto the floor. Pete jerked him, along with the chair, upright and squatted down to his eye level.

"I think you broke my nose!" Garrison held his hand over the mangled protrusion, warm, red blood spilling down his lips and onto his shirt. "What the fuck?"

"Did that hurt? Hmm, maybe I should've added an extra dose to your drink. You've probably built up a tolerance to most drugs. I thought for sure . . ." He watched Garrison's lids grow heavy, taking a moment longer to blink than usual. "There it is. I hadn't given it enough time to work. Sorry about that. I'm sure you give your girls plenty of time to receive the full effects of the drugs before brutalizing them. My bad."

"Guurls . . ." he began, his words sluggish and garbled. "I can get you—"

"I don't take things that don't belong to me, Garrison." Pete interrupted, letting Garrison's name roll of his tongue slowly. He traced the length of the gun with a leather glove-laden finger. "I am, however, here to take your life." He waited for the expected reaction, and wasn't disappointed. Garrison lifted his head, eyes wide with fear. A bead of sweat escaped his forehead, mingling with fresh blood as it traveled down toward his quivering lips.

"What the fuck did I do to you, man?" Garrison started to stand, but Pete shoved him back down in the chair.

He backed up, each step measured, without losing eye contact. "I'm here to take your life, just as you took the life of an innocent girl." He lifted the gun, aimed it at Garrison, and pulled the trigger.

Seth Morgan arrived home at three in the morning with a woman. He began to quickly undress her as they made their way down the hall and into his bedroom. He lifted her up, wrapping her legs around his waist and made his way to the bed. When he leaned back for the bed, they both plunged to the floor. "What the—" The bedroom furniture had been rearranged, bewildering him. He pushed the girl off of him and walked to the light switch on the wall. When he flipped it on, nothing happened. He flipped it up and down, but no light illuminated the room.

"Hello, Seth." Pete sat in a corner chair, dressed in black.

Seth whipped his head around to the corner and tried to let his eyes adjust. "Who the hell are you?"

"Send the girl away, we have something to discuss."

"Go on, go home." Seth nodded for her to leave.

She picked up her dress and shoes and backed out of the room, mascara staining her cheeks as she whimpered in fear.

Seth waited for her to shut the apartment door, hoping she was smart enough to call the police, and turned back to face the dark stranger in the corner. "Okay. What, do I owe you some money or something?"

"No, Seth. I'm here about a girl—beautiful, long dark hair, green eyes . . ."

"Katie. Haven't seen her in days. No one knows where she is."

"I do." Pete smiled.

"Wait!—" Seth held his hands up in surrender. "Please!"

Pete fired the silenced gun only once—between his eyes.

Chase Morris's body was left behind a dumpster in the alley by the liquor store. Pete hadn't planned on the knife Chase pulled, but after a brief struggle, Pete was able to complete the task at hand. He placed the gun in Chase's hand after lacing his fingers with gunpowder residue, and meticulously covered his tracks.

James Durand woke up in a haze. He tried to rub his eyes to clear his vision, but his hands and feet were bound to a chair. Looking around, he saw the familiar surroundings of his living room. He was startled when he saw a man standing across the room holding a gun.

"Who are you?" James groaned. "What do you want?"

Pete spoke in a calm and even voice. "I'm here about a girl. Let's see how long it takes for you to figure out who I'm talking about."

"I can get you any girl you want, man. Just untie me," he pleaded.

Pete ignored him and tried to evoke as much fear as he could, attaching the silencer to the pistol. He thought about how frightened Katie must have been. "She has long brown hair."

"Do you know how many of my girls fit that description?" James spewed. "Tell me her name and I'll get her for you."

"This is my favorite gun." Pete finished attaching the silencer before turning it over in his hand, admiring the shape and feel. "It's a Walther PPK. It's smooth and weighted with just the right balance. Did you know this is the same gun that James Bond uses?" Pete gave him a lesson on the gun, letting an ounce of hope settle in before firing a shot into James's left knee.

"Agh!" He screamed out as the mind-blowing pain raged through his knee and up his leg. "Fuck! What do you want from me?"

"Let's try again. The girl was about thirteen when you took her and forced her into this shit."

"Fuck, man. I didn't take anyone! All of our girls come to us. Mm—maybe it was Chase. I can help you find him." He watched as Pete lifted the gun higher, aiming it right at him. "Please, don't!" James screamed out as he felt the bullet rip through his right shoulder, sending a blinding hot pain.

"Here's your last clue." Pete stood and walked toward him. James's face was ashen and moist with sweat. *I wish Katie could see him now,* he thought. "She has green eyes."

James sat up taller, knowing exactly who he was talking about. "Katie! Her name is Katie. I can get her for you!" Desperation was revealed in his expression.

"No, James, you can't get her for me because you don't know where she is. You haven't seen her in days, have you?" He watched James's body shake with fear. "Do you know why you haven't seen her in days, James?" Pete paused for effect. "Because I took her home." He slowly circled around James as he spoke. "She has more money than you've ever seen in your lifetime, and she's happy." He finally stopped in front of him, squatted down to his eye level and explained. "You can't get her for me, but I can get you for her." Pete smiled sadistically before he stood and aimed the gun.

James's head lolled back immediately when the bullet penetrated his forehead.

Twenty-Six

Gram ran down the hallway toward Katie's room when she heard a blood curdling scream. Katie was curled up in a ball, hugging her knees, stuck in a horrific nightmare. "Katie! Wake up, honey. Gram's here—I've got you." She hugged Katie to her chest and rocked her softly. "You're all right, angel. It was just a bad dream. Do you want to tell me what it was about?"

Katie shook her head and wiped her tears. "No. I'm okay."

Gram stood and started to leave. She paused in the doorway and turned back around. "Katie, no one knows you here in Maine. You can forget your past and be whoever you want to be—a fresh start. We'll hire a tutor over the summer to catch you up on everything you've missed."

Katie nodded and smiled, uncertainty evident in her eyes. "Will you help me figure out who I'll be?"

"I already know who you are—a beautiful, smart, compassionate, strong girl. You just haven't figured it out for yourself yet." Gram looked into Katie's eyes. She didn't know how one could love another so deeply after only knowing them a few weeks, but she did. She would do anything in her power to protect her granddaughter, and help her grow into the magnificent young lady she knew she would one day become.

Katie stood on the edge of the small cliff looking out at the ocean. As the waves crashed into the cliff below it sprayed up stark white foam like a rabid animal hungry for her flesh. The wind sang a lonely tune in her ear as it whipped her hair around her face and implored her to jump into the raging water below.

"Katie," Gram shouted, breaking her gloomy trance. "Will you join me for tea, love?"

Katie slowly turned away from the ocean and walked back to the house.

"Katie-dear," Gram said as if it was one word—a nickname perhaps. "Would you like to see a psychologist? I know someone here in Maine. She's the best around, and I think she can help. You don't have to tell her anything you don't want to, but I think it's time you sought some healing."

"I thought I was supposed to forget about the past?"

"I thought it would be easy, but I underestimated what you've been through. I just can't bear hearing these nightmares wake you one more night, love—it's breaking my heart not being able to help you. Please, give it a try."

"Just talking, right?" The bond between Katie and her grandmother had quickly grown over the past few months. Usually relationships were built on time and trust, but something about Gram drew Katie in. She wanted to please her, make her proud. Maybe it was because she had saved her, or perhaps it was because she was the first person to show her love. Gram sat on the edge of Katie's bed each night, telling her how much she loved her and how happy she was they found each other. Of all the doubts that filled Katie—would she ever be a normal girl, would she make friends in her new school—Gram's love wasn't one of them.

"Yes, just talking. I'll see if I can get you in this week."

Twenty-Seven

Present day . . .

A two hour crying jag mingled with dry heaves left Katie's body exhausted. Her head felt like someone was taking a sledge hammer to it with every heartbeat. After pulling into Gram's driveway, she put the car in park, and eased out of the car. Usually she would skip up the stone path to the porch, but today she walked slowly, shoulders slumped, until she reached the door. Suddenly feeling like a stranger in the home she thought she'd spent her life in, she wasn't sure if she should knock, ring the bell, or just walk in like she'd always done.

Using the last bit of strength from her body, she opened the door, walked through the foyer and down the hall, following the sound of laughter until she reached the kitchen where her grandmother was. She was sitting at the table with someone—a man.

When Gram saw Katie standing there, she jumped up. Instead of the usual ecstatic look that would spread over her face, she looked worried. "Katie, love, what's happened? Why are you so upset?"

Katie moved closer and watched the strange man stand and turn to face her.

Gram introduced him. "Katie, this is a friend of mine—"

"Pete." Katie interrupting. The look of shock and sadness on both their faces confirmed Katie's nightmares were true. "Gram, we need to talk."

"Yes, we do." Gram's eyes filled with tears as she turned to Pete. Everything she was thinking and feeling was portrayed on her face.

"I'll call you tomorrow," Pete said. "I'm so sorry, Elizabeth." He turned to Katie, nodded his head, and took the side door out.

Katie took a seat across from Gram and waited for her to sit. "Please, tell me I'm wrong—or help me understand. A flood of memories assaulted me this afternoon—I remember details of a life that I didn't live. How is that possible? I also have clear memories of a childhood with you. I remember playing one-two-three-kick up the driveway, and songs we sang together. What about all of the pictures and toys?"

Gram tried to interject, "Katie—"

"How could all of those things have happened to me? And what about Branson? He thought I was—oh, God! We want children—can I even carry a child after everything my body endured? My whole life has been a lie. He has no idea who he's marrying."

Katie was spiraling out of control, and Gram needed to get hold of the situation. "Katie, listen to me!" She commanded her attention. "You don't have to tell him anything. Just go on like none of this ever happened. Don't you know that's what I've always wanted for you?"

Katie's phone buzzed with a text from Branson:
Where R U?

Katie ignored it and shut her phone off when it began to ring.

"You should at least let him know that you're okay." Gram pressed.

Katie stayed focused on the reason she had come—for answers. "Am I crazy? Do I have an alternate personality or something?"

"No, honey."

Gram and Katie sat for hours detailing Katie's past. Gram told her of her parents' death and finding out that she had a granddaughter. "When I found out about you, I asked Pete to find you. We're old friends, and he has powerful connections." Gram started a pot of coffee and sat back down. "I was so happy when he found you, but you were in a terrible situation. When he brought you to me, you were so frightened and lost. You'd been through hell and were shaken by horrific nightmares nearly every night. I thought my love for you would be enough, but it wasn't." Gram wiped the tears from her eyes. "So, I took you to a hypnotherapist and had your memories altered. I thought it was for the best—you would only have happy memories of a full life and be able to live the life you were intended."

Gram stood to pour coffee. Katie went to the liquor cabinet, poured some brandy into her cup, and sipped the hot, spiked coffee.

"How could you do that? What right did you have to try and control my life?"

"I didn't know what else to do," Gram said, her voice cracking as she pleaded with Katie. "Please believe me, I only wanted what was best for you. I just wanted you to be happy."

"I'm not sure how I'm supposed to live now." Katie's eyes became distant, contemplating her new situation. "I don't know who I am."

"You bloody well *do* know who you are. You're Katie Harrington. You're smart, compassionate, funny, beautiful, talented . . . shall I go on, or are you getting the point?"

The front door swung open, startling the two women. They watched as Branson rushed into the kitchen, relief washing over his haggard face. "Thank God." He exhaled. "Why didn't you answer my calls? I was worried sick." Noticing Katie's puffy eyes and tear-stained cheeks, he rushed to her side. "What's happened? Are you all right?"

Katie turned to face him, tipsy from two cups of liquored-up coffee. "I'm . . . okay. I'm sorry I didn't answer your calls, I-I just needed to see Gram."

Branson was confused. It wasn't like Katie to be gone when he got home from work, and it was definitely out of character for her not to phone or leave a note if she was going to see Gram. The way she'd been acting the past few weeks had him worried that something might seriously be wrong. He looked to Gram for any sign of what he should do or think.

"Branson, would you like to stay here tonight? Katie's had too much to drink to drive herself."

"I'd like to take her home, thank you. Of course, if you want to stay . . ." He waited for Katie's answer.

She shook her head slowly, feeling the effects of the alcohol. "No. We need to talk."

The drive home was silent, and Branson's mind roamed. He thought about every circumstance that would have Katie acting this way. *Is she having a breakdown? Maybe she's too stressed out? I knew the emergency room was too much for her. What if it's an illness—something incurable? Oh God, does she want to break our engagement?* He shook his head and looked over at Katie sitting in the passenger seat. Her eyes were puffy from crying. *It's bad, whatever it is.*

When they arrived home, Branson sat in the dark leather high back chair across from where Katie sat on the couch. "Katie, please tell me what's going on."

All the color from Katie's usually rosy cheeks vanished. "There are things about me that you don't know—things that I have recently learned about myself—things that will change everything."

Twenty-Eight

Katie inhaled deeply, trying to find the courage to speak. She twisted a strand of hair around her finger and held onto it tightly for security. "I don't even know where to begin."

"Whatever it is, we'll work through it together. Just spit it out, Katie."

She took another deep breath and blew it out audibly through pursed lips. "Apparently, Gram found me when I was sixteen. She had my memories altered to believe I had a wonderful childhood, but I didn't," she said, tight-lipped. "It all began when I was seven. My parents were heroin addicts, and I was forced into foster care. My foster parents were cruel and unloving. They beat me and Ally regularly."

"Ally, she's the girl from your dreams?"

"Yes, we were raised together as sisters." She took a moment to catch her breath and swallow back the growing lump in her throat. "When I say they beat us, you have to understand—it wasn't a spanking with a belt. They used wire hangers until our legs bled, or an extension cord. Once Rick, my foster father, got so mad he locked me in the basement for two days with no food and no electricity."

She left out the part about how he backhanded Ally for trying to get him off of Katie. He hit her so hard, she was unconscious for about ten minutes. Katie shivered when she thought about Rick's intentions. How could someone be so twisted and perverted?

Katie wiped the tears from her face with the back of her hand. She felt a massive migraine coming on, but ignored it. If she didn't get this all out now, she might lose the courage. She wanted Branson to have the chance to let her go before the wedding date got any closer. They would only have a few wedding gifts to return if they ended things now.

"Ally and I couldn't take it anymore, we feared for our lives. She came up with a plan to run away, and I agreed to go with her. She had a grand scheme worked out and made me believe the too-good-to-be-true plan. She met someone that promised to take us far away. He had jobs set up for us and promised we would never be without food or water again. I was too desperate and too young to see any fault in the plan, so I packed my bags and went with her." Katie had to take a moment. Her body was consumed with the shakes and she was finding it difficult to continue.

Branson stood and wrapped a blanket around her shoulders. "Are you okay to go on?"

Katie nodded her head diffidently. "We drove at night, and I think I must have been asleep when we arrived in California. When I woke up . . ." Tears began to stream down her cheeks and Branson handed her a tissue. "They drugged . . . and raped us." Katie refused to look at his face. She was sure he would be disgusted and would never have the desire to touch her again. Their love had been so perfect and pure, and now it was a lie.

Katie felt Branson's arms around her, pulling her in tightly to his chest. "My God, Katie. How could this have happened to you? I'm so sorry."

"My head is killing me." She rubbed her fingers deeply into her temples, trying to relieve the pain that throbbed through her head with every heartbeat.

Branson quickly returned with a glass of water and Motrin. Katie stood to swallow the pills and took the seat across from the couch, afraid to be so close to him when she shared the worst part of her past—the part that would have her returning his engagement ring and packing her bags. She began to cry at the thought of losing him, he had become her world and she had never loved anyone or anything so much.

"There's more." Katie paused to wipe her nose and swollen eyes. "I tried to escape—I did escape a few times—but was always caught. Each time they would rape and brutally beat me. Twice I thought I would die, and begged for the freedom of death, but he wouldn't kill me. One time I got away . . . I was gone for a couple of weeks, maybe. I stayed in an abandoned house. When he found me, he let one of his buddies handle me. I remember it so clearly now. He said, *'Do whatever you want, just don't mark up her face.'* None of them had a conscience."

Katie gulped each breath as the tears flowed. Once she could manage to speak again, she resumed the story she needed to tell. "As horrible as it was, nothing compared to watching one of the other girls get beaten because of me. He said every time I disobeyed him, he would make sure she suffered more than I did. He chose a girl named Piper. She was sweet and always kind to me. He forced me to watch her being beaten and raped. After that night, I knew that I would never try to escape again. I did what he asked of me .. . and sold myself to strangers."

Katie searched Branson's face, unable to read his expression. His lips quivered as he tried to contain his emotion. Tears pooled at his eyelashes, but she wasn't sure if he was angry, disappointed, or disgusted. She stood on wobbly legs and walked over to where Branson was sitting. His hands were clasped and his forearms rested on his knees. He wouldn't look at her when she approached, he remained still and tears spilled down his cheeks, leaving a pattern on his slacks.

Katie inhaled sharply and tried to swallow the sob that escaped as she removed the ring from her finger. "I'm so sorry." She placed the ring in his hand and ran out of the room to pack a few things, hoping to hear him behind her.

Nothing.

Katie packed enough to live off of until she could have someone retrieve the rest of her things. Her body moved mechanically, placing clothes and toiletries into a duffle bag. She was no longer able to cry as her body grew numb, a temporary defense from the overwhelming pain of heartbreak.

She couldn't bear passing him in the hallway as she left the house, but had no other choice except climbing out the window. When she returned to the living room, Branson was still sitting there in a daze. *I've ruined his life*, she thought. Without speaking, she walked through the room, into the garage, and stood there. *My damn car is at Gram's!* Katie sat on the steps, not able to think straight. She was alone and had no one to turn to for help at this late hour.

She walked outside and made her way to the end of the driveway. She pulled out her phone and dialed Gram. "Gram," she sniffled. "Can you come get me?"

"Sit tight, I'm on my way." She didn't have to ask how things had gone with Branson, the answer was in Katie's voice.

"Please, hurry."

A dull but painful ache crept up Katie's spine into her heart, spreading to her lungs and eventually reaching her head. The longer she sat there, the more intense the feeling became. *I can't stay here. I need to keep moving.* Katie stood and reached for her duffle bag. Her hands were trembling and the ache had reached her stomach, threatening to make her sick, as if she had lost her equilibrium and was suddenly falling, tumbling, down a steep staircase. *Move!* She commanded her legs.

Katie let the duffle bag drop to the ground after a few steps and inched her body onto a large rock at the end of the driveway. The air was cool, which normally would have her shivering, but she was statuesque as she sat there with the waves of numbness and loss battering her. She concentrated on breathing in and out as she let the disappointment of shattered dreams settle in. *We had plans—traveling the world together, children—two boys and two girls. How will I be able to erase him from my future? How will I survive this?* Katie thought.

She carefully lowered herself from the rock and began walking down the road. *Does he even care that I'm gone? Has he even looked to see that I'm okay? How can he be so cruel?* She felt fresh, warm tears spring to her eyes and shook her head in defiance. *I'm over it! I'm ready to move on! Branson who? Erased from future—check!* Katie made a checkmark into the air as she walked briskly down the road. All of a sudden the woods began to close in on her. It was dark, eerie and lonely. She wondered if it had always been this pitch black at night. *Surely the moon is able to break through the thick trees and light the path? Or maybe there is no moon tonight? Have you abandoned me, also?*

Oncoming headlights brought a wave of relief to Katie, but it quickly passed and darkness surrounded her again. The only sounds were of crickets, bullfrogs, and the lonely call of an owl in the distance. She walked slowly, her emotions toying with her.

Rage.

Sorrow.

Despair.

Rage.

Despair.

Gram's white Lincoln Town car came to a stop and pulled over.

Katie climbed in the passenger seat and set the duffel bag at her feet. "Thank you, Gram, I know it's late—" She was unable to finish before a wave of nauseating sobs erupted.

"I'm so sorry, love. He's a bloody wanker. I've always known he wasn't good enough for my Katie . . ."

Katie raised a hand in protest. "Please." As angry as she was at Branson, she couldn't hear Gram talk unkindly about him. This was her fault. If she hadn't run away from the foster home, maybe things would have been different. If she had only kept her revelations to herself.

Branson sat in the same spot for hours processing the information Katie had just shared. Everything he knew about her was wrong. He felt betrayed—it was as if he had just learned she was a Russian spy, sent to trick him into falling in love with her so she could obtain something precious. In this instance it was his heart. He instinctively reached for his chest as he felt the empty hole where it had been extracted. He could feel the empty thud mimicking a heartbeat every few minutes in the hollow space.

He let his thoughts run rampant. *Why did this have to happen? We were so happy and had our entire future mapped out. I've never loved anyone like I love her, why did she have to remember all of this now? And who the hell does Gram think she is, having someone's memory erased? I wish she had done a better job of it so Katie would never have remembered. My God! Who could inflict such cruelty on a child? If I ever find out who did this, I'll kill them myself.*

He let his mind go to the dark place of imagining another man's hands on the love of his life. He envisioned her cries as she was raped and beaten. A wave of nausea erupted and he instinctively stood to run for the bathroom. Something clinked onto the hardwood floor as it dropped out of his hand. He looked down to see Katie's diamond engagement ring. *What the—?* He looked around the room. "Katie?" He called through the house as he walked from room to room. "Katie—?" He entered the bedroom and saw that Katie's usually organized drawers were left open and in disarray. After searching the house thoroughly, he realized she was gone.

Katie climbed under the covers a little past two in the morning. Gram had given her something to help her sleep and she waited impatiently for it to kick in as she lay there in agony. She was barely aware of Gram coming in to check on her throughout the night, making sure she wouldn't do anything foolish.

Katie woke up to muffled voices and followed them to the kitchen. She overheard Gram say, "No, I don't want you to kill him. I'd like to kill him myself, but that wouldn't do any of us—" Gram stood. "Good morning, dear. I assumed you would sleep most of the day."

Katie tried to smile, but her face wouldn't cooperate. It took all of her energy just to breathe. She squinted as the sun filtered through the windows, burning her raw, swollen eyes. Pete was sitting at the kitchen table looking through the paper. He gave her a formal smile, giving away the fact that Gram had filled him in.

"I'll make a pot of coffee, if you think you'd like to stay up?"

"I can't sleep the day away. I think I'll be better off if I keep moving. I have to work tomorrow, so I need to get it together and move on." Katie picked up a pair of sunglasses off the counter and slid them over her eyes.

"I really don't think that's a good idea. Why don't you call in sick for a few days, and take time to heal, dear?" Gram said as she filled the coffee maker with water and added freshly ground beans.

"Maybe that's best. I'll call them now. Please, excuse me." Katie walked back down the hallway toward her room and returned a few minutes later. "Gram, have you seen my cell?"

"No, dear. Have you checked your purse?"

"Yes, it's not there. I guess I left it at home, I mean . . . I'll need to get a new one." She sighed, her eyebrows naturally turning downward, displaying sadness. "Has he . . .?"

"No, I'm sorry, love. He hasn't tried to call." Gram glanced at Pete, silently begging him to go along with her little white lie.

Before the pain could display itself across her face, she excused herself to the bathroom. Splashing cold water on her face proved to be more painful than helpful, so she slid the dark glasses back over her eyes.

Katie lowered herself into a chair across from Pete and studied his face. He was a handsome older man with salt and pepper hair, black eyes, and thick brooding eyebrows. He emanated danger, but she could see why Gram had been attracted to him. Katie wondered what Gram's life would have been like if she had followed her heart and married him. Gram never would tell Katie the reason she had denied him, but she had the impression it was because of his moral choices.

"Pete, may I ask you something?" Katie asked.

"Anything." Pete answered, then took a sip of tea.

"When you found me, did you ever see or talk to anyone . . . any other girls . . . I'm curious if you know anything about my friend Ally—did she get out?"

Pete looked up from reading the newspaper. He would love to tell her that if Ally had any sized brain in her head, she would have gotten out when he wiped the area clean of the controlling pimps, but he kept all emotion from his face and answered her without giving anything away. "I can't say for sure, my only concern was for you."

Gram poured Katie a large mug of coffee and set it down in front of her.

Katie sipped the rich black cup of comfort, slowly letting it bring some semblance of life back into her. *So this is what a zombie feels like—no heartbeat, no life, no reason to breathe,* she thought.

Time passed slowly over the next few hours. Gram brought a bowl of soup and crackers to Katie's bedroom, it was always her favorite when she was sick. Heart sick seemed to be good enough reason for soup. Gram encouraged her to eat, but Katie just stared out the window at the sea—it seemed to understand her. As the waves crashed against the rocks, it wasn't out of rage—it was a loneliness that only the two of them understood.

That night she watched the lighthouse in the distance as it flashed its light methodically. It seemed to be repeating the same phrase: *keep breathing . . . keep breathing.* Katie looked back to the heartrending sea and wished she had the strength to lose herself in it. *How hard would it be to let go of the railing and fall gently into the arms of the only one that has never abandoned me?*

Gram didn't abandon you. Katie's subconscious scolded her.

No, but she lied, and now my life is ruined.

She lied to protect you. She wanted you to have a chance at a better life. Think of where you would be if she hadn't found you and pulled you out of that mess!

I'd probably be dead, Katie agreed.

She looked around the room and saw the tray of food on the table. *Pull it together, Katie. She saved your life twice now, be strong for her.*

Katie slowly stood on shaky legs. Her muscles were stiff and unused. When she finally made her way into the library where Gram sat reading a book, she spoke in a hushed tone, "You've given me so much, Gram, and I'm sorry to ask for one more thing . . ."

"Please, Katie, you know you can ask anything of me and I'll try my best to oblige."

"I need to get away from here for a while, in order to heal. I'm afraid Branson will realize what he's done and come after me because of guilt. I don't want a pity-marriage, Gram. If you could've seen his face . . ." Katie was surprised at how quickly her body could replenish tears. "I—I'll never forget that look. Please, Gram, I've got to get away. Far away."

Gram rose from her chair and wrapped her arms around Katie. "My sweet Katie-girl—you're going to be just fine, you'll see. And yes, we'll get out of here. I'll make the arrangements while you pack a few things."

Katie rolled her small suitcase, along with Gram's, to the trunk of the white Lincoln and placed them in the trunk. After Gram pulled onto the interstate and headed south, Katie asked about her relationship with Pete.

"Tell me about Pete Savalli."

"There's nothing to tell. We're friends. He's happily married, and I won't do anything to disrupt that," she answered matter-of-factly.

"So why is he here so much, and why was he generous enough to let us stay in his cottage on the Outer Banks for as long as we like?"

Gram's manner revealed an untold story. Pained eyes turned toward Katie for a moment before concentrating on the road ahead. "We're dear friends, mature enough to put our romantic feelings in the past where they belong. He's done so much for us . . ." She trailed off.

Katie wanted to know every detail. She'd been deceived long enough and deserved to know Pete's involvement in her rescue and restoration. But the heartache displayed on Gram's face, and the distance in her expression, encouraged Katie to save the discussion for another time.

Twenty-Nine

The bar was nearly empty as Branson lined up his pool stick with the white ball. "Green six in the right corner pocket." He took the shot and missed.

"I hate to take advantage of you when you're down," Mike said, trying to lighten the mood, "but it's the only way I can beat you."

Branson ordered another round of beer for the two of them as Mike cleared three striped balls. "Clean shots, nice job." Branson handed his friend a long-neck Bud Light.

"Thanks." Mike sat and took a long drink of his cold, refreshing beer. "Your turn."

"I just don't feel up to it. Mind if I just sit here and enjoy my beer?" Branson rubbed his temples. He hadn't slept or eaten properly in days and it was starting to take its toll.

"We've been friends for years, right?" Mike paused for Branson's answer and continued when he saw his head nod slightly. "I'm going to shoot straight with you then. You look like hell, dude. I don't know what happened with you and Katie, but aside from sleeping with your best friend—which by the way hasn't happened—nothing is worth losing her over. You're obviously miserable without her, so drop your stubborn pride and go after her."

Branson shook his head. "I can't, man. I just can't"

"You can't or you won't?"

"I've tried. She won't take my calls."

Mike exaggerated a deep sigh. "You called. Real big of you. Is that how you proposed?" He shook his head. "You're just going to let the girl of our dreams slip away that easily?" Mike let the glare Branson shot him slide off his back. "Yeah, I said it. You remember how crazy I was about her in college, but she loved *you* . . . and now you're screwing it up. Or maybe you're just a coward?" Mike braced himself and wondered if through his liquid courage, he had gone too far.

"You're right. I'm a coward." Branson's shoulders slumped and he hung his head.

"Are you serious?" Mike was nearly shouting. "Pull yourself together. Is this the same guy that stood up to the gym teacher our sophomore year for picking on Al Smitty? Or the guy who stood in front of our entire high school playing guitar and singing a solo because of a dare? You've never lost a fist fight, but you're going to take the title of *coward* because you're too afraid to tell the girl you love that you're sorry? What the fuck?" He paid the tab and returned the pool sticks to the wall. "Let's go."

Mike pulled out of the parking lot and drove toward the interstate. "New London or York?" he asked flatly. "Choose wisely—I won't make the offer again."

Branson flashed Mike a look of hatred. "Who the hell do you think you are? You have no idea what—" He stopped and thought about the last week without Katie. He felt like he'd been beaten and left for dead. Every muscle in his body ached, especially the one in his chest. He didn't want to know what a life without her felt like. *Who cares about her past? I want her present and future. She's still my Katie—the person in her past was a helpless victim of child abuse and crime. Who are you, dude? When did you become so damn self-important and condemnatory? And look where it got you . . . death's door.* Without lifting his head he said, "York."

Katie sat in the soft white sand looking out over the ocean. She didn't feel the wind in her hair or the soft, warm breeze as it caressed her shoulders. The sweet aroma of salty sea air couldn't penetrate her senses, nor could she hear the sound of the waves lapping onto the shore. She could only focus on one thing—the sun melting into the horizon—symbolic of how she was feeling. A week had passed on the beach and hadn't dulled the hollow pain of her heartbreak.

"Katie!" Gram yelled from the back deck.

Katie slowly rose from her spot and walked to the house to see what Gram needed. "Yes, Gram?" she asked slowly, taking every effort to force words out of her mouth.

"I bought us a box of chocolates, let's try one." Gram smiled and handed the box to Katie. "You pick first."

Katie opened the box to see twenty four chocolates that had been bitten in half. Gram was nearly in hysterics from laughing so hard. Katie smiled and was surprised when she heard herself chuckle. "You're too much, Gram."

"It's so good to see you smile, Katie-girl. I thought I was going to vomit halfway through, but it was so worth it to see my sweet girl happy—even for a moment."

"I think this trip is going to be really good, Gram. They say the sea can heal all wounds—we'll see if it works on me too."

The sound of Katie's screams was something Gram would never get used to. She ran across the hall, waking Katie up and holding her in her arms.

"Gram," Katie sobbed. "He's gone . . . he's gone."

"There, now. I've got you."

Each night it was the same routine. She'd stroke Katie's hair, until her trembling granddaughter fell back to sleep, all the while silently cursing Branson Stone.

In the morning, Katie rubbed the remaining sleep out of her eyes, and got dressed. She was determined to walk the beach, keeping her mind busy and off of Branson. She chose her black bikini, tying the matching sarong around her waist, and joined Gram in the kitchen. "Good morning."

"Good morning, dear." Gram poured a cup of coffee and set it down on the table.

Katie took a sip, letting the warm liquid bring her to life, and said, "Thanks."

"You're still planning on taking a walk along the beach?"

Katie nodded, keeping the cup to her lips.

"Why don't you take a walk down to the pier? Take the camera with you and capture some pictures of the local birds for me, will you? I've always wanted to have a puzzle made out of a favorite photograph, and this seems like a perfect time for a puzzle." Gram had a plan and she would make sure it worked. Katie was already coming around after being there only a few days. She thought back to when she met the handsome young surgeon the previous morning at the supermarket. *"You just started your residency? Brilliant! My granddaughter is a nurse—just graduated from Yale."* Gram pulled out a picture and showed the handsome doctor. *"Isn't she beautiful?"*

He nodded his head and gazed at the picture. "She's stunning."

"Too bad she's here alone, mourning the loss of a dear friend. I've tried to get her to go out and meet some people, but . . ." She shook her head and placed the picture back into her purse.

"I'd be glad to show her around. I've got a few days off this week."

"Aren't you a dear? Would you? She'll be at the pier tomorrow morning, taking photos." She leaned in and whispered, letting him in on a few tips that would help his case. "It won't do you any good to mention our meeting each other. She likes a man that is confident and secure—and don't let her take no for an answer. She does enjoy a good game of chase."

As Katie stepped outside, the air was still. A storm brewed in the distance, but the clouds didn't move, revealing the storm's path. Taking her chances, she hung the Nikon D90 around her neck, and began walking toward the pier. She stopped and squatted down to get a level shot of a snowy white egret standing near the water's edge.

Several birds lined the roof of the pier, waiting for fishermen to either drop some bait or leave the remains of a gutted fish. Katie snapped pictures from different angles, zooming in occasionally to capture only their faces. She felt someone bump into her from behind.

"Excuse me, I wasn't paying attention," he said, a subtle trace of a Spanish accent.

Katie turned around to face the stranger. He was tall, with black wispy hair and intense dark eyes. He was undeniably handsome and the tattoo on his left shoulder told her he was a rebel. Gauging by his tanned skin, he was most likely a local. It only took one look into his eyes for her to know that he was trouble. He wore a camera around his neck and Katie chuckled at the happenstance. "It's okay."

"Are you shooting for The Cape?" he asked.

"The Cape?"

"The newspaper."

"Oh, no. Just capturing some shots for my grandmother. She's obsessed with the egrets. Do *you* work for the paper?"

"No, just a hobby."

Katie stole another quick glance of the stranger. When she caught him perusing her body, she stiffened. Instinctively, she turned slightly, so he wouldn't have the pleasure of viewing her full-on.

"What kind of camera have you got?" he asked, breaking the awkward silence.

"Nikon D90. I don't really know how to use it, I just take a lot of pictures and hope a few turn out."

"You can just set it on auto and it'll do all the work for you."

"Really?"

He smiled and his eyes locked on hers. Everyone that had previously surrounded them on the beach had suddenly disappeared, as the world instantly became still. She could see the power behind his eyes, but it was laced with kindness. Just enough kindness to keep her from turning and walking away. Her reverie was shaken when his hand touched hers, reaching for her camera. Her hand jerked back from the intrusion, but he smiled, and continued to change the settings.

"That should do it. Now all you have to do is point and shoot."

"Thanks," she said, hoping he would assume her rosy cheeks were from too much sun.

"Are you here on vacation?" he asked.

"Uh," Katie wasn't sure how to answer the question. It wasn't vacation per say, but any other explanation would send him sprinting down the beach away from her. For some reason she didn't want that. "Yes, my grandmother and I have a place for the summer. How long are you here for?"

"I live here, so I'll be here for a while." He leaned against the wooden railing of the pier and displayed a cocky smile.

"Nice." Katie looked down at her bare feet. *Nice? That's all you've got? Jeez!*

The stranger chuckled to himself. "I never asked your name."

"Katie."

"It's a pleasure to meet you Katie. I'm Aidan Romero."

Branson pounded on the front door and rang the doorbell several times. "Katie! Answer the door. I need to see you," he shouted.

After a few minutes, he walked around to the back of the house and repeated the process of banging on the door.

"She's not home." A lady appeared from the back of the house.

"Hello." Branson tried to calm his breathing, not wanting to frighten the petite woman standing there in gardening gloves. "I'm Katie's fiancé. Do you know when she'll be back?"

"You must be Branson," she smiled, her kind eyes washing over him. "I've seen pictures."

"Yes. Can you tell me when she'll be home? I need to see her, it's important."

She shook her head. "I'm sorry, but they'll be gone all summer."

"All summer!" He was tempted to shake the information he needed out of this woman, but resisted. "Where did they go? Please, you have to tell me."

"Mrs. Harrington didn't tell me where, only how long. I'm looking after the house while she's away."

Branson sank onto a bench and put his head in his hands. *I've lost her,* he thought. He slowly stood and walked back to the car.

Mike could tell by the look on Branson's face that it wasn't a successful trip. "Didn't go well?"

Branson shook his head. "She's gone. The lady didn't know where—only that she's gone for the summer. What am I going to do now?"

Thirty

The danger that radiated from Aidan was intoxicating as Katie walked along the beach beside him.

"Where do you work?" Katie asked, trying to guess his answer before he spoke. *I'll bet he owns a souvenir shop. No, he's too mysterious for that . . . he probably owns a nightclub.*

"Outer Banks Hospital."

Katie whirled her head around to look at him. "What do you do for the hospital?"

"I'm an orthopedic surgeon."

Katie raised one eyebrow, surprised. He certainly didn't look like any of the surgeons *she* had worked with in the past. Most of them were nerdy and unattractive. It was a stereotype, she was aware, but the surgeons in Maine fit the stereotype perfectly.

"Really? I'm a nurse." She was thrilled to have someone to talk to about the subject she loved most. It was nice to break the monotony of depression for a change.

"No kidding. What are the chances of two medical professionals carrying cameras around their necks meeting on a pier?" He laughed. "What's your specialty?"

"I work in the ER, or worked rather."

"You didn't like it?"

"Actually, I loved it. It's exciting and constantly challenging. I'm just taking a break." Katie squatted down, lifted her camera, and took a shot of a pelican skiing across the water as it landed.

As they continued down the beach, they shared stories about bizarre things they'd encountered in the hospital.

"It was insane!" Aidan spoke animatedly. "She actually came in thinking that she was having a gallbladder attack. She was nine centimeters dilated and never knew she was pregnant!"

Katie laughed, enjoying the story and the company. She felt the life slowly coursing back through her veins. "How do people not know they're pregnant?" A wave of sadness washed over her, remembering a time not too long ago when she hadn't been aware of her pregnancy. "Didn't she feel the baby kick? Or question missing nine months of her cycle?"

"I asked her those questions. She had a mild cycle throughout and instead of feeling the baby kicking, she thought it was gas. She said she'd always had stomach issues, so it didn't occur to her that it could be anything else."

Katie was so engrossed with the mysterious stranger, she hadn't realized they had walked past her cottage. "I better get back and check on my grandmother. It was nice talking to you, Aidan."

"You, too, Katie."

Surprised by how it felt to hear her name roll off of his tongue, she swirled the sand around with her toe before looking back up. "I see my Gram up ahead. Would you like to meet her?"

"I would."

Katie greeted Gram and introduced her to Aidan. "We met on the pier. He was taking pictures and we bumped into each other. He's a surgeon at Outer Banks Hospital."

"Hello, Aidan. My Katie's a nurse, a very good one. Did you tell him that, dear?"

Katie smiled. "I did. Anyway, he's on his way home. I just wanted to introduce you."

"Why don't you join us for dinner? I insist." She looked at Katie, urging her to agree.

Katie immediately saw the plan unfolding and wanted to object, but it wasn't Aidan's fault and she wouldn't embarrass him just to satisfy her need to foil Gram's scheme. "Of course. You should join us."

Surprisingly, dinner was more than tolerable, Katie actually enjoyed it. Gram wasn't too pushy as they dined on the back deck, watching the sun sink deep into the sea. Conversation flowed as easily as the wine and Katie felt relaxed and comfortable. Aidan stood to leave at eleven-thirty, thanking Gram for dinner. "I should be getting home. I can't believe how late it is, I hope I haven't overstayed my welcome."

"We enjoyed your company." Katie said shyly. It was true, and she hadn't had to hug herself to stifle the raging ache inside of her all day. She walked him to the front door. "Do you have far to go? I can drive you."

"I'm just a few blocks down, but thank you." He looked into her eyes and held her gaze for a moment. "I'd like to see you again. Are you free tomorrow?"

Katie knew it wasn't fair to lead him on. She wasn't ready for any kind of relationship, and wouldn't be for a long time. She had never loved anyone as deeply as she loved Branson, and if her heart ever healed—although she doubted it would—it would take a significant amount of time. On the other hand, she was tired of the constant pain that consumed her and diminished her quality of life. Aidan was the take-charge kind-of-guy that she craved right now. Although she was still in hurting, he brought air back into her lungs, and blood back into her veins.

"I might be," she said, regretting the flirtatious tone in her voice. "What've you got in mind?"

Aidan held her gaze for a moment before answering. *Be careful how you look at me sweetheart, you're putting some wicked thoughts in my mind.* "Lunch and a tour of the lighthouse."

"Sounds fun."

"I'll pick you up at noon. Goodnight, Katie." He brushed his thumb across her cheek before turning to walk away.

"Goodnight." She closed the door and exhaled the breath she had been holding. Not able to contain the smile that spread across her lips, she slipped into her bedroom and got in the shower to avoid Gram's knowing look.

The musky, warm aroma of the sea was invigorating as Katie sipped her coffee and watched the day begin. She observed a sand crab climb over a dune into a hole, while a thin older man in navy swim trunks and a white hat fished along the shoreline. As she sat there, her thoughts drifted to

Aidan. *He's very attractive, and he's a doctor.* She reflexively shook her head. *Put those thoughts out of your mind.* And then her mind roamed into the danger zone . . . *Branson.*

She thought about the way his lips tasted and how his hands felt on her body. She felt tears sting her eyes and the familiar pain begin to wrench her body into fetal position. *No!* She scolded herself. *Get up!*

Katie stood in the shower, letting the hot water wash her sorrows down the drain. She blow dried her hair and slipped on a pale yellow sundress. Aidan was waiting in the living room with Gram when she came out of the bedroom. "Hi. Have you been waiting long?"

"No, I just sat down. Ready?"

"Yes. Will you be okay, Gram?"

"Just fine. I'm going to relax and enjoy the sun. Have fun."

Aidan held the passenger door of his charcoal gray BMW Roadster open for Katie as she slid in, then jogged around to the driver's side. Katie's heart raced with exhilaration as they sped down the empty road in the sleek car. They ate lunch at a quaint restaurant with fresh seafood offerings, and lingered over dessert, talking about medical school, life in Maine versus life on the Outer Banks, and family.

"Tell me about your family, Aidan, and where are you from originally?"

"I was born in Argentina, but we moved to Georgia when I was thirteen. My parents divorced shortly afterward. I have a younger brother who's studying marine biology at Duke, he graduates next spring. My mother remarried and moved to Raleigh, and my father lives with his girlfriend in Georgia with no plans to ever marry again." He rolled his eyes. "My family is like a soap opera."

"Argentina? How exciting. What was your favorite dish growing up?"

"My mother used to make the best ham and cheese empanadas, and she was well-known for her Dulce de Leche, but my favorite dessert was the chocolate gelato from this little shop about two blocks from our house." Aidan smiled, remembering the taste. "What about you? Tell me about your family, and let me guess . . . your favorite childhood food was noodles and cheese, and for dessert you would have . . ." He thought for a moment as he looked into her green eyes. Little flecks of gold were visible just around the pupil. ". . . A chocolate sundae."

Katie thought back to her time with her parents. Chocolate sundaes never touched her lips as a child, and the only food memory she had was a can of Spaghetti O's. She knew she couldn't reveal any of that to Aidan, she would never talk of her past with anyone again.

"You're way off—I'm a vanilla girl!" Katie smirked.

"I doubt that." He lowered his eyes and smirked. "If I'm wrong, it's time you try something more exciting."

If he was trying to make her blush, he was doing a marvelous job. Katie swirled her spoon through the creamy panna cotta before looking back up. "I'm always game for trying new things."

"I'll have to remember that. Was I right about the noodles and cheese?"

Katie laughed. "You mean Mac and Cheese? I liked it okay, but my favorite is seafood. And my choice dessert would be Crème brûlée."

"Tell me about your family."

Tread carefully, Katie, she thought before answering. "My parents died when I was young, so it's just been me and Gram. We've had a lot of fun together through the years, and I wouldn't change a thing, except maybe a sister." She flinched as soon as the words came out of here mouth and she wondered if he noticed. To cover, she feigned the need to sneeze. Lying about her past was the plan, adding the idea of a sister was pushing too far. Now she had to hide the memories from her expression and continue. "I always thought it would be fun to share clothes and secrets." Katie kept the details to herself. She watched his face while she talked, judging by the few gray streaks running through his black hair, she noticed he was older. She spotted another tattoo on his wrist, making him seem more like a rebel than a surgeon. "What do you like to do for fun?"

"First of all, siblings aren't as glamorous as they sound. You most likely would've fought over clothes and *told* each other's secrets. Or like my brother and me—held them over each other's heads for blackmail." He took a sip of water and set it down. "As for your question, I enjoy running, weight lifting, and golf. How about you?"

"I play tennis and like to run—well, jogging is more my pace."

Aidan paid the bill and they left, heading toward the lighthouse. After parking, they walked along the sand covered path toward the tall black and white striped lighthouse, entering through a door at the bottom. They stepped in, waited for a family of four to get some headway in front of them, and began their ascent on a red metal, spiral staircase. Two hundred and sixty-eight steps later, they were leaning against the railing at the top of the lighthouse, looking out across the magnificent sea.

"It's a bit chilly up here." Katie rubbed her hands up and down on her arms as the wind whipped her hair around and chilled her skin.

Aidan wasn't sure if it was too soon to touch her, but he couldn't just stand there watching her freeze. He came up from behind and wrapped his arms around her, trying to relieve her shivering body. He felt Katie flinch beneath him, but she didn't pull away.

They stayed against the rail, watching the sea tempt two young kids on boogie boards, a flock of seagulls searching for food, and a kite surfer sailing through the water with the help of a strong wind. After about twenty minutes, Katie was ready to go. She turned around, thinking Aidan would instinctively back away, but he didn't. She found herself much too close to his face and didn't know how to get out of his hold.

She bit down on her bottom lip, trying to think about her next move, but it was too late. He leaned in and pressed his lips to hers. Electricity shot through her and traveled to each nerve ending. Her hands instinctively slid up over his chest and wrapped around his neck. As their tongues mingled, all sound and movement around them stilled, as if they were the only ones at the top of the lighthouse. She felt him moan into her mouth and she pulled away.

"I—I'm sorry." She slid out from under his arms and made her way to the bottom of the lighthouse.

"Katie, wait!" Aidan was right behind her and caught up with her in the parking lot. "I'm sorry, I know you're grieving and it's too soon. I shouldn't have kissed you."

"You know? How do you know?" Katie looked at him quizzically while she caught her breath.

"Your grandmother told me you had just lost someone and were still grieving."

"I don't know if grieving is the right word. I'm angry, I'm hurt, and I'm just . . . lost. I don't want to use you as a rebound. I thought we could just be friends, and then you went and kissed me, and I—"

"Rebound? That's an odd way of putting it. Was it your boyfriend that died?"

"Died? Is that what Gram told you?" Katie shook her head in disbelief. "That sounds like something Gram would do. I'm sorry, Aidan. It looks like you got caught in one of my grandmother's schemes."

"Please, explain to me what's going on." He was growing wary of the illogical talk of schemes.

"My boyfriend didn't die. He was my fiancé, and he's very much alive. I'm sure Gram thought it would be in my best interest to move on and meet someone new, but I—I'm sorry you've wasted your time. I'm sure a handsome guy like you won't have any trouble getting attention elsewhere. Would you please take me home?"

"Give me a minute, I'm still savoring the *handsome guy* remark."

Katie laughed. "I just told you that you've been set up and you would rather focus on a compliment?"

Aidan nodded his head. "Look, I don't like to be lied to, but I can't be too angry with the outcome. I've met a beautiful woman, who loves the same things I do, and I have to tell you, hanging out with you has proven to be more stimulating than time spent with Harold and Maude."

"Harold and Maude?" Katie looked at him quizzically.

Aidan chuckled, "My fish. They're good listeners, but terrible conversationalists."

Katie could feel it—her body began to relax and released a small amount of the dark toxin choking the life out of her.

Aidan opened the car door and shut it gently after Katie slid inside. She watched him walk in front of the car, around to the driver's side. He was good looking and good-natured. *There's no harm in spending time with him now that he knows the truth.*

"Is there any chance of reconciliation with your fiancé?" he asked before starting the engine.

Katie lowered her head and felt the brief spark of life being sucked out of her. "No."

"Okay then, today begins a new chapter for you. It's my mission to make you laugh until you ache." He grinned and pulled out of the lot.

"It's working." Katie whispered one night after dinner as she and Aidan walked along the beach. She held her shoes in her hand, enjoying the feeling of the cool, powdery sand under her feet and between her toes. The full moon illuminated the beach, revealing their seclusion.

"What's working?"

"My stomach muscles hurt from laughing so much." Katie looked down, suddenly shy.

They had spent the last three days together playing in the surf, jumping waves, and body surfing. They enjoyed long walks along the beach during the day, talking about anything and everything. Evenings held games of mini-golf, casual dinners, and an art show. He seemed to have the ability to sense when she needed a laugh and could pull out a great joke at just the right time.

Aidan slid his arm around Katie's waist and pulled her close to him. "I'm glad." He felt her body tense and released her. Shaking his head, he whispered, "too soon?"

Katie sighed. "I'm sorry." Katie looked into his eyes. There was an undeniable, strong connection to him. She wanted to let go of the heartache, and experience life again. But guilt played its hand wisely. How could she so easily be lured by someone, when her heart belonged to Branson? *Branson threw it away,* she reminded herself. Standing on her tiptoes, she asked, "Can we try that again?"

She began the kiss, but he took over. He felt her let go and get lost in the moment, returning his passion with the depth of her own. Aidan rested his forehead on hers, catching his breath. Her greens eyes and sweet disposition drew him in, and he was strangely attracted to her brokenness, wanting to mend her.

"Katie," Aiden exhaled.

"Hmm?"

"I have surgery early tomorrow. We should get going."

"Oh, of course." Katie held onto Aiden's arm as she slipped her shoes back on. "What have you got scheduled tomorrow?"

"Two hip replacements and a broken ankle. Actually, he shattered it. It's a mess and I don't know how long it will take to put the puzzle back togeth—I'm sorry, that's too much information."

"I like to talk medicine." Katie smiled.

Katie clicked her heels together, knocking most of the sand off of her shoes before getting into the car. She watched Aidan walk around to the driver's side, admiring his confident stride. There was something dark and mystifying about him, and Katie was sure it was the one thing she was most attracted to. Bach's *Minuet* filled the car with the enchanting, yet lonely sounds of the cello. Katie enjoyed the music along with the little sparks that traveled through her hand every time Aidan rubbed his thumb across the top of her knuckles. She laid her head back on the leather seat and allowed her mind to imagine a future with the mysteriously handsome surgeon.

After a tender kiss, Katie said goodnight, shutting the cottage door behind her. Before she could reach Gram in the living room, her phone dinged with an incoming text:

Sleep well, green eyes. I'll be dreaming of you tonight.

The text should have made Katie smile, but instead it felt like she had been sucker punched. *Green eyes. Branson used to call me that.* She couldn't bring herself to text him back, so she replied with a simple smiley face:

:)

"Gram, are you still up?" Katie whispered, walking toward the kitchen.

Gram was curled up on the couch with a book. "Of course, it's only ten o'clock. I waited to have a cup of tea with you."

"Good. I want to talk to you." Katie brought two cups to the table and waited for Gram to pour the water.

"So how's the doctor?"

"He's great. He makes me feel alive." Katie frowned. "Is there something wrong with me, Gram? How can I be attracted to him so soon?"

"There's nothing wrong with you, dear. You're young, enjoy your life. What are your plans for tomorrow?"

"He's in surgery all day. I thought I would take a long walk down the beach, try to gain some perspective. Do you mind if I take a day to myself?"

"Of course I don't mind, dear." Gram could tell Katie was still deep in thought, struggling with her feelings for Aidan. "Katie-girl, listen. I think I can help you decipher your feelings. When I was young and naïve," Gram twisted her hands and smiled, remembering her youth. "I fell in love with Pete. There was something about him that drew me in like a powerful magnet, but I couldn't marry him. When I found out that he . . . well, let me just say I couldn't deal with his line of work. I was crushed and thought my heart would never heal. Then I met your grandfather, Charles. He was kind, loving, a talented businessman, and he loved me. I knew I could raise a family with him and be happy. There were no sparks at first, but I learned to love him and it grew and grew over the years. Pete still makes my heart race, but I wouldn't trade my years with Charles for an increased heart rate any day. Besides, at my age it could kill you," she chuckled.

Katie sipped her tea. "Thanks for sharing that, Gram. I guess I'm in the opposite predicament. Although Branson was safe, we had electricity, too. But I don't have that choice anymore."

Thirty-One

The faint sound of a kettle whistling in the distance woke Katie with the promise of a steaming cup of her favorite tea. She stretched her arms and legs, stirring herself back to life before slipping out of bed and into her too-new house shoes. There was something about a pair of well-worn house shoes that had molded to your feet—they were so much more comfortable. These made Katie's feet slide back and forth, and it was an effort to keep them on.

"Good morning, Gram." Katie mumbled, sleepiness still present in her voice.

"Good morning, my dear. Sleep well?"

Katie shrugged her shoulders and held the cup to her nose, letting the aroma wake and refresh her senses. "Okay, I guess. You?"

"Yes, I slept just fine. The book I'm reading is good, but it makes me drowsy. You should pick one up today, it might help you fall asleep."

"Hard liquor might help, too." Katie grumbled.

"Katie Rose! I've never been opposed to an occasional nightcap, but only for pleasure—never for the wrong reasons."

"I know, Gram," Katie sighed. "I'll check out that little bookstore on the corner today."

"Good. I've been invited to lunch with a group of ladies. I didn't want to leave you—"

"No, you go and have a good time." Katie interrupted. "I'll check out the bookstore and then take a long walk down the beach. I could use some time to myself."

"All right then. I'll order dessert to go and we'll have a treat this evening."

Katie stood in the shower, letting the hot water soothe her stiff muscles. She used her thumb and forefingers to massage either side of her neck as she lolled her head to the left and then to the right. *Jeez, have I been that tense? There's no other reason for my muscles to be so sore, I haven't exercised in . . .* Katie thought back to the last time she did anything physical. She and Branson had gone on a long trail run, enjoying the fresh summer air, and then cooling off in the lake. She giggled to herself remembering Branson's attempted front flip that landed him on his backside.

The shop was a quaint shingle-style-home-turned-bookstore. Katie immediately loved it. Warmly welcomed by a petite blonde, and pointed in the direction of the fiction section, Katie was on the hunt for the perfect escape novel. She read the back covers of books that resembled her own life too much, and carefully put it back on the shelf. *Come*

*Back to Me, I'll Never Love Again, The One That Got Away &
Took My Heart With Him.* Katie replaced each book. *I've got
to get out of the romance section!*

"Excuse me," Katie asked the store clerk. "Do you have
any Stephen King on the shelves?"

"Sure, right over here."

Katie browsed through the selection and purchased *Cell.*
After thanking the clerk, she picked up a bacon, lettuce,
tomato, and avocado sandwich from the bistro next door
and drove back to the cottage to eat.

Most of the day was spent with her book on the beach,
reading the same few paragraphs over and over. Finally, she
set the book down, and began her walk down the beach,
thinking about her fast-growing relationship with Aidan.
She recalled the conversation with Gram about learning to
love someone. Katie was ashamed of using Aidan to help her
heal, what if he fell in love with her? Could she love him
back, enough to satisfy him? She fast-forwarded in her mind
to her future. *She was standing in the kitchen with her hair in
a messy bun, no makeup, and sweat pants stained with baby
food. The green glow of numbers on the microwave proved
that it was after midnight. Pouring another shot of Jack
Daniels, she watched the clock take her into the early morning
hour.*

*When she heard the front door slowly creak open, she lay
in bed, listening to her husband tip-toe through the house.
Closing her eyes, she pretended to be asleep when he snuck
through the bedroom and slipped into the bathroom. He spent
his nights with another woman, and she couldn't blame him.
She wasn't in love with him and had quit taking care of
herself. Any time and energy she had was used to meet the*

needs of her children. As soon as they were in bed, she began drinking.

Katie's reverie was broken by a Frisbee slamming into her thigh. "Ow!"

"I'm so sorry!" a girl said, running up to her. She looked to be around twelve with a sun-streaked ponytail.

"It's okay." Katie picked up the hot pink Frisbee and handed it to her.

Walking back to the cottage, she focused on her surroundings. Everyone on the beach was laughing, playing, and enjoying the ones they were with. Young couples were holding hands and looking into each other's eyes, families were building sand castles and taking pictures of their kids as they played in the surf. *I want that,* Katie thought as she picked up her book and climbed the steps of the back deck.

Gram was waiting inside the cottage. "How was your day, dear?"

"Nice. That bookstore is a gem, you should check it out. How was your lunch?"

"Really good. I'd like to take you soon, you'll love the food."

Katie fell asleep that night thinking about Aidan, and awoke in a sweat after a haunting nightmare. *She was tied to a chair, while Aidan leaned down, much too close to her face. He ran his tongue across her bottom lip teasingly and flashed the cocky smile she liked so much. He softly trailed his lips down her neck and shoulder, and continued the tortuous pleasure over each breast as she squirmed beneath the restraints. He whispered so low she strained to hear what he was saying. "What?" she asked. "I can't hear you."*

Aidan stopped traveling the line of her inner thigh and rested his hands on the arms of the chair. He leaned in close to her face and displayed an evil grin that made her tremble. "I said you're a filthy little whore." Katie began to cry as he continued kissing her inner thigh while mocking and degrading her, the tears slipping down her temples into her hair and eventually waking her.

Stumbling into the bathroom, she splashed cold water on her face, took a long drink of water, and slipped back into bed. *He'll never know about my past. Never!*

Tuesday morning was greeted with a quick rain shower. As Katie sipped her coffee, she watched the rain pelt the ocean as the waves grew angry and rolled in faster. They slung white foam onto the sand before receding and working up enough strength to repeat the process. After thirty minutes, the rain stopped and the sea calmed. It reminded her of a quick temper-tantrum a toddler would throw in the grocery store after not getting the treat he asked for.

A knock at the door startled Katie, causing her to whirl around. She slapped her hand over her chest and turned to Gram. "That scared me! Are you expecting anyone?"

"No."

Katie opened the door and was greeted by a large bouquet of flowers. She heard a voice say, "I've got flowers for Katie Harrington."

"Yes, that's me." Katie took the flowers and thanked the young man hidden behind the bouquet. She looked at the clear vase holding orange roses, pink Gerbera daisies, and green Fuji mums. After setting the bouquet on the table, she pulled the card and read it aloud.

Beautiful Katie,
I hope this brightens your day as much as you've brightened my world. Dinner tonight. I'll pick you up at 7:00.

"Lovely! Are you going to go?" Gram clasped her hands together, swooning.

Katie nodded, studying the flowers. They were bright and beautiful. She loved that he was thinking of her while they were apart. "I think I will. Aren't they gorgeous?"

Katie finally decided on a turquoise sundress and piled her loosely curled hair into a clip. As she was adding some lip gloss, she heard Aidan at the front door.

"Hi." She kissed him sweetly on the cheek. "Thank you for the flowers, they're beautiful."

"I knew you would like them. Ready to go?"

"Just let me grab my purse."

"I've had dinner delivered to my place. I hope you don't mind."

Katie's heart pounded as she contemplated being alone with him. Was her nightmare prophetic, or just her mind trying to trick her into remaining miserable? Trying to erase the apprehension from her voice, she answered, "Okay."

Walking into the foyer, Katie inspected her surroundings. The moon reflected on the ocean, visible through the glass living room wall. "It's stunning."

"Thank you. Let me show you around." Aidan took her hand and led her through his home. "This is the living room, kitchen, there's a half bath through there."

Katie was surprised at how simple and modern his taste was. The entire house was white, except for the kitchen, which boasted sleek black cabinets, black granite countertops, and stainless steel appliances. "It's so . . . clean."

"I like clean lines and a clutter-free environment." He led her down the hall and opened the door. "And this is my room."

His bedroom matched the rest of the home—spotlessly clean and modern. Katie didn't have time to look around, only to notice his bedspread was black with a white fur blanket draped over one corner at the end of the bed.

They sat down at the dining room table and enjoyed Chinese takeout by candlelight with great conversation. The more he talked, the more ridiculous her nightmare seemed.

"More wine?" Aidan asked, refilling Katie's glass of Pinot Grigio.

"Thank you. Dinner was delicious." Katie smiled, feeling the effects of the wine relaxing her.

Aidan got up from the table and returned with two small white, oval dishes. He set one of them down in front of Katie, waiting for her reaction.

"Crème brûlée!" Katie beamed. "You remembered."

After dessert, Aidan took Katie's hand, waiting for her to steady herself. "Sorry, I haven't drunk that much in a long time."

"Follow me."

Katie tensed, wondering what he had in mind, but relaxed when he led her outside. She followed him underneath the back deck to a large hammock. Aidan climbed in, making room for Katie. She stood there, her body language portraying her reluctance.

"It's okay. I thought you'd like to listen to the waves." He held up his hands in surrender. "Only listening, and talking."

Content with his pledge, she carefully slid in next to him, balancing her weight so they didn't topple off onto the sand below. Aidan guided her head onto his chest and wrapped an arm around her.

"Relax," he commanded.

Katie obeyed, and felt her muscles loosen. She could feel his strong chest and arms beneath her, and was taken aback by how much she wanted to touch him. Instead, she listened to the waves and let the rocking motion of the hammock lull her to sleep.

"Katie, wake up." Aidan stroked her hair and kissed her forehead. "We fell asleep."

"What time is it?"

"It's late, after two. We should get you home."

Gram was asleep when Katie came home, so she slipped into bed—sundress and all—and drifted off to sleep, the sound of the waves still rolling through her mind.

Wednesday afternoon, Katie drove to the hospital to meet Aidan for a late lunch.

"Can I help you?" A pretty blond nurse in green scrubs asked.

"Hi. I'm supposed to meet Dr. Romero on the orthopedics floor."

"Sure, it's on the—actually, just follow me and I'll take you up there."

Katie looked over the bubbly, petite woman and instantly felt comfortable around her. She had an addictive personality that reminded her of Maggie.

"May I ask? Are you his sister?"

"No, we're not related. We're—" Katie wasn't sure what they were. Was he her boyfriend, friend, heartbreak-curer? Before she could figure it out, the elevator door opened and she saw him. Aidan was standing at the nurses' station writing in one of the charts. She could feel the hormones raging inside of her as two nurses ogled him.

Katie nibbled on her sandwich as she and Aidan talked. She listened to his words, but her mind was too busy processing her newfound attraction to him. Whether it was jealousy prodding her competitive streak, or something completely different, she didn't care. She was only focused on making sure his attention was solely hers.

Thursday afternoon was spent shopping with Gram. Katie found a new bathing suit and a pair of sunglasses, while Gram tried on shoes. Katie cared less about shoes, she was most comfortable in her bare feet, while Gram was obsessed—she insisted every woman should have a pair of shoes to match every outfit. As Katie sat on a bench outside of the third shoe store, her phone dinged with a text from Aidan:

Hi beautiful! I have the weekend off. Spend it with me?

Katie's heart lurched in her chest. She wasn't sure what he meant by spending the weekend with him. It could mean dinner, putt-putt, a movie . . . or could he actually be asking her to spend the night?

What do you have in mind?

I have a house on Cape Hatteras. 2 other couples going. You will love it!

Katie contemplated the idea. *I don't know the other couples, but I'm sure it will be fun. Jeez, I wish I could talk to Maggie about it. I miss her so much. But I can't talk to Maggie—without telling her everything—I'll just have to make my own decisions. I don't know what to do.*

"Hi, dear, wait until you see these shoes—" Gram pulled a pair of brown leather sandals out of a bag and flaunted them as if she were trying to get the best price at an auction. "What are you so deep in thought about?"

"Aidan asked me to spend the weekend with him and two other couples on Cape Hatteras. I don't think—"

"Take a risk for a change," Gram interrupted. "Try something new."

"Who are you and what've you done with my conservative grandmother?"

"I didn't say go and act like a floozy! You're an adult with a good head on your shoulders."

Katie typed her answer and hit *send*.

Sounds fun!

Katie shaved her legs—twice—and made sure to pack her new black bikini. Before opening the front door, she gathered her bag and took a deep breath. "Hi, come in."

"I'm so glad you agreed to go this weekend. We're going to have a great time."

Katie was full of questions on the drive. "Tell me about the other couples."

"I've known Brad and Ryan for three years. Brad works in advertising and has been married to Sarah for almost two years. Ryan is a plastic surgeon and he's been dating Penelope—we all call her Penny—for four years. The girls are nice, and they'll love you."

"Have you rented this place before?"

"Brad and I own it. We originally bought it as an investment to rent out, but decided we liked using it personally. It was unsettling to have strangers in our beds."

Katie focused on those last words and wondered if there was a hidden meaning. If he didn't like having strangers in his bed, was he a relationship kind of guy? She wondered how many women he had brought to this place, and if the other couples would assume she was just another woman for him to conquer. Aidan pulled in the driveway to the large four-story home.

"Looks like we're the first to arrive," he said, helping Katie out of the car. He unlocked the front door and set their bags down. "Let me show you around."

The vast living room and kitchen were bright as the light shone through the glass wall that overlooked the ocean. "Wow, it's just beautiful," Katie said. "I can't wait to get on that beach!"

"Let's pick our rooms before the others get here, and then we'll hit the beach."

Katie hung on his words. *He said "rooms," he has no intention of sharing a bed with me.* She exhaled a breath of— was it disappointment or relief?

Aiden picked up the bags and led Katie up a spiral staircase to the second floor. "We have six bedrooms, one with bunk beds and—"

"Yes! Let's take the bunk beds. We can stay up late laughing and making prank calls." Katie laughed.

"If you're sharing a room with me, I think you'll find this one much more appealing." Aidan opened the door to the first room. Rich caramel walls surrounded a large king-sized bed, and glass sliders led to a balcony overlooking the beach. Aidan set the bags down and took Katie's hand.

"Wait—"

"Katie," he interrupted. "I'm just going to show you the bathroom."

She followed him into a large bathroom with a deep tub. "Nice. I could enjoy a glass of wine and a soak in that tub."

"I hope you will." Aidan took Katie out onto the balcony. There were two Adirondack chairs with a small round table between them.

Katie stood there watching the sea roll in, wondering if she had made the right choice, joining Aidan for the weekend. She was confused, knowing she should share a room with him, but she wasn't ready. She searched her mind for something safe. "Maybe you could join me for coffee out here in the morning."

"Sure. Let me show you the rest of the house." Aidan took Katie's hand and led her to the room next to hers. "I'll stay in this room. The room across the hall is the one with bunk beds, and the rest of the rooms are on the other side of the house."

He'd made the decision not to share a room with her, and now she felt even more conflicted. All of the signals informed her that he wanted her, but now he didn't? Katie looked around the room while Aidan set his bag on the bed. It wasn't nearly as regal as the room she would be sleeping in. "Aidan, we really need to switch rooms. Although, the floral pattern does wonders for your skin tone," Katie laughed.

Aidan laughed along, happy to see her relax a bit. "There's the smart mouth your grandmother spoke of." He took her by the waist and whirled her around to face him before winking. "I like it."

She found herself against the wall as Aidan's hands gripped her waist. His intense black eyes bored into hers, drawing her in like an unexplained force, convincing her to taste the delicious poison.

The heat from Aidan's breath on her neck, and the gentle kiss that barely touched her skin behind her ear made it hard for her to maintain balance. She heard him whisper *"Me Estoy enamorando de ti."*

Katie wasn't sure what he had just said, but the accent mixed with his mysterious darkness was causing her to quickly spin out of control. As the familiar stir swirled through her body, she slid her hands over the soft fabric of his blue shirt, gliding over each muscle in his chest and arms. He did want her.

Aidan's breath hitched as his body tensed under her touch. The way she was melting under his gaze sent a jolt right through him. Her eyes were a stunning shade of green against her flushed cheeks, giving him a glimpse of who she might have been before that bastard shattered her heart.

Not taking his eyes off hers, he slowly leaned in and claimed her lips. A quiet moan escaped Katie. Her fingers knotted in his hair as the kiss became more ardent, and he wanted more. He pinned her arms above her head and slipped his hand under her shirt, skimming over her ribs until he reached her breast. The feel of her leg wrapping around him to pull him closer had him fully aroused.

The distant sound of chimes immediately broke the gripping intoxication. "Was that the doorbell?" Katie asked, trying to catch her breath.

Aidan released her arms and rested his hands on the wall behind her, his eyes still burning with desire. "Yes," he exhaled. "They have a key, I think that was just a polite alert." He rubbed his thumb gently across Katie's cheek.

Katie ran her fingers through her hair and straightened her top. "Hey," she took Aidan's hand, flashing him a mischievous grin, "what *exactly* did you say earlier?"

Aidan softly kissed her forehead before answering. "I said I'm falling for you." He watched Katie's face to see how she would respond. He always believed in saying what you mean, life was too short to hold anything back. His parents never shared their feelings with each other or their children, and he was sure it was why they divorced. His mother said his father was too rough and didn't love her, but he knew the truth—his mother was seeing someone else.

Katie began to giggle until she saw the look on Aidan's face. "I'm sorry, I shouldn't be laughing. I just didn't expect that at all. I thought you said something dirty." Katie bit her bottom lip, forcing herself to be serious. "I really am sorry." She cupped Aidan's cheek in her right hand, stood on her tip toes, and kissed him sweetly, searching his face. "I hope you'll speak to me again in Spanish, it's really lovely."

"Mi culo poco inteligente." Aidan shook his head and led Katie down the stairs toward the awaiting guests.

"What did you say?" Katie pleaded.

"I called you a little smart ass."

"There you are!" Brad said, causing everyone to turn and look at Aidan and Katie as they came down the stairs.

"I'd like you all to meet Katie Harrington. Katie, this is Brad and his wife Sarah, and this is Ryan and Penny."

Katie shook each hand as they exchanged polite introductions. Brad Stewart had short brown hair, navy eyes, and a stocky build. His wife Sarah, whose smile captivated Katie, had shoulder length blond hair, kind brown eyes, and wore a preppy, plaid sundress that Katie immediately coveted.

The plastic surgeon, Ryan Russell, was tall and thin with brown hair, brown eyes, and seemed quite a bit more reserved than Brad and Aidan. Penny Hall stood next to him, smiling politely. Her black pixie cut and dark eyes gave her a regal bearing. Katie thought, *She's definitely well-suited for Ryan, they both seem a little uptight. Or maybe they're just shy.*

Aidan addressed the group. "After you settle into your rooms, I thought we would hit the beach, and then grill something for dinner."

Sarah spoke first. "We'll take the third floor bedroom with the Jacuzzi tub on the balcony." She smiled at her husband, and it was obvious to Katie they were still in the newlywed stage. "I'm planning to rent jet skis this weekend, if anyone wants to join us."

Katie's face lit up and she looked at Aidan. "That sounds fun!"

"I'm going to show Katie the rest of the house, and then we'll meet you on the beach. Brad, do you mind putting some drinks on ice?" Aidan took Katie's hand and showed her the rest of the main level and lower level. There was a small theater room with leatherback chairs and a large screen television, and a large room containing a pool table and foosball table on the lower level. Aidan opened the glass sliders leading outside. Two large round glass tables with cushioned chairs sat under a covered patio with fireplace, built in television, and two grills. Just past the patio were a rectangular pool, separate Jacuzzi, and a pale yellow building trimmed in white serving as a tiki bar.

"A tiki bar! I love it!"

"It's fully stocked." Aidan pulled out a barstool for Katie and stepped inside. "What can I fix you *bella dama?*"

"I'd love something sweet, like a Bay Breeze, and a personal translator, please."

"Bay Breeze coming right up." Aidan winked.

"C'mon, what'd you say? You could be calling me an ugly pig for all I know." She watched him pour vodka over the ice, then add cranberry and pineapple juice.

"Hardly. I said you were beautiful." Aidan handed her the drink and lifted his glass. "To an amazing weekend."

Thirty-Two

"How did you and Aidan meet, Katie?" Sarah asked. Penny stopped peeling the cucumber and turned to wait for her answer.

"We met on the fishing pier. We were both taking pictures of egrets and bumped into each other." Katie took a long sip of wine, preparing for the twenty questions that were sure to follow.

"Go on. We're girls, we need details." Penny smiled.

"Well, we each assumed the other worked for the newspaper. I mean, who goes to the beach to take pictures of birds, right?" Katie chuckled, feeling like the two women were closing in on her. "I told him I was a nurse . . . he said he was a doctor . . . he walked me home, and then my grandmother . . ." Katie rolled her eyes, remembering the entire set up. That bit of information would *not* be shared with anyone. "My grandmother invited him in for dinner, and here we are."

"Agh! You're terrible with the details." Sarah groaned. "Tell us about your first date—or the moment you fell in love with him." She set her knife on the counter and picked up her glass of wine, settling in for a magnificent story.

Katie wasn't sure how to answer that. She wasn't in love with Aidan. Lust maybe, but not love. She decided to tell them about their first date, and was very descriptive about lunch and the lighthouse, hoping that would satiate them so they could move on to something else. "Okay, your turn. How did you two meet?" She listened as Sarah told about falling in love with Brad the first time she laid eyes on him. She was very animated. Katie wondered if she could actually talk without using her hands.

Penny's story was more interesting. She had visited Ryan's office for rhinoplasty after breaking her nose in a car accident. "We fell deeply in love, and I was certain we would marry. I don't know why he's dragging his feet. We've been together for four years, now."

Sarah laid her hand on Penny's shoulder. "Have you told him how you feel? Does he know how much you want to get married?"

"No, I don't want him to feel trapped, like I have a hidden agenda. I want him to *want* me for his wife."

"Oh, Pen, guys don't think like that. You must tell him how you feel. As far as he's concerned, you're happy with the way things are, and that's good enough for him." Sarah picked the knife back up and finished chopping the tomatoes.

"Steaks are ready, ladies," Brad called through the open sliding glass door into the kitchen.

Katie ate almost all of her beef tenderloin, it was tender and buttery. She was having the best time listening to the others share stories and jokes while sipping on Chardonnay. Sarah and Penny treated Katie like they had known her for years, and she slowly became more comfortable around them.

"We're hitting the hot tub. Goodnight, all." Brad stood and lifted Sarah over his shoulder, her laughter echoing through the house as he carried her off.

As if it were a manly competition, Ryan followed suit, taking Penny's hand. "I think we'll call it a night, too."

Aidan and Katie shared a nervous laugh as they sat at the table alone. "More wine?" he asked.

"No, thank you. I'm going to have trouble making it up the stairs as it is."

"Come here," Aidan said, pulling Katie onto his lap. He kissed her softly, tasting the sweet wine on her lips. "Let's get wet."

"What?"

"The hot tub." Aidan nodded in the direction of the steaming water next to the pool.

"Oh, okay, I just need to get my suit." Katie stood, holding onto the table to steady herself.

Aidan held her arm. "I don't think you can make it up the stairs. You don't need a suit."

"Yes—I—we do!" Katie stuttered.

"Let's be bad," he whispered, leaving a trail of goose bumps on Katie's neck where his lips had been.

Katie raised an eyebrow. "Okay," she answered. "But you're not getting me naked."

The combination of hot water and too much wine conspired to put Katie in an uninhibited frame of mind. "This feels amazing." She sat next to him, rested her head back, looking up at the star-filled sky. Aidan's unsolicited touch normally would have surprised her, but she didn't flinch. He pulled her onto his lap, wrapping her legs around his waist, so they were facing each other. He found the spot behind her ear that drove her wild. "Mmm, that feels good, too." Katie instinctively wrapped her arms around his neck and pressed her body into his.

Instead of kissing her, he softly bit down on her bottom lip. He traced over her lips with his thumb, and locked eyes with her as he moved down her neck. When he grazed over the fabric covering her nipple, Katie closed her eyes, relishing the pleasure of his touch.

"Look at me," he commanded as he slowly traveled down her body with his hands.

Desire swirled through her as she felt his arousal growing beneath her. Obeying his command, she kept her eyes locked with his and felt his hand dip between her legs. His touch overwhelmed her, causing her eyes to close as her head tilted back slightly. When he slid her panties to the side and his fingers found access to her most intimate area, she searched for something to cling to. Her hands traveled across his thighs, resting just above the knee. As the pleasure intensified, she gripped his legs firmly and moaned. Katie was caught up in the spell Aidan had cast over her, forgetting where she was, and enjoying his skilled hands as they left a burning trail of heat behind them. The enchantment was broken when she heard a noise in the distance and her body stiffened. She inhaled sharply and looked around.

"Relax, baby, just let go."

Katie shook her head. "I can't, not here."

"C'mon." He helped Katie out of the water, and paused while he looked at her exquisite body. She had curves in all the right places, and her body was fit and toned. Beads of water trailed down between her full breasts and flat stomach. Her white lace bra and panties had become transparent, leaving nothing to the imagination. Aidan inhaled sharply, feeling his body respond. Impulsively, he reached out and chased a bead of water down her stomach with his finger. After drying her off, he lifted her into his arms and carried her upstairs.

Katie's eyes were closed, and he hoped she hadn't fallen asleep. "Katie?" he whispered as he gently laid her on the bed.

"Mmm hmm," she replied sluggishly, a smile playing on her lips as she stretched her arms over her head.

"I'll be right back." Aidan hurried into the next room to get protection, and when he returned, Katie was sound asleep.

He sat on the bed next to her, shaking his head in disappointment. After a moment, he carefully removed Katie's damp bra and panties before sliding her under the covers.

Warm buttery sunlight filtered through the blinds into the bedroom. Katie snuggled deeper under the covers, wanting a few more minutes of sleep. When the silky sheets grazed her skin, she realized she was nude. Startled, she tried to remember what happened last night. She vaguely remembered getting into the hot tub with Aidan and being carried upstairs. Katie lay there frozen, afraid to move. *Where is he? Surely he's not the kind of guy to leave*

afterward. Maybe he didn't want this, and he's graciously slipped out before I woke up. We'll just pretend it never happened. Shit! Shit! Shit!

Katie heard a soft knock on her bedroom door. She pretended to slowly wake up when the smell of coffee entered the room along with Aidan. She studied his face, wondering if he would mention last night.

"Thank you," Katie said, taking the cup of coffee and enjoying a sip. He was not giving anything away, and the silence was unbearable. "Aidan," she said slowly, staring into her cup of coffee. "I had too much to drink last night . . . did we . . .?"

"Did we what?" he replied, a sarcastic smile spreading across his lips.

"You know, did we . . ." Katie struggled to find the right words as panic started to swell inside her.

"Of course we did. All night long! You're an animal," Aiden said, watching Katie's reaction.

She immediately turned crimson and buried her face under the blankets.

"I'm kidding. You fell asleep. I prefer my partners to be active participants." Aidan laughed as Katie pulled the blankets down from her face and let the panic slowly wash away. "But have I ever told you how cute you are when you're sleeping?"

Aidan waited on the balcony while Katie slipped on a T-shirt and shorts. The beach was deserted except for a few birds fishing for breakfast. "This is pure bliss." Katie said, taking a seat and listening to the waves.

"We can come here as often as you like. Dr. Yewell and I have been talking about adding another partner, so I'll have more time off."

"Really? So it's just the two of you in your practice now?"

"Mmm hmm." Aidan took a sip of coffee. "He has a family, so I've been taking the majority of patients." He paused and focused on Katie's lips as she blew the steam from her cup. "Katie, I know things are moving really fast, and as greedy as I am, I'll only take as much as you're ready to give."

Katie took a drink and looked out to sea. She physically wanted him as badly as he wanted her, yet something was holding her back. "So, what are the plans for today?"

"We can do whatever we like. Brad and Sarah want to go jet skiing. We can join them, or we can hang out on the beach, go horseback riding, fishing . . . you name it."

"Horseback riding? On the beach?" Katie's face lit up.

"Okay, that's what we'll do." Aidan took Katie's empty cup and set it on the small table. "Come, sit with me."

Katie hesitated a moment, convincing herself to move. *All right, Katie, let go.* She took a seat on Aidan's lap, trying to let herself enjoy his embrace. It was uncomfortable at first, trying to let go of the pain and push her memories back, but the longer he held her, the easier it was. Maybe she was stronger than she realized, and could get through all of the turmoil without counseling as Gram had suggested. It was a lot for one person—a broken heart, terrifying past, and pretending it didn't have a massive effect on her—but if she could live through it, she could definitely heal from it . . . one day.

"I'm going down for a refill, want more?" Aidan asked, picking up her mug.

"I'll come with you."

Katie stepped into the kitchen as she overheard Penny and Sarah talking.

"Do you think she's the kind of girl that would share details?" Sarah asked.

"No." Katie said, rounding the corner with a smirk for the two ladies sitting at the island on barstools. She wasn't sure what would be worse, telling them the truth, or letting them believe she and Aidan were intimate.

"Because I haven't seen Aidan smile like that in—" Sarah looked up as if she were counting. "Actually, I've never seen him smile like that. I don't know what you've done, but that man is crazy about you."

Her words washed over Katie, bringing warmth with them that had Katie standing a little taller.

"Just be prepared," Penny said. "You're going to piss off a lot of women."

"*Really?*" Katie feigned ignorance. She had seen the way the woman looked at him when she showed up for lunch. "I guess he *is* quite a catch." She glanced over at him while he talked to Brad and Ryan. His khaki board shorts sat low on his hips and the soft cotton T-shirt accentuated his slim waist and broad shoulders. She let her mind linger on the words he spoke in Spanish the day before, and how close she had come to giving him everything. Her competitive streak began to tug, convincing her to play her hand carefully from that point on. *Other women might be ogling him, but I'll make sure his eyes are focused on me.* Her mind traveled to the hot tub and how she melted beneath his touch.

"Yes, quite a catch indeed." Penny glanced in Aidan's direction, and then back at Katie. "How did you do it?"

"Hmm?" Katie said, distracted, as she sought refuge by searching the inside of the refrigerator.

"What are you looking for in there?" Sarah asked.

"Oh, I—uh, I was looking for creamer." Katie stuttered. She preferred her coffee black, but it was the first thing that came to mind.

"It's right here on the table with the sugar." Penny smirked. "You must not have slept much last night." She giggled.

Katie was sure her face revealed all of her secrets, but before she could speak Penny saved her. "Katie, you're going jet skiing with us, right?"

"If that's what Aidan wants to do." Katie poured the dreadful creamer into her coffee and swirled her spoon around, watching it transform her dark brew into the color of caramel.

"Aidan, we're taking Katie jet skiing with us. Are you boys up for the adventure, or would you rather stay here and watch *Days of Our Lives*?"

Sarah was a smart-ass, and Katie connected with her. She caught Aidan's eye as he walked over, wondering if he would speak up about the horseback riding. He leaned in and whispered in her ear. "We've got all day tomorrow for horseback riding, let's go jet skiing." Katie nodded her head and smiled brightly.

Jet skiing was exhilarating for Katie. She sped through the water, turning into the wave to get some air, and squealing with delight each time. She watched while Aidan stood up racing through the water, and without warning jerked the steering wheel to the right, causing his jet ski to do a perfect three-sixty.

After a full day out on the water, everyone agreed that a night out would be more enjoyable than staying in. Katie showered, taking extra care to make sure her legs were shaved smooth. She chose a pale blue halter dress that hugged her curves just right, making her feel sexy. She was putting her earrings in when she heard the soft knock.

"Come in."

"You look beautiful," Aidan said, watching her. He kissed her on the cheek and waited for her to finish getting ready.

"Thank you. I'm almost ready, just a little lip gloss."

They dined at a local seafood restaurant enjoying oysters, crab legs with drawn butter, and the continuous flow of Chardonnay and conversation. Katie hoped she would have a chance to spend more time with these people in the future, they were all so much fun to be around and she felt at ease in their presence. She watched each of them as they shared stories and laughter, and eventually let her mind wander to a future with Aidan.

After dinner everyone else retreated to their rooms. "Let's take a walk on the beach," Aidan said, taking Katie's hand and leading her through the gate. Only a crescent moon, along with the stars, lit the beach, making it difficult to see the path in front of them.

"It's a beautiful night." Katie observed, trying to make small talk.

"It is. Katie, what's on your mind?"

"Nothing, why?"

Aidan stopped and turned her to face him. "You've been distant tonight. What's going on?"

Katie stopped, unsure how to respond. Every word spoken to Aidan had to be planned. She couldn't give too much away. He knew she was still dealing with a broken heart, but he didn't know she was also trying to tackle feelings of shame and unworthiness. The whole thing was a train wreck. She needed to keep him at a distance to protect her heart, but at the same time his desire for her made her feel wanted and accepted. She was definitely attracted to his confidence, the way he took control of every situation, rendering a feeling of security. In her vulnerable state, she craved someone willing to lead and guide her.

He wasn't shy about expressing his hunger for her, but she constantly had to fight the demons telling her she was only a body being used for sex. No matter how many times she told herself she wasn't that girl from the past, she was a Yale graduate, her demons spoke louder. *Whore!* She shook her head, trying to push the condemning voice away. After a deep, cleansing breath, she donned the protective mask, and answered. "You know me, I was just taking it all in."

"Forgive me if I don't believe you. I think you're still thinking about him."

Katie's heart tightened, as if someone was physically squeezing it. She had thought about Branson, but he wasn't the strongest factor she'd been tormented with at dinner. Admitting to thinking about Branson was much easier than telling him the truth, so she titled her head to the side and shrugged. "I'm sorry, Aidan. I'm trying. I really am."

"I'm not going to push you into anything you're not ready for, Katie. Just relax, and have a good time."

"You're a good man, Aidan." She sighed.

"Someone's gotta be the good guy in your life, beautiful." He winked.

Katie wanted to scream. Every time they took one step forward, they took at least three back. It was like a maddening game of Chutes and Ladders. Aidan was older and wiser, but she was perfectly capable of taking control and changing her situation. Stepping closer, she wrapped her arms around his waist. "Kiss me."

Aidan gazed at her for a long time, trying to gauge her mood. She was as fickle as any girl he'd ever encountered, but he didn't want to miss an opportunity. They came together like a compelling force, each taking as much as they could get under the light of the full moon.

Aidan pulled away. "Come," he said, taking Katie's hand and leading her toward the house.

When they arrived, everyone was in the living room waiting for them. "There you are, we've been waiting. Girls versus guys in a game of Catch Phrase!" Sarah held the game in her hand and seemed eager to get started.

Katie excused herself to the bathroom, certain her cheeks were flushed, revealing their foiled plan to spend the night together. *It's a sign,* she thought.

Promises of lunch and shopping with Penny and Sarah filled Katie's mind as they drove back to the Outer Banks. Katie felt alive again and couldn't quit smiling. Although, she hated leaving the house on Cape Hatteras, she couldn't wait to see Gram and tell her all about the weekend.

Katie leaned against the front door as Aidan kissed her goodbye. Each time she pulled away to leave, he pulled her back in close.

"I wish you would just come home with me," he exhaled.

"You can't have *everything* you want, mister." Katie winked. She gave him one more kiss and slipped inside.

"Gram! Are you here?" Katie called out.

"Yes, dear. I'm in the kitchen."

Katie sat for hours sipping tea and telling Gram about the weekend. Her cheeks were sore from smiling so much. "I guess I haven't used these muscles in a while, they're actually aching." Katie giggled.

"I can't tell you how delighted I am to see you happy again. I was thinking about going back to Maine to check on the house. I feel okay leaving you now. Of course, you're welcome to come back with me if you like."

"No, I'd rather stay." Katie couldn't bear being that close to Branson, or taking a chance running into him.

A petite blonde with a heart-shaped face looked up from the nurses' station and greeted Katie with a smile. "Can I help you?"

"Hi, I'm Katie. I thought I would surprise Dr. Romero with lunch."

The lady raised one perfectly plucked eyebrow. "And you're Miss—?" she asked, elongating the word until Katie filled in the blank.

"Harrington."

"You can wait in his office. I'll let him know you're here."

Katie waited, feeling foolish for coming to the hospital without running it by Aidan first. He mentioned having a light day, so she thought he might like a surprise luncheon, but now she stood in his office, second-guessing herself.

Aidan's office was organized. She chuckled when she saw that his bookshelf was alphabetized. She ran her fingers along the book edges and pulled one out, flipping through the pages illustrating uncommon breaks and how to treat them. She swung around when she heard the door open behind her. Aidan looked more like a doctor in his lab coat, taming the rebel look he usually presented. "Hi!" Katie smiled. "I brought lunch."

"You should've called first. I don't have time today." Aidan took the book from Katie's hand and replaced it on the shelf.

Katie felt the air being sucked out of her lungs and she needed to get out of there. Leaving the lunch on his desk, she breezed past him and got on the elevator. Aidan was on her heels and slipped in before the doors closed.

"You're angry?"

"It won't happen again." Katie affirmed, trying to hide the embarrassment.

"I'll walk you to your car."

"No, I'm perfectly capable on my own." The statement held more than one meaning, and she hoped he had understood.

"Katie, let me explain," Aidan began. "It's been a—".

"Please, Aidan, can we talk about this later? I-I, just, later ... please."

Without looking back, Katie hurried to her car and drove away. She didn't let the tears flow until she was out of the parking lot and away from prying eyes. *What am I doing? I have no business playing this role.*

Thirty-Three

The porch light was out, making it hard for Katie to unlock the front door. Thankfully, she had left the lamp on in the living room, the warm glow inviting. She began to brew a pot of tea when she heard a knock at the door. Too late for a delivery, the only reasonable conclusion was one of the neighbors needing something.

She considered the possibility of teens playing a prank, but quickly erased that idea from her mind. Whoever was on the other side of the door was persistent, knocking without pause. Katie hurried to the foyer, rested her head against the door, and with a voice filled with hope asked, "Who is it?"

"It's me," Aidan answered.

Katie exhaled, her shoulders slumping in disappointment. After a moment of gathering herself, she unlocked the door and swung it open.

Aidan held a large bouquet of red roses. "May I come in?"

"You should've called first. I don't have time." Katie started to shut the door.

"Katie!" Aidan held the door open. "I'm sorry lunch didn't work out. Today was a horrible day and you caught me in the middle of a disaster." Aidan slowly stepped inside and shut the door. "One of the nurses made a terrible mistake with one of my patients. I fired her only minutes before you walked in, which left me short two nurses." Aidan stepped closer and ran his hand down Katie's arm as he spoke. *"Mi mujer hermosa de ojos verdes, me perdonas?"*

Katie raised an eyebrow and folded her arms. "Did you just call me a smart ass again?"

"No," Aidan laughed. "My beautiful, green-eyed lady, forgive me?"

Katie relaxed, feeling the tension from the day slowly leaving her body. She placed the roses in a vase filled with water. "I was just making some tea, would you like a cup?"

Aidan took Katie into his arms. "What I really need right now, is you."

Katie spent the morning on the beach, watching families play in the surf. Her attention was focused on a couple with their young son, lifting him up over each small wave near the shore. His giggles made Katie smile every time. She couldn't help coveting what they had. Her mind traveled into the forbidden abyss, and although she knew she shouldn't go there, the pull was too great to resist. As the lump grew larger in her throat, she wondered if her child had been a boy or a girl. For a moment she allowed herself the luxury of imagining Branson on one side and her on the other, lifting their son over the waves as he giggled with delight.

Tears slipped down her cheeks, breaking her daydream. After wiping them with the back of her hand, she gathered her things and walked back to the cottage.

After a long hot shower, she started to pick up her book and settle in for an hour of reading. She glanced at her phone to see a missed call and voice message.

"Hi beautiful, are you free for dinner tonight? Call me."

Katie looked herself over in the mirror once more before opening the front door. As Aidan stepped inside, Katie smiled. He was devastatingly handsome in khaki pants, and a black cotton shirt that enhanced his strong upper body and made his eyes look dangerous. Just what she needed to distract her from her self-deprecating thoughts.

"Ready to go? I'm starving." Aidan twirled her around slowly. "You look amazing. I like this dress."

"Good. I'll let you borrow it sometime." Katie grinned, feeling more like her old self, and started for the door.

"That mouth is going to get you in trouble." Aidan whirled her around to face him.

Katie's grin quickly faded when she saw the predatory look on his face. She backed up, feeling for the wall with her hand and leaned against it for support as her equilibrium was put to the test. Aidan's hands rested on either side of her head as he inched closer to her. She barely felt his lips brush against hers, teasing, seductively. Closing her eyes, she breathed him in. He wore just enough cologne to entice her senses—a masculine, earthy scent that must have contained just the right amount of pheromones to drive a woman wild.

"Shouldn't we go?" Katie said.

Aidan didn't answer, instead he pressed his lips to hers. He moved tenderly at first, and then the kiss became more powerful. His scent, combined with the way he was manipulating her mouth, was doing a great job of convincing her to skip their dinner plans. She felt his hand slide down her waist, around to her ass. A low groan escaped her mouth, vibrating across their tongues as they explored each other.

In one swift motion, Aidan lifted her up, wrapping her legs around him, and carried her to the bedroom. "Hold on to me," he commanded, crawling onto the bed. He guided Katie's head down onto the pillow and trailed kisses up her neck until he reached her ear. Pausing there, he let his soft breath linger on her ear, until she emitted the moan he'd been waiting for. "Tell me what you want."

Katie paused, not sure what he was asking, or how she should respond. No one had ever asked what she wanted. Wasn't it obvious?

"I want you, Katie, but I need to know you want this, too."

Unable to form the words, she nodded.

Aidan ran his hand up her smooth leg, watching her reaction as he teased her through lace panties. Feeling how turned on she was only intensified his hunger. Helping her sit up, he removed her dress before laying her back down. She worked the buttons of his shirt as he hovered over her, stealing a kiss as she finished the last one.

Katie's head was spinning with desire as Aidan removed her bra and traveled over her body with his hands and mouth. She reached for him, desperate to make him feel the way she did, but he held her arms overhead and grinned mischievously. Being restrained had a suffocating effect on Katie. She gasped for air and tried to wriggle loose. "No, stop." She began to cry. "Please, stop."

"What happened?" Aidan asked, wide-eyed. He released her arms and sat up, searching her face for answers.

Katie couldn't speak, she only shook her head as the hot tears streamed down the sides of her face into her hair. When she finally settled down enough, she tried to explain in a shaky, high-pitched voice that was barely audible.

"I—I'm sorry, I don't know w—why I'm crying." She turned her head into the pillow. "I wanted this to happen—I—I really did." Her body began to shake as her crying turned to sobs. "I told you . . . I'll—I'll always be broken."

Aidan lifted her into his arms and held her trembling body against his chest. "Shh, you're not broken." He gently stroked her hair as she wept, and talked in a soothing voice until she tapered off and finally stopped crying.

"Well," Katie wiped her tear-stained cheeks with the back of her hands and scooted to the edge of the bed. "That's a story for your buddies. You can tell them about the lunatic you were dating." Not able to look him in the eyes, she pulled her knees to her chest and hugged her legs.

"*Were* dating?"

"Please don't try to be a hero, Aidan—just go. You deserve a whole person, not someone you have to piece together with super glue. I'm sick of being the injured party and I know you're sick of being the healer. "

"Actually, I spent most of my adult life studying how to heal, so . . ." he trailed off, not sure how to fix this situation. Women had always been easy to read and he never had to put much effort into wooing them to bed. Katie was the exception. "C'mon, I think we could both use a stiff drink."

Katie pulled her robe on and followed Aidan to the kitchen, watching as he poured two fingers of Dewar's into each glass. "Thank you," Katie said, "for the scotch, and for being such a wonderful man."

Aidan tapped his glass against hers, the sound of the ice cubes clinking against each other echoing through the small kitchen. "You're worth waiting for." *Although I don't think I can handle another episode like that.*

Katie finished her drink and asked for a refill. She felt foolish about what had happened, and her body was still swirling with a mix of desire, heartache, and shame.

Aidan topped off her glass, and then his own. "Know, that when I ask this, it's because I care for you, Katie." He swirled the liquid around in his cup. "Are you going to let that asshole destroy you?"

"Excuse me?" Katie gripped her glass so tightly, she feared it would shatter.

"When's the last time you went for a run, or played tennis? Have you allowed yourself to do any of the things you once enjoyed, or are you avoiding everything that might remind you of him? I know he's the reason you cringed at the mint chocolate chip ice cream. It's his favorite, isn't it?"

Katie wiped the tears with the back of her hand. She was surprised he knew so much. Had she really been that transparent? At least he didn't know the entire truth. "I haven't avoided everything. He breathes, and I'm still taking in oxygen." She tried to laugh, hoping to cease the conversation before it got any deeper, but it got stuck in her throat, mimicking a sob.

"I'm sorry," he said, pulling her into his arms. "Maybe I'm wrong in rushing you, but I believe you need someone who will shoot straight with you. You're a strong, capable woman, and you need to forget about that jerk so you can start enjoying life again."

Katie's head was spinning. She drew in a deep breath, and before she could filter her thoughts they came out of her mouth. "Do you think the Stepford Wives facility is still in operation? Maybe you can order up your perfect mate there!"

Aidan released her and stepped back. "What are you talking about? I don't want to mold you into something you're not. I just want to help you heal." He blew out his breath and shook his head. "Tell me what to do, Katie."

Of course he didn't know what she was talking about, and he never would. Emotion almost got the best of her, pushing her to tell him everything, but thankfully she hadn't. "When I figure it out, I'll let you know," she said, exhaustion settling into her bones. "Maybe we should call it a night?"

"Yes, of course. Good night, Katie." He kissed her cheek, a sweet gesture, presenting an undertone of friendship rather than romance.

Katie was pleased to have anything after the night she'd offered him. "Good night, Aidan."

Standing alone, Katie pondered what had just taken place. After another glass of scotch, she realized everything he said was true. She used to be strong and confident. If she could just heal her stubborn broken heart, and come to terms with her past, or at least block it from her memory again, then she could be everything he needed.

Katie picked up the phone and started to dial Maggie. She longed to talk to her best friend. She was desperate to hear her voice, get her advice on Aidan . . . ask about Branson. When she realized how late it was, she set the phone down and paced the room. As fatigued as her body felt from the crying jag, a chaotic restlessness possessed her. It was too late to go out or call anyone, and there was nothing on television. Without thinking it through, she picked up the phone and dialed Aidan's number.

Crap, what am I doing? She was ready to hang up before he answered, but it was too late.

"Hello?"

"It's me." Katie grimaced.

"I know."

"I'm sorry about tonight."

Aidan paused, searching for the right words. "I'm just ready for you . . . for *us* to move on."

Two cups of coffee and a long soak in the tub erased most of Katie's headache. As the storm clouds moved in, she was happy for a reprieve from the sun and an excuse to stay inside finishing her book. Stuck on the same paragraph, reading it six times in a row, she picked up the phone and dialed Maggie.

"Maggie," Katie sighed. The comforting yet upbeat sound of her best friend's voice pricked at her heart and filled her eyes with tears.

"Katie? What the hell? Where have you been and why haven't you called? Are you okay?"

"I'm fine. It's so good to hear your voice."

"Answer me, Katie. Why haven't you called me?"

"I couldn't, Maggie. You're my best friend, and I trust you completely, I just couldn't talk about what happened."

"Are you ready to talk about it now? What did he do to hurt you so much, Katie?"

"I don't want to talk about . . . *him*, okay? We can talk about anything and everything else, just not him."

"Okay, but you should know—"

"Please, Mags. I can't."

"Sure, okay. Talk. Tell me everything, and don't leave a single detail out."

"I've met someone." Katie exhaled, a mix of anxiety and excitement in her voice. "And I need your advice."

"Are you serious?" Maggie's voice raised an octave. She cleared her throat before continuing. "Are you sure you're not rushing into something? Or is this a rebound-type-thing? I've heard those are good and necessary, as long as you know your boundaries."

Katie tapped her fingers along the edge of the chair as her friend ranted. "I'm not sure of anything. All I know is he's mysterious, exciting, sexy as hell, and he's trying to help my heart heal." She took a deep breath in, filling her lungs for another round. "He's a little older, and confident . . ."

"Oh my God, Katie, go on."

"He's an orthopedic surgeon," Katie was careful not to give her location away in case a certain someone decided to try and reach her. "For a hospital here in town. He's originally from Argentina—I wish you could hear his voice."

"He sounds like a dream. So what do you need my advice about?"

"I don't know. He makes me feel things I'm not . . . familiar with. I look forward to being with him, he excites me, but—"

"He's not Branson?"

Katie flinched. "No . . . he's not. He's the exact opposite."

"But it sounds like you're into him?"

"Yeah, I'm just having a hard time letting go."

A dull ache radiated through Katie. She pulled her knees to her chest and hugged an arm around her legs. She needed to turn her focus back to Aidan before she was in fetal position on the floor, sobbing. Swallowing the lump in her throat, she shook her head, trying to erase the thought of Branson's intoxicating blue eyes. "Aidan makes me laugh. He brings me flowers and he took me to an art show." Katie sighed, happiness eating away at the sorrow.

"I'm happy for you, Katie. I don't understand what's happened or why, but I'm on your side."

"Thanks, Mags. I can't tell you how I've missed talking to you."

"Me, too. Listen, Katie, you should know, Bran—"

"No! Please, Maggie, I can't," Katie groaned. "It's too painful." She was sure Maggie had news of Branson moving on with another woman, or moving away. Whatever it was, just the mention of his name sent a searing pain through her chest. "How's your job? Tell me all about Gavin."

Katie felt a lot better after talking to Maggie. She sounded happy and blissfully in love. Although she was still confused about Aidan, Maggie had convinced her to follow her instincts and live on the edge for once. Katie had missed out on so much living during their high school and college years, there was nothing wrong with playing catch up.

It happened after dinner at Owen's—a romantic upscale restaurant in Nag's Head. Aidan ordered filet and lobster tail while Katie enjoyed scallops marinated in tequila, sugarcane, and drizzled with Key lime vinaigrette.

"Let's get dessert to go and watch the sunset," Aidan suggested.

Katie was delighted things were going so well. She could feel herself healing as she obeyed the good doctor's orders and had started running again. Although Aidan wasn't the best tennis player, he was able to volley back and forth with her, reviving her passion for the game.

Aidan laid a blanket on the sand and set the slice of Key lime pie between them. As the sun descended behind a few wispy clouds, swirling muted pastels across the sky, Katie felt it. She had experienced the lustful stirrings every time Aidan had kissed her, but laying back against him with his strong arms enveloping her in warmth and safety brought a whole new feeling. She decided Maggie was right, she needed to let go of the past and move forward with him. A thrill danced along her spine as she felt the freedom of her decision.

Aidan kissed the tender area inside of her wrist before looking into her eyes. "Spend the weekend with me in Cape Hatteras."

"Will Sarah and Penny be there?"

"No, just the two of us."

A mixture of trepidation and excitement taunted her senses. *Dive in, Katie.* "Okay, I'll go."

On Thursday, the beach behind Aidan's house was crowded with a group playing volleyball and several twenty-something's enjoying beer and loud music. Aidan encouraged Katie to enjoy the sun while he quickly made rounds at the hospital. He laid a towel over the lounge chair behind the house and told her to make herself at home. "I won't be long. I'll pick up lunch for us on the way home."

Katie lay there, watching the volleyball game with the drink Aidan had made for her. It wasn't the best piná colada she ever had, but it would do. Katie sipped the concoction, watching the team on the left dominate and finally win the game.

Feeling relaxed and a bit uninhibited, Katie rolled over onto her stomach and untied her bikini top. She dozed off and on as the sun blissfully warmed and bronzed her skin. She awoke with a start when she felt someone stroking her hair. Careful not to expose herself, she turned her head. "Oh, hi. You're back earlier than I expected." Katie smiled and tied her top before sitting up.

"Come inside. I brought lunch." Aidan wrapped the towel around her, protectively covering her. "When I think about those men ogling my girl . . . fantasizing about your naked body . . ."

Katie giggled and bumped his hip with her own. "You're silly. No one saw anything except a bare back."

"Maybe, but they envisioned more."

"Well, I can't be held responsible for that. Bikinis don't leave much to the imagination. Would you have me wear a turtleneck next time?"

"Would you?" He laughed.

"I have to admit, I like your jealous streak." She winked. "What would you like to drink?"

"Water, please."

Katie brought two water bottles to the table and sat down. She felt the beginnings of a headache, and tried to stifle it by rubbing her temples.

"Aren't you hungry?" Aidan asked, watching Katie pick at her salad with her fork.

"I've got a terrible headache. I'd really just like to take a bath and climb into bed."

"I'll run a bubble bath for you and get some Motrin." Aidan started to rise from the table.

"I'd like to go back to my place, change into my pajamas." Whether it was the sun or the crappy piná colada Katie's head was pounding and the only remedy for this kind of throbbing was sleep.

Aidan drove Katie home and walked her inside. He found some Motrin and brought it to her with a glass of water.

"Thank you. I think I'm going to skip the bath and climb right into bed."

Aidan kissed her on the forehead. "Do you want me to stay?"

"Thank you, but I'll be okay. I just need to sleep this one off."

"I'll pick you up tomorrow. I'm doing rounds early, so I should be here around noon."

"Mmm hmm." Katie nodded. "Can't wait." Every word spoken sent her heartbeat into her ears.

Aidan helped her out of her clothes and into bed, covering her up. As he turned to leave, he flipped the light switch off. "I'll lock the door behind me. Goodnight." He opened the front door to leave, but changed his mind and locked the door. He went into the kitchen, ran a washcloth under cold water, and placed it on Katie's forehead. Aidan removed his shoes and pants and slipped into the bed next to her.

"What are you doing?"

"I'll sleep here tonight. If you need anything, just ask."

Thirty-Four

After Branson learned that Katie had gone away for the summer, he concocted a plan. In the dead of night he came back to the Harrington home and searched for the hidden key he watched Katie use and put back so many times. Amongst the landscape rocks along the walkway, edging the roses, was a hide-a-key rock. Everything about the rock mimicked the others, and to the naked eye, no one would know it was a fake. He counted back from the front porch to the third rock on the left, and lifted it up. *Thank God!* The key was there.

Entering the Harrington home while they were gone felt wrong and intrusive, but he needed answers. The house wasn't completely dark as lamps set on timers illuminated the living room and one of the guest bedrooms. He searched the house for any clue of where they might have gone, starting with Katie's room. For a few moments, he sat on the edge of her bed, holding a picture of the two of them. It was the day they got engaged. Katie had insisted on having Gram take their picture in the exact spot by the cliff. Her arms were wrapped around this neck as they gazed into each other's eyes. The smile on her face revealed everything. She was insurmountably happy and in love.

Branson set the picture down and searched her room for any clues to where she might be. An unsent note to Maggie, a journal entry, or a receipt left behind. Nothing was found, except painful memories of how happy they once were. Next, he swept through the office, methodically checking each piece of paper and replacing everything exactly the way he found it.

The last room he checked was the kitchen. A small junk drawer containing pens, a calculator, roll of Scotch tape, and an envelope full of receipts was searched thoroughly, but offered no leads. Branson plopped into one of the barstools and leaned over, resting his head on the granite countertop. *Damn! Where are you, Katie?* Tapping his fingers along the hard stone, he tried to think of what he missed. Traveling back to the last vacation he took with his parents, he thought of their routine. *Packing list, airline tickets, mail . . . no, they always stopped the mail. Lamps on a timer, hire one of the neighbor kids to take care of the plants . . . emergency numbers! Gram must have left an emergency number for the caretaker I spoke to.* He walked to the far side of the kitchen, to the built in desk, and glanced at the contents surrounding the phone. "Yes!" he exclaimed, finding a pad of paper with emergency numbers listed.

Finding a scrap piece of paper, he jotted all three numbers down and made sure everything was back in its place. It was late, and he'd have to wait until morning to call, but at least he had hope to help him get through the night. Before he reached the front door, he dialed the first number. "Hello?"

"I'm sorry to disturb you at this hour, but I need to reach the Harringtons."

The call was a dead end as the neighbor didn't have any details of their travel plans, their only job was to watch the home from a distance and be willing to call authorities if a water line broke, or someone tried to burglarize the place.

The second number he dialed appeared to be a cell phone. Branson's heart beat against his chest, not knowing if Gram or Katie would answer. Instead a man answered.

"Hello?"

Branson's throat constricted and he remained silent.

"Hello? Is anyone there?"

"Yes," He cleared his throat. "My name is Branson Stone. I'm looking for someone and I thought you might—I found your number and I wonder if you know the Harringtons?"

"What's your concern with them?"

"I'm Katie Harrington's fiancé and I need to find her. Please, I know you don't know me, but I'm in love with her and I need to find her. If you know where she is, I'm begging you to tell me."

"Are you in York?"

"Yes."

"Meet me at the Maine Diner in twenty minutes."

Branson entered the diner and found a booth by the window. The place was unusually crowded for ten o'clock at night.

"What can I get for ya?" a waitress asked, chewing her gum like it was trying to get away from her.

"I'll have a cup of coffee, black."

Branson sipped the coffee and waited for the faceless, nameless stranger. He looked around the noisy diner and watched waitresses in matching T-shirts and aprons rush around delivering food and refilling drinks. He wondered how the man he talked to would recognize him. He wasn't the only lone stranger in the diner. Would he go table to table asking?

The bell above the entrance notified him of an approaching customer. A man with salt and pepper hair walked through the door, bringing a gust of wind in with him, and approached the table.

"Branson, I'm Pete." He took a seat across from Branson. "I'm an old friend of the family. I can help you find Katie."

"Old friend of the family" . . . that explains how he knows me. He must've seen pictures. Why haven't I seen or heard of him before? "I'm sorry, have we met before?"

"No, but I know who you are."

The tone in his voice and the darkness in his demeanor demanded respect. Branson didn't care who he was, or why he hadn't heard of him before. This man had answers that he needed, and he'd do whatever it took to get them. He could ask questions another time. "Thank you for agreeing to meet me. I've been going out of my mind. I've called Katie's cell, and the house—I know she's angry—but disappearing is extreme."

The waitress returned, still working on her wad of gum. "What'll it be, hon?"

Pete waved his hand, informing her he wasn't interested in anything on the menu, or her presence. Somehow, the way he waved her off didn't come off as rude, but the directive was made, understood, and followed.

"What are your intentions when you do find her?" Pete asked.

"To tell her that I love her." Branson ran his hand through his hair, his nerves were frazzled. "And I'm sorry."

Pete chose his words carefully. "Like I said, I'm an old friend of the family. Elizabeth and I go way back. I care for her deeply, and I know that she's doing what she thinks is best for Katie. However . . . I disagree. This is the second time she's tried to control two people in love, and I'd like to make sure this time turns out for the better."

Branson watched Pete's face soften as he talked about Elizabeth. It wasn't hard to figure out that the first incident he was referring to was between the two of them. "Thank you."

"Elizabeth and Katie are staying at my cottage on the Outer Banks." He slid a piece of paper across the table. "Here's the address. I expect you to do right by Katie. You made a mistake letting her go. Don't make it again." His eyes darkened as he gave the warning and Branson knew he would never want Pete on his bad side.

"I won't." He picked up the paper and studied it before shutting his fingers around it.

The smell of freshly brewed coffee drifted through the cottage and into the bedroom where Katie was enjoying the most restful sleep she'd had in weeks. She felt the pull and stretch of each muscle as she pointed her toes and stretched her arms overhead. After slipping into her robe, she ran her fingers through her hair—trying to tame the bed head—and stepped into the kitchen.

Aidan was over the stove, flipping pancakes. "Good morning," Katie whispered, her voice groggy.

"Good morning, sleepy head." Aidan handed her a mug of coffee. "Hungry?"

Katie nodded as she sipped the rich brew that promised to bring life to her fatigued body. "What time is it?"

"Eight o'clock."

"Really? I usually don't sleep that late. Don't you have rounds this morning?"

"I did, but I got it covered." He set a plate of pancakes in front of Katie and sat across from her at the small, round kitchen table. "How's your head?"

"I feel great. Thank you for taking care of me." Katie cut into her pancakes and took an oversized bite. She could only get halfway through them before she was full. Relaxing back into her seat, she sipped her coffee and watched Aidan. He was meticulous when he ate, cutting each forkful and then setting his knife down on the side of his plate while he chewed.

"I've got big plans for us this weekend." He flashed that cocky smile that was quickly becoming Katie's undoing.

"Oh?"

"Pack a bag and be ready in a couple of hours."

Thirty-Five

A new sensation distracted Katie's racing heartbeat as they approached the beach house in Cape Hatteras. She gazed at Aidan's right leg, his muscles flexing as he took his foot off the gas pedal and switched to the brake. Her eyes shifted up, noticing his hand as he shifted into a lower gear, slowing the car and eventually coming to a stop. She thought about spending the weekend in the amazing beach house with him, no distractions, no worries about prying eyes or knowing smirks. This new feeling wasn't the usual fear and uncertainty, it was a feeling of anticipation and possibility. Thoughts of his hands roaming over her body in the hot tub sent a warmth through her body that landed on her cheeks, threatening to give her thoughts away.

Aidan caught a glimpse of Katie, who seemed to be deep in thought. He saw the heat behind her eyes and a jolt of electricity shot through him. Nothing would stand in his way of having her this weekend. He was finally going to make sure she knew who she belonged with. After putting the car in park, he turned off the engine, and looked at Katie. "Ready?" The question held more than one meaning.

Katie wasn't sure who made the first move, but as soon as they stepped through the front door, they came together in a wild, primal haste. Aidan dropped the bags and pulled Katie with him as he shut the door, never losing contact with her mouth. She groaned when he pushed her up against the wall, almost knocking the breath out of her.

Katie cradled his face in her hands as they kissed. She pulled away when she saw movement in the kitchen. She froze.

"What is it?" Aidan asked, pulling his shirt down off of his face so he could see. As soon as the words left his mouth, he knew what Katie was looking at.

"Dammit, Maria!" he said under his breath, before turning to face her in the kitchen. The housekeeper was in her mid-fifties. She had a kind face and dark brown eyes that matched her hair color. She was as big around as she was tall, and it was obvious she didn't know what to do in this situation.

"Almost finished?"

"Yes, sir," she answered. "I just finished stocking the fridge. I'll be on my way now." She grabbed her purse and ducked out, avoiding eye contact.

Aidan rested his forehead against Katie's, hoping the moment wasn't completely lost. He chuckled and shook his head slightly. He took her hand in his, leading her toward the kitchen. "How about a drink?"

"Yes! Can we take them out to the beach?"

Aidan whirled a blender full of frozen mango daiquiris and divided the mix into two turquoise cups. "Beach friendly, and festive." He donned each with an umbrella straw and handed one to Katie.

"Ah," Katie sighed. "I could get used to this. Relaxing on the beach, watching the waves roll in and out. The sun warming my shoulders as I sip this delicious frozen concoction. All we need is Bob Marley."

"I've got some of his music on my phone . . ."

"No, now that I think about it, I like the sound of the ocean best." Katie covered her mouth as a yawn escaped. "Sorry."

"Are you tired?"

"Not tired, just sleepy. After effects of that massive headache last night, I guess?"

"I didn't have anything planned for this evening. How does a movie on the couch sound?"

"That sounds so good to me."

Moments later, Katie was in a sweat shirt and shorts, ready to cuddle up on the couch. She was in charge of picking the movie while Aidan prepared popcorn. After slipping *Skyfall* into the DVD player, Katie pulled a blanket up over her legs, and rested her head on Aidan's shoulder. She closed her eyes, for just a moment, to relieve the heaviness. Soon she experienced the sensation of floating and lifted her lids, peeking out through her lashes. "What? Where are we going?" she asked, realizing she was in Aidan's arms, traveling up the stairs.

"You fell asleep. I thought you'd be more comfortable in bed."

"No, I'm awake." She yawned, unable to open her eyes fully.

Aidan balanced her in his arms carefully, while working the comforter down with one hand. He laid her on the bed, covered her, and whispered good night.

Katie gripped the hem of his shirt as he turned to walk away. "Stay."

Sounds of grunting and heavy breathing reverberated through Katie's ears. The smell of cigarette smoke and cheap beer assaulted her senses, causing her skin to pebble with goose bumps. She wriggled out of someone's grip and started running down a damp, asphalt road. Her legs were so heavy, she had to grip her pant legs in each hand and make them move, as a puppeteer commanding the movements of his wooden doll.

Tripping over a pothole, she fell. The pavement came up to meet her before she could release her pants and brace herself for the fall. She felt the warm blood trickle down her chin before her nerve endings sent the message of pain to her brain. Pushing up onto her hands and knees, she reached for her busted chin to assess the damage. She pressed two fingers gently against her flesh, now slick with blood and peppered with bits of dirt and gravel.

The crescent moon offered little help guiding her path. She stood, looking down the road in front and behind her. There was no light, no sign of life, and nothing to signal the right path. She had to make a choice. Turn back or go forward. Neither seemed promising, and her body shook with fear. Her senses were heightened as she heard every noise coming from the woods surrounding her. Crickets played music together in tune, frogs cleared their throats, and owls delivered haunting questions that echoed through the air. The air was as thick as pudding, and Katie found it difficult to breathe. The moisture tickled her skin as it settled on her bare arms in a fine mist.

Finally choosing to go forward down the road, Katie took a step. Each step was a chore as coaxed her feet to lift off of the pavement and step forward. Dark figures began stepping out of the woods coming toward her. She begged her feet to move faster . . . to run from the demons trying to capture her. When they surrounded her, hands grabbing at her shirt, arms, and hair, she screamed. Blackness surrounded her like a fog. Flowing black material swooped in all around her, covering her, touching her, and grabbing at her. She felt their fingers on her, but no flesh was visible, only shadows and fabric. They were trying to suffocate her.

"Don't touch me!" she screamed. "Stop! Don't touch me!"

"Wake up." She heard a voice in the distance. It was pulling her, commanding her to take control of the nightmare, and wake up. *"Wake up, Katie."*

Opening her eyes, she tried to focus on her surroundings. The dark figure was there, in reality. Or was she still dreaming? He was too close to her, looming over her, ready to attack. "Don't touch me!" She flailed her arms, striking his chest.

"Katie! Wake up. It's me, Aidan."

"What?" She sat up, looking around the room, and then back to him. "Where am I?"

"We're at the house in the Outer Banks. You were having a nightmare."

Warm tears spilled down her cheeks. "Another nightmare? Oh, I'm so sorry."

"Another? Do you have them often?"

Katie tried to catch her breath and settle her emotions before she gave away too much. She racked her brain, wondering if she'd said anything during the bad dream. "Did I say anything in my sleep?"

"You were screaming, 'don't touch me.'" He wiped a tear traveling down her cheek. "How often do you have nightmares, Katie?"

She sighed, not wanting to have this conversation with him. He was her fresh start, her chance to keep the secrets of her past safely buried forever. If she told him the truth behind her nightmares, he'd drop her in a heartbeat. Worse than that, he'd look at her with the same expression Branson had. "I'm sorry, Aidan. It's the scary movies. I just can't handle them. I've been plagued my entire life with nightmares after seeing something frightening. Next time I'll remember to pick a comedy."

"We watched *Skyfall*," he said, confused. "James Bond . . . there wasn't anything scary in the movie. Besides, you fell asleep during the opening scene." He lifted her chin with his forefinger and thumb, looking into her eyes for answers. "Tell me what's really going on."

Lying wasn't one of her gifts, and she scrambled, trying to think of something. It wasn't fair to blame everything on her breakup, but it was the only thing she could think of on the fly. "It's because of . . . you know . . . I've been having the nightmares since . . ."

"The breakup?"

Katie nodded. She hadn't had to tell another lie after all, Aidan filled in the blanks for her. He pulled her into his arms, stroking her hair like Gram used to do. When her body finished trembling, and the flow of tears came to a halt, he lay down and held her until they both drifted to sleep.

Thirty-Six

"Are you up for an adventure?" Aidan asked as they finished an early dinner of arugula topped with pear, asiago cheese, walnuts, and thinly sliced steak.

"Sure, what've you got in mind?"

"You'll see. Yes or no? Once you commit, there's no backing out." He threw her a wicked grin, enticing her daring side.

Katie was intrigued. What could he offer that would be too frightening to go through with? She thought of the possibilities. Swimming with sharks would be scary, but thrilling. A night of karaoke didn't sound fun as she couldn't carry a tune, but if liquor was involved, she'd get through it. At this point in her life, the only thing that terrified her was cats and experiencing the pain of a broken heart again. The latter could easily be crossed out, as she would never fall so deeply in love again. A wall had been erected, fortified with rebar, and filled with concrete. She was perfectly content with what she and Aidan had—lust, intrigue, and *their* version of love, which was more of a friendship with benefits. Well, they didn't share the benefits part of the equation . . . yet.

"I'm in," she answered confidently. "No matter what."

Aidan took her hand and led her to the garage. When he opened the door, she saw the motorcycle. "Wow." She exaggerated the word. "What kind of bike is that?"

"Harley Davidson, Fat Boy. Have you ever ridden?" he inquired, pride evident in his voice as he ogled the bike.

"No." Katie circled the bike, afraid to touch it. The gas tank and fenders were the color of merlot, and the sleek black leather seat sat atop the shiny chrome workings of the engine, exhaust, and whatever else was needed to make it run.

Aidan handed her a helmet and helped her get it fastened. After sliding his own on, he straddled the bike and waited for her.

Katie's eyes traveled over the bike and then to Aidan. He looked like a biker—dangerous and masculine. A wave of distrust washed over her and she began to chicken out. She imagined watching the pavement come up to meet her, the pain that would sear through her as the road cut into her flesh, leaving horrific scars and broken bones. She remembered the feeling of her mangled chin from last night's dream and shivered.

"Are you afraid?" Aidan taunted.

"No!" She lied. The only thing worse than road rash was letting him know she was scared. She slung her leg over the bike and slid in behind him, wrapping her arms tightly around his waist.

"I haven't even started the engine." He laughed, enjoying her failed attempt to hide her timidity.

The engine came to a roar, startling Katie as she squeezed around his waist again. He slowly pulled out of the garage onto the driveway and waited for the door to close.

"Hold on tight," Aidan warned before barreling out of the driveway onto the empty road.

Katie made sure every part of her body was clinging to him as he sped down the road. With the wind against her skin, the landscape speeding past her, and the roar of the engine, her heart raced with a mix of fear and adrenaline. As they traveled further down the road, her body calmed and she began to trust his ability to ride. She concentrated on the way his body felt against hers. Focusing on the specific pressure points—his toned abs beneath her arms, where her knees hugged into his thighs, and his strong back against her chest.

Aidan traveled down NC-12 and turned around in the Hatteras Landing Shopping Center. The ride back was more leisurely as he took the scenic route. He enjoyed the sensation of Katie pressed tightly against him on the back of the bike. She was dependent on him for her security and the feeling was invigorating. When they returned he pulled into the garage and shut off the engine. Before he could ask what she thought of the ride, she climbed off and removed her helmet.

"That was freaking awesome!" Katie exclaimed. She set her helmet on the shelf and walked back to Aidan, still sitting on the bike. "Let's go again tomorrow! Can we?"

"Sure." Aidan put his helmet away and led Katie to the kitchen. He poured two glasses of Pinot Grigio and grabbed a blanket out of the linen closet. "Let's catch the sunset."

They walked hand in hand along the sandy path leading to the beach. Once a perfect spot was settled on, Katie spread the blanket on the sand, sat down, and took her glass of wine. They watched as bold shades of red, orange, and purple were painted across the sky, eventually becoming muted as the sun sank lower and lower. Just before the large orange ball melted into the sea, Aidan lifted his glass for a toast.

"To an unforgettable weekend."

Katie clinked her glass against his and swallowed the last bit of wine. The weekend hadn't started out as she planned, but they had two more nights in the house, and after the motorcycle ride, she had high hopes for it getting better. Aidan jogged back to the house and came back with the bottle of wine. He refilled Katie's glass, and then his own. When she was halfway through the second glass, he encouraged her to finish it. Aidan set the glasses in the sand and pulled Katie onto his lap facing him, wrapping her legs around his waist. He took her chin in his hand and gazed into her eyes for a moment before kissing her.

With arms wrapped around his neck, Katie enjoyed the kiss until he started to remove her T-shirt. "Whoa, what are you doing?" She quickly pulled her shirt back down.

"We're alone," he assured, and pulled her in for another kiss, while he slid the shirt up and over her head.

"What if someone sees us?" Katie whispered, her heart beating against her chest.

"It's dark." He lifted his own shirt over his head and tossed it aside before traveling over her breasts, kneading each one as their kiss became more ardent.

"Take off your shorts," he commanded, rolling her off of his lap.

Katie had never been modest . . . until now. She felt like a schoolgirl sneaking around. At the same time, she felt alive . . . and hungry for his touch. "Can't we move this inside?"

Without saying a word, he picked up the glasses. Katie's shirt was already back on when she picked up the blanket, shaking the sand off. With a hurried pace, they made it through the glass sliders and dropped off the items from the beach.

Aidan took her hand in his and led her upstairs, shutting the bedroom door behind them. Resting his arms on either side of her head, he locked her in place against the wall. He gazed at her for a long time, enjoying watching her squirm impatiently. Her breathing became shallow, causing her chest to rise and fall in a chaotic rhythm. His patience was replaced with an untamed ferocity. His plan to linger on her, taking his time to tease her until she was ready to explode was fading. He fought for the control he was on the verge of losing, when she focused on his lips.

Leaning into her, he skimmed his thumb across her bottom lip, watching her mouth part slightly. Inches from her face, his mouth brushed against hers. Katie arched her back, pushing herself off the wall, pressing against his body. Her hands came up to feel his chest, but Aidan grabbed her wrists before she was able to touch him, and placed them on the wall above her head.

A soft moan slipped from her mouth when he pressed his body into hers so she could feel his excitement.

"Tell me what you want."

"You," Katie pleaded. "I want you, Aidan."

With his free hand he swept her hair around to the side, exposing her neck. His hot breath tickled and burned her skin. She angled her head to the side, granting him more access. He nibbled on her earlobe, and then trailed down her neck with his tongue, sending ripples of desire through her.

His mouth never broke contact with her flesh as he worked his way up to her mouth. She was lost in his kiss, his scent, his bold confidence. She pulled back slightly, searching his face. Her mind was flooded with things she wanted to say—things she needed him to understand before they took this step. But with his mouth sealed over hers, and his tongue mingling with hers in a heated frenzy, she couldn't pull away, or form words.

Aidan gripped the hem of Katie's shirt and lifted it over her head, tossing it aside before removing her bra and traveling over her breasts. He unbuttoned her shorts, letting them slide to the floor, and waited for her to step around them.

She ran her hands over his bare chest, framing his outline as she took him in with her eyes. Her fingers gently glided down his abdomen to his khaki cargo shorts, and unfastened the button and zipper. Carefully, she moved the fabric over him, until they dropped to the floor. Her breath hitched when she realized he wasn't wearing anything under the shorts.

Aidan's strong hands rested on her hips for a moment before sliding up, following the curve of her waist, and over each breast. Her soft moan was the invitation he needed as he lifted her into his arms and carried her to the bed.

Katie swept her hair up onto the pillow as Aidan gently laid her down. The way he looked at her with intense black eyes and a slight knowing grin sent a surge of fear through her veins. Her body tensed, trying to push back the memories that now haunted her.

"Are you okay?"

"Mmm hmm," she answered, keeping her eyes closed so he wouldn't see the lie behind them. "Wait." She laid a hand on his chest, pushing him back far enough to look into his eyes.

"You can trust me, Katie."

His eyes softened and Katie tried to relax, realizing he wasn't the reason for her nightmares. He knew nothing of her past, and wasn't treating her as if he had any clue. "I know," she said, sliding her hand around the back of his head and pulling him back down to her. He traveled down her neck to her breast, flicking her nipple with his tongue and taking it between his teeth until she whimpered. When his lips met the flesh just above her ankle, she lolled her head back in pleasure and gripped the fabric of the comforter.

He took his time tracing his fingers up her leg, gently kissing her most tender areas. She had no idea that a man's lips just inside her knee could cause such a spine-tingling sensation. By the time he got to her inner thigh she was sure she would detonate. "Oh God, Aidan," she cried out.

He continued the exquisite torture, sending a sensation through Katie's body that she could only equate with the feeling of lava spreading through her muscles.

"I want you, baby." Aidan breathed into her ear.

"Take me," she pleaded.

Reaching down, he trailed over her stomach until he reached her lace panties. Katie heard the fabric snap on one side and then the other. In one quick motion, Aidan slid the remaining material from underneath her. He dipped two fingers inside of her, plunging deeper with each of her moans. Pulling out to drag his fingers across the bundle of nerves, holding all of her sexual tension, she cried out as the orgasm spurred her to body to quiver.

After tearing open a foil packet to make sure they were protected, Aidan lowered himself over her, resting on his forearms, and at the same time his mouth met hers, he was inside of her.

Wrapping her legs around his back, she encouraged him to move faster, harder. With each thrust, she whimpered in pleasure, hoping he would never stop. Her body began to shudder in frenzied spasms as another powerful orgasm soared through her, reaching every part of her body.

Aidan groaned into her ear as he found his release. He rested his forehead beside her on the pillow and let out a slight chuckle. "Damn, that was amazing."

"Mmm hmm." Katie kept her eyes closed, savoring the sensations that lingered in her body. Aidan caressed her skin and held her in his arms for the better part of an hour before taking her again.

Thirty-Seven

Afternoon rolled in like a speeding train. Katie lay in the sun soaking up the last bit of their time in Cape Hatteras, thinking about a future with Aidan. He brought feelings she had never experienced before—danger, intrigue, an intoxicating adrenaline rush, and he was constantly pushing her limits.

She sipped on her ice cold Bay Breeze and watched Aidan step out of the pool and walk over to her, all male and muscle. He leaned over and shook the water out of his hair onto her stomach, the wet spray cooling her off and making her giggle.

"Anything you want to do before we go?" he asked, lying back in the lounge chair next to hers.

"This is pretty blissful."

"It's been a great weekend, right?"

Katie agreed. The entire weekend was magical and unforgettable. They rode horses along the beach, swam and enjoyed cocktails by the pool, took long rides on the motorcycle, and relished exploring each other. She wondered how things would progress once they left the Cape.

Aidan walked Katie to the door of her cottage and kissed her goodnight. Her heart sank when she realized he wasn't going to pursue spending another night with her. She tried to convince herself it was because of his hectic Monday morning schedule.

"Goodnight," Katie said, unlocking the door. "I had wonderful time."

"Me too. I'll call you after rounds tomorrow." He kissed her again, long and deep before pulling away. "Goodnight, Katie."

Katie shut the door behind her and put on a kettle of water for tea. She dunked the bag monotonously into the cup of hot water, feeling restless and on edge. Sliding the cup away from her, she stood and decided to run a bath. Filling the tub with extra bubbles, the thick suds nearly spilled over the edge. Eager for the promise of washing her troubles away, she slipped into the steaming tub. She let the hot water along with the sultry tunes of Portishead relax her muscles and take away the tension until her fingers were pruned.

As she climbed into bed, she traced her fingers along her neck, remembering Aidan's touch on her skin. She knew she wouldn't sleep well that night, wondering if things would be different when she saw him next. Would the lustful passion last, or would they sink into the mundane rituals couples usually fell into? Her mind taunted her, reminding her that she'd have to hide the nightmares from him, hide her past, and heal on her own.

She let her mind wander further into the future, and tried to picture them married. It was too painful to envision children, but she saw herself attending functions with him, his hand on her back as he led her through a room full of his colleagues. Would she work at the same hospital, or another one? Maybe he wouldn't want her to work at all. He might have her stay home, making sure his house was immaculate and dinner was ready on time. And if he ever learned about her past . . .

Shaking that thought from her mind, she imagined him coming home from work, hungry for her. She let her fingers slide down her neck, over her right breast. Circling her nipple with the tip of her finger, and then letting her hand—along with her imagination—travel down her waist and over her stomach. She imagined Aidan's eyes locked on hers as he slid his hand over her silk panties, making her beg him to continue.

A knock at the door made Katie sit up in alarm. Her heart began to flutter, hoping Aidan had changed his mind about letting her sleep alone. She took her time getting out of bed, purposely making him wait. He loved playing games with her, testing her patience and vulnerability. The knock grew louder and more persistent as she walked toward the door, a grin playing on her lips as desire swirled through her. When she heard the voice on the other side, her heart beat against her chest erratically, threatening to explode.

"Katie, please open the door! I need to talk to you."

Thirty-Eight

Katie stopped in her tracks, unable to move or breathe. She could hear the *thud-thud*, *thud-thud* of her heart beating in her ears, as the room seemed to be moving around her.

"Katie!" His fist banged against the door.

She resumed her slow pace, walking the path to the front door, each step a difficult task. She knew it was going to be hard to see him, but she was also terrified he would leave before she did. When she finally made it to the door, she turned the knob until it clicked, and eased the door open.

The lump in Katie's throat wouldn't allow her to speak. She swallowed hard, and managed a barely audible whisper. "How did you find me?"

"It's a long story. I've been searching for you all summer."

An awkward silence filled the barrier between them. Katie couldn't believe Branson was standing there in front of her after all this time. So many emotions ran through her all at once, it was almost too much. She loved him with every fiber of her being, and she hated him for hurting her.

"Are you going to invite me in?"

Katie stepped aside to let him in, and shut the door before leading him into the kitchen.

"Are you alone? Is Gram here?"

"Why are you here?" Katie said stiffly.

Branson's subconscious scolded him as he watched her. Something about her seemed . . . *different.* He couldn't put his finger on what it was, but she had changed. She lacked her usual confidence and buoyancy when she moved. "Katie, I was an ass."

Katie nodded, trying to find her confidence. The last couple of months flashed through her mind—the heart-wrenching pain that choked the life out of her, finding herself again, Aidan . . .

A surprising rage washed over her. "I can think of harsher terms to describe your heartless, selfish, moronic stupidity," she spat. "But please go on—tell me *your* reasons for ripping my heart out. No wait, let me! You had a perfect world pictured in your mind. You'd marry the innocent woman you deflowered, present her so proudly at all of your business functions, and then tuck her away neatly in the hidden sanctuary in the woods . . . where she would bare and raise your perfect children . . . who make straight A's and wear their shirts tucked in . . ." Katie walked in circles as she talked. Her voice becoming louder as the rage took over.

Branson waited patiently for her to take a breath and pause long enough for him to get a word in edgewise. "May I speak?" He ran his hand through his hair and left it there, holding on for dear life. "I don't know what happened. I was sitting there, listening to what you were telling me— heartbroken for all you'd been through." He exhaled. "And then you told me about your life on the streets. All I could think about was the men that touched you. I was out of my mind—caught up thinking about how I would murder every single one of them. I didn't know what to do, or say, or think. I was numb, but I wanted to hurt someone. I needed to lash out. I fought to control the rage coursing through my body. The last thing I wanted to do was hurt *you*."

Katie turned to look at him, studying his face. His hair was disheveled and his face unshaven. His eyes were bloodshot and looked crazed as if he hadn't slept for days. "I walked right past you with my bags packed, Branson. You didn't say a word. You just let me go. Did you ever consider how hard it was for me to learn about the past? Did you think everything that happened was a *choice*? Because it wasn't! I was in hell! I was beaten, drugged, and ra—" She couldn't finish the word.

"I know you didn't have a choice, babe."

His words flowed through Katie like wasp venom, bringing a wave of nauseating pain with it. "Don't do that. Don't call me babe."

He saw the pain behind her eyes and watched as she hugged herself tightly. His heart shattered. "I was wrong to let you go—"

"You wouldn't even look at me." Katie interrupted. "I knew we would probably have a difficult road ahead, and I assumed we'd need some counseling, but I wasn't prepared to lose you completely." Katie felt the familiar sting of tears well up in her eyes. *No! Be strong!* "I'm going to be just fine, Branson. You can free your conscious, knowing that I'm not going to die without you."

Branson stood and walked toward Katie. He stopped short when he saw her flinch and back away. "I was in shock, trying to process everything. I should've pulled you into my arms, but instead I was selfish, dealing with my own feelings and needs"

"I've moved on. I've met someone." Katie cringed. As much as she thought she wanted to hurt him, it hadn't felt as good as she imagined. Instead, it wrenched her heart and made her feel worse. She silently begged him not to leave after hearing her words.

"You met someone?" Branson wanted to punch his fist through the wall. He drew in a deep calming breath and unclenched his fists by his side. "Do you have feelings for him? It's only been a couple of months, Katie."

Katie tried to be nonchalant. "He makes me laugh, and he's done a great job of helping me heal . . . and get over you." It came out a lot angrier than she planned, but the spew of her emotion gave her a jolt of life that felt a lot better than the hollow pain.

"All I want is for you to be happy. If he makes you happy, then—" He couldn't finish. "I'm sorry, but that's not true. He can't possibly be a good man if he jumped in so quickly. He moved in on you while you were vulnerable and—"

"You came all this way to lecture me about whom I date and how long I should wait before trying to get over you—after you shattered my world?"

The tension between them as they stood facing each other was thick as mud. Katie wanted to pound her fists into his chest and wrap herself in his arms at the same time. She wasn't sure how much longer she could hold herself together before sliding down to the floor and disintegrating into a ball of tears. The pain she felt being away from him wasn't nearly as intense as what she felt looking into his bloodshot, pain-filled eyes.

Branson slowly exhaled the breath he'd been holding. Her words pierced through his soul like a knife. "No." He tried to calm his shaky voice. "I came here to tell you that I'm sorry. I'm miserable without you." Leaning against the fridge for stability, he folded his arms across his chest, then dropped them by his sides again. "I was a fool for not pulling you into my arms and telling you everything was going to be all right. I should've gone after you when I realized you'd left, but I thought you might need the time to consider things yourself, and when you wouldn't answer my calls—" Branson's eyes were pleading as he made his case.

"You *never* called." Katie squinted her eyes, astonished he would lie to her.

"Yes, I did. I called your cell phone and left dozens of messages. I even called the house several—"

"Gram never told me you called the house." Katie shook her head, the realization suddenly rolling over her. *Of course she didn't.* "I lost my phone and had to get a new one." *I wouldn't put it past Gram to have thrown it into the sea.*

"Katie, please believe me when I tell you I've never wanted a trophy wife and perfect children—and you know I was shocked to learn that I was your first. At least we thought I was your—" Branson wanted to kick himself for bringing that up.

Katie looked down at her feet and whispered. "It was the first time anyone made love to me. You *were* my first."

"Please, come home."

Katie found her courage and looked back up. "Remember the guy in the bar that wouldn't back off and you punched him?"

"Yes."

"After it was over you said . . . I was worth it—worth fighting for. You didn't fight for me this time, Branson. You gave up on us so easily. It hurt . . . you really hurt me." Katie wiped the tears that spilled from her eyes with the back of her hand.

"I know." Branson lowered his head shamefully. "I'll spend the rest of my life making it up to you, if you'll give me the chance."

"I can't." Katie shook her head back and forth, deep in thought. "My whole life is a lie, Branson. You fell in love with someone who doesn't exist." Her body began to shake. She sucked in a deep breath trying to swallow the sob that threatened her throat. She had thought with every tear that fell, a little piece of Branson had been washed away, but she was wrong—her love for him hadn't diminished in the least.

"You're wrong about that. You hate the snow, your favorite color is slate blue, you drink your coffee black, but prefer a cup of Earl Grey with honey before bed—"

"But—"

Branson stepped closer, fighting the urge to hold her. "Sneezing makes you giggle, and when I kiss you behind your left ear, you come unglued. That's who you are, Katie. That's who I fell in love with."

"How can things possibly be the same, now that I remember my past?"

Branson wanted to shake her until she came to her senses. "Do you not understand the depth of my feelings for you?" He held her chin, forcing her to look into his eyes. "I'm sorry for all that you've been through, and all the pain I've added. Please believe me, it doesn't change anything. I fell in love with *you*. I want your past, your present, and your future." He looked into her sad eyes. Something about her revealed a change and he didn't know if it was the heartbreak or—as much as he wanted to deny it—perhaps she had fallen in love with someone else. "Have your feelings for me changed?" Branson asked, his eyes portraying the same pain that was reflected in hers.

She hesitated an instant, searching her heart for what it was she was feeling. She had just experienced an amazing weekend with Aidan, and undeniably developed feelings for him. It wasn't the deep love that grew over time, but it was powerful, raw, and indescribable. "I still love you, I always will." She squeezed her arms tighter around herself, fearing the ache would return. "But I don't think I could stand you looking at me with judgmental eyes, bringing my past up every time we had a fight. At least with Aidan I have a fresh start—I can keep my past hidden."

"Aidan?" The name rolled off of his tongue sneeringly. "So you'd rather live a lie with someone you barely know, than live in truth with me?"

The defeat in Branson's voice tumbled over Katie like giant boulders, crushing her to the core. Her mind was foggy as she searched for something to say. Nothing came—only an overwhelming exhaustion that made her question the ability of her legs to hold her up any longer. She felt for the wall behind her with her hand and leaned against it, resisting the urge to slide down into the floor. She longed for Branson to promise that everything would be perfect, that he was her knight in shining armor and had come to save her. Assure her that he would forget all that happened and never bring it up as long as they lived.

"I—I just wish we could go back to when our lives were perfect," Katie whispered.

"Our lives were never perfect, babe. We've endured a great deal of heartache together, and I have no doubt there will be more, but as long as we have each other to lean on we can get through anything." He paused, gauging her reaction. "My love for you has only grown stronger after hearing about the hell you endured. You are strong, brave, and . . . you're mine." Branson pulled her in for a long, hard, desperate kiss, hoping to satiate the hollow feeling in his chest. He felt her body relax and melt into his and he was overcome by the profound desire to protect and comfort her.

He could have kissed her all night, giving up all of life's necessities—food, water, oxygen—as long as he never had to let her go again. But he knew she was exhausted. "Let's get you to bed."

Katie nodded her head, barely able to keep her eyes open. She was physically and emotionally drained.

Branson helped Katie to bed and kissed her forehead before turning to leave.

"Branson!" Katie started to sit up. "Don't go."

"I'm not going anywhere. I'm going to sleep on the couch."

"Hold me?" Katie pleaded.

Branson slid in beside her and pulled her backside to him. He wrapped his arms around her and held her tight. As he listened to Katie's breathing settle into a pattern, it slowed and became calm as she drifted off to sleep. He stroked her hair, ran his hand down her arm, and kissed the top of her head every few minutes, cherishing having her back in his arms.

Most of the night was restless for Katie, waking several times to make sure Branson was still beside her. Each time, she snuggled into the dip in his chest that cradled her head perfectly and gripped him tighter. *He's here . . . he's really here.*

Fog surrounded Katie as the past twenty-four hours played out. She was with Aidan, horseback riding in the nude on the empty beach. Her arms were wrapped around his waist as her chest and stomach hugged into his strong back. She felt wild and free as they raced along, her hair blowing in the warm breeze. They climbed off the horse and ran into the ocean, diving into the water to cool off. Aidan took her in his arms, and she wrapped her legs around him as he began to make love to her. She lolled her head back, enjoying the feeling of him filling her over and over again. When she looked into his eyes, they changed from dark to clear blue. Guilt washed over her as she realized it was Branson. Had she been fantasizing about Aidan the whole time? He smiled at her and she saw the safety of his love. She began to move her hips, resuming the pleasure. Her eyes closed as he moaned and told her how much he loved her. Feeling him change around her, she opened her eyes to see Aidan's lustful gaze. "I'm going to drive your body wild." Confusion pervaded Katie as Aidan changed back to Branson. "No one will ever love you like I do."

Suddenly, she felt something jerk her out of his arms. "You want me." Aidan commanded, his dark eyes hypnotizing her as he easily led her out of the water. Looking from Aidan to Branson, she was unsure of what to do. She loved them both, wanted them both.

She clung to Aidan as she reached for Branson, pulling him out of the water with her.

"You must choose," Branson said, arms folded across his chest.

Aidan mirrored Branson's pose. "I won't share."

Katie didn't know what to do, she went back and forth looking for an answer from either of them, but they didn't move. All of a sudden Aidan raised his arms in disgust. "Whatever," he said as he climbed on the horse and galloped away.

Katie chased after him, her legs sinking deeper into the sand with each step, making it impossible for her to catch him. She turned to Branson who was walking down the beach in the other direction, farther and farther away from her. "Wait! Please don't go!" She shouted, but he didn't turn or slow his pace. "I've lost them both." Katie fell to her knees, rested her head in her hands, and let the tears flow.

Branson awoke to Katie's soft cries as she grasped at his shirt. "Hey, it's okay, you're having a bad dream." He stroked her arm until she calmed down and fell back asleep.

Thirty-Nine

Crying wasn't an option—yet. Katie would have to wait and let her emotional turmoil release when she had a moment alone.

Branson looked hopeful as he stood in her kitchen, busying himself with the coffee machine. "Good morning, I didn't see you standing there."

Katie pushed herself off of the door frame and retrieved the creamer from the fridge. "I haven't been here long. Need help with the coffee maker?"

"No, I've got it." He chuckled. "What are you hungry for? Pancakes? Eggs?"

"I'm not hungry. Coffee will be fine."

"You've got to eat something. Breakfast is the most important meal of the day. How 'bout we grab something on the way home?"

It dawned on her that he was probably starved. "If you're hungry, there are bagels in the fridge."

He looked at her, trying to read the emotion displayed across her beautiful features and in her demeanor. Taking a place against the wall next to her, he asked, "What's wrong, baby?"

She shook her head, unable to speak. How could she explain what was going on inside of her? He would bolt if he knew she was torn over which man to choose. "I . . . I need some time."

"Of course. We can take it slow."

"You don't understand. I need time to process. I have some things to sort out and I'm just not ready to come home."

Branson's exhaled a long, slow breath. "I see." Suddenly the happy tune on the radio was annoying and seemed to be mocking him. *Pocket full of sunshine . . . seriously? What the hell does she need to think about? I know I screwed up, but I thought we worked through all of that shit last night?* "How long do you think you need?"

Katie shrugged. "A couple of days, maybe a week?" *How long does it usually take people to make a life altering decision?*

"All right. Bart can handle the office while I'm gone."

Katie whipped her head around and looked at him with wide eyes. "You can't stay *here!* How am I supposed to be alone with my thoughts if you're right next to me?"

"I'm not going back to Maine, if that's what you had in mind." He wrapped an arm around her waist and pulled her closer. "Now that I have you back, I'm not letting you go. You belong with me, baby."

Did she? Katie let his words flow over her, caressing and comforting her. It felt so good to hear him say these things. Then she remembered Aidan saying something similar. His voice echoing in her mind, *"You are mine."* Both men sent her world into disarray. She needed to belong to *someone.* Branson *loved* her. He was every woman's dream of a devoted, faithful husband. Aidan *possessed* her. He made her feel desired and he pushed her, revealing a risky, sensual side.

Branson interrupted her thought process. "Tell you what. I'll stay in a hotel. You can have your space, while you mull things over." Part of him felt like he was losing his man card, resorting to this. But after the hell of losing her, he would fight for her no matter the cost. Before leaving, he made sure she knew how much he wanted her. "Dance with me?"

"Here?"

"Yes."

Branson took her hand and pulled her in close. The contact of his flesh against her pajama-clad chest ignited a fire inside of her, making it difficult to maintain balance. Their bodies clung to each other, floating to the sultry sound of Rihanna's voice as she sang about wanting her lover to stay. Their eyes locked on each other as Branson held her in his arms. Katie heard the words in the background and felt like she was living them. *"Round and around and around and around we go . . ."*

Katie wrapped one arm around his neck, never losing eye contact. She listened to the words of the song and reflected on how perfectly they told the story of her situation. She was sure he had picked this song to sway her, and dammit, it was working.

When the song stopped, so did time as they stood there looking at each other. Her body tensed when Branson leaned in. She tried to stay strong as he kissed her, not wanting to give him a false sense of security, but when his lips touched hers, she melted. After all the time apart, and everything she had experienced with Aidan, the spark was still there. His kiss was still unlike anything she had ever experienced, liquefying her muscles as he demonstrated the depth of his love. The buzz of her phone broke her enchantment, and she slid it into her pocket before Branson could see the text.

"One day," Katie said, walking to the front door. She opened it and leaned against the frame. "Give me one day without calling, or coming over. I need to be alone with my thoughts."

"Deal." Branson leaned in and kissed her cheek. "I love you, baby."

Katie shut the door before a tear escaped and slipped down her cheek. She had no clue what she was going to do. Maybe she was meant to be alone—maybe she didn't deserve either one of them? She pulled out her phone, remembering the awaiting text, and read it:

Busy day. I'll call you tonight.

Katie was disappointed and relieved at the same time. She longed to hear his voice and feel his hands on her body, burning up her flesh with his touch. But she also needed time to think and process. Her deepest musing came from being close to the ocean, so she grabbed a towel and headed outside. A warm breeze caressed her shoulders as she hugged her knees with one arm near the water's edge. She ran her finger through the sand, monogramming her initials onto the beach. As the water lapped against her feet, she contemplated her situation. Branson was her first love, and she reminisced about laying eyes on him for the first time, dating, and the first time they made love. She thought about the heartache they shared over losing a child, and how he held her and cared for her through her time of despair.

Her mind wandered to Aidan. He was devilishly handsome and electrifying. She experienced new things and feelings that were way out of her comfort zone, and time spent with him was exhilarating. She pictured an exciting life together—travelling the world, scuba diving, making love in the ocean.

Looking down the beach, she watched as a family of four walked along the shoreline. The kids were jumping over the waves and laughing. The girl looked to be around eleven with long blond hair braided down her back. She held her younger brothers hand, helping him jump. Probably three or four, with matching blond hair, he giggled and begged her to do it again.

Katie imagined the family was hers and Aidan's. Would he be a good father? Did he want children? Her head was spinning as she imagined her life with Branson versus Aidan. Both excited her, but in different ways. She erased her monogram from the sand, and replaced it with KRH.

Right next to it she scrolled KSH. *Katie Stone, Katie Romero. Mr. and Mrs. Stone, Dr. and Mrs. Romero. Ugh!* Katie ran her hand over the sand and sighed.

She imagined Aidan's hands on her waist as he held her against the wall, possessing her body and mind as he took her over and over again. He knew just how to manipulate her and bestowed an insatiable hunger inside of her. The way he looked at her ... but Branson ... the one she vowed to love forever. She recalled their first night together, how he had been so gentle and loving with her. She wanted him to be the only man that ever touched her. Their connection was magnificent. It was natural, deep, and made her feel whole.

She wanted a family, a home, security, and love. Branson could provide all of those things, but she also needed trust. He blew it in that department. He promised he wouldn't hold her past against her, but she couldn't get the image of his expression out of her head. Could she trust that he wouldn't hold it against her ten years down the road?

Could she trust Aidan? He was mysterious and controlling—but honest. If he didn't like something, he told her. He wanted her all to himself and couldn't stand the thought of another man looking at her lustfully. Wasn't that exactly how Branson felt after learning about her past? He was crazed thinking of someone hurting the woman he loved.

Katie dug her fingers in the dry sand behind her, and held the soft powder in her hands for a moment before letting it slip through her fingers. She tossed around the idea of a life with Branson versus a life with Aidan for hours and she hadn't come up with an answer.

Three glasses of wine on an empty stomach wasn't Katie's best idea ever. She started to get in the car, but thought better of it when she couldn't steady her hand enough to get the key in the lock. Instead, she walked the two short blocks to Aidan's house.

All the lights were out, and she hoped it wasn't too late. He had the OR booked for an early surgery, but she had to see him. Their phone call earlier was brief as he most likely took Katie's lack of enthusiasm for boredom. Usually, she loved hearing about the more difficult surgeries, but her mind was filled with confusion and grief. Maybe seeing him would give her some answers. She reached for the doorbell, and pressed it once. A light came on inside, illuminating a boxer brief clad Aidan as he walked toward the door.

"Hi, gorgeous, come in."

Katie stood on her tiptoes, wrapped her arms around his neck, and kissed him. The familiar sensation of electrifying pulses traveled through her stomach and down into her thighs as he kissed her back, his hands sliding around her waist and straight to her ass.

He pulled back and flashed her a wicked grin. "You've been drinking. And now you're here for a late night booty call?" Trailing his lips along her neck, up to her earlobe, he whispered, "I'm in."

Katie's body stirred, the familiar hunger and longing taking over her senses. It took every ounce of will power to make him stop. "Stop . . . please, I need to talk to you." Her words were breathless and filled with need, encouraging him rather than making him pause. "Aidan. Stop!"

"What? Why?" He pulled away, the frustration evident in his tone. "What's going on?"

"I didn't come here for a quickie. I said I need to talk to you."

"Oh," he said, his eyes sobering.

The reality of the situation poured over Katie like a cold shower—awakening her common sense. Was this relationship with Aidan purely sexual? Would a future together be possible? Once the desire hit a plateau, would there be anything left? There was no room in her twisted heart for regret.

Katie pulled herself out of his arms and stepped back, creating space between them. "Branson knocked on my door last night."

Aidan ran both hands through his hair. "And you told him to fuck off?" He hooked his finger around the ribbon that circled the waist of her blue sundress and pulled her in to him.

"Aidan," Katie put both of her hands on his chest, preventing him from pulling her in any closer. "Let's sit."

Katie sat on the couch and waited for him to join her. She let her eyes roam over his confused face. He was the man who helped her heal, the one that convinced her to laugh, run, play tennis, and experience life again. She felt a pit in her stomach, wondering if he would fight for her.

"I listened to what he had to say." She looked at the ground, unable to find the courage to look into his eyes. "He wants me back."

"Of course he does, Katie. Don't let him manipulate you. He had his chance . . . and he blew it."

"What exactly do you want from me, Aidan?" she asked, studying a tassel on a decorative pillow. "How do you see things going for us in the future?"

"I . . . Katie, we've only just begun getting to know each other. I can't make promises yet." Aidan stood and paced the room. "I can tell you that I don't want to lose you. I'd like to explore a future with you . . . slowly . . . over time. I don't think rushing things is a good idea for either of us."

"No, I agree. But I have to know . . . do you want a family one day? How do you feel about children?"

"I've never been around them. They make me uncomfortable, but I'm not opposed to the idea one day."

Katie let her mind wander to the future. She tried to picture Aidan with his son, teaching him how to fish, or tying his little girl's shoe before kissing her on the top of her head. It didn't fit. Damn it, they would have had beautiful children, too. Dark hair and eyes, olive skin . . . she was going to miss him terribly.

Her entire body ached from the impending heartache and tears filled her eyes. *I can't do it! I just can't.* Katie stood and wound a strand of hair tightly around her finger as she paced the floor. "I—I um . . ." Gauging the look on his face, he knew what was coming . . . more of the same Katie.

She wiped her tears with the back of her hand. "This is much harder than I thought it would be." She sat back down in a chair opposite Aidan, her mind reeling as she struggled for words.

"Don't do it, Katie." Aidan stood and walked to the picture window overlooking the beach. "You won't be happy with him."

"Aidan," Katie walked up behind him and reached out to comfort him, but let her arm drop down by her side knowing it would just make it harder. "You're amazing and I'll never forget what we shared."

"Stay with me." He turned and took her chin in his hands. "You can't deny that what we have is worth exploring."

"I want more, and you're not ready to give that."

"But—"

Katie held up a hand interrupting him. "I know it's too fast, too soon. I don't begrudge you that. But you have to realize . . . I *had* a family. I *had* the future I'd always dreamed of. That's what I need. I want a whole houseful of kids . . . running through the house, climbing into our laps to cover us in sloppy, wet kisses." She saw the dread in Aidan's face as he tried to smile, but the cringe lingered in his eyebrows giving him away. He'd probably keel over the minute a dirty little hand was pressed against his sparkling sliding glass door.

"You've already made up your mind." He dropped his hands and turned away, facing the large glass window that looked out toward the ocean.

"I—I'm sorry. You helped me heal and I experienced things I didn't know were possible. I've changed because of you. I've enjoyed being a woman. I love you, Aidan, but—"

"Spare me the bullshit," he said flatly.

Katie stiffened. The uncaring tone stunned her, releasing the vice grip from around her heart. "I'm sorry and I hope one day you'll forgive me," she said, keeping her voice level. "I gave my heart to Branson a long time ago, and I know we can't give each other what we both deserve." She turned to leave, swallowing the lump in her throat that made it difficult to breathe.

Aidan whirled around and pulled her into his arms. Before she could protest his lips were on hers with such desperate need it was uncomfortable. She pulled back and looked into his troubled eyes as he spoke.

"I'm not going to be here every time you need to be glued back together, Katie. He can't give you what I can—what you need. I know you, you're fragile and vulnerable. You need someone to push your limits so you can enjoy life. I want you . . . and you need me."

"You *have* pushed my limits, and I'm grateful to you for that, but I'm not fragile." She wiggled out of his arms, stepped back to get the full view of him. "Do you love me? I mean, really, truly . . . love me enough to give up everything for me?" she asked, watching his expression change. Finally—the chance to see him squirm under *her* gaze for once. It was a lot to ask, and she knew her own answer to the question. She couldn't give up her dreams for him.

"I—you know I do. I mean, we haven't known each other very long, but—"

"You and I are in lust, not love, Aidan."

"Don't diminish what we have." His eyes grew darker, something Katie didn't think was feasible. "Yes, there is a lot of lust between us, but I do care for you . . . deeply."

"I care for you, too, Aidan. I just don't think it's enough to sustain us long term." She turned to walk away.

"Katie!"

Aidan slammed his fist against the wall, causing her body to recoil in fear, but she resisted the compulsion to look back and closed the door behind her. Walking down the road, she took her time, pondering the night's events. A feeling of morose washed over her temporarily as she recalled the words they shared. Questions still loomed over her. Had she made the wrong decision? Would it have been worth it to give up on the idea of a family? To erase her past once more, and move on as someone without skeletons in her closet?

Nearing the pale yellow cottage, sadness was immediately replaced with joy. Branson was leaning against the front porch post waiting for her.

"What are you doing?" Katie asked, walking to the front door.

"You said one day. The day is over."

Katie unlocked the door, pulling Branson in behind her. After locking the door—just in case—she buried her head in his chest and wrapped herself in his arms. Not a word was spoken between them as Katie pulled away and removed his shirt. She kept her eyes locked on his as he pulled her in at the waist, untied the ribbon, and unzipped her dress. He slid the straps off of her shoulder, letting the thin material fall to the floor.

Katie stepped around the dress. Her body stirred in anticipation as Branson's eyes roamed over her as she stood in her bra and panties. She reached out and skillfully unbuttoned and then unzipped his khaki shorts, using both hands to slide them to the ground. She trailed a finger down his stomach, over his belly button, moving until she reached the waistband of his navy boxer briefs.

Not able to wait another moment to feel her skin, Branson pulled her into him and led her back against the wall. He kissed her hard and deep, concentrating on her taste, the way she melted beneath him. Unhooking her bra, he flung it across the room. With his free hand, he cupped one of her breasts. He could feel her breathing become heavy as he took her nipple between his forefinger and thumb, squeezing with just enough pressure until she released a soft moan. Keeping her hands against the wall, he rested his palms on top of hers and lightly trailed them down her arms, feeling her body quiver under his touch.

Katie lowered her arms and pulled him into the bedroom. She stood on her tiptoes and wrapped one hand around his neck as she kissed him with all the passion she had. When she pulled back, she slid her fingers into the waistband of his boxers and carefully lowered them down and over his bulging arousal. She guided him onto the edge of the bed and knelt down in front of him, trailing her tongue along the length of his impressive erection.

"Katie," he warned. With the emotion of having her in his arms again, and the length of time that had passed since he'd been touched by her—or anyone for that matter—he wouldn't be able to maintain control.

She peeked up at him through her lashes, and smiled before sliding her mouth over him inch-by-inch. *Oh, shit!* The site of her pleasuring him as her hair moved around the insides of his thighs nearly took him over the edge. The room began to spin as her warm mouth and tongue enveloped him, causing every muscle in his body to tense. He clenched the sheets on either side of him as he allowed another moment of the exquisite pleasure. In one swift motion, he lifted her off him and laid her on the bed. He hovered over her, caressing her magnificent body with his eyes.

Katie moaned with pleasure as his hand moved between her legs, feeling how turned on she was. He needed to taste her, to please her. Nibbling and kissing her thighs as he made his way to the destination he desired had her squirming beneath him. He felt her body tense when his tongue touched her, and relax again as he savored her. Her body writhed appreciatively as he moved at just the right speed and pressure, until finally she released the tension that had been building and cried out his name. He watched as the last of the aftershocks surged through her while she gripped the pillow above her head.

"I need you inside of me, now," Katie pleaded, trying to catch her breath.

Branson brought his body down on top of hers, positioned himself at her opening, and entered her with sheer primal need. They groaned in unison when their bodies became one. Neither of them could get close enough, or deep enough. Branson slid his hands underneath her hips, lifting them slightly as his pace accelerated. Katie pushed back, allowing him to sink even deeper inside of her. He was losing control. In one quick movement, he lifted her up and on top of him. He took her breasts in his hands as she lolled her head back and gripped his thighs. She slowed the pace, squeezing her muscles as she rose up, moaning in ecstasy each time she came back down. With each of her moans, it was becoming harder to fight the desire to let go and experience his release. Instead he rolled her over onto her back and resumed control.

"Branson!" It was so intense. How could something feel so amazing? The sensations were rapidly building inside of her as he moved faster and harder. She gripped his back with her heels and dug her fingers into his shoulders as he filled her up one last time before welcoming the earthquake together. Branson laced his fingers through hers and squeezed tight as the aftershocks reverberated through their bodies.

He felt Katie's body softly trembling beneath him. Her lashes were moist with tears as she kept her eyes closed, and his heart sank thinking she was filled with regret. "Hey, look at me."

The concern in his voice caused more tears to surface, and as Katie opened her eyes to look at him, they spilled down her cheeks.

"Are you okay?"

Katie couldn't speak knowing if she tried, a hyperventilating cry would erupt. She nodded her head instead.

"Talk to me, Katie," he whispered.

Katie reached around his back with both arms and pulled him back down to her. She hugged him tightly to her, hopefully erasing his worry. When she finally found her voice, she whispered into his neck. "I've never loved anything, or anyone, as deeply as I love you."

He grinned, relieved that everything would be all right, and covered her face in kisses. "I'll be right back." He kissed her before rolling off the bed and heading to the bathroom. When he returned, he knelt beside the bed in all his glory, holding her engagement ring. "I love you, Katie. Marry me?"

Katie sat up and whispered, "Yes!"

Forty

The smell of freshly baked apples and cinnamon reminded Katie she was home. Gram squealed and wrapped her arms around her when she stepped into the kitchen. "Oh, Katie, I'm so glad to see you!"

"You too, Gram," she answered flatly, her arms dangling by her sides as her grandmother continued to squeeze her.

"What's wrong, love?"

"Once again you manipulated my life. What gives you the right to keep doing this to me? I know you've explained the first time was to save me, but what's your excuse this time?" She searched Gram's face, waiting for the realization of her granddaughter's anger to register. "How could you watch me suffer all summer long, knowing what you did?"

Gram pulled out a chair and took a seat. Letting her chin rest on her folded hands, she shook her head. "I'm so sorry, Katie. I—I don't understand . . . what have I done?"

Katie slammed her hands on the kitchen table, the sting registering as it traveled from her palms into her wrists. Ignoring it, she let her anger spill over. "You knew Branson called. You lied to me!" She leaned in. "Why, Gram? How could you be so cruel to me? I trusted you."

"Please believe me when I tell you everything I did was out of love." She wiped the tears from her cheeks with the back of her hand. "You must know how much you mean to me. I didn't think he was worthy of you." She picked her head up, looking curiously at Katie. "How do *you* know he called?"

"We've reconciled, Gram. He—"

The shrill whistle of the tea kettle interrupted their conversation and broke the spell of Katie's fiery wrath. "I'll get it," Katie said, walking to the stove and turning the gas burner off. She pulled two cups out of the cabinet and poured the hot water over two Earl Grey tea bags.

After a sip of tea, the brewed leaves worked their magic, calming Katie enough to fill Gram in on everything that happened. Gram shook her head. "So, Branson broke into our home, rummaged through our things, and called every number on my emergency phone log until he tracked you down?"

"You make him sound like a crazed stalker. I thought it was romantic." Katie smiled, letting her mind roam for a moment before continuing. "Besides, Aidan wasn't as sensational as you wanted to believe."

"So, tell me how Branson won your heart back."

"He explained everything, Gram, how he really felt about me after learning the truth," Katie began, pausing to take a sip of tea. "When I left, I didn't give him any time to process all that I had just thrown at him, I just fled. I didn't realize, but his heart was ripped out, too. It was a lot for anyone to grasp, and I'm not sure I would've handled it any differently if the roles were reversed."

"All I've ever wanted for you, Katie-dear, is for you to be happy. I thought Aidan was the one."

Katie spoke clearly, enunciating each word. "Gram, Branson makes me happy. Why are you so set on me being with Aidan?"

"Honestly," Gram lowered her head and studied the cup of tea gripped between her palms. "He reminds me of Pete."

Katie was taken aback by the statement. Sadness filled her, realizing Gram still regretted breaking off her engagement to him so many years ago. How did she live each day knowing that her soul mate was sharing his life with someone else? Katie reached across the table and rested her hand on Gram's. "I'm sorry, I had no idea you were still in love with him. Have you told him?"

"No." She shook her head, not able to lift her head. "Of course not. He has a family. I would never do anything to damage what he's built. Lillian, his wife, is a wonderful lady. I respect her."

"I understand." Katie hesitated, choosing her words. "Gram, look at me." She waited for Gram to lift her head. "Aidan is nothing like Pete. Yes, he's exciting and mysterious, but he's very different." Katie's cheeks flushed as she recalled some of the things they'd done. She was sure Gram would see the difference if she shared those details. "Aidan and I were never in love. I'm not sure he's capable of loving someone the way you and Pete loved each other . . . the way Branson and I do."

"I had no idea, love. I thought he was crazy about you."

"I think he was, and I felt the same way about him, but it wasn't love. There was no security, no trust in our future. I don't regret the time with him. I believe I've grown from the experience, as well as accepting the truth about my past."

"You know everything I did was for your best interest? I just wanted you to have the life you deserved."

"I know you thought you were doing the right thing, but it wasn't, and it backfired. A lot of people were hurt by your manipulations."

"I would never purposely hurt you, love."

"I know that, and I'm grateful for all you've done for me. Please don't misconstrue what I'm trying to say. You've done so much for me and I have no doubt that I'd be dead if you hadn't rescued me when you did. However, if you hadn't erased my memories, I wouldn't have disgorged my entire past in Branson's lap, causing our separation. I'm thankful for my time with Aidan, but if you'd been there to push me into choosing him over Branson, I have no doubt that I'd be sitting across from my granddaughter one day telling her how I let the love of my life slip through my fingers."

The analogy wasn't lost on Gram. Her manipulations had caused her to lose Pete, lose her son, and almost caused her granddaughter to experience the familiar pain of being without your soul mate.

Shivers ran down Katie's spine and tears spilled over her dark eyelashes as she listened to the opera singers tell the story of Jean Valjean's death. Branson purchased tickets for the Saturday night show, and Katie was thrilled. She had always wanted to see *Les Misérables,* and although she memorized the lines from watching it on BBC, she had never seen it live. She was the first person to stand and applaud when the show ended, joined by everyone in the room.

"That was amazing! Just brilliant!" she said to Branson without taking her eyes off the cast during their curtain call.

"I'm glad you liked it." Branson smiled and watched her take it all in. Her tear-soaked green eyes had their sparkle back and his heart warmed seeing her so happy.

After the show they enjoyed coffee and dessert before he had to take her home. Katie decided she wanted to spend the time leading up to their wedding day with Gram, and although Branson agreed to her wishes, he was dying to touch her. Branson took a sip and debated on whether or not to ask her what had been on his mind for weeks. "Katie?" he asked.

"Hmm?" She looked up from her cup and smiled.

"I want to ask you something. If you don't want to talk about it, just let me know, and we'll move on."

"Sure, go ahead."

Branson hesitated, wanting to form his words in a way that wouldn't bring too much pain with them. "Do you remember the men that hurt you?"

Katie set her cup of coffee down and swallowed hard to choke down the warm liquid in her mouth. She wasn't expecting the question. "I think so."

He watched as her eyes shifted up and to the right, as if that's where she kept those kinds of memories. "Will you tell me their names?"

"Why?"

Because I'm going to kill them for what they did to you. "I just want to do some research—I'll feel a lot better knowing where they are. You know the feeling you get when you see a spider in the bedroom? You have to make sure you get it before you go to sleep, or you won't be able to close your eyes. I'd feel better knowing where they are—knowing that I can close my eyes at night, because they can't harm you."

"Can I be a part of the research?" Katie asked. She could have cared less about the four assholes, but was curious about Ally.

"Sure. I'll be right back." Branson went to the car to retrieve his laptop from the trunk. When he returned, Katie was deep in thought. He scooted his chair around next to hers and waited for the screen to come alive.

Katie took a deep breath and felt like she was uttering a string of curse words when she said the first name. "Garrison Ford."

Branson typed the name into the search field and frowned when he saw how many results appeared. "Hmm, this isn't going to be that easy."

"Try Garrison Ford, Vallejo, California."

Branson typed in the words and the results were narrowed considerably. They browsed through the list and clicked on one matching his age and description. Branson read aloud:

CALIFORNIA: POLICE ARE LOOKING FOR SUSPECTS IN THE DEATH OF GARRISON FORD. FORD'S BODY WAS FOUND SHOT TO DEATH IN HIS APARTMENT. ANY INFORMATION REGARDING THIS CRIME, PLEASE CALL LOCAL POLICE.

They both sat there looking at the screen in silence. Branson was the first to speak. "Good. The bastard deserved it."

"Chase . . ." Katie could see his face in her mind and began to tremble.

"Hey," Branson wrapped his arm around her, trying to comfort her. "This is too hard. Let's forget it."

"No, I'm okay. Look up Chase Morris."

They read the screen in front of them with wide eyes:

CALIFORNIA: AUTHORITIES HAVE IDENTIFIED ANOTHER BODY. CHASE MORRIS WAS FOUND SHOT TO DEATH BEHIND A DUMSTER NEAR WELL'S LIQUOR STORE. AUTHORITIES BELIEVE THE MURDER IS RELATED TO THE RECENT DEATH OF GARRISON FORD . . .

A similar news report stated the shooting death of Seth Morgan. Katie whispered, "One more . . . James Durand."

CALIFORNIA: AUTHORITIES ARE SEARCHING FOR A POSSIBLE SERIAL KILLER. JAMES DURAND, THE LEAD PIMP OF A WELL-KNOWN PROSTITUTION RING WAS FOUND DEAD IN HIS HOME TONIGHT. HE WAS BOUND, TORTURED, AND KILLED. POLICE CLAIM TO HAVE SEVERAL SUSPECTS, BUT NO PRINTS OR MURDER WEAPON HAVE BEEN FOUND.

Katie cupped her hand over her mouth and stared at the screen. "They're all dead . . . every one of them."

Branson was relieved, but disappointed that he'd been robbed of killing them himself. "Did you?" he asked, lowering his voice to a whisper.

"Oh for Pete's sake, Branson! How could I have—" She slapped her hand over her mouth again and drew in a sharp breath. "Surely . . ."

"What?" Branson asked eagerly. "Do you remember something?"

"No, I was just thinking." Katie wasn't sure she should share her thoughts aloud. She was surely wrong, but as her mind sorted over the details, it made sense.

"What? Tell me what you're thinking."

"What are the dates on all of those reports?"

Branson scrolled back through each of them, and noted the dates. "They were all dated in July—only a day or two apart from each other, seven and half years ago."

Goose bumps rose on Katie's arms and she rubbed them away with her hands. She spoke slowly, choosing her words carefully. "I'm not positive, it's just a guess really," she started. "I wonder if Gram's friend Pete Savalli had a hand in any of this."

"Pete? He's the one that helped me find you." Branson leaned back in his chair and let his mind trace back to his meeting with Pete. He was so desperate to find Katie, he hadn't paid much attention to the man. The only thing he remembered was how much he seemed to care about her and wanted her to be happy. "He seemed to care a great deal for you. Despite Gram's wishes to separate us, he wanted you to be happy."

"That's the thing. I remember when I met him, thinking he was a killer. I thought he was going to kill *me*! You know, one of those serial killers that want to rid the world of its filth." Katie looked down, ashamed that she was once considered filthy. Her memories were still hazy, but it wasn't a life she would wish on anyone. She wondered if there was something she could do to help victims of human trafficking.

Branson took her hand and gave her fingers a squeeze. "You're an amazing woman, Katie. I'm in awe of your strength and ability to overcome all the shit you've been through."

Katie thanked him with a warm smile. "Anyway, he admitted to having connections. He said that my foster parents would never be able to hurt children again—he said police would find all sorts of drugs in their home that he, or someone he knew, had planted." She shook her head. "I could easily believe that he killed those men, the timing is perfect. It was seven years ago when Pete found me and brought me to Gram. He could have had it done, or gone back and took care of it himself. But why would he do that? He didn't even know me." Katie shook her head, deep in thought. She vaguely remembered sitting on the plane with Pete. He was kind to her, but didn't put up with her bullshit, and she was smart enough to respect his sinister bearing. "Does it make me a horrible person to be a little grateful to him for it?"

"No. Does it make me a bad guy to feel cheated out of killing them myself?"

Katie kissed him for that statement. She hoped he would never take anyone's life, no matter how horrible they were, but it made her feel good all over to hear him say it anyway. "Can we look up one more person?"

Branson typed in the name Katie gave him and waited. Several choices were offered, and they clicked on each one. None led them to Ally.

"Well, no news is better than bad news, I guess."

"Who is she?"

"We grew up together in the foster home. She was three years older and treated me like her baby sister. She protected me, and comforted me when she *couldn't* protect me. She was with me when we were taken to California. Actually, it was her idea to run away. I hated her for what she got us into, but now I realize she was just a desperate kid herself." Katie's eyes moistened with tears. "I left her there with those monsters. When Pete came for me, I should have insisted we go back for her, but I didn't."

"I'm home!" Katie sang as she searched for Gram.

"In the kitchen, love."

Katie floated on air as she glided through the house and into the kitchen. The smell of Yorkshire tea filled her nose and made her smile. It was she and Gram's nightly ritual to have a cup of tea with honey before bed each night, and although the hour was later than usual, it comforted Katie to come home to the tradition. When she rounded the corner humming, she saw Pete sitting at the table and stopped.

Pete stood and flashed a warm smile. Gram was pulling another tea cup out of the cabinet. "Hi, angel, join us for tea and tell me all about the musical."

"No tea, thank you." Katie sat down and roamed over Pete's face for answers to her questions. She needed to talk to him, but not in front of Gram. *I wonder if Gram knows who he really is.* "So tell us all about the musical, dear." Gram took a sip of tea and waited.

"It was wonderful. The best I've ever seen. I cried, and then clapped until my hands were numb." Katie tried to stay focused on the conversation, not wanting to reveal her distraction. "We have to get the soundtrack so you can listen to the music, Gram. You'll love it." Katie stood and stretched her arms. "I'm going to go on to bed. Goodnight, Gram." She nodded at the man sitting at the table next to Gram, much too late, in her opinion, for a married man. "Pete."

"Goodnight," Gram and Pete answered in unison.

Katie kept still in the silence of her room, waiting for Pete to leave. When she heard his footsteps leading toward the front door, she slipped out the back and leaned against the side of the house. She waited for Gram to shut the door and jogged over to Pete's car. He jumped when he saw her standing there. "Holy—you startled me."

"I need to talk to you," she said, before slipping into the passenger side of his black Lexus.

Pete got in, shut the door and turned to face her. "What's this about?"

"Let's drive and talk. I don't want Gram to wonder why you're sitting in her driveway."

Pete drove down the long driveway and took a right. He found an empty lot and parked the car, but left the engine running. Katie looked around for any sign of life. A street lamp flickered at the end of the parking lot, matching the pace of her accelerated heart rate. What was she thinking getting into the car with this man? She was sure he was responsible for killing four men, and who knew how many others. He was a murderer, and she allowed him to drive her down the road to an abandoned lot.

After the car was in park, Katie hesitantly began the flow of questions, trying to steady her shaky voice. "Please, don't insult me by denying any of this, just answer my questions. I'm fairly certain that you're responsible for ridding the world of the four men that ruined most of my childhood." She waited for Pete to hold up his hand in defense and deny her accusations, but he remained still and kept his eyes on Katie, patiently waiting for her to finish. "If I'm right, thank you," she whispered.

"My question is, did you ever come across a girl named Ally? She had long brown hair and was a little shorter than me. We were raised in the same foster home. Although I hated her for getting me into that mess, I realize she was young, naïve, and just wanted out of that house of hell. I'm sure she didn't know that she was leading us into another level of it."

Pete paused, making sure Katie was finished. He knew he couldn't admit to the crimes, but he also knew it wouldn't hurt to tell her anything he could about Ally. "Anything said in this car remains here, is that understood?"

Katie saw the seriousness behind his eyes. He had saved her life, and he could just as easily take it back. She nodded her head, "Yes."

"Yes, I did make Ally's acquaintance." He wondered how much he should share with Katie. He only wanted to give her as much information as needed to satisfy her. "Ally's not like you, Katie. You were determined to get out and be something, and she didn't care. I did get her out of there, away from that lifestyle. I put her up in an apartment within walking distance to a local high school and helped her get registered for classes.

"She didn't finish high school. I was sending money every month for rent, utilities, and food. I had someone delivering cash, so nothing could be traced back to me. One month, he reported that she was pregnant and strung out. I went down there myself to see what I could do for her. After relocating her, we started all over again. She put the baby up for adoption, got a job at the local convenience store and was straightening herself out."

Katie exhaled and relaxed back into the leather seat. "Do you still send money?"

Pete gripped the steering wheel and drew a long, slow breath before answering. "No. She disappeared, and I haven't seen her since."

"Oh." Katie looked straight ahead, not sure how to process all that she had heard. "You're a good man. You've done more for her than anyone in her life ever has. You didn't owe either of us anything, yet . . ." Katie drifted off thinking about Ally, wondering where she was and if she was all right.

Pete cleared his throat and regretted his words as soon as they slipped out. "There's one more thing . . ."

Katie turned to look at him. Hearing the hesitation in his voice caused alarm to rise along with the tiny hairs on the back of her neck.

"Her child . . . my wife and I are raising her."

Katie's mind went numb trying to wrap it around what she had just heard. "You have Ally's daughter? How old is she? Does she look like Ally? Does she . . ."

"She's four years old." Pete scrolled through his phone and retrieved a picture. "Here." Passing the phone, he waited for her reaction.

Katie's eyes filled with tears as she saw Ally's long golden hair and mischievous smile in the picture. "She's beautiful. What's her name?"

"Her mother named her and we decided to honor her request." He delayed his answer for a moment, staring at the little girl in the picture, his eyes smiling gently. "Her name is Rose."

Katie wiped the tears from her face with the back of her hand and whispered, "Rose?"

Pete nodded.

"It's . . . perfect."

Forty-One

Katie studied herself in the full-length mirror. She held her arms by her side as she followed the strapless sweetheart bodice down to the opulent, sparkling, wide belt that cinched in her waist. The tulle skirt wasn't too full, but made her feel like a fairytale princess. She adjusted her chapel length veil and smiled. Everything was just as she dreamed.

After a light tap on the door, Gram entered.

"Oh my," Gram began, "You're the most beautiful bride I've ever laid eyes on." She walked slowly toward Katie. "I have one final touch." She pulled out a strand of perfectly round milky-white pearls. "I wore these on my wedding day as did my mother on hers." She fastened the necklace around Katie's neck and stepped back to admire the entire ensemble.

Katie stood in front of the mirror and let her fingers glide over the smooth round pearls. Gram had gone overboard telling Katie how important she was to her after the memories invaded her. She wanted her to know that no matter the past, she was a Harrington—loved and wanted.

Katie knew that Gram loved her, but she hadn't felt worthy of being part of her family, until now. Gram wanted her to wear the pearls that two generations had worn before her, and to Katie that was momentous. "They're perfect. Thank you, Gram."

Ava Maria drifted into the room, bringing an instant smile to Katie as she heard the string trio play Bach's version of the song. Katie's heart soared realizing it was almost time to meet her groom at the end of the aisle.

"That's my cue," Gram said, kissing Katie's cheek. "I love you so much, Katie-girl."

Katie looked herself over once more as she listened to *Ave Maria* end and *Jesu, Joy of Man's Desiring* begin. The bridesmaids would be walking down now and she would be next.

Pete tapped on the door before walking in and offering her his arm. "We're up." He thought about how much things had changed since the first time he met Katie. She was the epitome of sadness and pain. A frail girl with no hope. Her face had displayed only one emotion—defeat. Now he smiled as he looked at the beautiful woman standing in front of him. She was confident, and had a youthful, happy smile that he felt sure would never leave her. "You look exquisite."

"Thank you, Pete—for everything." Katie picked up her bouquet and took his arm. "I wish things had worked out differently for you and Gram. You would have made a wonderful addition to our family."

"They worked out as they should have. Your Gram and I have an unbreakable bond of friendship, and I thought you considered me part of the family anyway?" He smirked.

"Yes, I do." Katie walked with him down the hall to the door that led outside. She heard the string trio begin to play *Canon in D* by Pachebel. *It's time.*

Lanterns lined the long walkway to the gazebo by the sea, illuminating the path and adding a warm glow on the faces the guests. Katie clung to Pete's arm as he slowly walked her down the cobblestone path toward Branson. Butterflies tickled the inside of her stomach as she saw her smiling groom waiting.

The sea was calm as the windless October evening greeted her with a warm welcome. Fall colors of orange, red, and yellow were displayed in floral arrangements hanging from the lanterns that lit the path. Katie smiled at several familiar faces before looking ahead to her handsome groom dressed in a black tuxedo and charcoal gray ascot. His eyes carried her toward him, until she was close enough to see the wide grin displayed across his face and the dimples she hoped their children would inherit.

She was vaguely aware of the minister speaking and Pete kissing her cheek through her veil before taking his seat. Katie handed her bouquet to Maggie and relished the feeling of Branson's hands as they held her own.

Branson gazed into her eyes as he vowed to love and honor her for the rest of their lives. She tried to concentrate on the meaning of their vows and savor each moment on this perfect night. She wanted to remember the way Branson looked and how she felt. After they exchanged rings, the minister pronounced them husband and wife. Branson gently took her chin in his hand, lifting it slightly, and brought his lips to hers. The kiss was so soft and tender, mimicking the first time she experienced his lips. Her heart stopped beating and time stood still.

"It is my pleasure to introduce for the first time, Mr. and Mrs. Branson Stone."

Branson took Katie's hand in his as they walked down the aisle, surrounded by family and friends clapping and cheering.

"My wife." He pulled her in and hugged her to his side.

"It sounds so strange, doesn't it? I'm Mrs. Stone. Katie Stone. I like it!"

After pictures, cocktails and hors d'oeuvres were served on the patio. Katie popped a bacon-wrapped scallop into Branson's mouth. "Isn't that delicious?"

"Mmm . . ." he mumbled while he chewed, and then fed her one.

They walked around, greeting everyone as they sipped cocktails and sampled the food. Servers walked around with stuffed crimini mushroom caps, grilled beef brochettes with an Asian dipping sauce, and mini Maryland crab cakes.

Dinner was served inside. Katie and Branson were introduced again as they entered the dining room and shared their first dance to "At Last" by Etta James.

The party flowed easily and all traditions were observed, starting with a heartfelt yet hilarious toast from Mike. "A toast to my best friend and his bride. He's either the luckiest bastard alive, or a genius to land such a woman. Welcome to the dark side, Katie!"

Maggie was next as she recounted youthful adventures through tears. "I used to make fun of her for listing out her life goals, but she was focused and got everything she dreamed of. I remember the first time she saw Branson. It was the first time I witnessed an actual hyperventilation episode!" She wrapped up her speech between sniffles with, "I love you both and wish you every happiness."

Branson stood and raised his glass. "First of all, a personal thank you to each of you for attending our wedding tonight. Some of you have traveled a great distance to celebrate with us. Now, a toast to my beautiful bride." He looked at Katie with adoration. "Thank you for choosing me. You have brought joy to my sorrowful mind, peace to a raging soul, and love to my desolate heart. Time will never diminish the depth of my love for you."

Katie's heart melted at his words, and all she could think about was getting her hands on her delicious husband. She kissed him before clinking her glass with his and taking a sip of the bubbly champagne.

Branson leaned over and whispered in Katie's ear. "Have we been polite long enough? I can't wait to get my hands on you."

"I'll meet you in the lobby." Katie stood and shared a look with Maggie, letting her know it was time to wrap things up. Before meeting Branson in the lobby, she changed into a casual cream dress. She looked outside and saw the crowd waiting for them. "They're standing out there like an army waiting to attack."

"I know. Maybe we should have chosen bubbles instead of birdseed. Just hold on to me and run!" He laughed as they held hands and ran through the spray of birdseed. Once in the safety of the car, they waved goodbye to friends and family and began their adventure as husband and wife.

"Whoa!" Katie giggled as Branson lifted her up into his arms to carry her over the threshold of their honeymoon suite. He set her down, hung the do not disturb sign on the door and looked around the room. A tray holding chocolate covered strawberries and two champagne flutes was displayed on a table near a freshly lit fire. Branson lifted the bottle out of its ice bath. "Champagne, Mrs. Stone?"

"Mmm, yes please." She lifted a card from a large bouquet of white roses. "These are from your parents. How lovely."

Branson handed Katie a glass before clinking his against it. "To us."

Katie took a sip and set her glass down. "Well, it's late, we should get some sleep." She tried her best to contain the smile that begged for release. She was rewarded with the dumfounded and defeated look on Branson's face and giggled. "I'm kidding." She hung her suit jacket over a chair before taking Branson's glass and setting it down on the table. "We can sleep on the plane."

Katie felt the heat rising as she held the gaze of her gorgeous new husband. He didn't take his eyes off of her as he reached around and slowly unzipped the back of her dress, pausing to trail kisses down her neck and shoulder.

"Holy—" Branson inhaled sharply as he stood back and admired her white lace thong. His body responded immediately. He had planned on taking his time with her, slowly savoring every inch of her body, but it had been two months since they had come together intimately and he was losing focus quickly.

Katie closed the space between them and began unbuttoning his shirt. She slid it off into the floor and ran her hands over his broad shoulders, gliding down over every muscle.

Branson pulled her in and kissed her. The kiss began softly, tenderly, but quickly escalated into a wild hunger that nearly took him over the edge. He felt her fingers knot in his hair, and one of her legs wrap around him pulling him closer. Without taking his lips from hers, he quickly unhooked and removed her bra. There was desperation in his haste as he helped Katie finish removing his clothes. Not willing to have any space between them, he led her around the furniture to the frame of the bed.

Katie felt his hot breath against her ear and moaned. He guided her back onto the bed, sending chills along her spine as he gave equal attention to each of her breasts. His hands and mouth traveled down her stomach until he reached her white thong and slid it off.

"You are all mine," Branson whispered.

Katie tilted her head back and closed her eyes, enjoying the sweet rapture of his touch. She was completely consumed in the exquisite pleasure of their bodies and souls becoming one.

"Is it possible that it's even better now that we're married?" Katie rested her head on Branson's chest and listened to his racing heartbeat.

"It's definitely more intense. We should test the theory." Branson pulled Katie on top of him and the miracle began all over again.

Marriage was exhilarating for Katie. She loved hearing the lady at the front desk refer to her as Mrs. Stone, and signing her new name to the room service ticket. Lovemaking seemed new and uninhibited, with bottomless levels of energy.

They honeymooned in Bali, and spent the first four days either in the room or lounging under large cabanas on the beach. They snorkeled the startling clear waters of Nusa Lembongan where they took underwater pictures of coral, turtles, and colorful fish, including a large Mola Mola.

On Saturday they visited the Tanah Lot Temple and watched as the sky was transformed into a mad artist's canvas with bold strokes of orange, red, and purple splashed across the sky as the sun melted into the sea.

Katie and Branson enjoyed horseback riding along the shoreline, shopping in the village markets and hiking through bamboo lined forests. They sampled the intense and beautiful flavors of traditional Balinese cuisine.

"I really want to try it, but I'm nervous." Katie scrunched her eyebrows together at the thought of drinking something so revolting.

"We have to try it. They say it's the best in the world. Besides, it can't hurt you or people wouldn't drink it."

"Maybe it's considered the most expensive coffee in the world for a reason—no one will buy it!" Katie hesitantly smelled the steaming black cup of coffee. "It doesn't smell like poo, it actually smells divine."

The man serving the Luwak coffee laughed before telling them about the process of gathering and cleaning the coffee beans. "Civets, a weasel-like animal, are let loose in coffee plantations at night. They eat the high-quality coffee berry, and release the coffee bean. The harvested coffee beans are then thoroughly washed and roasted over a fire."

"By release, you mean defecate." Branson laughed.

"Yes, but trust me—it is the best coffee in the world."

Katie and Branson counted to three and sipped the brew at the same time. "Wow, it's really good." She looked at the man behind the counter. "Anyone ever get sick after drinking this?"

He shook his head. "No."

On the last day of their honeymoon, Branson ordered massages overlooking the beach. As they enjoyed the relaxing effects of the deep tissue massage and the sound of the sea, Katie said, "I wish we could live like this forever. Can't you see it—you, me, on a deserted island making shelters out of palm fronds. You could fish for our food and I would make luscious desserts from coconut and papaya. Mmm."

"Don't tempt me. This has been heavenly, but it's not over yet."

The massage ended but Katie was too relaxed to move. Branson sat up, took a long drink of water and helped her up. "Let's have a drink by the pool before dinner."

Katie slipped on a white chiffon dress for dinner. It hugged her curves and was a nice contrast against her skin that had been deeply bronzed by the sun. She ran a brush through her hair once more before applying a hint of lip color. "Mmm, don't you look handsome," Katie said as she watched Branson finish buttoning his white linen shirt. His freshly shaven face was tanned and gorgeous, and Katie couldn't resist running her hand over his cheek.

Branson pulled her in for a soft kiss and smiled. "Don't get me heated up before dinner. I've gone through a lot of trouble to make tonight special."

"Oh?" Katie's curiosity peaked.

"Let's go." Branson took her hand in his and led her out to the beach where a table for two was elegantly set under a white flowing canopy. "Dance with me, Mrs. Stone?"

"I'd love to."

Branson held Katie close as they moved to the romantic melody that flowed from the guitarist standing in the distance. Candles were scattered along the sand, providing a warm glow. The crescent moon provided enough light to glimpse the daunting sea.

"I love you, Branson. I can't imagine being happier than I am right now."

They feasted on fish dressed in a light citrus sauce and a sampling of delectable desserts. Branson took the champagne out of ice, grabbed the two flutes, and stood. "Let's finish this in our room."

Branson took Katie's hand and led her through the candlelit path back to their room. He filled the two flutes, champagne bubbling over the top and spilling onto the tiled floor. "Oops," he smiled, handing her a glass. "To us."

"To us," Katie agreed before sipping the liquid. The taste of ginger, toasted hazelnuts, and apricots lingered on her tongue, tantalizing her taste buds. She set her glass down when she saw the look in her husband's eyes.

"Branson," Katie whispered in breathless anticipation as his lips found hers, soft yet urgent. Her body felt like it was melting into his, leaving her dizzy with desire. She stepped backward, finding the bed with the backs of her legs and pulled him down with her, arching her back to feel his body press into hers.

He began at her knee, slowly moving his hand up her silky-smooth leg. He moaned when he felt for her panties and found her nakedness instead, her body revealing how much she wanted him. "God, Katie." He exhaled. "I don't think I'll ever get enough of you."

"Good." Katie finished the buttons on his shirt, under a watchful eye, and slid it off his shoulders. She worked fervently to get his khaki pants off as he lifted his hips while tracing his tongue over her ear. "You're rendering me useless, Mr. Stone." She arched her back and moaned in pleasure as he caused goose bumps to cover her body while jolts of surging electricity soared through her.

Branson kicked off the last leg of his pants and continued where he left off. He loved watching her body respond to his touch, hearing her soft moans. Her body was a wonderland to touch, taste, and enjoy. He helped her sit up so he could slide the dress over her head and then guided her back down. "So beautiful . . ." He softly kissed the space between her neck and shoulder, making his way down to her full breasts. ". . . and all mine."

Katie was overcome with need as her hands roamed over his magnificent physique. His kiss was enough to send her into another dimension, and his touch had her body aching and spiraling out of control.

She felt him grin against her mouth before entering her. With matched moans they became one. Katie cried out in sheer pleasure as her body trembled and shattered in delicious bliss. Branson gripped the headboard with one arm and groaned into the pillow as wave after wave erupted through his body.

He held her tightly in his arms as they fell asleep listening to the waves gently crash onto the shoreline and the lonely whistle of the wind coming in through the open sliders.

Forty-Two

Christmas Eve filled Katie with an excitement she had trouble containing. She busied herself preparing tomorrow night's dinner as Maggie had suggested and set the dining room table. Her nerves had gotten the best of her and went straight to her stomach.

"I just can't eat anything, love, my stomach is in knots."

"You'll make yourself sick, if you don't stop for a moment and nourish your body. Just sit and have half a sandwich with me." Branson set a plate on the kitchen bar.

Katie took a few bites and hurried back to the kitchen to make the brown sugar and pecan topping for the sweet potato casserole. Her stomach felt terrible and she headed for the bathroom. *Don't let me get sick now!* She silently prayed. *What did Gram used to give me to help? Crackers and ginger ale—I know we have crackers, maybe Sprite will work.*

"Are you okay, babe?" Branson asked. "It's just our family—please relax."

"I'm okay, I always get a stomach ache when I'm nervous. Crackers will help."

"What can I do? Give me a task." Branson insisted.

"Um," Katie thought about what was left. "You could set out the wine glasses and a tray for appetizers."

"Done. What's next?"

"One last thing." She hung her monogrammed red plaid stocking on the mantle and hung Branson's matching green plaid next to it. *Three or four more would be nice.* "I got one for Jackson and little Rose, too. I know they're not waking up here, but I wanted to have something for them. I got Jackson trucks and cars and some of those super hero characters he likes to send flying across the room. I got Rose a doll, some fake makeup, a plastic cell phone, and a slinky. Can't you see her sending a slinky down the stairs? Hmm, let's eighty-six the slinky. I don't want her falling. Oh, and silly putty—remember silly putty?"

"They'll love it, babe."

With Branson's help Katie managed to get everything done and decided to retire early. "Come to bed with me—we can watch a movie together."

"Sounds good. I'll get the movie and meet you in there."

Branson returned with *It's a Wonderful Life* and two cups of hot chocolate. "I don't know if your stomach can handle it or not?"

"I'm feeling much better now that everything is done. Thank you." Katie took the cup, sipping slowly.

Branson inserted the DVD and climbed into bed. "This movie has always been a Christmas Eve tradition in the Stone house."

"Perfect. I love it."

Katie was asleep twenty minutes later.

Branson stroked Katie's shoulder and arm. "Wake up, darling. It's Christmas."

Katie slowly opened her eyes and grinned. "Merry Christmas, my love." She flung back the covers, alive with a renewed sense of energy and excited to start ripping into wrapping paper. "Let's open presents!"

Branson plugged in the lights to the tree, started coffee for himself and a cup of cocoa for his finicky bride, and joined her in the living room. She was giddy with happiness and it was contagious.

Katie handed him an elegantly wrapped shirt box. "Open this one first."

Wrapping paper was strewn all over the living room as Katie and Branson sipped their morning mugs of comfort and relaxed into the soft leather couch. Katie finished her cocoa and produced a wrapped package. "I almost forgot about this one, it must have gotten hidden under all of the paper." She handed the wrapped shirt box to him.

Branson ripped the paper off, opened the box to view the third shirt she picked out for him and was confused. "What's this?"

Katie didn't answer. Instead she watched as he picked up the framed picture and stared at it. When she realized he wasn't going to get it, she whispered, "It's our baby's first picture."

"Are you serious?"

"I wanted to tell you as soon as I found out, but I had to be sure that . . . well, the doctor says we have no reason to worry—everything looks good." Katie knelt down in front of

Branson and looked into his eyes. "Are you as happy as I am?"

Branson took Katie's hand and helped her to stand. He lifted her into his arms and twirled her around. "We're going to have a baby?"

Katie nodded her head excitedly.

Branson set her down gently, treating her like a china doll.

"I'm not going to break," she said.

"How do you feel?" He looked her over. This explained why she had been so tired lately.

"I'm scared," she began. "What if I'm not a good mother?" She let her mind travel to the past. Her first impression of a mother was a selfish drug addict that never had a kind word for her, and the second was the cruel, psychopath Maxine that had taken her in for purposes only God knew. She didn't know how to act around children, what if she screwed up their life, like her mother had hers? Panic washed over her face and the room spun slowly around as a wave of nausea filled her.

"Hey, look at me." Branson sat her down on the couch and knelt in front of her. "I've seen the way you are around Jackson. He adores you and he's comfortable with you. He trusts you because you love him and you're a good person. You'll be an amazing mother, Katie. Gram has had more influence than anyone from your past, I think you'll take her love and compassion with you. You couldn't be a bad mother if you tried."

"I hope you're right." She placed her hand over her stomach. "I already love this baby so much."

Branson sat down and wrapped an arm around Katie, rubbing her belly and imaging their child growing inside the love of his life.

Katie leaned her head on his shoulder, savoring the moment. She felt protected, loved, and hopeful—it was everything she'd always wanted.

About the Author:

Eleanor Green resides in Tennessee with her husband and two children. She enjoys the things everyone else does—reading, writing, cooking, gardening—but is also an adventure seeker.

Terrified of cats, passionate about hot tea, allergic to being cold.

Still left on her bucket list: getting lost in Italy and being invited in for dinner by a sweet family, eating a scorpion, and swimming with the dolphins.

Eleanor also writes under the name Lisa Poston Murphy.

Email: contact@authoreleanorgreen.com

Website: http://authoreleanorgreen.com

Facebook: https://www.facebook.com/AuthorEGreen

Twitter: https://twitter.com/AuthorEGreen

www.ingramcontent.com/pod-product-compliance
Lightning Source LLC
Chambersburg PA
CBHW030401180626
46812CB00005B/1880